A
CONTROLLING
INTEREST

A CONTROLLING INTEREST

A
NOVEL
BY
PETER ENGEL

ST. MARTIN'S PRESS
NEW YORK

Library of Congress Cataloging in Publication Data

Engel, Peter H
  A controlling interest.

  I. Title.
PS3555.N39C6   813'.54   80–23185
ISBN 0–312–16919–1

To M., K., A., K., M.

book one
ROLLING HIGH

1

The slopes of the elegant Swiss ski resort of Gstaad, and the private ski club in its valley, belong exclusively to the young, the rich, and the beautiful. A fat man, an ugly girl, a small child or an old woman would each look totally out of place here.

Valentino, the handsome, talented Italian designer, keeps a house in Gstaad. Suzy Chaffee, ex-Olympic skier and sometime Chapstick girl, sleek and sexy in her Bogner jumpsuits, skis here. Jackie visits, as does Bianca, occasionally. . . .

Walter Cort's house lay outside the village itself, high on the side of the valley. The location sometimes made life difficult for Mortimer, Walter's invaluable house manager, who looked after him whether he was in his New York apartment, his house on Cape Cod, or here, high above this valley in Switzerland. The house was so out of the way that Mortimer often had trouble hiring servants—they didn't want to work so far from town. But the setting gave Walter a far longer view than was common in the Alps—he hated the feeling of mountains looming over him, pressing in. He needed space to move, to feel free. When he skied, he felt as though he could conquer the mountains; with enough speed, he could elude even the most lowering cliff or ominous overhang.

Mortimer glanced at the Swiss cuckoo clock over the mantel. It was almost four; his boss would probably be taking his last run. Mortimer calmly rose from the easy chair, automatically smoothing the pillows, making sure the velvet nap was unruffled. He folded the newspaper he had been reading and replaced it in the wrought-iron holder next to the bookcases. Taking a pair of binoculars from the shelf above the stereo, he went onto the balcony.

Adjusting the binoculars carefully, he started to scour the distant slope. Systematically scanning backward and forward, Mortimer was as determined and methodical as a mine sweeper. Even through the glasses he had to squint from the glare of the sun on the diamond-powdered slopes. After a few moments he found what he was looking

1

for—a serpentine formation of six dots skiing in single file just below the skyline. Steadily but very slowly, the dots crossed the white expanse, their motion almost imperceptible—like the minute hand of a clock which advances without ever appearing to move. He nodded with satisfaction. That was Mr. Cort all right. He'd be back within the hour. Mortimer lowered the binoculars and went sedately back into the house to turn on the roast. Walking through the dining room, he couldn't help glancing at the liquor cabinet. Even after six years, the desire was still there. . . .

High on the slope, speed and chance were paramount. The three men and three girls hurtled through the dunes of loose snow. Sometimes they were up to their necks in the clouds of powder sprayed up by their skis; seconds later, as they hit a giant mogul, they would fly several feet clear of the ground like some strange species of giant locust leaping and gliding. Then, touching down again, their legs would compress like steel springs and they would crouch on their skis, compact as balls.

Walter Cort led the group at a furious pace, his face rigid with concentration. His hawklike nose and strong chin glistened with melted snow; his goggles and the white snow crust over his hair made him look like something out of science fiction. He chose only the steepest inclines and attacked them recklessly. Occasionally, hitting an unexpected bump or an invisible valley, he would wobble precariously. Once he teetered on one ski for yards before recovering. But he would not slow down, and gradually he drew away from the others until he was twenty yards ahead, a low projectile with a snow cloud swirling six feet high in its wake.

"Hold on, Walter," one of the girls cried out. "Wait for us." He braked sideways, throwing up a great cascade of snow. The others caught up with him. Resting on their ski poles, they panted and grinned at one another.

"Sorry, folks, was I running away from you?"

"Walter, you're crazy," the girl said, her not-quite-cultured English voice full of admiration. "No one should be able to ski like that. Not . . ."

"Not at my age?" he asked cynically.

"I wasn't going to say that."

"No? But it's correct." His voice, deep and faintly accented, was barely short of breath. "I'm practically an old man."

"You are not," the girl said. "Forty-four's young. Anyhow, you do everything as if you were twenty." She leaned over to touch his elbow, her eyes suddenly hooded and private. "Everything," she repeated softly.

"You ski as if you're fleeing from an avalanche," one of the men interrupted.

Walter looked at him with surprise. "Perhaps I am," he said softly. "Come on," he added briskly, "we've another hour to the bottom."

"You're in a hurry?" the girl demanded.

"Yes, Judith, my dear. When you know me better, you'll realize I'm always in a hurry."

"I know you well enough after three days to know that's not always true," she said. "But if you want to rush home, then so do I."

"Okay," he said, patting her bottom. "Then let's see who gets there first." With a flick of his ski poles, he turned his skis downhill and was instantly off, rushing ahead through the virgin snow.

She was as graceful and elongated as any Modigliani nude. As she slept, her long blonde hair spilled over the flowered pillowcase onto the crumpled sheet.

Beautiful, thought Walter Cort. He interrupted his methodical progress toward getting dressed to study her, enjoying her slender youth, the bikini marks across her jutting hip bones, the thin lines of her obviously trimmed pubic hair, the knowing yet childish face . . . Lovely to look at, he reflected, and exciting to play with—on the slopes and in bed.

The really thin ones aroused him the most. When he entered them, he always felt a surge of power, as if he could fill them so completely they must become his slaves, and he their total master. It was different with larger women. When he entered them, he felt vulnerable, almost engulfed.

Not that he'd ever met a woman he really considered his equal. He loved women, loved them all; whether fat and old, or young, sexy, and desirable. He enjoyed them enormously. He was always happy to watch them, often by the hour, as they dressed and primped, perfected their makeup or concentrated on blowing just the right touch of untidiness into their carefully casual hairstyles. He loved to watch fashion shows, too, partly for the clothes themselves, but more for the parade of elegant, sensual, graceful females who presented them. He collected models, and playgirls like this one, showing them off with pride in the most expensive restaurants of New York, Paris and London, as other men showed off their paintings or paraded their horses at Ascot.

Although Walter loved women, he viewed them essentially as playthings. Indeed, that was a large part of his enjoyment. They charmed and excited him. They made him laugh. But even the sharpest of them could never compete with him. Certainly he employed several bright, well-educated women in his business, two in quite senior positions. But he would entrust none with any delicate negotiations—or any negotiations at all, for that matter. They were either not clever enough, or too bitchy, Walter thought. The only business they were really good at, he reflected rather bitterly, was taking his money. They all seemed instinctively competent at that. In the old days, before all the wealth and success, few women had really seemed to care about him. And they always left him soon enough.

Looking down at Judith naked on the bed, he felt himself start to get hard again. Such a beautiful picture, so innocent, so sexual. He shook his head impatiently, walked to the mirror and meticulously adjusted his tie. Twenty-five dollars that tie had cost, and worth every penny, he thought. That's just how life is, he reflected. You've got to keep pushing, keep fighting for more. . . .

"I'm leaving," he told the girl. Her eyelids fluttered. He bent down and kissed her flat, almost concave belly. Incredible how fresh she seemed, considering how much she knew, considering the experiences she'd had—everything from getting married as a crazy kid of fifteen to working as a top London stripper, if he could believe what she'd told him. She had certainly amazed him last night, almost instantly finding precisely the right spot to lick, and continuing relentlessly until he could not possibly hold back any longer.

While he had still been basking in the afterglow of that pleasure, she had dug into the pocket of her jeans, which lay crumpled beside the bed, and had pulled out a vial of cocaine. Expertly she had shaped the powder into four tidy, narrow lines on his polished bedside table, extracted two bills from his wallet and rolled one for each of them to snort through, all in a few seconds. He remembered that the bills she had used were fifties—and that they had disappeared into her jeans with the unused part of the cocaine. Fair enough, he thought; after all, it was her coke. He used it rarely, and never kept any around. Finally, when the zingy energy of the drug had hit them, she had attacked his body, cursing and screaming at him, until he was hard again. He had come that second time as violently as any sex-starved sailor, and she with him, her nails clawing deep into his back.

"You sleep as long as you want," he said to her now. "When you're ready to leave, Mortimer will drive you wherever you're going. If you need anything before you go, just let him know."

As always, Walter was sure Mortimer would handle the girl appropriately. From the very first day six years ago, when Mortimer had answered the ad for a house manager, he had handled everything in Walter's private life perfectly. Acting as travel agent, chauffeur, butler and general factotum rolled into one, he had exhibited imperturbable dignity in every situation. Whether he was hiring servants, cleaning the house himself when they didn't turn up, supervising the kitchen, ejecting a drunken guest or rushing to catch a plane, Mortimer always looked as if he had been sent straight from Central Casting to take the role of an English "Gentleman's gentleman"—and his name, which Walter guessed he had made up, confirmed the impression. No one except Walter had any inkling of his history.

"Will I see you again?" the girl asked sleepily.

"Of course," he said automatically. "When I'm next in Europe." But he doubted it. The casual way he had picked her up on the plane coming over from England made it unlikely. He wasn't even sure whether he had enough information to find her again. He remembered writing her name and a telephone number somewhere because he recalled thinking what an inappropriate name she had for such a sex kitten. Vickie or Toni would have been normal. But no, she was called Judith. And if he remembered right, her last name was equally unimpressive: Katz. Judith Katz. Oh well, he thought, if he really wanted to find her, that would give him enough to go on. But he probably wouldn't—although he had to admit that this one was wilder, skiing and screwing, than most.

"You never know," Judith said, stretching her arms above her head so that her whole body elongated even further and her breasts formed perfect ovals on her chest, "maybe I'll see you in New York or at your place on the Cape you were telling me about. I love sailing almost as much as skiing."

"Bienvenue à bord Concorde. Welcome to the Concorde," the pretty, efficient stewardess greeted Walter Cort as he inclined his head to enter the sleek plane about to depart from Charles de Gaulle Airport in Paris. She glanced at his boarding pass. "Three B—right there."

"Yes, thank you." It was the seat he always chose, preferring the front compartment of the plane because it was less noisy, and an aisle seat to avoid being hemmed in.

"You are just in time," she said. "We shall be leaving in a few moments."

Almost immediately the doors closed and a small, powerful vehicle, all engine and wheels, started to push the plane away from the gate. Minutes later the Concorde's own engines took over, and the plane taxied quickly onto the runway.

"Please sit back and relax," the stewardess said over the intercom. "We shall be airborne shortly. However, we shall not be supersonic until we have reached twenty thousand feet and are clear of the area where our noise would disturb." While her cool voice with its delicate French accent was pleasing, it was distant, as efficient and inhuman as the plane itself. Computerized, Walter decided. "You may watch your progress on the clock face," she explained. "We shall travel just under Mach I, the speed of sound, for about ten minutes. Then we shall accelerate until we reach Mach II, and cruise at that speed for three hours until we are close to New York. . . ."

Walter tuned out the rest of the speech. He had heard it many times before. Sitting back in his seat, he contemplated the last few days. It had been a good week. His business deal had closed on schedule, with fewer problems than he had anticipated. Almost fifty grand on that one, not counting expenses, which hadn't been excessive. Just a few "friends" to cut in on the deal. That was part of most European deals. And both the skiing and Judith had been superb. He should take the time to ski more often, he decided. His muscles were stiff; he was out of shape. But there was never enough time. Even after these three days he felt jumpy. There was so much to do in the office, so much paperwork to catch up on, so many deals . . . then tonight there was the governor's party. . . . "Fleeing from an avalanche," his friend had said. Yes, Walter thought, that's exactly what my life feels like. He wondered whether he would ever lose that sense of impending crisis.

The terrified ten-year-old dashed across the street. His ferret-face pulled tight in a soundless scream, he half-jumped, half-fell into the ditch at the edge of the sidewalk. He pressed himself into the ground amid the trash, which, now that the Nazis had killed the mayor and half the city council, littered the streets.

"Run!" his mother had screamed at him when the knocking started. "Get out!"

But he couldn't. He just couldn't run off to be so totally alone. So he lay in this ditch, barely daring to raise his head.

An eternity passed before the soldiers brought his mother out of the house. The boy noticed that her hair was mussed and her clothes torn. He couldn't understand why, because she was always so neat. She seemed to walk in a trance, the men shoving her to move faster. He watched, overwhelmed with loss, as they loaded her into their truck and then rumbled away with her. At that moment, simultaneously wrenched away from love, childhood, and even from the normal trappings of civilization, he was forced to become an animal, like a rat, destined to live always on the edge of panic.

The first days of his new life were the worst. He ran endlessly, hugging whatever cover there was until he reached the caves in the forest where he had often played hide-and-seek with his friends. Only a week before his father had told him that bands of Jewish children hid there.

"If anything should happen to me, Walter, look for them. It's the only place you might be safe."

"But what should happen? We're not Jewish."

"Your mother is, so you are. Anyway, to them we're Jewish because we're not against the Jews."

"But that's not fair."

"Criminal, but there it is." His father had shrugged in resignation.

Whenever Walter thought about his father, he remembered with rage that habitual, pathetic shrug of willing passivity. Never would he submit like that, he had vowed.

It took twenty-four hours for young Walter to find the band of kids and its tough, gangling, reticent, seventeen-year-old leader. In fact, it had been the gang who found him, springing from behind the bushes where they had been hiding and surrounding him. They were threadbare and bony, but he soon learned that they were the wiliest of scavengers.

"Name?" the leader demanded.

"Walter Kortinowiecz."

"Age?"

"Ten."

"You're too young and small," said the leader, looking down at him with distaste.

"Have you no relatives?" the girl beside him demanded. She seemed no larger than Walter himself, but she held herself so tough and erect that to him she seemed invincible.

"My father said to go to the caves."

"And I say you're too small."

He never knew how he knew it, but suddenly Walter realized he was being tested. "Fuck you," he said belligerently, his tiny face quivering with the effort of holding back the tears. "They're my caves too. If I'm too small, try to throw me out."

"Good. You got balls. They killed both your parents?"

"I . . . I think so." Walter could hardly understand the question. Killed? The word was more incomprehensible than horrifying. Suddenly he was shaking violently. "They killed my Dad last week. And yesterday I saw them take my Mommy away. . . ." He felt more empty than sad, and he couldn't understand why his body was racked with such violent, shivering spasms. If only the leader didn't notice and order him to leave.

"Poor little bugger," said the leader more gently. "I know. They got all my family, too."

"Don't they come here?"

"They try, but we're too tricky for them. Anyway, they don't think we're important—just a bunch of kids."

"You got food?" Walter realized he had eaten nothing since the day before.

"Of course," said the girl. "We steal what we need and find lots of stuff in the forest, too. Don't you know?"

"Yes, I know about mushrooms and things. I've been coming here all my life."

"Then you know the caves?" the leader asked.

"Of course. Hide-and-seek."

"That's it. Only it's always us hiding and them seeking . . . And it's no game."

From that day until eighteen months later when the leader was shot while trying to steal bread through a farmhouse window, Walter stayed as close as he could to the older boy, worshipping him, depending on him absolutely. But when the nightmares came and he woke up crying for his mother, it was always the girl, Rebecca, who would hold him in her arms, comforting him back to sleep. "Becca," he would murmur; "Becca, Becca," over and over. He would clutch tightly at her hand in his sleep.

Little Walter and Rebecca were only a few feet away when the leader was hit by the bullet. They saw him collapse, an arc of blood spurting from his face. And although Walter had seen many others die —adults and children killed by Nazi bullets or clubs—he went into shock, and couldn't make himself move. If his resourceful friend could be killed so easily, what hope was there for him? Through months of deprivation he had believed that his leader—and therefore he himself —would live. Suddenly he realized he had been utterly wrong.

"Get away! Come on, for God's sake!" Rebecca pulled at his sleeve. "He's dead. There's nothing we can do."

"No," he insisted. "We must help him." Slowly, inundated by his loss, he moved toward the body.

"Run," she cried one last time. "They're coming!" Then, daring to wait no longer, she ran off, tears streaming down her face. She was fourteen.

He was not sure whether the men had faces or only jackboots and riding britches and swastikas on their arms. He felt more relief than terror.

"*Jude?*" the closest of the jackboots demanded. "Jew?"

The boy shook his head automatically but they didn't believe him. All those dirty, thieving kids from the forest were Jews.

"*Weg mit Ihm.*" "Take him away," the German sergeant ordered. Young Walter was goose-marched to the town center, where a stockade of rough wooden posts served as a pound for captured Jews. His terror actually helped him. Without it he might never have survived the anguished, overwhelming sense of loss he felt at his leader's death and his abandonment by Rebecca.

It was the routine of death at Auschwitz that almost destroyed Walter, nearly seducing him into the same acceptance of his own passing that brings the terminally ill peace before death. Men prayed or moaned or shrugged their acquiescence as his father had shrugged, and Walter almost joined them in their acceptance. But because he was young and surprisingly healthy—and the children in the forest had instilled in him a powerful sense of rebellion and survival—Walter never quite gave up. He remained alive during the first month only because his number happened not to be called. But gradually he regained his determination to live and, even as starvation shriveled his body, his soul hardened into a knot of hate so unrelenting that it enabled him to pretend to enjoy even his captors' grossest demands. He knew that he had to survive to avenge.

When the Americans finally walked into the camp, there were only a few survivors. All were emaciated and most were disfigured almost beyond humanness. Many of the guards had fled. But one, blond but no longer arrogant, lay dead on his bunk with his testicles stuffed into a gaping hole gouged in his stomach. This act of revenge, by a group of the boys the blond guard had frequently raped, had been instigated by Walter. He felt cleansed afterward of at least a small part of his disgust.

One of the American liberators, Sergeant Jimmy Kowalski, was neither an admirable nor a tender man. His human contacts for most of the twenty-six years before he had enlisted in the army had been limited to a quick Saturday night fuck with his wife and, even more to his liking, the raucous camaraderie of getting drunk with his buddies whenever his funds allowed. In the army his life had changed little. Saturday-night sex with an occasional whore was very much the same as it had been at home, and drinking with the boys remained his favorite pastime. He had enlisted too late to see any heavy combat, or to experience much hardship.

But even through Jimmy's thick brain the horror of Auschwitz exploded, leaving him for a while sickened and sensitized, a mass of undefined remorse. At the end of the first day of cataloging the toll of torture and death, of herding the barely living into recovery wards, he was moved to deep feelings he could barely tolerate. By the time he ran across Walter, the last in a long line of inmates that day, Jimmy had been left totally vulnerable. So when Walter, bedraggled and emaciated kid though he was, insisted that he was a free man with the right to leave the camp, Jimmy Kowalski for the only time in his life felt compassion. Exhibiting the only altruism he would ever show, he rescued Walter Kortinowiecz and allowed him to move into the building where he was billeted. "My fellow Polack," he called him, renaming him Cort because, although Jimmy Kowalski was Polish-American, he had no inkling of his ancestral language.

A few months later, when Jimmy was mustered out of the army, he adopted young Walter officially and took him back to Brooklyn, New York.

Back home, Jimmy Kowalski quickly returned to the lazy, mindless self he had left behind. Usually he was unemployed—and drunk. When he did manage to get out of bed and stay sober, he took occasional odd jobs. From those, and his Social Security, he kept himself supplied with beer and an occasional fifth of cheap bourbon on weekends. He was the very picture of a slob, always belching, his pendulous belly hanging over his pants. Often he would beat his wife on Saturday night instead of having sex; it seemed to satisfy him more. In his adopted son he took no interest whatsoever.

Walter Cort arrived in the United States a fourteen-year-old who had survived impossible odds through a combination of luck and stubborn will. He was small and bony from years of starvation, and as sly, quick and suspicious as a coyote. Beneath his survivor's exterior, however, young Walter desperately craved the love and warmth he only dimly remembered—and he found none in either Jimmy Kowalski or in Jimmy's slovenly, resigned wife.

Harry Grass met Walter on the day Walter arrived in Brooklyn. It was typical of Harry to seek out the latest new face in town. A year older than the newcomer, Harry was already a fast-talking, hand-waving promoter, always in the center of everything. He held the leadership of his gang, the Bozos, through salesmanship and a constant flow of entertaining ideas. He looked and talked like an adult. Even his body, not much taller than Walter's, had already set itself into the stocky, rotund shape it would hold for the rest of Harry's life.

Walter, in total contrast, was a puny, reticent, undersized kid. Except for a certain sinewy resilience, he seemed at first glance hardly more than a child.

Harry was fascinated. He'd never met anyone like this new kid who spoke little English and who, they said, had survived a Nazi concentration camp. "Where d'you come from?" he demanded, pulling Walter into an empty doorway.

"Poland." Walter was terse with suspicion.

"Christ, another Polack!"

"You not like?"

"Oh, I don't give a shit. Polack, Schmolack. . . ."

"No understand."

"Don't worry about it, kid. How come you moved here?"

"I live with Mister Jimmy Kowalski, and Mrs. Kowalski. He rescue me from Germany."

"Thought you said you were from Poland."

"They moved me to concentration camp in Germany."

"Christ, I heard about those! Poor bastard, did you have a hard time?"

"Yes." Walter had learned that there was no way of communicating how hard.

"Where's your parents?"

"Killed by Germans." Walter's voice was factual, unemotional. It moved Harry to admiration. The kid was cool.

Harry examined the thin boy before him carefully. He had never known anyone whose parents had been killed. It made an impression. And the kid was older than he seemed. He'd be okay. "Come to the clubhouse after school," he invited. "I'll show you around."

Walter Kortinowiecz, rechristened Wally Cort, had won his first battle in the United States without even realizing he'd fought it. He had been accepted by the most important person in the area. It was a victory he would repeat frequently, an ability to secure people's trust even though he rarely gave his own.

It did not take Wally Cort long to be fully accepted by the Bozos. He was smaller than most of them—although he grew rapidly during his second year in America—but he was the fastest and wiriest of them all. Soon he had a major "rep" for clambering across roofs and scrambling over backyard fences. His English improved very fast, too, so that within weeks he was able to hold his new friends spellbound with the horror stories of his survival. Within a year he was Harry Grass's most valuable lieutenant.

Sitting on the Concorde, speeding back to New York thirty years later, it seemed nightmarish but unreal.

"Ladies and gentlemen," he heard the stewardess say, "shortly you will feel a slight impact as we pass through the sound barrier. It's perfectly normal, nothing to be concerned about."

"Fast enough for you?" the man next to him asked excitedly.

Walter nodded but did not bother to reply. No, he thought, just before he fell asleep, probably not. His life was still full of risk; every new deal was a new chance for failure. However much he tried, he seemed unable to build anything permanent or find anyone he could *really* trust. However quickly he moved, the avalanche was still there, ready to catch him if he faltered for even a second.

2

The next morning in New York was crystal clear, cold, sunny: marvelous. Even in New York, the weather seemed to assure the city's battered residents, winter would eventually turn to spring. In celebration Walter Cort decided to walk the fifteen blocks to his office. He liked the exercise. Watching the hurrying, worried-looking people crowding the sidewalks, he felt superior, a graduate among the freshmen, only there to observe. It was a feeling of confidence and security in which, when it was with him, he reveled.

Walter strode past the expensive brownstones of New York's East Side, south on Park Avenue with its glass skyscrapers, and downtown toward his office high in the Pan American Building. His strong chin, sharp nose, wiry black hair and piercing eyes gave him a look of fierce determination; his superlatively tailored suit, slender, polished shoes and skiing tan shouted wealth; and his easy stride and air of authority plainly indicated a fine family heritage. He could almost hear the passersby envying him his birth. If only they knew what an imposter he really was, he thought. . . . But today he didn't care. He was a successful entrepreneur with money in the bank, a thousand deals in front of him and the world ready to do his bidding.

Walter walked through the tunnel under the newly gold-leafed Helmsley Building, across Forty-fifth Street, through the revolving doors of the Pan Am Building and up the escalators to the elevator floor. He felt at home here in this huge marble hall full of scurrying people. Was he not, after all, one of the bosses of New York's complex, competitive business establishment? He waved to the elevator man, who swelled at the fact that he was recognized by Mr. Cort, and punched the elevator button to the forty-fourth floor. One button for every year of my life, Walter thought. He had moved from a lower floor into these offices shortly after his birthday two months earlier, and it amused him to think of his life as a progression upward, equal in years and floors. Would he continue to grow? Damn right! And then, cynical as always, he pricked his own enthusiasm by asking: What else is there?

The elevator doors slid open, and Walter emerged into the offices of Walter Cort, Incorporated, the company he used as the umbrella for his business ventures.

"Good morning, sir." "Good morning, Mr. Cort." Friendly, but respectful voices greeted him as he strode swiftly toward his office.

"Good morning, sir." Caroline, his private secretary, was pleased to see him; the mornings moved slowly until he arrived. She hurried into his office after him. "Harry Grass has been calling. He wants to discuss the Von Ackermann deal before you call Germany."

"Okay, you'd better get him."

She hurried out again and made the call, and Walter held the phone receiver away from his ear to blunt the harshness of Harry's voice. "Harry?" he asked after a second. "What can I do for you?"

"On the Von Ackermann deal, I heard things are getting fucked up." Unlike Walter, Harry had never lost his rasping Brooklyn tone of voice, his appalling grammar or his love of obscenity. "So what's going on? I wanna know."

"Sure; after all, you started it. . . ." Walter liked to give credit. He had found that people generally liked praise, and it cost him nothing to give it.

"I didn't do nuttin' important," Harry said, automatically declining the compliment. "Only told Charles to contact you." Praise was rarely free, he had learned years ago. A request usually followed fast.

"That's starting it," Walter insisted. "But if you say not . . ." He paused significantly.

"All right, already. So I started it."

"Damn," Walter interjected in mock annoyance, "I was beginning to think I wouldn't have to share my fee for once."

"No way, Wimp. But from what I hear, if you don't get with it, there won't be no fucking fee."

"I've told you a million times, Walter, not Wimp. Walter."

"Okay, Wimp."

Walter laughed in spite of himself. It was their traditional argument. How he had hated the name as a kid; how puny it had made him feel. Now he wasn't sure. It seemed reassuring: a sign that Harry really was a reliable old friend. He pulled himself back to business. "Well, it's like this," he started. "Charles DuPont has been running Clarendon, the French mail order company, for five years. He's built it up and made a big profit. Now he wants to buy out his partners but he hasn't the money."

"Yeah? Well, it ain't easy getting money on frog deals," Harry said.

"It's difficult. But I got the Von Ackermann group involved. He's a real pig, but his people understand France and they're always looking for investments. So I suggested they put up six million for forty-nine percent of the company . . ."

"Clarendon's outside their normal range," Harry interrupted even more abruptly than usual. He always hated to waste time, and difficult deals were a mug's game. "They go for appliances and shit like that."

". . . and in addition, I threw in a hooker." Walter took no notice of his friend's abrasive tone. When Harry became too combative, the best thing was to ignore him. "They'd have the right to lend Clarendon

money against consumer receivables at top interest rates. Von Ackermann would be more interested in that than in the acquisition itself."

"Makes sense," said Harry, instantly changing his view. "So
why're they backing out?"

"They're not. No, the problem is that now that the deal's almost
done, they're not sure they need us in the middle."

"Oh, shit. But I started it—"

"So I hear," Walter interrupted dryly.

Harry's laugh was so abrupt and cynical it sounded more like a
cough.

"That's the trouble with that type of finder's business," Walter
continued. "We put the deals together, but afterward no one believes
we did anything." If only I owned something myself, he thought
angrily, instead of always depending on others.

"Ain't we got a contract?" Harry demanded, interrupting Walter's thoughts.

"Of course we do. But do you want to sue Von Ackermann?"

Harry grunted. "Sure. After I'm done boxing Ali."

"I suppose we can hope Charles doesn't double-cross us."

"Yeah," said Harry doubtfully, "some hope." He barked out his
brief laugh. "You're doing fine, kid," he added. "Keep it up. Which
reminds me, how're the broads?" But he had no time to wait for an
answer. "See ya," he said, and hung up.

Instantly the phone rang again. A second later the buzzer
sounded. "It's Frankfurt on number three," said Caroline.

"Thanks." He picked up the phone. "Hello?" There was only
static on the other end of the line. Walter's slender fingers drummed
impatiently.

"*Jawohl?*" The German crackled harshly into Walter's ear.

"Hello, can you hear me?" Walter demanded, leaning forward, his
face as set and concentrated as if he was about to attack a precipitous
ski slope. "Hello, I want to talk to Heinrich Von Ackermann."

"Speaking." The voice seemed to float out of the telephone.
"Walter?" he pronounced it with the flat vowel sound and German V
—*Vulter*. Walter could not quite suppress a shiver of revulsion at the
sound. Long ago he used to wonder whether it was worth doing business with Germans at all, since he hated them so. But why cut off his
nose to spite his face? West Germany had become the richest country
in Europe. And his fluency in German gave him an advantage, even
though he never spoke the language unless he saw a real benefit for
himself. So he had started doing business there, and over the years, he
had made a great deal of money at it. Often he squeezed his German
opponents far more ruthlessly than if they were any other nationality.
It gave him considerable satisfaction.

"Listen, Heinrich," Walter started to say, "I gather the deal with Charles DuPont is going forward." No point in showing any of his doubt. Von Ackermann would take it for weakness. "You're calling me about it?"

"Yes, we want some reassurance." Von Ackermann's voice was deep and gutteral, but he was entirely fluent in English. "Is he able to run that business? Is it a safe deal?"

"Of course it is. I wouldn't have suggested it otherwise."

"Well, my dear fellow, you might have. After all, you claim you deserve a big fee . . ."

Instantly Walter's fears multiplied. Claim, the bastard had said. "That's right," he said quickly. "But we've already invested a great deal of our own time and money speculatively, so . . ."

"Oh yes, so you have said," the German responded agreeably, admitting nothing. "By the way," he added, "where is Charles?"

There it was—the reason Von Ackermann was calling. He wanted direct contact. "No idea. He said he'd call me later today. Anything I can do?"

"No," said the disembodied voice, trying unsuccessfully to sound casual. "No, I just thought it could be helpful to get together with him." Von Ackermann was not a subtle man.

"Happy to arrange that anytime. Just let me know when and where and I'll be there."

"Fine. Good talking to you. Good-bye." The line went dead.

Walter hung up slowly. For a few moments he ruminated. He knew he couldn't keep Charles DuPont and Von Ackermann apart much longer. And when they did get together, they might well decide they could do without him. It was precisely the problem he had faced almost every time when he first started arranging mergers. Most of his so-called clients tried to welsh on him in those days. Now he had it a little easier. He had quite a strong reputation in the business community, and merger partners were reluctant to anger him or treat him unfairly. But that ruthless bastard Von Ackermann wouldn't think twice about double-crossing Cort. Oh, the hell with it, Walter decided. He couldn't spend all day worrying about any one deal when he had so many others to look after. "Caroline," he called, seeing her walking past, "where do we stand on that English garment deal with Raymond Mitty?"

"We owe him prices," Caroline answered promptly, swinging herself to a halt on the door jamb. "We got them in yesterday, so I'm preparing a telex." She saw Walter smiling broadly. It made his normally craggy, tough face, break into a twinkle. She loved the contrast. "What's so funny?" she asked, wondering whether it was something she had done.

"It's when I think of Mitty. . . ."

"The King of the Wide Boys?" Caroline asked, using the cockney expression she had learned from Mitty himself.

"That's it."

"Yes, I met him when he came over last year. He's like a street hawker who's made good. And his English accent's so thick it has to be phony."

"It is. But he's a damn good *schlock* artist. He'll sell anything that moves if he can buy it at the right price."

"Where does he sell the stuff?" Caroline asked innocently. She loved to get Walter talking. For one thing, the deepness of his voice and the indefinable, almost mysterious middle-European undertone of his accent never failed to fascinate her. For another, it stopped him from giving her dictation.

"Factory compounds. At the pit head of coal mines. Anywhere there's a captive audience and he can get permission to set up. Then he sends in his saleswomen with market stalls and they sell off everything that moves, from cookies to cosmetics."

"Everything . . . ?"

"Enough," Walter interrupted. "I've some letters to get off." He was always irritated when he caught his secretary at her trick of diverting him. Not that he could get too angry, for in most respects she was wonderful to him, loyal and caring.

"Oh, yes. I just remembered," Caroline said quickly. "You got another call from Harry. He's going to be out of town, but he says that on Clarendon you should offer Von Ackermann another deal. He doesn't have one to suggest at the moment, so he'd like you to handle it."

"For Christ's sake," Walter exploded. "Where does he think I'm going to get a deal from?" Caroline knew better than to say anything. "Oh, well," he said, his anger ebbing as quickly as it had risen, "I'll see what I can do." Funny, he thought, how Harry's always the one who sets up the deal and I have to follow it through. It had always been like that, ever since they had been kids together in the same run-down section of Brooklyn. Harry Grass had been the one with the ideas, the one who knew people, while he, feisty little Walter Cort, was the one who carried out Harry's schemes.

"Come on, Wimp!" Fifteen-year-old Harry yelled from across the street. "For Christ's sake, get a fucking move on!"

"Where we going?" Wally Cort demanded. "What we gonna do?" He crossed the street to where a dozen loutish teenage youths waited.

"Wait and see." They all slouched off together laughing loudly, swearing, nudging each other with their elbows.

"Where we going?" Wally repeated, his voice higher pitched than the others, his accent strongly foreign. "We're not going to Coney Island again, are we?" he demanded suspiciously. "Last time I almost got caught."

"Course not," Harry reassured him. "Anyway, they didn't get you, did they, Wimp?"

"Only 'cause I snuck out the back when they wasn't looking." He shuddered at the memory of stealing hot dogs from Nathan's. He had wriggled in, the only boy small enough to squeeze under the gap in the back wall, while the others waited outside. It wasn't the first time, so he hadn't been too worried. Then the dog they hadn't known about had started to bark; and the old man came rushing around the back . . . Fortunately the old guy tried chasing the bigger boys when they fled, giving Walter just enough time to sneak out the back entrance.

"So where we going this time?" Walter's steps slowed.

"Come on, keep up."

"Listen, I ain't going nowhere till you tell me where."

"To get candy at Bonomo's," Harry explained reluctantly.

"Yeah," the other boys chimed in, "Turkish Taffy."

"How are you going to do that then?" Walter asked suspiciously.

"Through the skylight. Come on, Wimp. We'll explain when we get there."

"Fuck you! You mean *I'm* going through the skylight."

Harry stopped to stare at him. "You scared?" he asked in a withering tone.

"No, of course I'm not scared. Asshole." He felt his stomach contract. Why me? he wondered. Why is it always me that has to take the risks? But he was proud that they wanted him with them, needed him. He'd do almost anything to stay their friend. "What did you say that for?" he accused Harry. "Scared! After all the places I've been? Asshole." But while he blustered, he could feel his fear, like acute dyspepsia, writhing in his stomach.

"Okay, Wimp. I didn't mean it. Okay?"

The Bonomo warehouse was a long, gray, single-story building, its roof edges only eight feet from the ground. The boys had no difficulty hoisting young Wally onto the corrugated roof. Crabwise, he scampered diagonally up the roof to the skylight. The rest of the boys fanned out around the building to give warning if anyone came too close. In moments Walter had the skylight pried open and was dangling inside, reaching for the cases of candy.

He was sliding the fifth case down the roof when he heard the sirens. Instantly his companions fled, leaving Walter totally exposed on the vast expanse of the roof. The scream of the siren came closer every second.

For a moment Walter's panic paralyzed him. Visions of another sort of police so petrified him that he could only squeeze himself flat against the ribbed metal. Then, with a sudden wild rush of adrenaline, he was on his feet and running at top speed over the dangerous, sloping roof. Without pausing, he leaped into space, grunted once as he hit the grass, rolled and, without losing momentum, disappeared down Coney Island Avenue toward the boardwalk. He ignored the fiery pain in his ankle. Within a minute he was engulfed by crowds. Only when he was quite safe did he allow himself to limp—and to vomit from fear. But besides the panic, there was pride, too. He'd gotten away, hadn't he? In spite of the terror. Like he'd always gotten away from them in the end.

Later that evening, Harry had slunk over to Walter's tenement. He'd knocked tentatively on the apartment door. Normally he would have just yelled from the street, so the fact that he had climbed the three flights of stairs was proof that he had a bad conscience.

"Shithead. Where'd you go?" Walter demanded as soon as he saw his friend.

"I'm glad they didn't get you," Harry said in a gentler tone than Walter could ever remember his using.

"No thanks to you! So where were you when the cops came?"

"There wasn't nothing we could do," Harry said lamely. "Anyhow, I knew you'd get away." He had looked at his little friend with admiration. "You always find a way."

The memory faded. He's still doing it, thought Walter. Thirty years later, and he's still doing it.

"It's England on the phone now," Caroline interrupted his thoughts. "Raymond Mitty."

"Hello, Raymond . . ." Walter started.

"Hello, old boy." The musical-comedy voice of Raymond Mitty seemed to come from next door. "I say, how *are* you?"

"And I say, I'm fine."

"Good show!"

"What can I do for you?" Walter asked, knowing that the small talk would continue indefinitely if he didn't push for substance.

"Nothing much, old boy. I was just wondering about those gauchos."

"The what?"

"The gauchos. You know, those strange pant-skirts your birds wear."

"Birds?" Walter was mystified.

"Women, females, old boy. We call them birds."

"Oh, yes, yes." Walter suddenly remembered the garments that were giving him such problems.

"Your office said you had ten thousand dozen at eighty cents each."

"No. They're eighty-five cents," said Walter quickly. Raymond tried it every time.

"Oh, eighty-five cents was it? Okay. You still got 'em?"

"I don't know," said Walter, knowing perfectly well that it was merchandise he had been unable to get rid of anywhere in the world. "Let me ask Caroline." He pushed the hold button and waited a few seconds. It was all a game, he reflected, this bargaining. He quite enjoyed it, although at times it made him feel foolish, like a grownup playing kids' games.

"Yes," he said after an appropriate delay, "she says we still have them. We got an offer for seventy-nine cents, but we turned it down."

"Lovely, I'll take them. Eighty-one cents?"

"You can have them at eighty-four cents." Walter hoped the relief in his voice was not apparent. At a purchase price of seventy-five cents each, only five percent of retail, the gauchos had looked like an excellent buy four weeks ago. He'd taken the whole lot for a hundred thousand dollars, convinced he'd move them in hours. But then the colors were wrong, sizes were a problem, the whole thing looked like a disaster. After a while he started fretting that he might not be able to sell them at any price, let alone at a profit. So now his relief was great. If Raymond would pay eighty-four cents, Walter would actually make a profit of nine cents per garment—over ten thousand bucks.

". . . 'Fraid I can't go that high," Raymond said, dashing Walter's high hopes, "I'll go for eighty-two cents."

"Christ, you're a tough bargainer, Mitty. But I can't sell them for that." Walter feared that if he accepted Mitty's price too readily, the Englishman would think there was something wrong and back off. "I'll split the difference," he said, "eighty-three cents."

"You're on. Eighty-three cents. A hundred and eighty day credit. Okay, old boy?"

Walter's heart sank. "Christ," he said, "what do you think I am? A goddamn bank?"

"No," said Raymond Mitty with a chuckle. "A fellow who paid seventy-five cents apiece for gauchos he can't sell. I'm giving you eight thousand dollars profit as it is."

"And then killing me with just as much interest expense," Walter interrupted.

"Never mind, old man. It's better than nothing."

"Ninety days, then," said Walter. "That's long enough."

"Sorry, old man. A hundred and eighty."

"Fuck you," said Walter, but without rancor. He knew it was the best he could do. So forget it and on to the next deal. That had always been his philosophy. "Okay," he said. "Deal's done."

"Fuck you too, old man," said Mitty pleasantly. "See you soon. Have a happy."

How could he sound so inane and be so sharp? Walter thought as he put down the phone. He beat me on that one from the first sentence. He chuckled to himself, pleased that he had at least broken even. He hated it when he lost money, not so much because of the loss itself—he could afford that these days—but because it gave his neuroses a field day. Was he losing his grip? Was it worth it? "Show me a good loser, and I'll show you a loser," Harry Truman had said. Walter Cort was just as poor a loser now as he had been in the early days, when every loss was a calamity.

For the rest of the morning Walter worked on a series of local calls, Caroline arranging one after the other swiftly and precisely.

"Bartalini on line one, Mr. Cort. You wanted to talk to him about the advertising on the cameras." Walter, picking through his memory like a computer sorting index cards, would start talking as if the subject had been at the front of his mind all day.

"Furgeson of International Plastics on line two. He says your consulting offer sounds fine, but he wants to talk price. . . ." "On line three, sir, it's Jonathan Gold. He wants to know whether you're still interested in the building contract. . . ." "The mayor's office on line. . . ."

Occasionally Walter asked for information before taking a call, and Caroline hurried in with the file. Sometimes in the middle of a call he buzzed twice on the intercom and she arrived on the run. "Get oil contract," he scribbled without interrupting his conversation. When she rushed back with it, he smiled, mouthing "Thanks."

At the end of each conversation, he rattled off a summary into a dictating machine. He had long ago learned that these summaries (or perhaps the widespread knowledge that he made them) helped other people's memories as much as his own.

By noon Walter Cort's voice had become grating. He ran his fingers through his hair and massaged his forehead. "No more calls for a while," he told Caroline.

"You made enough money for this morning?"

"I need to do some dictation."

"Susie called earlier, asked that you call her back."

"Which Susie?"

Caroline shook her head. "How should I know?" she demanded petulantly. Why was he always so casual about his women? she wondered, as she had many times before. Why did he act as though women were nothing more than inanimate objects?

"Mad at me?" he asked innocently, smiling.

"No, but when it comes to women, you just never seem to know what's going on."

"Oh, I know *what,* Caroline, it's just that I have a little trouble remembering *with whom.*"

She laughed in spite of herself. It was the only thing she disliked about him. He had so many girls, and he sent them flowers, gave them lavish gifts, took them to "21" and The Four Seasons, and spent fortunes flying them to meet him in Rome, Acapulco, Gstaad—but he never shared himself with them, never gave them his feelings: only his things. As far as Caroline knew, she was the only female he ever really paid attention to, she and that damned dog of his, she thought cynically. Or was she merely a professional secretary, another piece of expensive office furniture . . . ? No, we have a special relationship, she assured herself. I'm not pretty or slim like the others, but at least I'm reasonably bright, she thought, proud of her 137 IQ. At least he respects me as a person. It was just that sometimes, especially late at night when she couldn't fall asleep, she found herself wondering what it would be like if she were just a little more attractive.

However, Caroline was wrong in thinking that her boss had never formed a close relationship. There had been a girl once, long before Walter had money or success. Harry Grass had introduced them.

"Hey, Wimp, you ever met my cousin Rachel?"

"You know I never."

"Come on over then."

Walter shuffled his feet. At seventeen, only just reaching physical maturity and still short for his age, he felt terribly self-conscious with girls. "Nah, I'm busy."

"So how busy could you be?"

"I said I'm busy."

"So come over after school. She's a real looker."

"For Christ's sake . . ."

"Only trouble is she's too small for me, Wimp. Hell, she's shorter than you are."

"Hello, Walter, how are you doing?" Mundane words, but her voice lilted, and he could still recall his surprise at being called Walter.

"Walter? Who the fuck's Walter?" Harry Grass demanded. "He's Wimp."

"He's Walter to me," Rachel said with dignity.

"See. Asshole. Like I told you," Walter said proudly to Harry.

"Walter." He grinned at Rachel. "Thanks. Come on, I'll buy you a hot dog." To his astonishment, he didn't feel at all shy with her.

"You gonna *buy* one?" Harry asked in feigned amazement. "You never paid for one yet."

"How do you get them then?" Rachel asked.

"Slides in under the wall in back."

"I'm gonna buy one this time. You want one, Rachel?"

"Yes, I'd love one. And I'm glad you're not going to crawl around on your belly for it."

They walked down the street, Rachel and Walter together, Harry the odd man out.

"You got money?" Harry was still surprised that his friend would actually stoop to buying food. You *took* food, the gang always assumed, you *bought* real things—and only if you couldn't steal them.

"Enough for a couple of hot dogs."

"If not, I got some," Rachel said.

"I don't want your money." Walter was instantly defensive.

"How'd you get money anyhow?" Harry demanded noisily of Rachel. "Girls ain't suppose to have money of their own." He was willing to say anything to keep from being ignored by the other two. "Bet you didn't get it wriggling on your stomach."

"What d'you mean?" Walter asked suspiciously.

"I mean . . ." Harry hesitated.

"He means," interrupted Rachel haughtily, "I probably got it lying on my back."

Instantly Walter erupted in anger. "Leave her alone, you son of a bitch," he snarled at his friend. "You talk to her like that again and I'll smack you one." Later he would not be able to understand why he had become so incensed. He had met the girl barely ten minutes earlier; and anyhow, what Harry had said was not so bad—as a rule, no one cared what you said to girls. But, against all expectations, that particular insult made him so mad, he was ready to fight.

"Hold it, Wimp. Hold it!" Harry Grass laughed teasingly. "I was only joking. It ain't true she does it on her back. Rachel only does it standing—" Before Harry could continue, Walter's foot smashed into his groin.

"Christ!" Harry shrieked as he fell to the ground.

"You leave her alone, shithead," Walter said coldly. "Next time I'll kick 'em right off."

"Christ sake, Wimp." The boy on the ground was holding himself and writhing. "Christ sake, help me."

"Okay, but no more cracks, you hear?"

"Okay, Wimp, okay. Just help me up."

In the following months it was usually Rachel who organized what they did and where they went. She did it subtly, never seeming to dominate.

"A movie?" she would ask softly. "There's a Jimmy Cagney on. Or the club?" She hated the broken, dirty storefront his gang called the club. "Harry and you could shoot pool." It was a makeshift game with used-up tennis balls on a wooden table.

"Movie," he would order. "I don't want to go to the club again." At the club he always felt as if he had to compete for her with a dozen other boys. Not that she ever flirted, but she was friendly with the other gang members, and he was secretly convinced that one day she would throw him over for one of his larger, better-looking mates.

"Okay," she would say, pleased with how she had manipulated him, careful not to show it.

At the movie he would sit as close as possible to her and she would let him touch her almost anywhere he wanted, drawing her careful line only if he tried—as he did every time—to insinuate his hand under the elastic of her panties. That touch, which he longed for until his groin ached, she consistently forbade. Eventually he almost gave up hope and made only token attempts at "going all the way."

"Do you love me?" she asked one afternoon, as they walked through the park, laughing and scampering like children.

"Sure."

"Say it."

"I love you, Rachel. I love you a lot." He stopped, wondering at the unexpected question, and saw her looking at him with strange and distant eyes. She seemed not sad or afraid but isolated and solemn, as if she were enjoying some great tragedy. He moved closer to her, tentatively putting his arm around her shoulders.

"I love you too." She turned toward him and kissed him, first gently, then demandingly, her tongue probing deep into his mouth. His desire for her rose as violent as rage. He grew so large that his underpants felt painfully tight. Roughly he pulled Rachel's body to his. But instead of pulling away as she normally did, she shared his sudden passion and clutched at his hips with both her hands, gyrating against him so that he forgot his discomfort in a mixture of amazement and love, desire and pride.

Locked together, they fell to the ground, kissing and clutching at one another. Briefly he looked up to check that no one was too close, and realized with delight that they were lying in a depression in the ground just deep enough to be hidden and alone. That there were others beyond the rim of their private saucer did not bother them. Privacy was rare in their ghetto lives; even this much was a luxury.

"Rachel," he managed to whisper, "Rachel, I do love you."

"Hush," she whispered back. "I know." She withdrew from him slightly so that she could wriggle higher and pull his face down to her breasts. Then, to his astonishment and delight, she started to unbutton her blouse.

The instant she had her blouse open, and her bra, miraculously hooked in front, undone, he was nuzzling and sucking at her nipples, overwhelmed almost to tears, while she moaned and pulled at his hair, stroked his ears, pushed her pelvis at him in a way he had dreamed about. She had let him touch her breasts and marvel at their perfection before. But this was different. She had never helped him take off her things. There was a new passion in her which he could not understand but only adore.

After a few minutes he dropped his hands across her flat belly and surreptitiously started to lift her skirt. He did it by degrees so that she would not be forced into stopping him too soon—the rules between them up to then had been clear. But now, instead of pretending not to notice, she was lifting her hips to help him. There was a sense of urgency and seriousness in her, he started to realize. When he touched her panties and she responded by groping for him, his heart flooded with a gratitude even greater than his desire.

She helped him pull her underthings off, as if he had done it a hundred times. For the first time he felt the indescribably beautiful, soft roughness of her hair. He could have lingered there, playing with it for hours. But she was in a hurry now, and when he was too slow to please her, she helped him along, undoing his pants with a matter-of-fact practicality which made him gasp.

Before he had any idea of what to do next, she was holding him in her perfect hand. Then she was moving herself against his shaft, rubbing its length along her warm wetness, while he lay on his side, his eyes tightly closed, trembling, trembling.

For one awful second he recalled the camp and the guard, the jackboots, a different kind of sex. . . . He opened his eyes in momentary horror, but when he saw her, he forgot everything again but his love and desire.

"Wait," she commanded. "I've got to put something on you." And while he watched incredulously, she leaned over to her purse and pulled out a condom. "I stole it from Harry's jacket."

Walter thought it was the cleverest, sweetest act he had ever seen. "Christ, I hope he doesn't need it," he giggled.

"Of course not. He's never had a girl."

"He's had hundreds."

"Just boasting. It's not true."

She slipped the rubber onto him and leaned over to kiss him.

"And you?" The question was torn from him by an absolute need to know.

"Of course not," she said, and laughed. "But it's time."

Before he realized he had even moved, he was on top of her, and in an instant deep inside. Then their hips were pumping together in an instinctive coupling that was a triumph for both of them—of ecstasy, of tenderness and wild abandon, of making love.

The next day he heard from Harry that his cousin Rachel and her family had moved away. "Down South," Harry explained. "She sure didn't want to go. Made a big scene last week when they told her. But her dad says there's no work for him here so they don't have no choice. Goddamn shame, good-looking broad like that. Probably won't see her again."

"Time for your lunch date," Caroline said, interrupting Walter's thoughts. "The Friar's Club. You're meeting Fred Pogue."

The Friar's Club not only *is* a famous institution in New York, it looks like one. Its granite facade bespeaks importance; and its carved oak door implies that it is a privilege to be allowed to enter, a privilege not easily earned. Inside, the club is detailed with turn-of-the-century luxury: high-vaulted, decorated ceilings; massive doorways; and a staircase of carved and polished wood. Heavy Victorian furniture fills the bar and dining rooms. As befits the world's leading show business club, its ambience is upbeat and full of noise. Walter enjoyed it for its informal cordiality, its good food and friendly, efficient service. The only annoyance was the constant interruption of the loudspeaker: "Calling Friar Milton Berle to the phone, please. Friar Milton Berle. Calling Friar Joey Adams to the phone, please. Friar Joey Adams. . . ." The litany was impressive, but interruptive.

"Has Fred Pogue arrived?" Walter asked the man taking the coats.

"I think—"

"Welcome. How you doing?" Fred's cheerful voice interrupted the answer, instantly catching Walter up in its good humor. He was a great, untidy bear of a man. His loose suit seemed to hang on him like a set of drapes and his hair, silver gray and thinning, was windblown and messy. People often mistook him for a grandfatherly small-town college professor. At the Friar's, strangers observing his marvelously mobile, expressive face, thought he must be a character actor or a comedian. But on closer contact, his sharp eyes and keen street sense gave away the fact that he was a businessman. Beneath his untidy, almost comical exterior hid a tough competitor who bargained hard and who was rarely bested in a deal. Nevertheless, most of the time he was cheerful and warm, his round, flattened, versatile face covered with a grin. "Come and libate with me."

"Do what?"

"Libate. Have a libation. Drink, my friend, drink!"

Walter, looking like a terrier next to Fred's St. Bernard, accompanied his friend into the dining room. They sat down opposite each other, Fred against the wall, his head just below a picture of Frank Sinatra.

"A Perrier for me," Fred called to the waiter.

"Is that all you're having?"

"Drink for me only with mine eyes . . . I'm dieting. Damn nuisance! But if I don't, I balloon." He blew out his cheeks, made a cute, silly face, poked at his belly with his forefinger and, to Walter's amusement, gave a precise imitation of the Pillsbury doughboy.

"The latest theory is that it's your parents fault," Walter said, laughing. "It's the size of your fat cells. If your mother pushed food into them while you were growing, they remain easily expandable."

"Yeah? I'll tell her. She'll be so pleased to have something new to blame herself for," Fred sighed tragically. "You don't know how lucky you are not to have expandable fat cells," he added. "I suppose your mother. . . ." He stopped, acutely embarrassed at his faux pas.

"I took a bit of a slimming cure as a teenager," said Walter lightly. "I used to run a lot," he added sarcastically, "for my health. . . ."

"Calling Friar Fred Tarter to the phone, please," the loud speaker interrupted, "Friar Fred Tarter."

"He's one of my main competitors."

"You barter agents all called Fred?" Walter asked facetiously. "And all members of the Friar's Club?"

Fred Pogue smiled. "Several of us belong. That's because barter's so closely connected with radio and television," he explained. "When a station has advertising time they can't sell, they'll swap it for almost anything rather than waste it. After all, there's nothing deader than yesterday's unsold advertising time."

"And I suppose they can't just cut their prices without destroying their market."

"Absolutely. If they did that, no one would pay full price."

"So they camouflage the discount by swapping against merchandise?"

"Sure. That way the station seems to be getting its full price— but the buyer gets his discount anyway because the merchandise he swaps isn't worth nearly a hundred cents on the dollar."

"I'm aware of that part of the deal. A couple of my clients do that with you. But I've never really known how the TV or radio stations use the redundant merchandise."

"That's where barter agents like me come in. We act as a clearing-house. We take in the merchandise and barter it against other stuff."

"Like what?"

"All sorts of things. Hotel rooms, rental cars, furniture . . ."

"Huh?" Walter was becoming confused. This was a field he—and most other businessmen, for that matter—knew little about. "Is it as complicated as it sounds? And where does the chain stop; when do you make your money?"

Fred grinned complacently. "You do need to know what you're doing," he admitted. "And you've got to have the capital to hold on until you finally end up with something you can sell for cash." He held his breath like a man under water. "Sometimes it takes a while before you can come up for air," he gasped.

Walter laughed. "You seem to be breathing okay at the moment," he commented.

"Oh, indeed," Fred nodded his head vigorously, making his cheeks flap. "I just made me a small fortune. . . ."

"As opposed to the large fortunes you usually make?"

"Oh, no, barter agents don't usually make large killings on a single deal. We aim for a small percentage made frequently. But this one was different."

"Tell me about it," Walter said indulgently, knowing that nothing would stop his companion from doing just that.

"Well, what happened was that I discovered three unrelated facts. And when I put them together—bingo!" His eyes glinted with the excitement of the memory. Energized, his whole body seemed to lose its flabbiness and become tighter, more in control.

"Go on." Walter was infected by the other man's excitement.

"Well, first I discovered that a certain soft-drink company was spending about a million dollars a year on telephone-equipment rental. I also found out that their cola syrup only cost them about twenty-five percent of their selling price. And finally I was told that there were several potential customers for syrup who didn't buy from them but would at a cut price . . ."

"So how did those three pieces of information help you?"

Fred Pogue smiled broadly. "I offered the cola company ten years of telephone equipment for ten million dollars' worth of syrup."

"Which only cost them two and a half million!"

"Right."

"They must have been delighted."

"They were pleased," said Fred in classic understatement. "Even though I asked for the full two-and-a-half million of the syrup up front, that was still a hell of a lot cheaper than a million dollars cash a year for ten years." He sat back and smiled at the memory.

"Well, go on, what happened? Did they agree?"

"Oh yes, they had to agree."

"And then?"

"Then I approached a huge user of Pepsi-Cola syrup, and asked at what price they would switch to our cola and buy ten million dollars of the syrup.

"And?"

"And they said seven million dollars." Fred was talking at full speed now, his hands sweeping across the table. "Then I went to ITT," he said dramatically, "and asked them how much would they charge for the ten years of equipment. I held my breath for three weeks while they calculated." He stopped breathing again to demonstrate. "Finally, they came back with their answer," he said, letting out his breath with a rush and relishing his punchline. "Their bid was six million dollars!"

"And you were looking at a million-dollar profit," Walter said in awe.

"Less a few expenses."

"But why couldn't the cola company deal directly with ITT?"

"Because ITT doesn't want cola syrup!" Fred looked utterly triumphant.

"What a fabulous deal. The cola company saved a bundle on their telephones. ITT made a large sale. The cola user bought at a good price. And you made a million dollars. Everyone won!"

"That's how good barter deals work." Fred beamed.

The waiter served their food; the loudspeaker intermittently blared out the names of the famous and near-famous. The two men ate their lunch and enjoyed each other's company, speaking of many things.

"I'm delighted you had time for lunch," Walter said as they were finishing their coffee. "I learned a lot more than I knew before about barter. I'm sure it will come in handy for some of my clients—which clears my conscience for having eaten too much."

"If we tried as hard to lose weight as we try to find excuses for why we can't, we'd all be as skinny as ghosts," Fred laughed. "Someday someone is going to invent a diet that an ordinary mortal can stick to. Every diet on the market now is made for an *average* person—and there aren't any of those. If only someone would develop a diet for *real* people—not average ones—then even *I* would lose weight."

"That would be fantastic. Whoever did that would make millions —and deserve it."

Walter would remember his remark many times in the future, often with great bitterness. But for the moment it was insignificant, mere lunchtime chatter.

As Walter walked back to his office—down Madison Avenue instead of Park for a change—he felt a rare sense of contentment. He window-shopped in the attractive but affordable men's shops; loitered at construction sites every few blocks, observing the giant cranes that seemed so top-heavy but were nevertheless able to lift steel girders as if they were matchsticks; jumped to safety as a city bus, belching fumes, rode onto the sidewalk, barely missing pedestrians; and felt at peace. Perhaps it was because he had enjoyed his lunch with Fred Pogue, or because the girls swinging along the avenue were so pretty, or just that the weather was so perfect, with a cool breeze and a blue sky. Or perhaps today his panic was simply better-covered. He felt confident in every possible way. Almost.

"Why the fuck did I agree to make that speech?" Walter Cort demanded angrily of his secretary. "When's it scheduled?"

"Next Thursday afternoon," Caroline said flatly. "I've planned for you to go up to Boston the day before—you'll have a dinner meeting the evening you arrive and see the First Boston Group the next morning." She knew his swearing meant that he was thoroughly annoyed. Usually he left the vulgarities to his friend Harry Grass.

"I hate giving speeches," said Walter petulantly. "Especially at the Harvard Business School. Those students act so damned superior." But even as he complained, Walter realized that his annoyance was excessive. Damn it, he thought, speaking to the business school was supposed to be an honor, not a nuisance. "Okay," he said decisively. "I'll dictate my remarks while I drive out to see Associated Products tomorrow."

Caroline pouted. "I hate it when you dictate in the car. All I hear on the tape is traffic noises."

"And occasional screams of pain?"

"Those too."

"Probably the best part of my speech," he said, and chuckled. He was used to Caroline's complaints. "Anyway, what's next?"

"You're all heart, aren't you?" she said, not really bitter; actually she admired the fact that he used every moment of his day productively. "Your accountant called to offer a coal shelter," she continued. "I don't know what that means—"

"It means a black hole underground . . ." he started, wanting to cheer her up.

"No it doesn't," she interrupted, amused. "It means something to do with taxes. I just don't know what."

"It's complicated." He loved to explain, to teach. It made him feel generous, giving. He sometimes wondered whether that was one reason he had become a consultant. And Caroline was an apt pupil. Totally unlike Judith—and all the others, for that matter, who wouldn't have understood one word. "The way it works is that you invest a certain amount in a coal mine," he explained, "let's say forty thousand dollars. But you only put up about a quarter, say ten thousand, in cash. You pay the rest by giving a promissory note. Then you deduct the whole forty as expenses against your income."

"But that means you're deducting more than you put up."

"That's why it's a tax shelter. It means that if you're in the fifty percent tax bracket . . ."

"You put up ten thousand in cash and get back twenty thousand from the government," she concluded triumphantly.

"Exactly."

"So what's the catch?"

"One is that you may have to pay off the note at some point—although, of course, the shelter organizers claim you'll earn enough from the coal mine to cover it."

"But if you earn it, isn't that more taxable income?"

"Sure. But it's income that's delayed a few years. And you can always shield it through another tax shelter. You keep doing it until a year when you have little other income and don't have to pay high taxes."

"Or until you drop dead!"

"At which point you don't care quite so much."

Caroline laughed.

"The only other catch is that the government might disallow the whole scheme."

"Might? Why can't you be sure?"

"Because the way the tax laws are written, they're so convoluted that they have to be interpreted by the courts. So before at least one typical case goes to court, no one really knows what the interpretation will be."

The telephone interrupted. Efficiently Caroline jotted a message onto the telephone pad and added it to his pile.

"Who was it?"

"Western Union. I've written it on your note pad," she pointed out, acidly.

"You can't tell me?"

"A message from a Judith." Caroline's voice was glacial. "She says: 'We'd have had even more fun if I'd been awake that morning. See you soon.' "

With three hours to spare before dinner, Walter Cort elected to visit the Harvard campus. It was a crisp, bright afternoon. Spring was fighting to emerge; the forsythia was budding. Altogether it was perfect weather for a stroll. The taxi deposited him just outside the campus, and he walked around the wall and in through the main gate.

A wave of emotion filled him—a mixture of awe and pride. That he, Wally Cort of Brooklyn, Auschwitz, and places in Poland that he could scarcely recall, should be invited by the masters of this hallowed institution to impart *his* knowledge to *them* seemed at once ironic and flattering. He watched the students sauntering in the sun, looking so expensively casual—and somehow so much *cleaner* than at other schools—and decided again that this was what a university should look like. Even the ugly, neo-European buildings seemed appropriate. The grotesque Widener Memorial library, with its 1914-era Grecian pillars; the squat, dark red, looming Seever Hall with its foolish rounded portal; the commemorative chapel with more Grecian pillars, and a garish, silly white steeple as sharp as a lance; and the huge modern Science Center, like an oversized ocean liner of gray-lilac marble with a shiny observatory cupola perched on top—all, surprisingly, seemed to blend into an eclectic whole connoting learning and dignity. Graceful trees, their trunks and limbs forming natural sculptures, and carefully arranged paths crisscrossing between patches of lawn added to the effect. The perfect setting, Walter concluded cynically, to serve the only true gods: learning and wealth.

In spite of the bustle of students everywhere, there was something soothing and restful about the Harvard campus. The serenity of wisdom? No. Not letting even something as intangible as a sense of awe upstage him, Walter quickly amended his thought: more likely, the bliss of ignorance.

Walter emerged from Boston's Drake Hotel—traditionally elegant, reeking of money: antique carpets; mink wraps and coats subtly touched with fragrance—into the cool afternoon sunlight. Ahead of him was the Boston Common, as genteel as New York's Washington Square was noisy. On either side of the hotel stretched English-style townhouses, many holding bookstores or boutiques selling antiques, carefully understated china or stuffy, matronly fashions. Walter's glossy maroon Ferrari, ostentatiously awaiting him at the curb, with his driver lounging carelessly against the hood, seemed garish in these surroundings, nouveau riche in the extreme. Walter loved it!

"I'll drive myself. Thank you. No need to wait." He always enjoyed the sensation the car created. Here in stodgy Boston he was particularly amused to see the slightly disapproving frowns of the passersby as he tooled along, driving a little too fast. Nor was he disappointed when he reached the Harvard campus. Even here, where money and the display of it was commonplace, the car was noticed. There was something aggressively sexual about its long, low profile and maroon gleam. Asking directions to the business school from a rather disdainful-looking young woman, and not understanding her complicated instructions, he cheerfully invited her to "hop in and show me." Throwing her Ivy-League reserve to the winds, she did so, and reveled in the luxurious decadence of the $70,000 car.

It turned out that the business school was several city blocks away from the main campus, and Walter had the impression that she purposely took him the long way around to show herself off to her friends. But he was a few minutes early, so made no comment. When they finally reached the business school, the doorman took one look at the car sliding up to the curb and hurried down the steps to greet its driver.

"It's fine to park here," he greeted Walter, pointing to the no-parking zone. He pronounced his words with the typical elongated Bostonian vowels: "paaak." It sounded a little like a bleating sheep, Walter thought. Immediately he was annoyed with himself. He hated prejudice in all forms, but especially in himself. Silently he apologized.

The doorman held open the door of the Ferrari as if he were a host welcoming an honored guest to his domain. Walter, skilled from practice, hoisted himself out of the low-slung seat without apparent effort and walked up the steps and into the building. In the foyer a young man, more formally dressed than most of the students, stepped confidently toward him.

"Welcome to the business school, Mr. Cort," the urbane student greeted him. "I am the president of the Speaker's Committee, and it is an honor to have you visit us."

"Thank you." Walter was impressed by the young man's polish. No wonder Harvard MBAs got such exorbitant starting salaries. Thirty-four thousand was last year's average, he had heard. This fellow certainly looked worth it. He couldn't help comparing how rough Harry and he had been at the same age—just a pair of gas-station grease-monkeys trying to figure out how to buy the station for nothing. Harry had finally figured it out. Leverage, they called it here at Harvard; buying a company with its own assets. In those days neither Harry nor he had ever heard of the word.

The amphitheater was crowded when Walter and his guide entered.

"There's a lot of interest in what you have to say. Usually we get executives from large companies, not . . ." the young man hesitated, looking for the right word. "What do you call yourself?"

"Entrepreneur best describes it."

"A taker-in-between?" the young man asked doubtfully.

"I see what you mean. Perhaps *entredoneur* would be better. A giver-in-between." They both laughed.

"I think it's time for me to introduce you." The young man walked to the podium. "Ladies and gentlemen, I'm honored to introduce to you an entrepreneur who does not, as the word implies, take from between; he does quite the opposite: he adds to deals and cements them. He tells me he would prefer to be called an entredoneur. But perhaps he would be happiest to be known as an entre-activateur—an activator-in-between . . ."

Walter realized that the introduction, and hence his earlier conversation, had been rehearsed. A nice piece of manipulation, he thought: Subtlety 101.

". . . and so the title of Mr. Cort's talk today is 'Venture and Adventure Capital,' " the young man was concluding. "May I present one of New York's most successful entre-activateurs, Mr. Walter Cort."

There was a polite round of applause as Walter walked to the stage.

"A clever and erudite introduction, for which I thank you," Walter said into the microphone. "It is fitting that, at Harvard Business School, the study of business can be combined with plays on the French language, points of business philosophy, or whatever other recondite games entertain you." He paused to survey his audience and to underline his next sentence. "But I'm afraid those are the hobbies of the academic world, not the realities of the business world," he said emphatically.

"This is the second time that I have talked here at a Harvard Business School meeting," Walter continued. "Frankly, I am astonished to have been invited back. I think it is only because no one present at my first talk was consulted. Or perhaps it is that everyone who studies at Harvard recalls their time here through such a rosy haze of later success that they feel happy even about me . . ." He paused for the mild ripple of laughter and took a drink of water. Cynical faces gazed up at him. These young people were bright and alert, but already too world-weary for their own good.

"You see," he said, "as presentations go, my first one here was a disaster. I was asked whether I thought that Pareto or Keynes had a greater influence on modern business thinking. And I was forced to answer that I had no more than a general idea of Keynes's theories, and even less of Pareto's. My secretary thinks he plays third base for the

Red Sox." There was some more light laughter.

"The fact is," Walter stated firmly, "that no economist, no social theorem, no book about advertising or marketing, nothing I have read —except perhaps technical matter written about accounting and law —has very much influence at all on the business world."

There was a rustle of annoyance from the audience. "You would doubt that, of course," Walter said, overriding the growing hostility. "No doubt you would point out that Harvard students are more successful than average students—indicating that, contrary to what I've just told you, the theories taught here are applicable out there." A few heads nodded in agreement. "But no," Walter continued, "you all know that those who enter the business school are superior in the first place: you are the elite. And of course you don't lose that advantage here. But it's because you are *good,* not because of the theory you learn, that you succeed."

"You see, the business world deals with hard practical issues of how to make money, how to get promoted, how to beat your competitor. There aren't many useful theory books written about that. Maybe a few novels by people who have done it, but that's about all. As a friend of mine pointed out, if the study of economics showed the way to succeed in business, then universities wouldn't need fund-raising drives . . .

"Economics departments don't make money because they have other interests," a woman's voice challenged. "The thinking process of economics applies."

He looked up in surprise. It was unusual for the students to interrupt before question time. "Does it?" he demanded. "I doubt it. But there's an easy way to check: If it makes money, the thought process is valuable in business; if not, it's not." Walter was searching the auditorium to find his questioner. The tall, arrogant blonde in the top row? Or just below her, the foreign-looking girl in the jeans? No, she probably had an accent. He couldn't tell; they all looked equally incensed at his words. "So you tell me," he challenged, searching the area from which the voice had come. "How valuable is your thinking? How much money have you earned with it?"

"None yet." He almost missed her the second time. When he finally realized it was the tiny, round, feather of a blonde he was even more surprised by the firmness of her voice. "But I will." She said it with flat emphasis.

She looks as fragile as a bird's egg, he thought. "You sound as if you will, my dear," he said indulgently, and noticed that she blushed at the compliment.

In fact, the blush on Katherine Anne Rochester's face was not pleasure but a flash of anger at his condescension. She had only interrupted because she was interested in what he said. He spoke well and threw a vigorous challenge at the class—better than those corporate men who couldn't stop boasting about their companies' administrative practices and steady profit growth. She wanted to make sure he noticed her, always anxious as she was to widen her contacts. So why did he have to patronize her? Dear, indeed! These damn men, she thought for the millionth time. Just because she was petite—how she hated that word—it didn't mean her head was empty. When she said she would make money, she damn well meant it.

"But how will you make your money?" Walter continued his question. If she was impertinent enough to interrupt him, she could take the consequences.

"I haven't decided yet."

"But you are developing a plan?"

"No, not yet. I am still studying those business theories you decry." Thinking she was winning the argument, or at least holding her own, she was gaining confidence.

"But if the main theoretical objective of the individual in business is to make profits—and if you are not formulating any profit-making plans—then surely you are studying the wrong theory," he closed in on her. "Back to your lessons, young lady."

The whole class laughed. Katherine Anne Rochester, known as Katy by almost everyone except her mother, went pink with embarrassment, and bit her lip. He was wrong, the bastard, even though she hadn't expressed her point clearly. Of course there were practical considerations in business. That's why Harvard used a case-study method. But there was such a thing as valid theory, too. This Walter Cort was so superior, damn him. Katy decided she wasn't going to let him off that easily.

"My brother is studying medicine," she said. "But he is only in his first year, so they do not let him operate. Yet he is learning how to be a practical doctor." She was pleased with her answer. "First the theory, you see. Then the practice," she concluded triumphantly.

"It is a point of view," Walter conceded, impressed that the girl was managing to stand up to him rather well. "But a weak one, I'm afraid. Doctors, you see, learn technique, not theory. That's like a businessman learning accounting, which, as I said, is fine. Moreover," he added with a small chuckle, "unlike businessmen, doctors get paid for failure—whether the patient lives or dies." He smiled at the class before turning his attention back to the girl. "As a matter of fact," he said, grinning, "when your brother and you both graduate, he'll probably make more money than you do—which will make him a better practical businessman!" Walter paused for effect. "Oh *dear!*" he added lugubriously, with precise comic timing that made the entire class roar with laughter. Katy, annoyed at being so unfairly bested, could meanwhile only glower at him, silent.

"The fact is," Walter continued, ignoring the young woman now and concentrating his persuasion on the rest of the class, "if I make a hundred thousand dollars, and you make only twenty, I am five times better than you as a businessman. Of course, I realize that the equation becomes more complicated if yours is the start and mine is the end of my efforts. But, although the arithmetic can be made as complicated as you like, the principle maintains. The amount we earn is what measures us as businessmen."

Katy almost interrupted the lecture for a second time. ". . . and women," she muttered angrily.

". . . in the eyes of God, we may be measured by different virtues. As politicians, it's votes that count. As surgeons, we are—or at least we should be—measured by the lives we save; as lawyers, by the accused criminals we incarcerate or set free. But, I repeat, as businessmen, we are measured by the money we earn and by nothing else at all." He closed his notes with a snap. "And that is my point of view," he said with a smile. "Some colleges are starting to share it now. More of them are appointing businessmen to offset the preponderance of academicians on their faculties. But many schools of business still disagree with my views. That's why I've kept my remarks short, so that we can have plenty of time for discussion—and plenty of time for me to convince you!" There was a rustle from the audience when he said that, and he noticed several annoyed expressions on the young, scrubbed faces in the audience. From somewhere on his left he heard a voice whisper: "Fat chance!" He ignored the taunt, but it angered him. What did these students know about how tough it was to be successful? There was no theory to fall back on when the banks wanted to foreclose or Big Julie's garbage company was trying to put you out of business by threatening your drivers. That's when you sweated with worry through sleepless nights—and succeeded, or didn't, depending on many things, including luck as often as not, but never including anything in a book these kids read at Harvard. "Any comments or questions?" Walter demanded brusquely.

"Make money for *whom?*" Katy demanded sharply.

"For ourselves, of course. Who else?"

"For our stockholders." For our families, she wanted to say, for our rich relatives who sneer.

"Our success as businessmen—"

"I object to the term," Katy interrupted.

"What term?" Walter asked in surprise.

"Business*men.*"

"I do apologize." Walter's voice was entirely polite, but no less sarcastic for that. "Businesspersons." There was a snicker around the room, and to Katy's annoyance, several of the female students joined in it.

"Our success as businesspersons," Walter continued, "depends on how much we earn ourselves. The chairman is viewed as more important than the junior because he earns more for himself—even if the junior, through some brilliant marketing stroke, earns more for the shareholders."

"If an entrepreneur who owns a factory supplying hubcaps to Detroit earns more than the president of General Motors, does that mean he's a more successful businessman?" Katy demanded.

She might look fragile, Walter realized with surprise, but there was intelligence and some damned stubborn toughness inside that eggshell.

"The president of General Motors earns about a million dollars a year, plus a huge amount in deferred benefits," he started to explain. "Moreover, he's pretty much assured that his income will continue for a fixed number of years. No doubt you have recognized that such low-risk income is worth more than the hubcap maker's high-risk income. So the question whether the head of General Motors or the hubcap entrepreneur is a better businessman may be like asking whether Christ or Buddha is the greater saint. However, if the entrepreneur clearly makes a hell of a lot more than the president—not by luck or inheritance, but by acumen and hard work—then, yes, he sure is a better businessman. . . . But I must admit it's a good question. And I think, within limits, I could make a fair case for a differing view."

Damned if I could, Katy was thinking with grudging admiration. She looked him over carefully and decided she liked the lean determination she could see in his face. He seemed the sort of man who could help her make the money she wanted so urgently. "And if the hubcap maker does it by breaking the law?" she demanded, thinking he might have trouble getting out of that one.

"Ah, my dear," he said, tired of the argument, "on that I think I'll take the Fifth!"

Once again the whole class laughed at Katy Rochester. But while it angered her, she couldn't help being impressed, as well. Yes, he certainly was the sort of man who could help her. She'd make a point of meeting him after the lecture. If nothing else, it might give her the chance to get some of her own back. She certainly wasn't going to take it lying down, this Walter Cort's offhanded way of making a fool of her in public: not like her father would, not if she could help it.

Katy Rochester was barely eight when she first realized that her father was a charming but essentially worthless man. It was the greatest shock of her life. And the fact that it happened so casually somehow heightened its impact. She walked into the living room of their solid, Victorian home in Boston while her father and her grandfather were deep in conversation. Neither man noticed her as she lurked silently between the high-backed overstuffed chairs.

"It is bad enough that you have never done a day's work in your life, young man," she heard her grandfather say sternly to her father, who stood, head hanging, like a naughty schoolboy. "But that you should now willfully use my name to overdraw your bank account, leaving me to make good, is unconscionable."

Young Katy did not really understand what her daddy had done wrong, but she knew from his whipped, guilty expression—and from Grand-Dad's anger—that it must be very bad. It was not her grandfather's sternness, though, which shocked the little girl, but her father's acquiescence. Why doesn't he argue? Nobody can talk to my daddy like that. Yet her father just nodded and kept hanging his head. "Yes, sir," he answered at last. "I'm truly sorry. I don't know what came over me. I shall not do it again."

"I shall inform the bank to allow you no further overdrafts," the old man said wearily, "so you won't be able to indulge in this particular foolishness again. But no doubt you will find some other way of defrauding me. One day, you know, you will push me too far and, losing patience, I shall apply the only solution left to me—the law."

"Yes, sir." Her father, godlike in her eyes up to that moment, slunk out of the room while the little girl, dismayed beyond all imagining, ran up to her bedroom, buried her head in the pillows of her four-poster, and cried hysterically. When Nanny, who normally did not hold much with medicine, found Katy, she was so concerned for the little girl that she prescribed warm milk and honey, two aspirins *and* a teaspoon of tonic.

The full pattern of her father's wastrel, playboy ways did not become clear to Katy Rochester until many years later. By that time her grandfather had been dead for a few years and her father had squandered most of his inheritance. Fortunately the legacy that her grandfather bequeathed directly to her was enough to assure her a fine education. In her high school years she attended Hotchkiss, the magnificent private school in the rolling, green countryside of Connecticut. So well-endowed was the school that it had over an acre of grounds for every student enrolled—and twenty-one tennis courts, two ice-skating rinks, an eighteen-hole golf course, a college-caliber science center and a theater to rival most on Broadway. There she distinguished herself —in spite of her diminutive, cherubic appearance—by being a terror at tennis and near the top of her class in academics. After Hotchkiss she entered Sarah Lawrence College. She chose it partly for its reputation as a center of literature, theater, philosophy and the arts, all of which fascinated her. But, as she admitted to herself later, she was just as impressed by the fact that it combined the advantage of having an unusually beautiful, serene campus with the excitement of being only a half hour from New York. However, after a year, the college's arcane, theoretical profundities paled for practical-minded Katy, and she transferred to the University of Pennsylvania and a tough economics course with a minor in accounting.

In her spare time she became assistant editor of the school newspaper and was elected vice-chairperson of her class. To her intense annoyance the top jobs at both the newspaper and in campus politics eluded her because too few people believed that such a dimply, dainty body could house a spirit as strong and determined as hers.

She was even more annoyed when she found, following graduation, that there were practically no positions available for petite blondes looking for tough competitive jobs in finance.

"I don't think you'd have much *fun* here, dear," or, "You know, we're a pretty straight, nose-to-the-grindstone bunch. I don't think you'd like it," were the sort of comments she heard from personnel managers again and again.

"I'm sure I *would,*" she would insist, trying to convince each one of her hardness, her toughness.

"Well, I'll certainly keep your application in mind. Let me think about it. . . ."

But she never heard from any again. Eventually, having no better alternative, she took a job in an advertising agency, first as a copy assistant and then as a copywriter. Almost at once it became evident that she was one of the few willing to stand up to The Client, an almost mythical beast, it seemed, of tremendous rapacity. In fact, the client was represented by a rather shy young man with the title of brand manager who, as she succinctly told her cohorts, didn't know his ass from any other hole and was desperately anxious to be told which it was.

"I told him."

"You told him what?" the account executive, an equally indecisive young man, asked in horror.

"I told him which advertising campaign he preferred."

"Christ!"

"And he loved it."

"Thank God. But don't ever do it again."

Since she would not take such orders seriously, she knew she had to leave. Even though leaving was largely her own decision, she felt awful about it. Here she was, fresh out of school on her first job, and already she was practically getting fired. Wasn't this exactly the pattern one would expect from her father's daughter—instability, ineptness, an inability to get a decent job or hold it? She was deeply shaken by the experience, afraid to look for another job. What if she failed again? That, surely, would prove that she had inherited her father's shortcomings. Instead, with some of her grandfather's money left, she applied to and was accepted at the Harvard Business School.

During her first year at Harvard, her combative nature, intelligence and compulsive ambition placed her third in her class—which, in view of her looks, was an astonishment both to her professors and her peers. In her own estimation her newfound success atoned for her failure at her first job; she almost forgave herself.

Now, at the end of her second year at the business school, Katy was back to casting around for career alternatives. She had decided long ago that she *had* to earn money—and lots of it. To build back the family fortune her father had squandered, to regain power, to repair the damage to the Rochester name. Above all she simply had to prove to herself that she did have her grandfather's strength; that, after all, it ran in the family. . . . Perhaps her father would have been strong, too, if there had been any need.

The trouble was she didn't know *what* she wanted to do. With an MBA from Harvard, jobs would be easy to find, particularly in view of the ever-growing circle of business contacts she had carefully nurtured for future use. They included all those her family still had, plus a whole network of Harvard friends, their fathers, faculty members and other acquaintances. Whatever business she decided to enter, she was bound to know someone who would be useful.

But what business? The question frustrated her. Not a single direction seemed obvious.

"The only thing I know for sure is that I'll never make it in some hyperconglomerate," she had told Helga, her roommate and closest friend. "I can't stand regimentation. I want to do my own thing."

The two girls had been sitting in their college dormitory room. Helga, using the unlimited allowance that her father gave her, had gotten the Harvard-provided furniture thrown out and had arranged for the room to be furnished by the decorating department of Filene's. As a result, the room looked stylish, correct, luxurious—and sterile. Or at least so Katy felt. She hated it.

"Regimentation is good," Helga replied. "We Germans understand that."

Katy laughed. Her friend was forever pretending to be either a sauerkraut hausfrau or a Wagnerian diva. In fact, she was tall, slender and beautiful, as infinitely distant from any caricature of a German as Katy could imagine.

"Still you know what I mean," Katy insisted. "I want to be free!"

She threw her hands wide and pretended to flap like a bird. "Is that so unreasonable?"

"Totally."

"No, it's not. All it takes is to find somebody with vision. Someone to give me an exciting job."

"Try the Mafia. Blonde broad with initiative seeks interesting position. Dislikes discipline but good at French and Greek."

"I wish you'd come up with some sense," Katy said in exasperation. "What are you going to do?"

"I'm going into my father's business. It combines corporate regimentation with parental control. The best of both worlds."

Before dinner there was an informal cocktail hour. Walter stood at the center of a small ring of students, discussing many topics. The sturdy leather armchairs reminded him of the staid decor of a bankers' club, and despite their youth the students seemed to carry all the ponderous self-importance which suggested a banker's image. They behave as if they're at least my peers, my seniors, perhaps, he thought, annoyed at their presumption, but admiring too. Every one of them must have been voted most likely to succeed at whatever high school he attended, Walter decided—but not one of them has ever seen a school as bad as the one Harry and he went to. Walter could still remember his relief when they finally graduated.

"We're on our way, Wimp," Harry had crowed. "The bastards can't stop us now."

"Yeah? Well, we've still got to prove it."

"I'll set it up; you get it. That way we'll both do okay." Harry had made good on his promise regularly ever since.

I haven't done so badly on my end of the bargain either, Walter thought. He wondered whether these self-possessed young people would live up their apparent promise as thoroughly.

At the edge of the group surrounding him, two young men started to talk quietly together, assuming he couldn't hear them. But his hearing was unusually acute.

"Did you get anything out of this guy for that paper?" the first of the two outsiders asked.

"Nah."

"So is he giving summer jobs?"

"Nah." The second man's vocabulary seemed limited.

"Then what the hell are we doing here?" the first man wanted to know.

Puts me firmly in my place, Walter thought.

"I'm sorry I interrupted your lecture," Katy said as she pushed through the group.

"Hello, businessperson," said Walter good-humoredly, noting that she had interrupted his conversation without the slightest hesitation. Tough chick.

She grinned, arching her neck to look up at him. She couldn't be more than five foot three, Walter realized, a good six inches shorter than he. He noted how her breasts jutted as her head bent back. Nice. Spring was busting out all over.

"I'm Katherine Anne Rochester," she was saying. "Of the Boston Rochesters," she added, half-facetiously. "My friends call me Katy."

"I suppose I should call you Miss Rochester, then."

"You may call me Katherine; that's a compromise."

"Hey Katy, you interrupted an important discussion," said a tall handsome Jamaican man with a deep lilting voice.

"Now Clifton," she said severely, "we have been taught to judge objectively. And obviously you can't be objective when you're judging how important your own discussions are. To determine that we would need some statistically significant market research. So while you put that in motion, I'll just talk to Mr. Cort. Okay?" She turned her back on the now tongue-tied Clifton. "I am graduating this year," she said to Walter. "Near the top of my class—which may be damning by faint praise," she added, smiling over her shoulder at Clifton. "I liked your answers, Mr. Cort," she added. "I . . ."

Walter was starting to feel almost as dominated by Katy Rochester as the poor Jamaican she had just disenfranchised. "So did I," Walter interrupted.

"So did you what?"

"Liked my answers."

"Good, then we agree." She smiled at him now, just as she had at Clifton, with a mixture of real warmth and slightly chiding superiority. I am woman, and I know about you poor boys, her smile seemed to say.

Amazing what strength she has, Walter thought.

"And I liked your conviction that success is measured by results," Katy was continuing. "It's . . ."

"Hardly original."

"But obviously sincere, which is more important."

"So you are going to. . . ."

"Look for a job where I can make money," she smiled. "Just as you advise."

"I might have an opening," he said on the spur of the moment. He found her bright and attractive. No harm in offering. He could always refuse later if he couldn't find anything suitable. Anyhow, she'd probably not come.

"I shall come see you in New York and discuss it. Thank you for the invitation. May I have your card?"

He extracted it with a smile. "I look forward to seeing you." What a remarkable girl.

Yes, Katy was certain, Cort was just the sort of man she had been looking for. Strong, but above all someone who knew how to make money. No doubt he'd be delighted to teach her, Katy thought wryly as she left the business school building; even though he didn't realize that yet. She grinned to herself as she strode off across the campus. That's no problem, she assured herself; she'd let him know soon enough!

Walter continued to talk to the students for another ten minutes. Then, seeing the crowd thinning, he started to wonder whether he too should leave. Instantly the personable young club president was at his side. "I'm sure you'll be wanting to leave soon," he said. "You must have a host of deals brewing."

"I do," Walter agreed. He didn't bother to add as they walked down the steps, that not one of them was easy, that not one would consummate without his constant pushing, cajoling, fighting. Nor did he try to explain how essential making those deals was; if he let up for even a moment, his whole company could go straight down the drain.

"Thanks for coming," the young man was saying.

Walter slid into the seat of his Ferrari and started the motor. "Take it easy," he called as he started to move away. Then he wondered, with a touch of bitterness, whether he'd ever be able to follow his own excellent advice.

It took Walter only a few minutes after leaving his business school host to find the Massachusetts Turnpike. Traffic was light, so he pushed the Ferrari's accelerator to the floor. The motor roared its appreciation, and bounded forward. Within seconds the car was moving down the three-lane highway at a hundred miles an hour—and straining to go faster.

The green, rolling countryside seemed to recede as the car ate hungrily at the road, and the traffic signs flashed past almost too rapidly to read. As he overtook other cars, he would hear the *whooooosh* he normally associated with vehicles moving toward him in the opposite direction. He'd probably get a ticket, Walter realized, but it would be worth it. He adored the speed, and the release it offered.

Thank God he'd decided to stop off at his house on the Cape tonight rather than drive straight back to New York. He could sleep late, lap up the sea breeze tomorrow morning, and then drive back to New York over the weekend, whenever it pleased him. He'd have to go to the office for a few hours, but he could do that anytime. He hoped

Mortimer had brought the dog. She always looked so funny romping down the beach, like a fleck of surf that had taken on a life of its own in defiance of wind and water.

Normally, it was a three-hour drive from Boston to his home on Cape Cod, but Walter arrived in under two. Either there had been no traffic cops on the road or they had been too slow to catch him. It was only eleven when he reached his sandy driveway. The night was cold but clear, and the sky was bright with a thousand stars. He could see a dim reddish light in his bedroom at the top of the old house, which he could not explain. And he could hear rock music, which seemed strange. Downstairs, however, the usual lights all blazed their welcome. Mortimer would have a snack ready, and a brandy.

As he got out of the car, slightly stiff from the drive, he could smell the sea. Tomorrow he would go sailing. There was always a good breeze at this time of year, and he enjoyed feeling the cold, hard spray from the whitecaps hit his face. He never felt lonely when the wind was strong. He loved to wrestle with the boat, endlessly curbing its desire to yaw away from the tight, keeling angle to the wind which gave him the greatest speed.

Feeling tired but mellowed, he walked toward the front door. As he reached it, he was pleased to see that the two whaling lights he'd bought had been installed. Three hundred dollars apiece—originals from a boat that might have sailed with Melville—and worth every penny. That's what money was for, wasn't it, to buy beautiful things? He pushed open the door.

"Thank God you're here," Mortimer quietly exploded the moment Walter entered. "It's that girl!"

"What? Which girl?" Walter could not imagine what Mortimer was talking about.

"That Judith," Mortimer continued indignantly. "That English girl from Switzerland. She turned up this afternoon saying she'd called your office and they told her you'd meet her here. Since you hadn't mentioned it, I thought I'd better check, so I went to call Caroline. The next thing I know, this Judith has sneaked upstairs and there she is in your bed and refusing to leave. She's been there for hours. Every time I try to force her out, she just lies back and, and . . ."

"And what?" Walter asked, curious as to what could so fluster his usually imperturbable house manager.

"She . . ." Mortimer blushed crimson, which Walter viewed with total astonishment. "She *touches* herself," Mortimer said in a rush. "Every time I come into the bedroom to tell her to leave, she lifts up the bedclothes and . . . and . . . touches herself . . ." Mortimer paused for breath, fighting to regain the dignity for which he was renowned. "It's . . . it's outrageous," he said, expelling air with as much force as might any shocked Victorian dowager. "Outrageous!"

Walter barely controlled his urge to laugh. "I'd better go and take care of her," he reassured Mortimer, certain that there would be only one way to do that. He could feel himself start to get hard. She had *chutzpah,* this Judith, he had to admit. No phone calls, no begging for dates. Just walked in and got into his bed. He had to admire her.

Slowly he started to climb the stairs. He could clearly hear the sound of rock music now coming from the bedroom. He wondered what sort of a crazy night Judith had in store for them.

As he opened the bedroom door, the blast of music deluged him like a breaking tide. The bittersweet mixture of incense and marijuana smoke filled the room as densely as steam in a sauna. The lamp next to his bed was draped with a red cloth, which threw harem shadows around the room. "Welcome back!" she said, "I suppose Mortimer told you I've been waiting for you—getting ready, you might say—all afternoon." Naked, she flung back the covers and smiled.

As usual, Walter was the last person left in the office. It had been after eight when he returned from his last meeting. Now, an hour later, he had still handled only half the day's papers. Only the old Ukrainian cleaning woman, rattling her bucket in annoyance that she would again have to skip the boss's office, broke the silence. Why did he always have to work late on the days she planned to "do" him?

Walter felt a certain kinship with the old woman who so often shared the emptiness of his evenings, sometimes late into the silent night. Not that he objected to working late. It was necessary. Moreover, he truly enjoyed his office. The powerful impression it made on visitors—awe, envy, admiration—invariably gave him a boost. And just being there bolstered his self-esteem. For there was no doubt that it *was* impressive. For one thing, it was large; for another, it gleamed with chrome, mirrors and glass, none showing the tiniest smudge of fingerprints. And it was strikingly and expensively decorated: an orange carpet of extraordinary depth and shading, a set of blue tapestrylike drapes and, scattered everywhere, pillows of the same blue and orange shades. The space-age desk sunk in the center of the room to form a "conference space" bespoke a tongue-in-cheek Hollywood attitude toward office design. Nor was it easy to take seriously the two computer consoles flanking the desk—each complete with a control panel, operating lights and a screen. One had a high-speed printing unit attached to it; the other was incorporated into a television/stereo complex. The office couch was of a soft white material, which looked brand new. In sooty, grimy mid-Manhattan, Walter had to have it changed every few months to keep it so fresh-looking.

But the most spectacular aspect of the office was the breathtaking panoramic view of Manhattan's skyline, sparkling in the evenings with a billion lights. The view spread across the two glass walls of the office as across a giant movie screen.

Shirt open, tie halfway down his chest, hair wiry and disheveled, his face gaunt, Walter looked slight and unimposing. He sat hunched quietly over a business report which tomorrow he would have to present to the president of one of his largest client companies. An observer would never have been able to tell how worried he was.

"For the five reasons enumerated," the report concluded, "we strongly urge against the proposed acquisition."

Walter rubbed his forehead. His basic credo was to act. Now he was forced to recommend against action, and he hated it. On top of that, he could practically hear his client then objecting to the fee. "Why the hell should I pay a hundred thousand bucks for you to tell me to do nothing?" the old bastard would snort.

But the acquisition was suicidal. No one could justify a purchase price of thirty million. Phony profits and overstated assets. "Close to fraud," Walter muttered angrily. "Why haven't *they* seen it?"

He looked up from the paper, leaned back in his chair and stretched his arms back over his head, trying to ease a persistent ache in his neck. The distant rattling of the cleaning woman's pail was replaced by the tinny sound of her transistor radio. "Is that all there is?" he could hear the voice of Peggy Lee. "If that's all there is my love, then let's go dancing. . . ."

Walter was overcome by a sense of loss so strong that it gave him a physical reaction that almost felt like hunger. His stomach hurt with emptiness. What am I doing here? he asked himself. What's the point? As if in sympathy, the tinny radio repeated the question, "Is that all there is . . . ?"

The telephone startled him.

"Yes," he barked into the receiver.

"Where the fuck have you been?" Harry Grass demanded angrily. "I got the biggest sonofabitch deal ever, hot as a celibate nympho, and you I can't find. I gotta talk. Your place in an hour."

"It's ten o'clock already," Walter objected.

"Okay, half an hour then." Harry hung up abruptly.

Walter had to laugh. When Harry was on the trail of something he wanted, he was like an irritated terrier digging after a rabbit he knew was down there somewhere. "Tenacious," that was the word that described Harry best, that and "impatient." With a sigh he switched off the lights again. In the darkness his face seemed to lengthen, and become more austere.

"Harry's been in a hurry from the day he was born," Harry's mother loved to proclaim. "I always said even then, didn't I, that he'd make it big. But I mean *big!*" She loved to boast about her successful son. "Didn't I?" She nodded her large head and her cheeks bounced in an orgy of agreement.

Harry Grass's mother, as her son was forced to admit to himself about the time he turned fifteen, was a lazy, fat, greasy woman. But she was easygoing and kind, able to put up with the noise and mess which always filled their four-room tenement flat. She brought up half a dozen children with a mixture of love, benign neglect and only occasional frenzies when their misbehavior forced her to rise out of her lethargy. She was surprised but tremendously proud when one of them became rich.

"He was walking before he was even a year," Mrs. Grass added, more impressed with this than with the fact that Harry had taught himself to read by the time he was five.

Not that Mrs. Grass was wrong; Harry had indeed been in a hurry all his life. Even as a baby, he pushed his food into his mouth with both hands and filled his crib with candy wrappers, clothes, newspapers, anything he could lay his hands on. Later it was money, women and, above all, influence. He learned from an early age to collect people: as a teenager, football stars and cheerleaders; as an adult, politicians, company presidents and judges.

By the time Harry was five, he was quite used to fending for himself. Most of his day was spent on the streets. He was at ease with the bustling life, the noise, the constant hubbub that went on day and night around the crumbling tenement stoops and rusty fire escapes. There, he played and fought with his friends, begged or stole apples from the stalls in the market three blocks away, burned newspapers for the excitement of it—but read the funnies before setting them ablaze. He went home only to sleep or for meals—which consisted mostly of stew or hot dogs.

On his sixth birthday Harry entered the first grade in the local elementary school. While his friends expended their energy playing softball in the prisonlike school yard, Harry breezed through the reading primers—and then got himself in trouble by using the time designated for learning to read to devour detective stories: Perry Mason, Mickey Spillane, Carter Brown—they all fascinated him. Eventually his teacher realized it was foolish to try and stop him. Thereafter Harry was allowed to educate himself on cops and robbers, and dream of how he would grow up to be another Mike Hammer.

When Harry finally did get interested in the softball games, instead of merely joining he organized them into contests. Participants had to contribute five cents each toward proper bats and balls, and the winning team kept the equipment as prizes. Inevitably it was Harry who was captain of his team, Harry's team which won and Harry who inherited the best baseball equipment on the block. By the time he was through elementary school, Harry was the big man to know.

Initially high school was a setback for Harry. It was an enormous institution, with buildings and staff equally worn out by generation upon generation of disinterested, disrespectful students. A third of the desks and many of the windows were broken, and the whole place smelled stale—a mixture of the odors of dirty bodies, rancid perfume and sweat. The corridors seemed endless. When they were empty, they banged and echoed with every footfall; but filled to bursting between classes, they were intimidating, a mayhem of rushing, pushing teenagers.

Overnight Harry found himself demoted from top dog in his elementary school to anonymous freshman. On his first day he got his nose bloodied by a senior for showing insufficient respect. Several times he was hurled against the stone wall of the corridor as a gang of older students asserted their right of way. But the eclipse of Harry's power lasted less than a week. By then, having found a rarely used storeroom —one of dozens of such rooms scattered throughout the sprawling building—he moved out part of the cleaning supplies kept there to a janitorial department closet—and sold the rest. With the proceeds he paid for a door sign, lettered in the same style as all other school signs, which announced, Freshman Class Club Room. Underneath it read, Harry Grass, Club Coordinator. He also installed a new lock to which only he had the key. No one ever questioned his right to use the room, not even the senior boy who had bloodied his nose and who, in later years, became a delivery man for a milk company Harry Grass controlled.

Harry's club, which he christened the Bozos merely because he liked the sound of the name, became his power base, establishing him as the leader of the freshman class. By the time he was a senior, he ruled the school. By then, too, Walter Cort had become his key lieutenant and part of every scheme Harry started, and the tiny storage room had become merely an adjunct to the storefront the two friends had managed to have donated to the Bozos. The sign on its door, weathered but, unlike most school surfaces, never defaced, remained intact until the day Harry graduated. As his last official student act, he donated the clubhouse to the janitorial department, who were most grateful because they had long lacked enough space for their cleaning supplies.

Harry started his first business on his eleventh birthday. It was a newspaper delivery route in the opulent Sheepshead Bay section of Brooklyn. He bought it for five dollars from an effete fifteen-year-old.

"I'll pay you a dollar a week," he explained to the boy. "It's worth more that way cause you can't spend it so fast. Otherwise I'd pay for the whole thing now, but that wouldn't be right."

"Okay," the boy agreed, confused but amenable.

Harry gave him the only dollar he owned in the world. Within ten weeks Harry's route had increased from twenty-five homes to two hundred, and he employed three older boys to deliver the papers. Generously, he paid them three-quarters of the profits. The week before Christmas Harry called on all his clients personally. Donning his Sunday best, he walked sedately up each neat path and knocked on the typically ornate front door of the Brooklyn wealthy. "It has been a privilege to deliver your paper this year," he would say to whomever answered. "I trust our service has been satisfactory. And may I wish you a very Merry Christmas." Invariably the homeowner, startled by such a small boy with such a big speech, would give a bigger Christmas tip than he had intended. In all, Harry collected one hundred and thirty-seven dollars—which he did not share with his employees. For the first time in his life, he was rich.

Throughout the rest of his school years, Harry held countless jobs, and to each he brought a particular business flair which earned him money. Once he and Walter became friends, they entered into most of these ventures jointly.

By the time Harry and Walter graduated, they had accumulated a nest egg of almost three thousand dollars, an unheard-of amount among their high school peers and, for that matter, among their parents and most of their parents' friends. Harry owned two thirds of the money. Briefly he toyed with using their capital in trafficking drugs, which were fast emerging in his neighborhood. But seeing the violence of the pushers and the human waste of the addicts, he opted for cleaner opportunities. Instead he informed Walter that they should work in a gas station.

"Why do you want us to do *that?*" Walter demanded.

" 'Cause we gotta learn how the fuck it works, Wimp, that's why."

"Huh?"

"So we know how to run it when we take over."

"Sure. I get it. And once we got the station, then we'll buy Esso, right?"

But Walter's objections were mild. He knew that Harry's schemes were rarely as scatterbrained as they first seemed.

"First we gotta figure out from inside how a gas station works, and how to make an extra buck. I got lots of ideas."

"I'll bet your first one is that I do the work while you figure."

"Nah, I'm gonna work on this one."

"That'll be a change."

"Yeah? Well, what's the point of working if you can make money thinking?" It was one of the few times Harry expressed even the most elementary philosophy. Normally he talked only of hard facts and money-making schemes. Walter looked at him with surprise. "I checked it out," Harry continued quickly. "That cut-rate Buy-Rite on the corner is best for us."

"Sloppy, isn't it?" Walter knew the station's half-drunk owner kept it in a thoroughly run-down state. He considered for a moment, then said, "yeah, I suppose you're right," answering himself. "That's what gives us our best chance."

"You read me," said Harry, slapping his friend on the back.

"Does he want help?"

"He don't know he does," Harry laughed. "So we gotta explain it to him. We're not regular workers, see, we're apprentices. We're gonna work cheaper than anyone who ever applied."

The two boys worked day and night at the station, pumping gas, changing tires, learning how to repair cars. It was a dirty, untidy place, littered with old tires, rusty metal junk, old oil cans and paper trash. The Buy-Rite sign had lost two of its letters and read Bu -Rit. The other boys who worked there moved slowly and sullenly, doing as little as possible. The owner, drinking constantly, alternated between swearing at them without effect and snoring loudly in the broken armchair in the oil-smudged office.

After a few weeks Harry and Walter were the only employees left. They did everything better and faster than the owner had ever seen. In addition they started to sell snacks, car accessories, batteries, anything their customers wanted, using their capital to buy the products and keeping the profits for themselves. The owner didn't object because it pulled in more customers.

Within three months the owner hardly ever came to work anymore. When he did, he was pleased to see that tire sales (the only accessory the boys did not handle for their own account) as well as repairs and gas sales were rising steadily. Satisfied, he would return home to his bottle.

It was after they had worked at the station for almost half a year that the boys made their move. For once the owner was sober on one of his visits.

"Good to see you," Walter greeted him in his polite, charming way. "Feel up to talking a little business?"

Harry Grass lounged at the corner of the garage, his hands in his pockets, chewing a double-size wad of gum.

"Sure. What you boys want? You wanna raise?" The owner looked at them condescendingly. Dumb kids. He'd gladly pay them double what they were earning.

"No, thanks. But we'd like a share," said Walter politely. "A share of any extra profits we make from here on in."

The owner looked amazed. "You want a share? You're fucking crazy. I don't give no shares. It's my station."

"Yeah," said Harry phlegmatically. "But that's still what we want." He continued to chew.

"Half the extra profit we make, starting now," Walter explained. "But you don't have to pay wages anymore," he added before the owner could object again. "So you make the full profit you're getting now plus our wages before we get a cent."

"I don't get it." The owner was confused but greedily intrigued.

"Well, since we've worked here, the station's profit has grown to about eight hundred dollars a month. But we think we can still do better," Walter explained. "So we'll guarantee you a full eight hundred a month profit, plus our wages of two hundred dollars, before we take out anything for ourselves. We only want half of anything the station earns over that."

"How do you mean?" The owner remained suspicious.

"It's simple. We take no wages from now on. Instead, we'll take half of anything over a thousand bucks a month the station earns. So if the station makes fourteen hundred dollars a month, you'll only be paying us the same two hundred you're paying us now, half of the extra four hundred.

"Yeah, and if it makes a lot more than fourteen?"

"It won't," said Harry roughly. "Not this shitty station."

"It does seem unlikely, doesn't it," said Walter. "And remember, you'll be getting half of the extra anyhow."

The owner looked at them slyly. "Okay, I'll go for that," he decided finally. "Half of anything over a thousand."

"Oh, yes, one more thing," said Walter smoothly, "we want a simple employment agreement . . ."

"What's that?" The man was instantly suspicious again.

"He means that if you kick our ass out, you gotta pay us six months of what we were earning," said Harry.

"I gotta do what?"

"Look," said Walter reasonably, "we don't want to build your station to a higher profit and then get nothing for it. So if we leave, all you've got to do is pay us what we would have earned for the next six months."

"No fucking way. I'll kick your asses out anytime I want, and I ain't paying nuttin'."

"Okay, we'll put it another way," said Walter. "If you kick us out, or we leave for any other reason, all you do is pay us the extra over a thousand dollars you actually earned for the previous four months. Christ, man, that's fair."

"Fucking right, that's fair," said Harry.

"Not four months," said the owner slyly. "That's too much. I ain't paying no four months. Maybe two."

"Two fucking months, that's a shitty deal," said Harry sullenly. But if the owner had been alert, he would have noticed that he was no longer slouching.

"Well, it's all I'm giving," said the man, his chin jutting.

"Three months," Walter suggested tentatively. "We'll take the last full month before we leave and we'll figure out the extra over a thousand bucks the station actually earned—and you'll pay us three times our share of that."

"Or you can start running your fucking station without us," Harry added aggressively.

The owner hesitated. The last thing he wanted to do was go back to pumping his own gas. "Okay," he finally agreed reluctantly, "three months."

"Fine," said Walter. "I'll write up the papers so we can all sign, just so there's no misunderstanding."

"Okay," said the man. "You're on. We don't need no papers."

"I'll get them ready anyhow," said Walter as the man started to leave. "Bring them around to your house this evening."

Neither boy moved as the man got into his car and drove off. But the moment he was out of sight, Harry jumped up and down in delight. "We did it, we fucking did it!" he crowed. "Now we'll get the fucking station for sure."

"We sure did," said Walter, acting calmer but feeling just as excited.

The papers were duly signed by the owner and notarized, and the boys readied their plan. For three months they held profits static, barely inching above a thousand dollars each month. As a result, they earned nothing for themselves. Progressively, the owner's smile turned to a jeer. "You boys got to work a little harder," he would tell them. "Otherwise you's gonna starve."

But the owner had no idea that even before the boys signed the agreement, profits from cigarettes had risen to $350 a month and soft drinks to an additional two hundred. Nor had he an inkling that during those three months Harry and Walter successfully raised profits in every conceivable respect except those the owner could see. At the same time they pushed every repair job they could get, every opportunity for the sale of tires, into the fourth month. Finally they collected all the capital they could find and readied it for their onslaught.

The fourth month started with a warm summer day. An independent auditor was present at six o'clock that morning to make sure the books of the previous month were closed and that a physical inventory of everything in the station was taken. The boys didn't want an argument later with the owner.

The auditor returned just before midnight on the thirty-first day of that month to take another inventory and officially close the books on the month's profits.

Between those two visits, Harry and Walter worked longer and harder than ever in their lives. They sold gas at such low rates that lines formed half a block long from the station. And to every customer for gas they peddled automotive parts, cigarettes, anything they could. They managed to repair fifty-four cars, charging an average of over fifty dollars a piece. They sold an astonishing twenty-four thousand dollars' worth of gasoline and, even more remarkably, eight thousand dollars of other automotive materials. In addition they sold almost a thousand dollars' worth of cigarettes and soft drinks, and two thousand dollars' worth of other items. And for the first time every penny of the profits they made went into the station's books. As a result, in that one month the two boys succeeded in making sales of $37,700 and profits of $6,400. They slept all day following the final audit.

On the morning of the second day of the fifth month, they were ready for their confrontation with the owner.

"We've decided to cash in on last month's profits," Walter explained to him. "Our agreement is that you'll pay us three times half of all last month's profits over a thousand dollars."

"Yeah. Why you wanna go, boys?" the owner asked in his superior tone. "Not making a go of it? Tell you what, I'll give you back your old salary—a hundred bucks each month."

"No, I think we'd prefer to cash out," said Walter blandly. "We figure you owe us eight thousand, one hundred dollars."

"Huh?" said the man, shaking his head to clear it of the whiskey fumes. "Huh?"

"Last month we made six thousand, four hundred dollars of profit."

"What? Are you crazy? You couldn't."

"I'm afraid we did," said Walter.

"Fucking right," said Harry, again lounging in his favorite corner. "Fuckin'-A right."

"Six thousand four hundred?"

"We have an independent auditor we can call in if you doubt it," said Walter. "Here are the books."

The man was stunned.

"Which means that you've got a profit of five thousand four over the thousand bucks we agreed. So half of that is two thousand seven. And three times that is eight thousand one hundred."

"We'd like it today," said Harry while the owner was still shaking his head in disbelief.

"Well, I don't know that I—"

"Today," Walter repeated just as sternly as Harry. "The contract says we're to be paid the moment we leave."

"Give me a few days," the man begged.

"Why?" Walter asked. "You know you can't find it in a few days any more than you can now."

"You couldn't find it in a fucking year."

The man looked at them with bewildered eyes. "You know I don't have that kind of money," he said, his tone a whine. "You gotta wait. There's no way of getting money out of me like that. I ain't got none. Not that kind of money."

"Then we'll take over the gas station," said Walter.

Suddenly the man started shouting. "You won't take over my gas station. I'm the owner. I keep it—"

"Not anymore," said Harry. "Not if you don't pay your goddamn debts."

"But it's worth a hell of a lot more than eight thousand bucks."

"Yeah," said Walter, "it probably is. So I tell you what. We'll take half the gas station now. Fifty-one percent. And we'll buy you out for an additional ten thousand dollars over the next year. That's fair."

They argued most of the morning, but in the end the owner, knowing he was beaten and increasingly anxious to get back to his bottle, capitulated. "Okay," he said, "ten thousand bucks over the next year, and it'll be all yours."

"It's fifty-one percent ours now," said Walter.

"Right," said Harry Grass. "Dead right. It will be all ours after we pay the ten thou."

"Okay," said the man weakly. "Okay, you win." Eventually, after the papers Walter had drawn up in advance were signed, he left.

This time the boys did not jump up and shout with joy. Instead, solemnly, they shook hands.

"And that's only a start," Harry Grass said. "Only a start."

That he used no obscenity to underline his point impressed Walter as nothing else could.

When they sold the gas station three years after they acquired it, each young entrepreneur made about forty thousand dollars profit. Harry banked a quarter of his. He used the rest as the down payment for several small grocery stores, which later became the foundation of his real estate business. Walter, choosing a different path, opened a tiny office in Manhattan, just large enough for a beat-up desk and a card table for his secretary/assistant. His intention was to make deals.

"We'll buy anything if we can sell it at a mil more," he would tell visitors. "And we're super salesmen. So what have you got? We'll pay top dollar."

Those had been arduous years for Walter. The forty thousand dwindled to ten before the business even started to become profitable. And for years after that each deal was a major gamble which he could hardly afford to lose. When he did lose, the feeling was always the same: panic, anger, an acute loss of self-confidence—followed by a desperate struggle to make good, to save himself. There were many failures.

On one occasion Walter bought a thousand slot machines at forty dollars apiece, only to discover that Big Julie, the local garbage kingpin, wanted the machines at a lower price. He insisted that Walter come to visit him.

"So why would I sell them to you for less than I paid for them?" Walter demanded, sitting in Big Julie's dirty office, trying to ignore the stink which rose from the dump outside.

"Well, look at it this way," Julie explained. "We's in the protection market as well as in garbage. It ain't quite kosher, but it's more profitable. And you're in a business where you need protection. . . ."

"I wasn't aware of that."

"Now you is. Believe me."

"I believe you." Looking at his huge, tough host, Walter did.

"So I want them machines. Twenty bucks."

"That's ridiculous. . . ." Walter tried to keep the desperation out of his voice. In the end he managed to bargain Big Julie up to $33 a unit, leaving Walter with a loss of $7,000.

It wasn't only the crooks who were crooked, though. In later years Walter would often recall how, not long after the slot-machine fiasco, he was just as mercilessly cheated by his own bank manager.

"We're here to help," the banker told him, looking grandfatherly and bland. "You need financing for the merchandise you want to buy; we want to lend you the money." The deal had progressed quickly. "All we need is your signature on these papers," the banker explained, looking owlishly over his steel-rimmed spectacles.

Walter looked the papers over. "But they show me giving my personal guarantee," he objected. "If something goes wrong, *I'm* on the hook in addition to the company."

"Of course. That's how it always works. But it's just a formality.

We'd never actually sue you unless you were trying to welch," the banker explained kindly. "In any case the inventory you're buying is worth more than your debt."

"And the loan's only for thirty days."

"Don't worry about it. We'll roll it over if you wish. Moreover, you said you already had a buyer."

Walter trusted the banker. It had never occurred to him that, behind the professional, blue-suited facade, there lurked a gangster quite as tough as Big Julie himself. So he signed the papers and borrowed almost two hundred thousand dollars—more than he owned in the world—to buy a parcel of musical instruments. He wasn't too worried because it was quite true that he already had a committed buyer for a large part of the instruments.

When the buyer backed out, after procrastinating for almost a month, the bank manager refused to extend Walter's loan by one extra day. And when Walter tried to remonstrate, the banker refused even to answer his phone.

Ironically, it was Big Julie who saved Walter from bankruptcy, although not from a big loss. "I'll take 'em off you for twenty grand less than you paid." Walter had no choice. "So how come you bought them in the first place?" Julie asked Walter after the deal was completed.

"I thought I had them sold," Walter admitted ruefully.

"Who to?"

Walter told him.

"Pretty dumb, kid," Julie commiserated. "No wonder you got took."

"What do you mean?"

"Didn't you know him and your banker friend is cousins?"

Fortunately, not all Walter's deals went badly. Often he made money, sometimes a great deal. And as he learned the ropes better each year, and learned also to control his panic when things went wrong, he grew steadily in wealth and reputation.

"I got a hot one," Harry said without preliminaries the moment he entered Walter's house. "Red hot."

Harry was all business tonight. "Magnatel had a board meeting yesterday," he rushed on, leaning forward in his chair as if he wanted to pounce.

"The German electrical people?"

"Yeah. Biggest electrical-machinery group in Europe. The thing is, they've decided they want out of the household end of their business."

"Out of it?" Walter interrupted. "But that's a sizable business."

"Right. And they want out." Harry's voice was full of excitement.

"Sell it, spin it off. Anything. Just so they can get out." He paused long enough to gulp a breath. "No more hair dryers, razors, mixers," he continued. "All they want to keep is their big industrial crap."

"That's a hell of a decision," Walter interrupted. "Are you sure?"

"Damn right I'm sure. One of their directors called me. It's about three hundred million dollars of sales they got. But they've never made money in the States, and they're losing their ass in the Vaterland."

Amazing how wired in Harry was. Walter never ceased to be astonished at how many people his friend knew.

"They've made a little in the rest of Europe," Harry was saying, "but for the whole bundle they've never pulled out much more than a break-even. So it's really worth shit to them." The hair around the shiny bald spot in the center of his head practically stood on end, and his voice was as harsh and rapid as a sportscaster's. "So Friday they decided they'd do better concentrating on their industrial stuff where they make a fucking fortune . . ." Harry was on his feet now, as wound up and emphatic as if he were presenting concluding arguments to a doubtful jury. "That's why this guy called me," he finished triumphantly. "To help them sell."

Walter looked at his friend quizzically. "Okay," he said. "Wonderful! Magnatel has decided to spin off its small appliances. So what?" But Walter already knew what Harry had in mind. And although the thought was crazy, it *was* exciting. He'd long wanted to get into something solid, stable . . . Well, here was his chance. In spades! But no; he forced his momentary elation down. This was far too big. "Definitely not," he said, not waiting for Harry's response. "There's no way for us to acquire them."

"There fucking is!" Harry disagreed pugnaciously, legs apart, bristling like a game cock. "I'm telling you. See, they gotta make one sweet deal to get *anyone* to buy—"

"But why?" Walter demanded. "It's very valuable even if it's not making much. The name alone is worth millions; just think what you could do with it if you ran it right. I tell you, Harry, the buyers'll swarm. Bees to the corporate honey pot."

"No."

"Why not?"

"Because they put a condition on it that'll screw up the swarm, that's why. They've decided they won't sell to anyone else in Germany. Losing face or something. They figure it's all right to sell out to us Americans, but it'd be an admission of failure if they finked out to some other German company."

"That does make it more difficult. Even so, there must be a dozen—"

"There ain't. For a start, no one who's in the business now could touch them because of the Feds."

Walter immediately understood what Harry meant. The Federal Trade Commission enforced far-reaching rules to impede any acquisitions which might reduce competition. Generally the rules meant that two companies with important market shares in the same product category could not merge, since they would then become allies instead of competitors. Since Magnatel held a major position in virtually every area of small appliances, any merger with another appliance company would probably be stopped.

"And there ain't many companies keen to get into a new area right now," Harry was saying. "With the economy all fucked up, most of the big companies want to stick in their own backyards."

"So . . ."

"So, Magnatel's as available as a whore's twat," Harry laughed briefly. "It's a once-in-a-lifetime opportunity, Wimp. All you gotta do is put together a group . . . No problem." Harry Grass rocked back on his heels as if waiting for applause.

"For Christ's sake, Harry, you're out of your mind. You're talking a hundred and fifty million bucks even if they're not making profits."

"Shit, man, a hundred million at the most," Harry disagreed.

"Oh, fine. Then you're right, there's no problem. I figure we could raise at least five million between us. So if we can get it for a hundred, we're a mere ninety-five million short. Now I see how easy it is!" He paused. "Like I said, you're out of your mind."

"Yeah," said Harry, "maybe so. But you must admit it could be an opportunity."

"Phenomenal. I've no doubt about that. But too big for us."

"Maybe so," said Harry. He paused and then, casually, as if he had just thought of it, he added, "But it would interest Von Ackermann."

Instantly Walter understood where Harry was leading. Here was an opportunity to dangle a really large prize in front of the greedy German. By offering him the chance to participate in Magnatel—even if the deal turned out to be more promise than fact—they might induce him to give them their share of Charles DuPont's Clarendon deal. The trick would be to get their Clarendon fee before Von Ackermann realized that they really didn't have a chance with Magnatel.

"And this one he won't think he can do without us," Harry pointed out with relish. "He figures he can cut us out of Clarendon because we didn't bring nothing except the idea and the contacts, and in his mind that's worth shit. But with Magnatel, he needs us in the middle 'cause they won't sell to no fucking Krauts."

"We've got to make it plausible, though," Walter said thoughtfully. "That bastard's been around long enough to smell rotten bait five miles against the wind."

"I've set up a meeting with the Magnatel people for Tuesday."

Harry's voice carried no inflection. "In Frankfurt."

"And booked seats on Pan Am, I suppose?" Walter couldn't help chuckling. "How do you know I'll go?"

"TWA."

"Asshole," said Walter, feeling suddenly a deep and satisfying sense of comaraderie with his old friend.

Harry slapped him on the back, grinning. Then, turning serious, he studied his friend closely for a second. "Too bad it's in Germany," he said.

"Yeah," said Walter in heartfelt agreement. "No point in missing out, but you're right. Too fucking bad it has to be in Germany." He looked at Harry with gratitude for his understanding.

Harry hadn't changed much over the years, Walter reflected. Paunch a little rounder, cheeks fuller, more jowly. He wished he had the same ebullient self-confidence that let Harry move in every conceivable circle of business without ever giving up his aggressively Brooklynese manner. They'd been through some incredible ups and downs together, but Harry had never felt the same need Walter had to pretend to be something he was not. Through it all—even when they were both practically broke and Walter was desperate—Harry had always remained confident. Now he wore his success as obtrusively as his six-hundred-dollar suit of light blue raw silk. Yes, the trappings had changed, but the fundamentals about Harry had remained the same over the years.

Was he the same, too, Walter wondered. Certainly not, he concluded. Gone was the excessive suspiciousness of his youth, at least about people he could trust—not that there were many. In those days he had trusted no one—and usually been justified, too, he recalled. He was easier and more relaxed now, no longer jumpy as a cat. One thing had not changed, though. From the first day they met, Walter had always admired his friend's self-assurance. He admired it still. Perhaps if they really could make a deal with Magnatel. . . .

"So how're the broads?" Harry's harsh voice broke through Walter's thoughts, startling him.

"Waiting for me all over town," Walter answered carefully. He had trained himself never to let involuntary reactions show. Self-control pays. "And all I get to see is you."

"You supposed to be with one now?" Harry got a vicarious thrill out of Walter's exploits.

"Sure. Probably creaming for me right now. Probably climbing the walls."

Harry looked at him with a mixture of amusement and pity. "You poor prick. When're you going to find yourself a wife?" he asked, pushing himself to his feet. "A good woman, like my Martha." His harsh voice sounded suddenly soft. "Someone you can give a shit about."

"A wife?" said Walter. "Not a chance. Not for me. I can't even get over being surprised that you've turned into such a model husband."

"I have, haven't I," said Harry pleased. "Who'd a thunk it."

"But Harry's just a . . . ." Her mother had searched for an acceptable word, "just a *trader.*" No point in antagonizing the girl. Martha was too headstrong for her own good as it was. "Not up to your class at all."

"So was Grand-Dad," Martha had pointed out. "And Harry's very smart." Her tone had been quiet but implacable. Eventually, seeing no alternative, her mother had agreed.

"He should realize how lucky he is to get you. I'll help him a lot in his business," her father had stated ambiguously.

In fact, Harry had accepted no help at all from his father-in-law over the years. As a result, the two men had been able to become close friends.

Martha, too, had been thoroughly pleased with her choice. Harry turned out to be just as virile, energetic and exciting as she had hoped and a lot more solid than she had expected. Only once in all those years had she even been tempted. . . . She was still shocked to her core that it had been another woman who had so involved her.

But then Wilma had been an extraordinary woman. Martha could still remember how impressed she was at that lecture where she first saw her . . . Wilma, with her prematurely white hair, beautifully tailored suit, was barely thirty but already a well-known authority in the emerging field of sex education. Doctor Willie, the newspapers nicknamed her. They wrote about her frequently, mentioning her in a half-titillating, half-serious way.

"How many of you feel embarrassed when I say 'sex?' " Wilma had demanded, her voice cultured, charming, assured. Her audience of matrons shifted in their seats uncomfortably. I hope she doesn't pick on me, each member thought. "Too damn many!" Wilma said with a smile. "And yet you, I, all of us, are sexual creatures. We make love, think about making love, are preoccupied with love and sex and marriage and men and getting pregnant—all of it—constantly. So how can you be uncomfortable . . . ?"

They were radical thoughts in those days. But as she got to know Dr. Wilma Matthias better, and to admire that incisive mind and steel-edged charm, the ideas started to seem more natural to Martha.

"She could sell *two* tails off a donkey," Harry would complain with a mixture of admiration and distrust. "Why d'you see so much of her?"

"She's fascinating. Anyhow, you're gone such a lot. And it's lonely just being with the kids."

Too fascinating in the end. For a few weeks, before she came to her senses, Martha had thought she was so in love with Doctor Willie that she could never again live without her. Only a few weeks, but of high adventure, full of risk and elation and despair.

But the boys were still young, and Harry was a perfect father. He was strong and loving with them, brooking no nonsense but admiring their highjinks and bailing them out efficiently if their energy got them into trouble. In the end she couldn't give up all that, or destroy so many lives. Still, she had often wondered what it would have been like with Wilma.

Although Martha's education was limited to a BA from a college designed for "finishing" girls, not really teaching them, she had learned from Wilma to love reading history and visiting art galleries.

"You're becoming a fucking intellectual," Harry had told her.

"Don't use that word please, honey," she had responded automatically, nevertheless pleased with the compliment. If only he knew from where her interest stemmed!

"Okay," he had agreed pleasantly. "An *ordinary* intellectual. I like it. Gives the family class." Harry's lack of education always bothered him. Whenever he found himself unable to avoid the company of people he still insisted on calling fucking intellects, he either became tongue-tied or excessively brash. It was the one situation that made him feel inferior.

"You do well in other things," Martha would reassure him. "They're just as important." No intellectual snob herself, she believed strongly in the value of business and hated people who put it down. Usually, she had noted, they were the sort who had inherited too much money from ancestors who had of course earned it in just the ways their offspring chose to deplore.

Over the years, too, Martha had learned a great deal about Harry's business. They often discussed his forthcoming deals, and she frequently gave him a valuable sense of perspective. Today Martha Grass was a plump, placid soul with solidly middle-class values and impeccable manners. Harry loved her passionately.

"You could do worse than get married, you know, Wimp," Harry refused to leave the subject alone. "The trouble is you're still a fucking adolescent. Literally," he added with a grin.

"For Christ's sake, Harry," said Walter, stung by the criticism, "what the hell would I do with a wife? I get all I can stand as it is."

"That's not why," said Harry Grass shaking his head. "Every broad has a cunt. A wife is different. . . ."

"No cunt?"

"I'm being serious. A wife is not just for sex. Far more. For solace . . ."

"Ten-dollar word, Harry. You'll lose your union card if you run around giving out with words like that."

"Yeah," said Harry, walking to the door. "I'll be more fucking careful." He grinned, waved and left.

Solace, Walter thought. Not a bad word at that. Oh well, he could do without it. You never knew where you stood once you started looking for that sort of help. Look at Rachel. No, he was far better off with girls like Judith. There were always more of them, so you didn't care if you lost one.

Slowly he started to climb the stairs. Briefly he considered calling Judith. She was staying in New York and would probably come over even though it was almost midnight. And she'd be fun. She certainly had some wild ideas. But solace wasn't part of them. He grinned at the incongruity of the thought. Money, sex, coke. All of that. And whipped cream in strange places, or leather fantasies, or . . . But solace, no. Not that a little might not be pleasant once in a while.

He decided not to call. Wildness was not what he wanted tonight. He wanted sleep. He only hoped tonight he wouldn't have the dream that often plagued him. Maybe a short walk with Bundle might cheer him up. His dog was always delighted to go out with him. He whistled quietly, and instantly there was a frantic answering bark. Then he could hear the sound of Bundle's toenails scratching and sliding on the slippery floor as she took the corners too fast, desperate to reach him. She burst into the hallway, a tiny bundle of hysterical white fluff, and slid to a stop at his feet. Throwing her head back, she panted and yipped with delight. To Walter, it looked as if the dog were laughing.

"You want to go for a walk?" he asked unnecessarily as her excitement mounted. "You'll burst your sides laughing one of these days," he said to her indulgently. "Come on, then. Once around the block." She wagged her tail so hard it made her rear end skid back and forth on the parquet flooring. "You don't ask me for much to be happy, do you?" he said. "And you'd love me just as much for scraps as for steak. An unusual female!" He patted her on the head and then opened the door. In an instant she was outside. But when he didn't rush out after her, she hurried back and gave him a gentle nudge. "Okay," he said, "I'm coming."

As they walked around the block, she never strayed more than a few feet from his side. And when he returned to the house, she wagged her tail in what he thought to be an uncannily human version of saying thank you.

Slowly Walter walked up to his bedroom. The dog accompanied

him quietly and went to lie on her cushion in the corner of the room. Maybe Harry had something after all with his solace, Walter thought again as he undressed. But he doubted it. Life was too tenuous to rely on anyone—except maybe a dog. Security was an illusion, it was only strength that counted. Still, if he could get Magnatel, maybe he could afford to settle down. Maybe.

5

Katy Rochester decided against calling Walter Cort before going to see him. The worst that could happen if she arrived unannounced was that he would be busy or out. Hell, she thought, I can always come back. I've got nothing else to do. Nevertheless, it was with considerable optimism that she presented herself, dressed in an impeccable, well-cut Lord & Taylor suit, at the receptionist's desk. She'd done some research on Walter Cort, Inc., and its many activities. And unless she was missing her bet, this was just the sort of company she was looking for. Somewhere in all the deals must lie her opportunity for making money —real money, the kind of wealth she craved.

"I'm here to see Mr. Cort," she said, approaching the modernistic, kidney-shape reception desk. "I'm Katy Rochester."

The receptionist looked at the names on her list and found no Katy Rochester. "Is he expecting you?"

"He invited me to visit him," Katy hedged.

"Just a moment." The girl telephoned through to Caroline. "There is a Miss Katy Rochester to see Mr. Cort," she said.

"Who?"

"Miss Katy Rochester," the girl emphasized the "Miss" just enough to give Caroline the hint.

"Never heard of her," said Caroline. "Is she another one of his . . . friends?"

The receptionist looked Katy over carefully. She had seen a number of girls trying to invade Walter's privacy. But no, this one didn't seem the type. "I don't think so," then giggling, she added, "but with him, you never know."

Caroline did not allow her amusement at the receptionist's cheekiness to be heard. The receptionist was presumptuous. Give any one of them an inch, and they always took a mile. "I shall inquire whether Mr. Cort wishes to see Miss Rochester," she said with cold formality. She punched the hold button and then Walter's intercom. "There's a Katy Rochester to see you."

"Who?" His tone was an exact duplicate of the one she had used.

"Katy Rochester," she said, enunciating clearly.

"Never heard of her," said Walter. "And I'm busy."

Caroline called the receptionist back. "Tell her to go away," she said succinctly.

"My pleasure," the receptionist replied. It was not often she could exercise power in her job, so when it happened, she liked to make the most of it. She hung up and turned to Katy. "He won't see you," she said sweetly. "His secretary says to go away."

Nor was she disappointed. Katy looked back at her disbelievingly and started to blush. "You mean he's busy at the moment?"

"No, I mean he's not going to see you at all, honey."

It was the "honey" that did it. Without that extra goad Katy might have left. But no receptionist was going to call her honey . . . of all the arrogant . . . ! Katy controlled herself with an effort. "Evidently you have made a mistake," she said calmly, but in a voice cold with rage.

Immediately the girl lost confidence. "I don't think so," she stammered, startled by her visitor's harsh tone.

"Fortunately they don't pay you to think," Katy said cruelly. "Now you call back his secretary and tell her Katy Rochester is getting fed up with waiting."

"Yes, ma'am," said the girl quickly.

"What?" Caroline asked in astonishment when she heard the message.

"She really is," said the receptionist, looking worriedly at Katy. "You'd better . . ."

"I'll talk to her."

The girl handed Katy the phone. "It's his secretary."

"Thanks." Katy took the proffered receiver. "Hello, I'm Katy Rochester. Walter met me at Harvard and asked me to visit him." She spoke rapidly, slightly emphasizing her use of his first name. "I can see him now," she added, "or if that's inconvenient, why don't you suggest a better time?"

"Of course." Caroline completely changed her view. "Let me ask him. Sorry about the confusion. I'll call you back in a second."

"Fine," said Katy and hung up. She smiled at the now completely cowed receptionist. "She'll call back," she explained.

Caroline buzzed Walter. "Mr. Cort, Miss Rochester is still here. She sounds very determined. Says you met her at Harvard and invited her to see you."

"Oh yes," Walter remembered now. "You're right, she is a determined one."

"What shall I say?"

"I'd better see her briefly."

"I'll interrupt you in fifteen minutes?"

"At the outside."

Caroline punched back to the receptionist. "Send her in," she said without explanation. "He'll see her right away."

"Mr. Cort will see you right away," the receptionist said with awe. "Through that door, down the corridor. It's the corner office. His secretary will meet you . . . and sorry," she added contritely.

"That's all right," Katy answered as she turned to leave, "honey!"

Katy's first thought as she entered Walter's office was how much more spectacular it was than she would have expected for the intense, serious man she had met at Harvard. She clucked to herself with a New Englander's dislike for both ostentation and waste. But he knows what he's doing, she realized—bolstering his status.

Her second thought, more urgent than the first, was that this man was altogether too arrogant. She'd have to find a way to take him down a peg or two if she was ever going to work here. For God's sake don't go and say anything trite, she warned herself. Looking around his superb office, she realized he must have heard all the ordinary compliments a thousand times. Carefully she examined the room. In the far corner, almost hidden behind a modernistic statue, she noticed a neatly framed picture of a gas station.

"Extraordinarily impressive," Katy said blandly, waving her arm to encompass the room. "But tell me, what's the gas station all about?"

Walter looked at her sharply, taken by surprise. "Oh, that's how it all started," he explained. "You're observant."

"In a gas station?"

"Your stereotypes are showing, my girl," he said. "I'm Brooklyn and gas station, not Boston and business school."

Katy Rochester noted the word "girl." For a second she thought of overlooking the insult. No, she decided, now was the time. "Now see here," she started, "I'm no girl . . ."

Walter merely raised a single eyebrow. She couldn't stop herself from blushing.

"I'm a *woman*," she went on, refusing to let the blush interrupt her sentence, "and a Harvard Business School graduate. I'm here partly because you invited me, but mostly because I've decided I'd like to work for Walter Cort, Inc. My reasons are, first, that I could learn a

66   PETER ENGEL

great deal about the entrepreneurial world in which you have obviously
been successful." She again waved her hand around the office.

"Obviously."

"And second, that I can earn money for you."

She's quite attractive, Walter was thinking, when she gets that
stubborn look. He was reminded of a tiny Thai boxer he had once seen
in Bangkok who had first smiled cheerfully at his opponent and then,
with exactly this girl's look of determination, had kicked in his teeth
and balls, all in one efficiently executed piece of the mayhem they call
boxing in Thailand.

"Well?" Katy felt forced to break the silence. "What sort of job
did you have in mind?"

Her question pulled Walter out of his reverie. He considered her
for a moment. She might be amusing to have around. But no. He could
see that she would probably make trouble in the end. "Look," he said,
"I know I said I might have a job for you, but it was a spur-of-the-
moment offer. Since then I've looked around. And frankly, there's
really nothing for you to do."

"Of course there is!" she interrupted briskly. "At least a million
things. . . ." Having decided she really wanted a job here, she certainly
didn't intend to be turned down now.

"All of which you can handle?"

If he expects humility, Katy thought, he's in for a hell of a shock.
"Yes," she said with certainty. "All of which I can handle—and probably better than anyone else." She paused. "Except, possibly, you."

Walter had to laugh. One couldn't help liking this brash, pretty,
ambitious girl. "I'll say this," he allowed, "if your competence is close
to your confidence, you'll be fantastic."

"Excuse me, sir," Caroline poked her head into the door. "Your
next appointment is in five minutes."

"Thank you," said Walter, "but you'll have to delay it. I'll be
another half-hour with Miss Rochester."

"Very well," said Caroline primly, pursing her lips in annoyance.
"I'll try, but you're very busy."

"Half an hour."

"Yes, sir."

"Tell me what you studied at Harvard." Walter leaned back in his
chair and placed his hands behind his head.

Christ, she thought, now he's going to play interviewer. "Economics, accounting, business law, business theory, decision making and
corporate games," she said rapidly. Then she too leaned back in her
chair, hands behind her head, mimicking Walter's pose.

"Goddamn it," Walter said as he laughed, "you really are
cheeky."

"Yes." They both broke their poses and smiled.

"That's an impressive list of studies, but we sell experience in the consulting business, not theory."

"You explained that thoroughly at Harvard," she said drily. But you have other young people working here."

"They only do what they're told."

"That's what I want to do."

"You want to do what you're told?" Walter said in exaggerated disbelief.

"Up to a point," Katy hedged.

"That's the problem. Your point and my point are bound to be worlds apart."

"Look, I know I don't have experience. But I want to learn. Perhaps we could start with you explaining exactly what your company does?" Always get them talking about themselves, she had been taught by the business school placement service. Ask questions, even if you know the answers.

"Well, one important thing we do is consulting," Walter started, unable to resist an opportunity to teach. "For example we help our clients, who are usually the big multinationals, launch new products."

"Why can't they do that for themselves? They must have big staffs."

"They do, but they're often not available for new projects. And they don't want to hire new people in case the project fails. So it's more practical to retain us until they know how it's faring."

"But that means that if it goes well and they hire people, you're out of business."

"Wrong! That means we're in a position to accept *new* business!"

Katy laughed briefly. "But it must make it difficult for you to keep growing. After all, how many new projects are there?"

"You're right," Walter agreed. "That's the limitation." How often he had worried about precisely that problem! "That's why we do other things."

"What sort of things?"

"Well . . ." Walter searched for something that would demonstrate to her how much she had to learn. "For example, we're starting to do some barter business with one of the largest people in the field, Fred Pogue. He brings the expertise, we bring the leads. It's one of the most exciting businesses I've ever explored."

"Media or goods and services?" she asked succinctly. It was a field she knew something about, thanks to an excellent presentation she had attended at Harvard.

Walter was astonished. The area was largely new to him, so her

offhand knowledge was surprising. "Goods and services," he said
weakly.

"A friend of mine did a deal with shortening," she explained,
remembering an example from the lecture and lying about her close-
ness to the deal. "He swapped about thirty-five million pounds of
shortening for eleven million in cash and four million in goods and
services, which only cost him two and a half."

"What sort of goods?"

"Things like hotel rooms, moving expenses, furniture, corrugated
board, automobiles. . . ." Katy reeled off the remembered list, delighted
that she had been able to take charge of the interview. This was going
better than she had hoped. "Now," she said, following up on her
advantage, "don't you think we should get back to the subject?"

Walter laughed. "Which is?" he asked, teasing her.

"My job."

"You're very bright," he complimented her. "And—"

"If you say pretty," she interrupted, "I'll scream rape."

"Okay, Okay." He laughed again. "And I love your epaulets."

"Huh?" She had no idea what he meant.

"Giant chips," he explained, grinning. "On both shoulders."

"Oh, I see." She smiled back at him. "I *am* a little sensitive."

"A little," he agreed.

"So do I get a job or not?" she demanded.

"Very well," he said capitulating. She could certainly be a useful
addition, he decided. And she'd be fun to have along on the occasional
business trip. He amused himself imagining what she would say if she
could read his thoughts. "You can start Monday as my assistant," he
said. "I'll pay you twenty thousand a year." Walter knew it was a
ridiculously low starting salary for a Harvard Business School graduate.
He still half-hoped she'd turn it down.

"You'll pay me twenty-five," said Katy promptly. "That's still
outrageously low."

"I said twenty."

"I know you did, but that wasn't a serious offer." She grinned at
him. "You meant twenty-five."

Again Walter had to laugh. "Yes," he said. "I guess I meant
twenty-five."

Katy's elation surprised her. Certainly it was satisfying to have
talked Walter into giving her a job. But that hardly explained the
degree of pleasure she felt. After all, she didn't even know what the
job would be; and by Harvard standards, the pay was pitiful. Yet she
felt ready to sing. She almost skipped down the street.

Her elation lasted all afternoon. Even the depressing fact that she was alone just before a weekend hardly dampened her spirits. As she strolled through Central Park, watching harried young matrons dragging their squalling brats behind them, she wanted to hug herself. She felt so *wonderful!*

By late afternoon, however, Katy's self-congratulatory mood was wearing thin. She wanted company. No, not company, friends. *A* friend. Company was easy. All she had to do was look up acquaintances in the black book of her contacts. She always carried it, neatly organized by geographic area. But a *friend,* that was different. Friends you couldn't organize like contacts . . . Oh, what the hell, she thought. Contacts for money, contacts for fun, even contacts for sex. Since that's all she had available, it would have to do. First some phone calls to arrange somewhere she could go to meet people, then a bath.

Resolutely Katy Rochester went into action. This evening she would have fun, she decided. *Fun!*

By seven-thirty Katy was luxuriating in her bath, soaping her breasts, between her thighs, lifting her hips out of the water so that the foam could build a mountain over her pubis. She wondered whether she would meet anyone interesting this evening. The thought roused her, and she touched and stroked herself in the warm bath water, feeling herself rise to a small shuddering peak, a prelude, she hoped, to what might happen later.

The party to which Katy Rochester had arranged an invitation was in a downtown loft, a culture shock after the solid, professional, West Side area where she had borrowed an apartment from an out-of-town girl friend. The taxi took her down Broadway and through the theater crowds around Times Square. They were surburban crowds, she noticed, but interspersed with the indigenous hustlers who lived like lice off the visitors. The cab continued past Forty-second Street, with its porn films and sullen drunks, where suburbanites would never dare show their faces and the junk-ridden flotsam of the city congregated; through the empty garment center, which, during the day, would be jammed with boys jostling pushcarts of dresses down streets and sidewalks; into the northern part of Greenwich Village, where Katy could see the boys holding hands, one pair kissing passionately on a street corner; and then eastward, toward Washington Square, still the center of Greenwich Village and meeting place for the area's artists, near-artists and freaks, even though the square itself was now flanked by expensive apartment buildings and conservative New York University. There the taxi got caught in traffic and for the next ten minutes inched its way down MacDougal street, thronged with an equal mixture of tourists and long-haired, artistic-looking residents. Katy knew that most of those, although they looked the part, were not artists at all. They were entrepreneurs who hid their shameful calling behind a camouflage of headbands, superbly scruffy jeans and even, where the tourist trade necessitated such dated ornaments, beads. What they sold was as diverse as the young men and women looked identical, ranging from the homely T-shirt (with or without salacious, funny or merely sick slogans) to the more exotic hallucinogenic drugs. A bazaar atmosphere prevailed: hawkers vended "hand-made" leather purses on the sidewalk; greeters invited passersby into "genuine" coffee houses; and a three-card monte artist performed to a crowd of his own shills and a few genuine marks. A thin cloud of hamburger grease hung in the air.

At length the cab reached the end of the block and turned left on Houston Street and right again into Soho—"South of Houston."

A few moments later the cab stopped on a deserted street in front of an apparently abandoned warehouse.

"You mean this is where you want, lady?" the cabdriver asked in a thick Brooklyn accent. "Looks like a pretty tough area for a girl like youse."

"I can take care of myself," she said coolly, paying her fare.

"As you like, lady." The cabbie was offended. "It's your funeral." He gunned the motor and screeched off.

Katy shrugged her shoulders. What the hell. But as she turned away from the curb, she observed three black youths lounging across the street, staring at her. Defiantly she stared back, but when one of them pretended to start toward her, to her acute embarrassment she found herself scampering into the building. It was dark inside, and although the stairs were serviceable they seemed dangerous. She could not stop herself imagining that the teenagers were climbing after her. Fervently she hoped she had come to the right place. To return downstairs again, alone. . . . She refused to finish the thought.

Out of breath, she reached the top landing. Thank God the door was ajar. She could hear the noise of the party in full swing. Hesitantly she entered.

"Hiya, honey!" A young blond giant clasped her around the waist, half-sweeping her off her feet. "Come on in, I've been expecting you." His voice—and his silliness, Katy thought—was pure Ivy League. "I'm Jake," he announced enthusiastically.

"I'm Katy."

"Jake and Katy, Katy and Jake; Jake and Katy, Katy and Jake; Jake and . . ." he kept repeating. She broke away from his clasp, realizing he was too high to make any sense, and found herself in the midst of a group of dancers swaying systematically to the disco beat. For a few minutes she retired to a corner to observe. Did she want to be at this party at all, she wondered?

"Hiya, honey." The words were the same, but this time it was a woman a little older than herself who smiled at her. "Come join us." Katy realized that all the dancers in this group were female. Stiffly she started taking a few steps, barely letting the music touch her. Gradually it forced its rhythm onto her: She loved to dance, and disco was the sound that broke through her New England inhibitions best. Its beat was strong but neither as violent as the acid rock of a few years ago, which frightened her, nor as sensual as the Latin dances, which made her feel embarrassed. Disco, with its mixture of formal choreography and safe, insistent rhythm, encouraged her to get lost in herself.

Katy danced for several minutes, letting the music warm her as she would let the water from a hot shower thaw her out after a cold day's skiing, before she realized that the girl who had greeted her was now her sole partner and was ogling her intensely.

"I'm going to get a drink," Katy said quickly, feeling extremely uncomfortable. The girl looked disappointed but did not follow as Katy hurried away.

At the bar a group of young men were jostling to reach the wine and sangria. One of them approached Katy. He seemed gentle and shy. "Can I get you a drink?"

"Please, I would like that. Red wine."

But the illusion of his reticence was shattered as he grabbed her bottom and pulled her toward him. "What do you *really* want?" he asked suggestively.

"What I really want," she said, looking him full in the eye as he tried to push himself against her, "is for your mommy to take you home."

He let go as if she had become scaldingly hot. She poured her own wine and walked to the opposite corner. The remnants of her elation evaporated as she looked over the milling, on-the-make crowd, saw the marijuana cloud eddying around the room and felt hopelessly lonely. What am I doing here?

"You seem to feel as out of place as I do." She looked up to see a somewhat older man in a conservatively tailored safari jacket and well-cut jeans.

"Yes," she agreed noncommittally.

"I'll commandeer some wine if you'll grab those two chairs."

"Fine." She went for the chairs fast before someone else got them. A few moments later her new escort returned, a full bottle of wine in one hand. "Look," he said, pointing at the two glasses he carried in the other. "Real glass."

"Damn." She laughed. "I like my wine in plastic."

He poured them each a glass. "To the observers," he toasted. "May we never lose our cynicism."

"What makes you think I'm a cynic?"

He merely raised an eyebrow, mocking.

"Yes," she said, "I see what you mean."

"Perhaps another twenty minutes here?"

She considered him for a moment. "Yes, at the most," she decided. "I'm celebrating this evening, and this hardly seems the place."

"Obviously not a new love."

"A new job."

"Worth celebrating?"

"I'm serious about work." She felt able to speak to this stranger, who seemed bright enough to comprehend but distant enough to be no threat. "I'm no cynic in that respect."

"Then it will have to be dinner."

"If you like."

"It passes the time while we get acquainted. I'm old enough to dislike sleeping with strangers."

"We're not in bed yet, you know," she said.

"Not yet," he agreed. "Let's go and have dinner."

His name was Ray Michaels, and he was a stockbroker with inherited money, reasonable intelligence and little imagination. He had no idea what he wanted to do with his life. What he did, following the path of least resistance, bored him. His apartment, which they reached after a pleasant enough dinner, was as well furnished as a suite at any expensive hotel, and just as impersonal. When they undressed, he folded his pants neatly across the ottoman at the foot of the bed. And when they made love, he seemed as organized and detached as when he folded his pants. His foreplay was standardized, a routine he had mastered as thoroughly as the buy-sell procedures he executed at work. Her body, healthy and normally responsive, reacted mildly. The sensations of his entry and careful, steady thrusting were pleasurable, almost comforting. He did everything correctly but without inspiration.

"Will you come?" he asked politely.

"Perhaps not this time," she said, as if declining a cucumber sandwich at an English tea party.

How different it will be once I'm rich! The thought came to her quite unexpectedly, and with it she felt the sexual tension, totally missing previously, start to mount. Captains of industry, politicians, financeers would be her partners then. Ruthless men, tough, dynamic. She moved her hand to where Ray Michaels was still dutifully thrusting and started to massage herself.

"Harder," she demanded. But although it was Ray who responded, Katy was thinking of quite a different sort of man: powerful, strong . . . Her fingers tugged at her labia and massaged her clitoris while her fantasies, a kaleidoscope of office orgy scenes, filled both her head and her pelvis. She imagined what it would be like to be fucked by some tycoon of industry on a board-room table—*her* board-room table. . . . With a smile of pleasure, which Ray Michaels completely misunderstood, she reached a most satisfactory orgasm.

Walter arrived home late and alone. Tomorrow he would take Judith to Saratoga. She loved to gamble, and there was a huge party planned for the evening. But tonight he would enjoy his solitude.

He showered, poured himself a glass of red wine, opened some cashew nuts from the snack cupboard and turned on the television. For half an hour he watched the news, then he read some papers for the next day's meeting. By eleven o'clock he was sleepy; by eleven-thirty, his day was complete.

He was nearly asleep, his mind almost still, when unexpectedly he started to think about Katy Rochester. The thought startled him awake. He grinned as he recalled his interview with her. Sharp, that one, he thought. I wonder what she's doing now?

Suddenly he had a vision of Katy lying in her bed, perhaps alone, perhaps with a man. What would it be like having her in this bed, he wondered. His hand moved toward his now-hard penis. Her breasts would probably pucker and point when he touched them . . .

His hand started to move up and down faster, and the desire to come, totally absent a moment earlier, filled him. What would it be like, he thought, to wake up with Katy, to feel her body pressing against him? He could feel his semen gathering to spurt and was just lifting the bedsheet out of harm's way when the telephone rang.

"Hello," he barked. "What d'you want?"

"I been figuring who'd be most likely to come up with really big money for Magnatel," Harry Grass said without preliminaries. "None of the banks'll go for it because there's no loan security."

"We don't even know the price yet, or whether they'll sell to us," Walter objected wearily, "and already you're getting it financed. Aren't you going off a little prematurely?"

"Better than not getting it up at all. Also, I got an idea," Harry continued. But his tone did not sound very enthusiastic.

"You don't sound like it's a very *good* idea."

"It's good. We'll get more money from him than anyone." Harry grunted to show he was nevertheless displeased. "Anyhow, I don't see no other alternative, so Kashi's an easy first." Harry's voice emphasized his distaste.

"The Arab?" Walter had heard the name and knew that he made his headquarters in England. He had heard that Kashi was very rich but somewhat unsavory.

"Yeah, the fucking A-rab."

"And you don't want to?"

"No, man," Harry replied seriously. "I sure don't. What with you working with the Krauts, and me with the A-rabs, the fun's going out of this deal." Suddenly he snorted his characteristic laugh. Over the phone it sounded like a small explosion and made Walter grimace and pull the phone away from his ear. "Oh, what the fuck, it's all money," Harry said, past hesitation now. "We might as well. Anyhow," he added, "I'll let *you* negotiate with the pig."

"Is it worth doing?" Walter wondered aloud. Distracted, he ran a hand through his wiry black hair.

But Harry was adamant again, his brief, rare moment of doubt over. "Of course." It was not in his character to drop out of any opportunity. Even years ago when they had hardly dared dream of being rich, Harry had been single-minded about his goal. "It's what we do, ain't it?"

"Will you ever stop?" Walter asked into the telephone and rolled onto his back in the bed.

"When I drop dead." Harry was about to hang up. The conversation had become too philosophical for him. "Hey," he asked his inevitable question as an afterthought. "How're the broads?"

Walter laughed.

"You got one with you now?"

"No," said Walter, "as a matter of fact, I don't. But there was a girl I was thinking about."

"You oughta settle down," said Harry and hung up.

Just conceivably, Walter thought for the first time, Harry might be right.

Katy Rochester arrived at the office the next morning at eight-thirty sharp. Glimpsing Walter, she tried to say hello. "I was thinking about you last night . . ." she started.

Walter smiled at her but hurried past, saying merely, "Good morning. Caroline will tell you where to go."

"He didn't tell me a thing about what you'll be doing," Caroline lamented. "I've arranged a desk for you, but all I can think of is for you to read the consulting studies we've done this year." She handed Katy a foot-high pile of paper. "This should take a few days to wade through. By then I should know more about what he wants." She said "he" in a deferential whisper, wanting to make sure this new girl shared in the general awe about her boss.

A long way from being screwed on her board-room table, Katy thought with amusement, and started to read.

It took her until late the next afternoon, even working half the night, to finish. Most of the studies were typical of those she had worked with at Harvard. The difference was that here she felt the tension of reality. Also, she noted, every one of the files she had read concluded with a proposal for vigorous action. That dynamism, almost like a signature of Walter Cort, Inc., was lacking in the theoretical solutions the business-school students proposed.

If that's what he wants, she thought as she left the offices that evening, I'll give him action. It was a childish promise, she realized ruefully, full of bombast. But even as she scornfully told herself to grow up, she knew that somehow she was going to get involved with Walter Cort. Not for love, not necessarily for sex—although that might be exciting—but for the power he exuded, for his strength, his dynamism. And, of course, for his money.

The silver-gray Buick—Walter felt a Cadillac or Lincoln was too obvious, and on principle he would own no Mercedes—picked him up at the main entrance to his building and whisked him to the East Side Heliport. His driver, elegantly named Nathaniel Washington Soames, placed the Mark Cross suitcase onto the helicopter and walked back to the car.

"All set, sir."

"Thank you, Nathaniel," Walter said, stumbling over the word. "Goddamn it, why can't you get a more pronounceable name?" he said, half-jesting, half-irritable.

"They can pronounce it in Harlem," Nathaniel answered in the same ambiguous tone.

Walter laughed and walked without stooping toward the helicopter. He had once measured the height of the rotary blades and found that they easily cleared his head. Thereafter he had stopped ducking when he entered the machine, and sometimes even waved his arm above his head when he had an appropriate audience. To his left the river glistened like oil. Ahead loomed the Fifty-ninth Street bridge, in front of it the aerial tramway that moved people over the river from Manhattan to Roosevelt Island. The helicopter, dwarfed by the bridge, pulsated in noisy defiance, an angry insect not in the least intimidated.

The trip to Kennedy Airport, up the East River, across the borough of Queens—Walter could see the rows upon rows of tiny houses crowded together, and the cars crawling down Queens Boulevard—almost directly over Shea Stadium, and finally to the sprawling airport, delighted Walter. And the sense of importance he derived from having a private helicopter fly him either to his company plane or, in this case, to an international jet, boosted his ego every time. Harry, by contrast, had arranged for one of his teenagers to pick him up at his Brooklyn house and drive him to the airport in the two-year-old family Ford.

The 747 circled several times over Frankfurt airport and eventually landed with a bump. Walter and Harry, alongside two hundred other weary passengers, stumbled their way down the steps, across the wet tarmac and into one of the waiting buses. It was a gray, drizzly morning.

Belching diesel fumes, the bus bounced to the terminal building, where Walter and Harry were jostled into the arrival hall by their now-impatient fellow travelers. Carrying their expensive briefcases, they walked down the seemingly endless airport corridors, taking care to pick up their feet at each step so as not to catch their toes in the tiny "teeth" sticking up from the hard rubber floor, knowing from past experience that this would jar their ankles. After a while they stepped onto the moving sidewalk. Walking forward at a comfortable saunter now toward the baggage area, they nevertheless moved as rapidly as if they wore seven-league boots. When their bags arrived, they placed them onto carts advertising Dr. Meuller's Sex Shop and trundled them past bored customs officials into the outer lobby. There they were met by a driver with a neatly labeled sign, Herr Cort, who hurried them into a large black Mercedes for the trip to the city.

"Efficient," Harry said,

"Yeah," Walter grumbled, "but why the hell is it always gray in this goddamned city?"

Harry was used to Walter's complaints about Germany, and merely grunted.

"I think it's to give the architecture the right backdrop," Walter continued. "Teutonic bleak."

"Who gives a shit, as long as we make a buck? Anyway, it's better than Brooklyn."

"I prefer Brooklyn," said Walter with conviction.

The Frankfurter Hof Hotel, traditionally one of the elegant hotels of Europe, had moved its main entrance from the archway through which its elite clientele used to sweep into the lobby, to a side entrance where there was more room for the tour coaches to park. Seeing the size of the Mercedes, the porter forgot the coaches, however, and sprang to attention. Then, carrying their bags as gingerly as if they might explode, he obsequiously followed Walter and Harry into the lobby. The registration process was also rapid.

"Magnatel company has announced to me your arriving," the assistant hotel manager said politely. "I believe we have arranged everything, to give you maximum comfort." He bowed and rubbed his hands, reminding Walter of a housefly.

After they registered, they were escorted to their rooms down long corridors, first wide, then narrowing as they reached the newer section of the hotel. Their rooms were airy and large, full of silk chairs and reproductions of French period furniture. There were also large baskets of welcoming fruit. Walter placed his outside the door, knowing that if he did not, by evening the whole room would soon smell of overripe apples. Nevertheless, he was flattered. However often he stayed in such luxury hotels, he would never fail to compare them with his Brooklyn beginnings—and revel in the difference. That was what life was all about.

Half an hour later, revived by showers and changes of clothes, the two men were completing their preparations for the day's work over croissants and coffee in the ornate hotel dining room.

The doorman at the Magnatel building, a square, gray edifice of neither charm nor originality, managed to appear both austere and fat. He barely looked up when Harry Grass and Walter Cort entered; they didn't wear hats or black overcoats, so they couldn't be important. Only the sight of an important man—a dangerous man, in his terms—was likely to arouse him. Was he not, after all, a dangerous man himself, shop steward for the Office Workers and Maintenance Gewerkschaft?

Walter nudged Harry. "Watch," he said under his breath. Slowly removing his raincoat, he strolled over to the porter. Suddenly he threw the coat across the desk. "Doctor Schatten," he barked.

The result was galvanic. Hearing the name of Magnatel's chairman and chief executive—the Herr Geschaeftsführer—the porter leaped to his feet so fast his chair crashed to the floor.

"Jawohl," he stuttered. "May I be permitted to announce . . ."

"Cort and Grass," Walter said in clipped tones. Then he turned away, no longer interested. He winked at Harry.

"Yes sir, *jawohl,"* the porter stammered. "Immediately."

Dr. Schatten's secretary hurried out within seconds, stretching out her hand to shake theirs in the American way, as she had been taught. Harry responded cheerfully, but Walter, ignoring the proffered hand, clicked his heels and merely inclined his head fractionally. The secretary's smile withered. "Please follow me," she said very carefully.

"Ah, how pleasant to see you. How kind of you to come. I hope you had a comfortable and convenient journey." Dr. Schatten looked lean and hungry. His body was bent and, even at this time of the morning, his face was grayed by the shadow of his beard. It made his cheeks look cadaverous. Not an impressive ad for their electric razors, Walter thought. Dr. Schatten's hair was thin and graying; dandruff covered the shoulders of his charcoal suit. The man was monochromatic, Walter concluded, noting as well that Schatten's attempts at being affable appeared to be costing him considerable effort.

"You must forgive my limited knowledge of your language," the Magnatel executive continued, evidently pleased to be able to show off his English vocabulary. "I have assiduously endeavored to study it, but my command is still far from impeccable."

He smells of 4711 cologne, Walter was thinking. They all do.

"Your English is damned good," said Harry, making a last-minute effort not to say fucking good.

"It will improve," said Walter coldly. Then, fearing he had taken his rudeness too far, he added. "During our negotiations, I mean, as will our German."

"Ah, yes, negotiations. Perhaps the time has come to invite our chief financial officer in . . ."

Old enough to be culpable, Walter was thinking. In Germany Walter "graded" people by age: sixty and over, clearly responsible; forty to sixty, tarnished; under forty, in theory, innocent—in spite of the fact that their parents were murderers.

"Perhaps a cup of coffee?" Dr. Schatten was continuing his forced geniality. "We can take it to our conference room." He led the way to a large but surprisingly drab room next to his office. There they were joined by Magnatel's chief financial officer, a hatchet-faced young man whose English had unexpected Cockney overtones, and the round-faced, older, pompous chief counsel. While coffee was served the conversation ranged from the weather to that specifically German businessman's game of tracing heritages.

"Ah, yes." Dr. Schatten threw his head back to dramatize his memory process. "I recall that there was a Rhinehardt Cort at the Deutsche Bank."

Walter winced at the smell of Halizon breath freshener which accompanied Dr. Schatten's every utterance. The damned man smelled like a Bangkok bazaar. "Not related to me, I'm afraid," he said.

"He was part of the Munich Corts. His sister was working for the I.G. Farben, I believe."

"Really? I thought the sister married and went to live in north Germany," said Walter, who had never heard of the woman. "Was not her husband involved in the shipping industry—before their divorce, I mean?"

"Did they get divorced?" Dr. Schatten became highly interested. "I didn't know."

Harry coughed to cover his snort of laughter. But his amusement ended fast. They'd lose the deal for sure if Schatten, who was a windbag but no fool, discovered what Walter was doing. "And you, Dr. Schatten," he interrupted, "have you led the Magnatel company for long?"

"I have worked here, Mr. Grass, since shortly after the war; but my role as Magnatel's leader is only two years. That is why we are embarking on a changed corporate policy. I have long felt it is in our best interests to divest ourselves of our consumer-products division, and now, at last, I am most gratified that my views have been heard."

The negotiations had started, but neither Walter nor Harry said a word. Long ago they had learned that silence could be a powerful weapon. Let the other guy chatter on—just ask a few questions to keep him on the track—and sooner or later he'll say something to hurt himself.

The silence lengthened.

"Yes, so it is." Dr. Schatten felt forced to continue. "Small appliances do not fit into our long-term corporate policy. In fact they are even manufactured in different factories, one here and one near New York, in New Jersey."

Still silence from the visitors.

"Even though, of course, the small appliances are an excellent business . . ."

"But how profitable?" Walter questioned.

"Not very profitable." Dr. Schatten was too experienced to lie. Obviously these two would find out the truth soon enough. "In fact," he continued smoothly, "we have not been able to do much better than break even." Why did he feel so uncomfortable with that Cort fellow? The other one wasn't so bad, but. . . . He shook his head clear of this thought. "You see," he explained, "it just isn't commensurate with the rest of our business to run something based on advertising. We are not marketeers; we are industrialists. However, I am confident that a marketing group, especially an American one, could do far better than we. You people are so *good* at marketing." His tone suggested that being good at marketing was somehow less than respectable.

Walter felt his anger flash, but he allowed no sign of it to show.

"I understand," Dr. Schatten continued, speaking directly to Walter, "that you are indeed a marketing specialist. Is it not so that you advise some of the most sophisticated multinationals how to improve their marketing?"

"Quite true."

"And what would you advise us?" Dr. Schatten tried without success to sound bantering. "After all, our name appears on all our small appliances as well as our large. We want no harm to come to it."

Here was the key question, Harry and Walter both realized. Magnatel would only sell to a group they trusted to keep their good name intact. That would be almost as important as the price to be paid for the company.

"Absolutely," Harry answered confidently, the Brooklyn accent, which in New York he wore aggressively like a badge of office, now muted. "We would fully agree with that. So by providing those widely used marketing supports needed—and with maximum efficiency—we would in fact strengthen your name." He smiled and sat back in his chair, confident that he had nicely confused the issue.

"Very interesting." Dr. Schatten tried to look as though he understood, while his two assistants, who had sat as nonparticipant as blocks of wood, blinked and shifted uncomfortably.

"Confusion to the enemy," Walter thought. It was the favorite saying of old Edward Ball, DuPont's key trustee and probably the toughest negotiator south of the Mason-Dixon line. Walter almost laughed in Schatten's face. Instead he leaned toward the chairman. "Which about summarizes our point," he said with a great show of sincerity, "and explains clearly why we would be the ideal candidates to acquire your division." He too sat back in his chair, looking complacent. "Don't you agree?"

The partners' negotiating attack almost worked. Before he really knew what was happening, Dr. Schatten found himself not only ready to sell to them but close to begging them to buy. "Well," he said at length, playing for time to figure out how the roles had been reversed, "you clearly bring with you considerable marketing skills . . ." He paused to light his pipe, "and considerable negotiating skills, too," he added with another attempt at levity. "So if we agreed to sell to you, you would undoubtedly make a great deal of money. A great deal," he repeated, starting to feel more confident again. "You see, the one thing we *have* done is build the reputation of our name." He ostentatiously examined a sheet of figures in front of him. "In the last five years," he said impressively, "we have spent over two hundred million dollars in advertising."

"Impressive," Walter admitted.

"Forty-five million last year alone."

"And the value of the company's factories and other assets is also large?" Harry knew that the value was low compared to the company's sales volume.

"Quite substantial. After subtracting all liabilities, our net assets still amount to about forty million dollars."

"Only forty million?" said Harry, feigning disbelief. "Less than you spent on advertising in one year?"

"Ah yes," said Dr. Schatten. "We are not a capital-intensive industry. That's one of our greatest advantages."

"Really," said Harry. "An advantage?" He clucked his tongue. "Forty million dollars net worth, and forty-five million dollars on advertising," he repeated, as if trying to understand an incomprehensible fact.

"And they break even," Walter added.

"I guess you have to call that good performance, considering how much advertising they have to spend to get their sales." Harry was apparently addressing himself only to Walter.

"We are asking one hundred and twenty million dollars for the division," Dr. Schatten interrupted the partners' dis?ussion abruptly. "Forty million for the tangible assets, and eighty for the goodwill of the name."

"How interesting," said Walter politely.

"No kidding," added Harry.

They both realized that the figure was high but not unreasonable. We'll be lucky to bring it down to a hundred, Walter thought, while Harry, always the scrappier of the two, thought, so now let's see how far is down. . . .

Dr. Schatten remained silent, realizing that without knowing how, he had again been put at a bargaining disadvantage. His two assistants said never a word.

"Funny," said Harry, "we had assumed that we would be buying the business for around book value. But that's so damned low." He looked at Dr. Schatten with disappointment. "You see, in America our auditors believe that a company's goodwill is only a valuable asset if that company is making a profit."

The young financial officer was just about to interrupt, but it was Walter who spoke first. "But Harry, there has to be some goodwill," he admonished, "even though there aren't any profits."

"I suppose," Harry conceded, looking glum. Then he brightened. "I guess you're right," he said. "In fact, now that I think of it, I myself once acquired a company with goodwill equal to almost sixty percent of its tangible assets."

"You did?" It was Walter's turn to look amazed. "That must have been tough to finance."

"Yeah, a real bitch," Harry reminisced. "We had to get a hell of a lot of help from the seller."

"On this deal we want all cash," said the chief financial officer, trying to help his leader.

"Of course," Harry laughed as if the suggestion were a wonderful joke. "Fucking right."

"Don't we all," said Walter, joining in the laughter.

The financial officer did not understand what was so funny. But since he had no sense of humor, he rarely knew why people laughed anyway, so he joined in.

"There is no advantage to us in selling if we do not get cash to build the rest of our business," said Dr. Schatten furiously. "We are asking a hundred and twenty million dollars in cash."

There was a long, tense silence. "And we, Dr. Schatten," said Walter Cort finally, "are prepared to offer cash for the book value, and a note for the same amount for the goodwill."

"Unacceptable," Schatten announced firmly. "You must improve the offer."

Got him, Walter thought. He didn't reject it outright. He'll settle for not much more than our offer.

Harry, sensing the same, jumped in for the kill. "I said some goodwill, not the moon," he said to Dr. Schatten. "My partner has just offered to pay as much for the goodwill as for the tangible assets of the company. Our board of directors would cut our balls off if we told them goodwill was more than that." He snorted with amazement. "They'll make a lunge at 'em as is."

Thank God for Harry, Walter was thinking. He could always count on him.

This time it was the German chief counsel who was about to comment, but again Walter who spoke first. Time to stage a partner's argument, he had decided. "I think we can go a little higher, Harry," he said, his voice almost pleading. "Maybe ninety million?"

"And I don't think you can go any goddamn higher." Harry was adamant. "Eighty's too damned much as it is."

"Look, the company's got a fantastic name. You yourself said we'd have to pay for that goodwill."

"And no profits." Harry's voice was rising.

"That's because they haven't run it efficiently."

"So?"

"So that's our speciality."

"If it's our speciality, why do we have to pay *them* for it?"

Dr. Schatten watched with astonishment as the two men argued. Cort was saying everything he wanted to, taking all the wind out of his sails.

"Look, Harry, I think we should go higher."

"And I don't."

"Eighty-seven, five?"

"No."

"Eighty-five?"

"Oh shit, I guess so. But we're gonna have a hell of a lot of problems."

"Eighty-five," Walter said turning back to Dr. Schatten. "Forty cash up front, the rest over five years."

"No, definitely not," said Dr. Schatten. "We cannot accept below a hundred million dollars, and it must be all cash." He seemed unwilling to budge further.

"That will not be acceptable to our side," said Walter, wondering whether he was bluffing too far.

"Then there will be no deal," said Dr. Schatten, and his colleagues were certain that he had said his final word.

"We would like to caucus," said Walter. "Would you excuse us?"

"My pleasure," said Dr. Schatten automatically, making it obvious that he felt no pleasure whatsoever. "Please feel free to use this conference room. We shall withdraw."

"Can we go any higher?" Walter asked the moment the Germans were out of the room.

"We don't have to," said Harry exuberantly. "We're doing great. He's gonna bite at eighty-five."

"Glad you think so."

"What they won't do is defer," said Harry, ignoring his friend's doubts. "My guess is the old fart means it when he says all cash."

"I agree with that. But as for the price, Harry, the deal's just too good. At that price we'd be stealing it . . ."

"I know it, I know it!" Harry could hardly contain his excitement. "But I'm sure we can get it."

"Okay. If you think so. . . . So what's the next step?"

"It's time me and the Doc had a word. In camera, as they say."

"The old divide and conquer routine? Convince him to come down to eighty-five and then talk me into all cash?"

"Right on, Wimp."

"Okay," said Walter, "see you back at the hotel."

"Alone, Dr. Schatten," Harry Grass waved the financial man and the lawyer away as if they were children. "I wanna see you alone."

Dr. Schatten hesitated. "Very well," he said at length, his geniality gone.

Harry turned his back and gazed out the window. Only after he heard the door close behind the two departing executives did he slowly turn. He made sure to remain in silhouette; perhaps the light from the window would blind his adversary. Every advantage helped. "We are going to settle for eighty-five million," he said in an utterly cold voice.

"Why do you think so?" Schatten's voice became more gutteral.

"I don't think, I know."

The doctor's smile made his face seem sinister. "You *know?*" he repeated sarcastically. "You are arrogant, my friend."

"I know many things. Many things from many sources."

"What things?"

"You said you joined this wonderful company *after* the war, Doc. I don't think that's true."

For a split second the German chief executive looked worried. It was only a shadow which passed over his face, but Harry caught it and knew he was on the right track. Amazing what you can do with bluff, he thought. Most of them have skeletons. "I think you worked here during the war, Doc," he continued accusingly. "I'm fucking sure you worked here."

"And if so, what then?" For the first time, a *w* turned to a *v*. "So vat?" he asked again.

"So what did Magnatel do during the war? Why don't you explain?"

"There is nothing to explain."

"There's about a thousand bodies to explain," said Harry, his voice rising. "There's experiments in electricity to explain. There's—"

"Those had nothing to do with me!"

"Then you knew about them?"

"I don't know what you're talking about," said Dr. Schatten, pulling himself together with an effort. "What do you want?"

"Eighty-five million, Doc, just eighty-five million and no more," Harry said very slowly and clearly. "That's what we're planning to pay."

"Perhaps it is not so unreasonable . . ."

"Yeah, Doc, perhaps it's very reasonable."

Immediately Dr. Schatten was in total control again, his smile almost warm. Harry could hardly believe the transformation. Within seconds the German's face relaxed from pinched, ratlike guilt to its former confidence. "Very well," said Dr. Schatten, sounding infinitely relieved. "Then we shall make a deal." The *w* was full and anglicized. "Eighty-five million dollars. But I'm afraid I must insist on cash."

"No. A deferred payment."

Dr. Schatten walked slowly up to Harry Grass. He seemed tougher, more sinewy than before. "No," he said in a firm, loud voice. "Cash!" Then, still keeping his face close to Harry's, he added in a reasonable tone, "I cannot agree to a deferred payment if the price is only eighty-five. There would be questions. There is no point if there are questions. There is no point at all for either of us unless I make a deal which I can push through."

"Okay, Doc," Harry said cheerfully, knowing he had reached the limit. "Eighty-five mill, all cash. You're on."

"Then we shall shake hands and act like gentlemen?"

"Yeah," said Harry. "Act like gentlemen."

"Damn good, Harry," said Walter.

The two men were in Walter's hotel room. Shoes off, ties slipped below open collars, they sat facing each other, their feet resting on the ornate coffee table between them. In the center of the table, flanked by their calves, sat an ice bucket cooling a half-empty bottle of wine: Bernkastler Doktor und Graben, the best the Moselle Valley had to offer. The only thing Walter really appreciated about Germany was the wine, and he had decided to splurge. Seventy dollars was an outrage, of course. But the treat was justified, and he could afford it.

"Not bad, Wimp," Harry agreed. "This stuff's not bad, either." He poured himself another glass.

"We've come a long way together, haven't we, from the gas station?"

"Yeah, and we got a long way to go," Harry said. Nostalgia made him uncomfortable. "Eighty-five million dollars to go. I couldn't get no deferral."

"It's better than I expected. In fact, it's a hell of a deal. I never thought he'd go below a hundred. How did you do it?"

"We had a little chat." No point in revealing the details of Dr. Schatten's capitulation. It would just upset Walter, and he might duck out if he knew. Why take that risk. . . .

"A little chat?"

"Yep, a little talking, a little convincing, a little pushing—and eighty-five million dollars in cash sitting on the end of a string. Told you, Wimp. Told you he'd go for it. So now we've got it."

"Got it?" said Walter, suddenly annoyed at his friend's smugness. "What do you mean, got it? Hell, all we've got is the chance to pay eighty-five million dollars. That and some far-out hope that some damned Arab buddy of yours will come up with the money. Christ, the bastard won't even see me till next week. His office says he's tiger hunting."

"Pussy, more likely," said Harry cheerfully. "Not much to go on, I admit, not when your best bet's some fucking A-rab. Still, it ain't impossible and you have to say it wouldn't be a bad deal if we could pull it off." He grinned at Walter, enjoying the understatement.

"No, it wouldn't," said Walter, trying to block himself from feeling too deeply the impact this deal would make on his life. "No," he repeated softly, failing to contain his fantasy, "it really wouldn't be bad."

7

Katy Rochester arrived every morning at Walter Cort, Inc., at precisely eight-thirty—and sat. After several requests from Caroline, Walter would suggest some work, usually reading or simple analysis. He was totally offhanded about her, making it offensively clear that he didn't give a damn whether she stayed or left. The rest of the time Katy read the *Wall Street Journal, The New York Times, Fortune*—any business publication she could lay her hands on. At five o'clock, bored and frustrated, she returned to her apartment.

The most exciting thing that happened during the first week was that Harry Grass visited, creating a hubbub of activity, and swearing loudly about Magnatel and a bunch of other deals which didn't even have names.

"What is Magnatel?" Katy asked Caroline. "I haven't seen a word about it in the files."

"Just something Mr. Cort's working on with Mr. Grass." Caroline had no intention of revealing anything even remotely confidential. And, snoop as she might, Katy could find no clues.

By the third week Katy was ready to scream. Everything was going wrong. Not a single one of her daydreams was materializing. Her job, which, in spite of Walter's initial hesitation, she had expected to be fascinating, was hopeless; her living situation, now that her roommate had returned, had been reduced to a claustophobic "efficiency"; and her social life was empty and celibate. The stockbroker she'd met at the Soho party called once, but Katy turned him down. Even after sleeping together she feared she might not recognize him. Once she went to a smaller party with business school friends, but it was a total bust: Each of them had a far more exciting job than she, and she ended the evening frustrated and envious.

Why do I stay then? she wondered. What's so special about Walter Cort, Inc.? But she would not answer herself honestly that the only reason she stayed was Walter Cort's dynamism—and he was rudely ignoring her. Instead, rationalizing, she tried to convince herself that it was the entrepreneurial spirit of the whole company that intrigued her. Any day now, she assured herself, she would find the business excitement she sought.

Her rationalizations, however, crumbled completely by the fourth week. Walter was rarely in the office: Yesterday, it had been Pittsburgh; tomorrow, she heard, he was flying to England. Damn it, Katy Rochester, she scolded herself, is this how you're planning to waste the rest of your life? She determined to make one final effort.

"Time to go home," Caroline said as the day dragged its way to five o'clock. "See you tomorrow."

"I can't go yet," Katy lied. "My date's calling me here."

"Okay, then, have a good time."

Katy waited until the office was empty except for Walter, who was still working, and that grumpy old cleaning lady rattling her buckets outside his office. Knocking once on his door but not waiting for a response, Katy bounced in.

"Hi," she said brightly. "I'm Katy Rochester, late of the Harvard Business School. I'm your personal assistant, and probably your best-read employee. I'm here to explain that, as an assistant, I would like to assist." She looked at him appraisingly to reassure herself that he was not becoming too angry. "I know you warned me that there was nothing to do, but you're going out of your way to prove it. So I figured I'd push a little. I suppose the worst you can do is fire me."

"I could spank you."

"That wouldn't be the worst." She grinned impishly.

"You really are a brash creature," he said indulgently.

"I'm a businesswoman bored to tears," she said carefully.

"You're free to leave," he said, his tone practical.

"What a sad situation it is," she said, feigning sorrow, "when the president of a company that lives off ideas can't think of one damn thing that needs doing—especially when there are dozens."

"What do you mean?" Walter's tone was neutral. He wasn't sure whether he should be angry or amused.

"Harry Grass was in here yesterday, shouting about why nobody could give him no 'fucking help.' I assume he's important. So if you can't give him 'no fucking help,' maybe I can."

"I'm not going to touch that suggestion with a ten-foot pole," Walter grinned.

Inevitably, Katy blushed. But she refused to acknowledge her embarrassment. "Tell me about Magnatel," she demanded, stabbing in the dark at the name Harry had mentioned. She was rewarded to see Walter's eyebrows rise briefly. "Why do you want to acquire Magnatel?"

Walter was caught with his guard down. "It's like climbing Mt. Everest," he started.

"Because it's there?"

"Yes," he said. "It would be a hell of a challenge to actually run something, not just advise."

"And a lot of work."

"Right,"

"Could we handle it?" she asked, testing him with the "we."

He noticed, of course. "Yes," he replied. "I believe 'we' could."

He placed just a hint of emphasis on the word. She smiled, relieved.

"Will you get it, then?"

"Not a chance," he said despondently, allowing his disappointment to break through. Instantly he covered his tracks. Never show emotions inadvertently; being vulnerable is dangerous. "Not a chance in the world," he repeated lightly. "It was only a daydream. Wouldn't really be smart. Far too many eggs in one basket."

"Still, you're trying," she commented blandly, realizing that, in spite of his protestations, he wanted it intensely.

"Oh, sure. I have a motto: First get the job, then turn it down. That's the only reason we're trying."

She knew he was lying. "I heard this deal ties in with something called Clarendon," she probed.

"Yes, distantly." Walter's desire to teach got the better of him. "You see, on Clarendon we're finders for a tough German business man called Von Ackermann. . . ." Walter started to explain.

But Katy Rochester barely heard. Von Ackermann! Good God, was all she could think, good God! At last! Here's my chance. The chance I've been waiting for.

Raymond's Review Bar in London, the only place Meshulem Kashi was willing to meet Walter Cort, was a high-class strip joint masquerading as a private club. It lay in the sleazy Soho section of London, not far from Piccadilly Circus with its pimps and prostitutes and certified addicts collecting their nightly fixes from the all-night chemist shop. Walter entered Raymond's from an alleyway leading past a porn cinema and a couple of sex shops. At either end of the alley slouched dirty-looking men trading perversities.

In contrast, Raymond's entrance looked like a posh, upper-crust theater lobby. Walter had to buy a year's membership for five pounds to be allowed to go upstairs.

"Yes, Mr. Kashi is waiting." The girl behind the bar pointed at the closed velvet drapes at one end of the room. They were a deep maroon. The rest of the room was dark red, velvet mostly, with slightly worn gold trim.

"How will I recognize him?"

"Oh, you can't miss him," the girl said in an ostentatiously refined accent. "He's a large gentleman." Suddenly she giggled.

"Large?" Walter wondered about the giggle.

She blew out her cheeks and hung her arms anthropoidally away from her body. " 'e's bloody 'uge," she said in pure Cockney.

And indeed when Walter pushed his way through the curtains, he was confronted by a mountain of a man, so obese that his flesh seemed to festoon itself over the edges of the armchair in which he sat. He was a round, greasy giant with enormous diamond cufflinks, a silk scarf knotted around his fleshy, layered neck, and tiny feet encased in superbly polished, handmade alligator shoes. As Walter approached, trying to mask his surprise, he found himself enveloped by a pungent cloud of incenselike perfume, which rose, together with the smell of sweat, from the outsize body.

On either arm of the chair, pushing into the fat man's flesh as into a feather pillow, sat a girl. Both girls were young, with skirts pushed high and breasts thrusting. In front of this grotesque tableau, on a table carved with serpents and sea nymphs, rested an enormous bowl of nuts and a giant snifter of brandy.

"Mr. Cort," boomed Meshulem Kashi. "Even though we have never met, I recognize you. You have that look of vague distaste new acquaintances of mine usually evidence." His voice was strongly British, evidently the result of an English education, but tinged with just enough Arab undertones to make it seem alien and dangerous. "Go!" he shouted at the girls, pushing their rumps so vigorously that they stumbled as they left. "Later I will call for you," he cried after them.

"Sit down, sit down," he bellowed at Walter, waving at a nearby chair. "Another brandy for Mr. Cort." His orders seemed to roll over one another like waves breaking. "Now," he boomed at Walter, "you want money, right? Everyone wants money."

"I have a business proposition," said Walter, keeping his voice dry and precise, trying hard not to be overwhelmed by the sheer size and power of Kashi. "A business proposition with an excellent return on your investment."

"Of course, of course. They all promise that, the proposals I hear."

"I can only speak for myself," said Walter, determined not to be patronized. "Would you care to hear my proposition, Mr. Kashi, or not?"

"That's why I invited you here." Walter was relieved that Kashi was no longer holding court.

"We have made an offer to acquire the Magnatel small-appliance division from its German parent," Walter began. "The division has sales of some three hundred million dollars, and an excellent reputation. Surprisingly, we have been able to persuade the parent company to sell it for an astonishingly low eighty-five million dollars. Now we are working out plans to find the best way of financing it."

"You mean you haven't been able to raise what you need," said Kashi. "No one comes to me if there's another choice. To you Western businessmen, I'm just a fat Arab, only good enough when all else fails —or perhaps if you have some money to wash. Then you give up your scruples. . . ." His voice was matter-of-fact, but there was no concealing the bitterness beneath.

Walter was about to deny the accusation when he realized how accurate it was. "Yes, I suppose you're right, Mr. Kashi," he said. "We prefer to do business with those we know. But then wouldn't you?"

"Good response, young man," Kashi said immediately. "Of course I would. You're clever. We'll do business together." He paused to gulp his brandy and stuff his mouth full of nuts. "So, how much do you want?" he said, spitting pieces of nuts onto his ample chest as he talked. "How much?"

"Let me tell you the facts first, Mr. Kashi. The net worth of the company is—"

"Forty million dollars. Don't take me for stupid, Mr. Cort. Men have called me many names, but no one has yet called me a fool."

Walter, startled, barely succeeded in hiding his surprise. "I was just reminding you of the background," he said coolly, "to point out that the net worth of the company is not its main asset. The name is. The consumer recognition."

"I'm told you will run it?" Kashi interrupted.

"Yes."

"That gives me some faith. Not much faith, but a little. You are reputed to give sound advice. I hope you have given yourself some."

"I have."

"I assume you will also invest in it?"

Until that second Walter had not even considered the matter but even as Kashi asked the question, Walter realized that he had no choice. No investor would put money into this venture unless Walter led the way; it would be a matter of principle. "Of course," Walter assured him. "I wouldn't miss the opportunity."

Their conversation was interrupted by the tuxedo-clad club manager sidling up to Kashi. "Excuse me, sir," he said sotto voce, "the Tigress is about to commence."

"The Tigress!" Kashi boomed. "Mr. Cort, business can wait; the Tigress cannot. You will shortly see something exalted. But first I must relieve myself. In anticipation, so to speak. Wait here, I shall return."

He heaved himself out of his chair one limb at a time. First he moved one huge thigh forward, then the other. Next he levered forward his belly so that his whole center of gravity advanced. Finally, pushing down onto the arms of the chair and grunting, he struggled onto his legs like a terminally pregnant cow. "Wait here," he commanded again, panting slightly from his exertions. He waddled through a door marked Men in gold leaf.

Finding himself suddenly alone was a great relief. Walter had expected nothing remotely like this. Harry should have warned him.

The manager who had alerted Kashi a few moments earlier hurried back in. "The Tigress is getting restless," he said urgently.

Before Walter could respond, Meshulem Kashi boomed from inside the men's room, "I shall be there shortly. Tell her I have interrupted a most important business meeting to attend her," he ordered.

"Yes, sir." The manager hurried out through the drapes.

The door of the bathroom swung open with a crash as Kashi emerged, hitching up his immense pants. "Come," he boomed to Walter. "Follow me." He waddled ahead through the bar and into the auditorium, where sat rows of men, their eyes riveted on the empty stage. The curtain near the back of the stage was down and the house lights glowed dimly. In front of the stage, in the center of the auditorium, was an armchair obviously reserved for Meshulem Kashi and next to it was a smaller chair, apparently for his guest.

Kashi lowered himself into his chair, arranged his limbs, pulled his pants away from his crotch, glanced at Walter to make sure he too was settled and waved his readiness to the manager waiting in the doorway. Immediately the lights dimmed and the curtain rose.

At first there was nothing but blackness and the roll of jungle drums. "I can promise you something fantastic," said Kashi in a stage whisper which could be heard throughout the auditorium. "Fantastic!"

As Walter's eyes grew accustomed to the darkness, he could vaguely sense someone in the center of the stage, moving rhythmically to the sound of the drums. Unexpectedly two disembodied white-gloved hands, glowing brightly fluorescent under black light, emerged to float in the darkness. They hovered gracefully in mid-air for a moment, the movement picking up the beat of the drums. Then they slowly started to caress what Walter soon recognized as the back of a nude woman. They moved up and down her torso, first over her shoulders, then to the small of her back, finally over her buttocks, defining the crack. Although the body remained invisible, the caressing hands outlined it so accurately that it took detailed shape in the audience's imagination. Then it seemed to turn, and the hands started to caress the front of the invisible girl into vivid existence: first the breasts, beautifully formed, with sharp nipples which the white fingers seemed to twist; then the slender waist; the long smooth hips; and finally, inward over the mons veneris . . . The audience sucked its breath in a hiss when the hands started to explore insistently at the invisible but now clearly defined slit.

Then the fingers were still. After a second a pinpoint spotlight of gradually increasing intensity picked out the very center of the face. At first just the thick sensuous lips with the shiniest imaginable lipstick, then the two green eyes—just enough to show the ecstasy on those lips and in those eyes. As the spotlight gradually widened, Walter saw the hair, a mane of brilliant red which gave the whole head a wild sensuality as taut and dangerous as any jungle cat.

There was a crescendo in the drumming, and then, suddenly, total silence. The lights on the stage rose, revealing the most magnificent female Walter had ever seen.

"Fantastic!" Kashi rumbled in awe as the girl stood, utterly still, clad from her hips down in a skin-tight leotard with a tiger pattern.

Her nipples stood erect. Her mouth, half-open, was wet and shiny with desire.

As the light rose further, Walter realized that the girl was in a cage. She gripped its bars desperately.

The silence seemed to last interminably until, finally, it was shattered from offstage by the wildest of screams, followed by the full blast of pounding rock music. The woman's magnificent body started to sway, first slowly and then faster and faster, until it glistened with sweat, and the wild red mane swung as if in a storm. The metal bars seemed to melt with her heat and Walter realized that she was able to push them apart until she could just emerge, rubbing her body against the bars as she slid between them. As if by accident a hook on one of the bars caught at her leotard and, as she wriggled to be free, it ripped the thin, mottled fabric off her body, leaving it hanging in tatters around her thighs. With a final struggle she was out of the cage. The remaining rags of her costume had ripped further and she kicked them off impatiently. Then she stood there, at the center of the stage just in front of Walter and Kashi, proudly nude.

Now began a wilder, more erotic and uninhibited dance than Walter had ever imagined. The girl's body seemed engulfed, physically assaulted, by the inundating music. Forced on by its beat, she twisted and writhed. At first she merely stroked her body, but as the music grew louder and more violent, she started to claw at her breasts, her thighs, harder, crazier, wilder. She moaned and cried as she reached peaks of excitement, each higher than the last, until her body was shaken by wave after wave of orgasm and the music reached the threshold of pain. . . .

At last, when the tension, the sound level, the violence, had reached the extreme edge of the bearable, suddenly, shockingly, there was again complete silence. The girl was utterly immobilized. For a second time stood still. Then with one final, overwhelming scream of animal release, the girl collasped, sobbing and totally spent. The house lights went black.

"Holy Allah!" Walter heard Kashi murmer. It seemed like a prayer.

When the house lights went on, the girl had disappeared. Nothing remained but a fake cage of silvered rope.

"For that I might give more than for your lousy company," Kashi said as he again pushed himself to his feet. "But I shall finance your company anyway."

"I agree, she was fantastic," said Walter. He could not remember feeling as excited. The girl was incredible; her performance theater of the highest order. A man would have to hate women a lot not to be turned on by that, Walter thought. So, for that matter, would a woman.

"I have offered unreasonable sums to have her," said Kashi.

Walter believed it. "Perhaps she's bargaining," he suggested.

"Perhaps," Kashi rumbled with laughter. "But I have offered a quarter-million dollars for a week. That is as far as I shall go."

"Would you really pay that much?"

"Wouldn't you if you could?"

"Maybe," said Walter, realizing that in Kashi's world two hundred and fifty thousand dollars was an affordable amount.

They moved back to Kashi's semi-private club room. Slowly the fat man turned to Walter, "Thirty-five million I shall lend you," he said. "No more, but thirty-five because I like you. Against the security of all the fixed assests currently in Magnatel. At the same prime plus two percent that you would get from a bank. The papers will be at your hotel in the morning." Walter was about to respond when Kashi interrupted. "The other girls," he boomed. "Bring back the other girls."

"It's not enough," said Walter flatly.

"That's all I have," said Kashi.

"Oh, come now." Walter's face reflected his disappointment that Kashi would sink to such a transparent lie.

"Let me correct myself," Kashi was instantly apologetic. "Of course that is not as much as I, Meshulem Kashi, have available. But I do not put my own money in except for ownership. I never lend. This money is from, let us say, American friends, and those are the funds of which I have no more."

"Now I understand." Walter had heard the rumor that Kashi was Mafia connected. Did this, and his earlier comment about washing money, prove it? Walter decided to ignore the question. Mafia money was no worse than Middle Eastern money, anyhow. For that matter, some of the greatest American fortunes were pretty filthy at their start. As long as he kept control of Magnatel, he didn't care where he borrowed the money. "Nevertheless, thirty-five is not enough," he repeated with determination.

The two blondes who had been sitting on his chair returned, accompanied now by a redhead almost as lithe as the one on stage.

"Not her," Kashi said, pointing at the new girl, irritable for the first time. "I want no seconds." Immediately the red-haired girl left. She showed no disappointment.

"If I use my own funds in addition, it would be as an investor, not as a lender," Kashi said, his tone now that of an ordinary businessman. He completely ignored the two girls wriggling into his lap.

"I believe we could agree with that in principle," said Walter carefully. "The terms would have to be discussed."

"Not much." Kashi suddenly boomed with laughter. "The terms would be exactly the same as for you." He looked at Walter with a grotesque version of an impish expression on his face. "I would put up six million on that basis if you put up four." His eyes looked hooded and speculative.

Walter considered for a moment. The same-terms clause seemed acceptable. But the investment was too much. He decided to voice his concern. "That's—"

"That's all you have," Kashi interrupted. "And you'll probably have to get some from your partner Harry Grass." He laughed uproariously again, his belly bouncing in unison with his gonglike, reverberating laugh.

The drapes parted and a stunning black girl joined the two blondes.

"That's better," Kashi said. "Will you join me, Mr. Cort?"

"I. . . ."

"Perhaps not," said Kashi. "Don't be embarrassed. I understand. Girls are available all over London, and without ten-ton Kashi to go with them."

Christ, I wonder what he does with them, Walter thought, and then quickly dismissed the idea before his imagination could picture the scene. "I have to think," he explained. "About the money, I mean."

"You will accept, my young friend. You have no alternative."

Possibly Kashi was right, Walter reflected as he said good-bye and hurried away. If he wanted to acquire Magnatel, Kashi was his best, possibly his only choice. If he wanted to. There, too, Walter realized, he seemed to be giving himself no choice.

Kennedy Airport is as hurried, efficient and rough as the rest of New York. In the baggage-arrivals hall there are large metal turntables onto which the incoming bags are pushed from underground conveyor belts. People groggy from long flights, excited to be in America—and in New York at that—mill around them. Long lines form ahead of customs officers. The whole process can seem interminable.

Walter's mind was on completely different things as he moved slowly across the airport, trying to avoid the jostling and ignoring the noise so that he almost missed her. In fact he would have, had not his porter almost collided with her, so that they found themselves walking side by side.

"Katy! What are you doing here?" His initial surprise was mild. Airports were so much a part of his life that he unconsciously assumed they were as normal a locale for everyone.

Katy blushed scarlet. "I'm just, eh, coming from . . ." she stammered, about to say Chicago but realizing at the last second that they were in the International Arrivals Building, ". . . from Dublin," she said recovering quickly. "I've a cousin there."

"So that's what you do when I'm off working," he said, "go for a quick week to Dublin." His tone was bantering, not accusatory, but he clearly wanted an explanation. He wondered why she seemed so flustered.

"I'm afraid we had a death in the family," she said sadly, confident that he would not pursue it. People, she had often noted, rarely probed when death or dying was involved. She'd used the technique before to avoid questions.

"Oh, I'm sorry," he said. But to her surprise he wouldn't let it rest. The explanation sounded too pat. She hadn't looked as if she were coming from a funeral. "Your cousin?"

"My grandmother," she said, realizing that she'd have to be more thorough in her excuse. "She used to stay with my cousin twice a year. To go fox hunting. Tough old lady." Katy stopped as if overcome. It was quite convincing. "But this time she fell," she continued, managing a catch in her voice. "And it killed her."

"Oh, I am sorry," Walter was convinced now, and therefore contrite. "Can I give you a lift? Nathaniel's picking me up."

"Oh, yes. Please. I was only gone twenty-four hours and I'm exhausted."

"I know the feeling."

"I can't imagine how you manage it," she said with admiration.

"You develop muscles for traveling. I suppose you do for most activities."

"I guess." She sounded dubious.

The limousine pulled up smoothly, and Walter's driver stored the bags. They both entered the car and relaxed into the comfortable leather seats.

For a few moments neither of them found much to say. Then as if hitting on a completely new subject, one that had come to her just that second, Katy broke the silence, "Oh," she exclaimed. "I've been meaning to ask you about your barter business. I hear you've got some big deal going—cars against television time?"

"Yes, with my friend Fred Pogue. I thought we might give it a try. I have a few friends in Detroit. . . ."

"Fascinating." She looked at him with saucerlike eyes. "Could you buy a whole company like that?" she asked naively, as if the thought had only just struck her. "A company that spends a lot of money on advertising."

Walter looked at her with total astonishment. "I don't know," he said, his brain racing. "I've never thought about it." He paused to let the enormity of the idea sink in. She had no inkling of what she had said, of course, but it was pure genius for all that. It might just work, too. "I suppose so," he said noncommittally. His head pounded with excitement. If he could make a deal with Fred to swap Magnatel appliances for the forty-five million dollars of media the company used annually, he could raise tremendous amounts of additional cash. The appliances wouldn't cost Walter more than thirty-five percent, seventeen million at the most. . . .

For the next half-hour Walter's brain raced with ideas. He hardly said a word until the limousine had pulled into the parking lot and was waiting for them to alight. "Come," he said then to Katy as he jumped out. "We've both got work to do. But from now on I want you to play a more active role. We'll get together tomorrow morning and I'll give you a number of projects, interesting ones this time." He steered her through the garage and into the Pan Am building.

"Thank you," she said, looking at him with a surprisingly calculating expression.

"Fine," he answered distractedly. If only Fred will do it, he was thinking.

Fred Pogue's country house was strange but imposing. Situated on four acres—rolling acres, the real estate ads would have said—it was a turn-of-the-century mansion reminiscent of Newport or "back country" Greenwich. The main portal—"doorway" was far too ordinary a word to do it justice—was framed by rows of wooden pillars, making the house look like a misplaced plantation manor. On either side stretched the building's wings, housing a number of guest bedrooms and then, successively lower, servants' quarters, playrooms and garages, ultimately petering off into tool sheds. Someone had built an observatory dome on top of the main house, so that the whole building looked to Walter like a low, untidy pyramid. In front of the house, redeeming its untidiness, was a superbly neat circular gravel driveway surrounding an impeccable lawn centered by a magnificent rose garden in full bloom. On either side of the house, as far as the eye could take in at a glance, stretched a forest of white birch. Above, the sky was a postcard cliché: blue as technicolor, with fleecy white clouds scudding dutifully by.

Fred Pogue, dressed in absurd Bermuda shorts far too big even for him, stood in his portal, arms stretched forward like a politician greeting the crowds. He quite glowed with pride in his residence.

"Hail, Caesar," shouted Walter, alighting from the Ferrari.

"Friends, Romans, countrymen! Lend me your ears," Fred bellowed back.

"Christ," said Harry, struggling out of the other seat of the low sports car. "Fucking intellects."

"Who's your iconoclast friend?" Fred laughed.

"Iconoclast, is it?" Harry was panting from his exertion. "Damn right. I come to bury Caesar, not to praise him." Harry snorted his typical laugh.

"He's a closet intellectual, has been for years," Walter was amused at Fred's surprise. "He only says 'fuck' as a disguise."

"Fuck you," said Harry, sounding quite belligerent.

"I thought you were bringing all our womenfolk." Fred was always uncomfortable at the two friends' bickering. He was never quite sure how much was real and how much ribbing.

"They'll be along shortly. They took the limo," Harry said. "Martha's scared of the Ferrari."

The three men entered the house. Walter's first glance took in an exorbitantly expensive Turkish runner in the hall, a Greek head on a pedestal, marble tiles and an original Dufy watercolor. A quarter of a million bucks of stuff, at least. They walked through the passageway onto the patio at the back of the house. To the left the swimming pool glittered aquamarine in front of the tennis court; ahead lay another perfectly manicured lawn, this one surrounded by low evergreen shrubbery artfully placed in front of the birch trees.

"Connecticut's answer to Monticello," Walter commented.

"Thank you," said Fred, obviously very proud of his property. "We like it." He only hoped he'd find a way to keep it from his creditors. The business had really got a hell of a lot worse in the last few weeks. He'd been making too many debatable deals—anything to cover his overhead—and he was being left with too much inventory. It looked good on paper, but he just couldn't turn it to cash.

"Mother'll like this too," Harry said, referring to his wife. He had called her Mother from the day, twenty years ago, when they first learned she was pregnant. However much she protested, he rarely called her anything else. It was one of the few subjects the two of them disagreed about. "I bet she gets on my back about getting a spread like this."

"Why don't you?"

"I'm no gentry," said Harry, looking surprisingly bashful. "I belong in Brooklyn. So does Mother, for that matter. She ain't no cocktail party gal. We'd be out of place. . . ." He paused, embarrassed at saying so much. "We just finance a few of them second mortgages for rich folks who ain't got the money," he added feistily.

"Why don't you two guys change," Fred suggested, pointing to the dressing room at the side of the patio. "Then we can have a quick swim."

"You mean the pool's for swimming in?" Harry pretended astonishment. "I thought it was the town reservoir."

The men went to change, emerging a few minutes later. Fred took one look at them and started to laugh.

"What's so funny?" Harry demanded.

"You're perfect," Fred said. "Both of you. Perfect to type. Just look at you."

Harry was wearing Bermuda swimming trunks with a Hawaiian pattern of red hibiscus and green leaves on a yellow background. His rotund figure was white, his belly accentuated by the low-slung band of the trunks. On his arm he wore an enormous gold watch. His sunglasses had large frames of two-colored plastic. On his feet he wore blue jogging shoes and white ankle socks. And under his arm he carried a sheaf of papers.

Next to him, as if imported from the French Riviera, Walter was tanned, sinewy and athletic in a light blue bikini. On his feet he wore expensive thonged sandals. His rimless sunglasses were pushed nonchalantly over his forehead.

Harry looked at Walter beside him and then at himself. He too started to laugh. "Fucking right, Wimp. You look . . . absolutely smashing," he said in a dreadful imitation of an English accent.

Walter draped an arm nonchalantly over Harry's shoulder, "And you, my friend," he said gently, "look like exactly what you are: one of the most successful businessmen in Brooklyn."

"I tell you what you don't look like," said Fred, still laughing, "you don't look like boyhood friends."

"But we are," said Walter seriously.

"Sure are," Harry agreed, just as seriously.

There was a small commotion inside the house. "The girls are coming," Harry announced.

And indeed a short while later the men were interrupted by girlish shrieks. "It's fabulous, Harry. Harry, it's fabulous!" Martha cried.

Harry turned. "Here it comes," he said under his breath.

"Oh, Dad," she called, "can't we get a country house like this?" The three men laughed.

"What are you laughing at?" Martha asked suspiciously. "Oh, I know—you told them I'd say that, didn't you?"

"I sure did, Mother."

"Well, it's not fair that you know what I'm going to say before I even think of it myself," she said crossly. Now everyone laughed.

Janet Pogue and Martha Grass, two ladies of a certain age, looked very similar. Janet's hair was somewhat more stylishly cut; and, subtly, she seemed more at home in the elegance of the surroundings. But both women wore one-piece swimsuits over their pudgy figures. Both were in their middle forties. And both exuded a sense of contentment, or perhaps just solidity, which announced to even the casual observer: "I am a wife, a mother, a matron—and proud of it."

"Where's Judith?" Fred asked.

"She's . . ." Janet started.

"She's waiting to make an entrance," Walter interrupted. He had hardly spoken before Judith appeared at the top of the steps leading down to the patio. Backdropped by the elegant country home, she was breathtakingly beautiful. Tall, with her slender, voluptuous figure adorned with a tiny bikini bound together with chains, she posed for her audience. Her arms decorously covered her breasts, her legs were slightly crossed in the traditional Venus emerging stance, her golden hair ruffled gently in the breeze. The whole picture was of such exaggerated innocence that it quite screamed its invitiation. She held the pose just long enough, then sauntered toward them, the three-triangle bikini aggressively emphasizing her sexuality.

"What happens when she goes in the water?" Janet whispered.

"There's not much that could happen," said Fred.

"Come on, everyone, let's go swimming," said Judith approaching the group. "Why are you all just standing there?" She gazed at them with knowing, innocent eyes.

"Bitch," said Walter, and smacked her bottom, making her jump and squeal. "You know damn well. Come on." He ran for the pool and dived in a graceful arch. Judith waited until his head emerged and then, like a little girl, leaped from the side, curling herself into a ball and landing with a splashing thud beside him, squealing with laughter.

The four others, seeming much older, lumbered after them. The men dived in gracelessly; the women clambered down the ladder, rubbed water over their bodies, and then, with a slight gasp, dunked their shoulders under the surface.

When it was time for their business discussions, the men went back into the house.

"I think I've had enough sun," Janet said. "Do you mind if I lie down? I could stand a snooze. I don't often get the chance."

"Sure," said Martha, "I'll doze right here. This is too good to miss."

"Ooh," said Judith as Janet left. "I love it here." She stretched out sensuously on her air mattress. "The sun really turns me on. It reminds me of the south of France. I lived there with an old guy once . . . He wasn't so hot, but I loved the sun!"

"I like it too," said Martha, lying down awkwardly on the mattress next to her. She had not been this close to another woman for years. Not since that time on the beach where Wilma. . . . She would not allow herself to finish the thought.

Judith half-rose and took off her bikini top. "Do you mind?" she asked, dangling the tiny garment over Martha's face. "They can't see anything from the house when you're lying down."

"Of course not," said Martha, but her eyes were not watching the bikini but the girl's perfect breasts only a foot from her face. She couldn't take her eyes off them. The little triangular patches of white on the bronzed body, each with its delicate pink nipple, gave her an indescribable feeling of tenderness.

"Do you feel it too?" Judith asked. "The power of the sun?" She moved her upper body slightly so that her breasts rippled. "It makes my body feel alive. All over." Her nipples tightened, the areolas becoming puckered, the tips whitening slightly.

"Yes, I do," said Martha, her breath shortening. Quite aware of Martha watching her breasts, Judith edged closer. "Here," she said, "why don't you take off your swimsuit too." Martha was about to object but the girl wouldn't let her. "I'll help you." She pushed Martha's swimsuit down over her breasts, lingering just a shade too long on the breasts themselves. Her fingers were surprisingly cool.

"Christ," Martha muttered to herself, starting to get wet, and then realized in embarrassment that she had said it out loud.

"They are beautiful, too, you know," said Judith, touching the left nipple. Instantly it became hard.

Involuntarily, as if seeking support, Martha's hips pushed themselves downward into the hard surface under her air mattress. Christ, she thought again, Christ, I can't believe this is happening.

"Your suit does look silly clenched around your middle like that," Judith said. "I'll pull it off." Giggling, she crawled down her mattress and onto Martha's. "The mattress sort of grabs at my knees," she laughed. Hanging, her breasts seemed larger. They swayed as she moved.

Martha was quite incapable of answering. Not for years could she remember a desire as powerful as the one surging through her; and when the girl, making a game of it, pulled at her swimsuit, her desire became so intense she almost reached orgasm that moment.

"What am I doing?" The words were torn from her as the swimsuit slipped down over her hips.

"Soaking up the sun," said Judith in a reassuring voice. "Don't you like it?"

"Christ!" said Martha, shocked but powerless. "I've never felt anything like this."

"It's okay to feel." Judith smiled at her.

Martha felt her body, her nipples, her breasts, her loins, become tense as steel. The cool hands of the girl stroked her, and the path they traced seemed both hot and cold. An indescribable sensation went through the older woman as she lay back, her thighs gradually spreading under the insistent, irresistible strokes of the experienced younger one.

When, gently, Judith bent down to kiss her between the legs and her tongue started to flick where no man had ever been allowed to put his mouth, Martha could not stand the sensation for another second. "Stop," she moaned. "You must stop! I can't stand it."

But now the cool hands were clasping at her thighs and the tongue flicked on inexorably. After only a few seconds of protest, Martha's body arched and she was absolutely overwhelmed by an orgasm beyond any intensity she could possibly have imagined. It went on and on. "Stop. For Christ's sake, stop! Please!" she screamed, even wept. But Judith held onto the writhing, bucking body like a leech and her tongue barely changed its rhythm, only speeding up slightly while another and yet another orgasm racked Martha's body, leaving her ultimately so exhausted that, when the girl finally stopped, her face wreathed in a triumphant smile, Martha lay almost unconscious in the afternoon sun.

". . . so you see, the proposal is quite simple," Walter was concluding in the office Fred kept as a tax deduction in his east wing. "We can acquire Magnatel for only eighty-five million dollars. We've raised the first forty-five." Walter had no intention of going into more detail than that with Fred. He'd work out the question of his four-million-dollar investment with Harry later. "We can finance much of the rest by bartering for our first year's media."

Fred Pogue's large mobile face for once remained impassive. Never look too anxious for a deal, however much you need it, was his philosophy. "Who's your backer?" he asked.

"Arab money," Walter said.

"Arab?" Fred looked like a giant grizzly bear aroused from sleep: slightly bemused but dangerously suspicious.

"Meshulem Kashi," Harry explained. "I guess you've heard of him."

"I have," said Fred acerbically. "The Saudi Mafia. No doubt he's got the money." He looked less bemused now, but grimmer. "But is he reliable?"

"Totally unreliable, unbelievably obese, dreadfully vulgar, and in every respect undesirable," Walter assured him, grinning. "But he'll give us a banker's check drawn on the First National City Bank of New York."

"I see what you mean." Fred's face began to beam.

"The question remains whether you can make the barter deal we want," Harry interrupted, getting impatient.

"Okay, so take me through the details," said Fred.

"It's very simple. We sell you forty-five million dollars' worth of any appliances we make. You pay for them with media."

"Do you have enough manufacturing capacity?" Fred wanted to be sure the basics were all there before he allowed his enthusiasm to mount.

"That's one of Magnatel's main problems: We have so much excess capacity our overheads are choking us."

"Fine," Fred said, his bearish look now changed from grizzly to teddy. "I mean, fine for me. Now, tell me, where can I sell your stuff once I've got it?"

Walter barely hesitated. "To any account not now purchasing from us," he said easily, hoping against all expectation that he could duck the real question.

"Anywhere in the world," Harry added, hoping the same.

"What about the people who *are* buying from you?" Fred asked, as they knew he must.

"Well, now," said Walter, trying to sound innocent, "we'd *prefer* you not to sell to anyone who's buying from us now."

"I can see how you'd prefer that," said Fred drily. "But what you'd be saying is that I can only sell to buyers who are not in the market for appliances." He laughed uproariously. Then, suddenly as tragic as a clown, he shook his jowls in resignation. "I don't think we could accept that," he said sadly.

"And we can't let you sell to our regular clients," said Walter heatedly.

"How about you agree two ways," Harry intervened, thinking fast: "One, you agree not to sell anything to our major customers; and two, to our small customers you sell only *extra* over what they'd normally buy."

"What's major?" Fred demanded, looking almost sleek in his sudden intensity.

"Anyone who bought more than fifty grand from us last year."

"And what's extra?"

"Anything over last year's buy plus ten percent for normal growth."

"Okay," said Fred, letting out a huge sigh and instantly losing all semblance of intensity. "I'll go along with that." He puffed out his cheeks, making himself look like an oversized Winnie the Pooh. "Now, let's talk price. What will you charge me?"

"Our cost," said Walter Cort promptly. "Of course."

"What cost?" Fred demanded, knowing that cost could be calculated in many ways. Cost including just raw materials and labor could be half the price of cost including factory and administrative overheads.

Walter laughed. "You know damn well what I mean. I mean that we would charge you the full cost of raw materials, packaging and labor, plus an apportionment of all other factory and administrative costs, including utilities, rent depreciation, indirect labor, supervision, management, research and development. . . ."

"If you charge me all that, I'd rather buy at Bloomingdale's!"

Walter grinned, enjoying the bargaining process, especially since he felt confident that these were now just details.

"I'll buy at the best price you sell to your best customers . . ." Fred stated.

"Done," Harry interrupted fast, trying to close the point.

". . . Minus ten percent," Fred continued imperturbably.

"That's more than our profit," Walter objected, immediately starting to worry again. If Fred wouldn't pay at least best selling price, the deal couldn't be done after all. "Our best selling price *is* cost."

"Why would you sell at cost?" Fred demanded. "Aren't you trying to make a profit?" He looked as suspicious as ever.

"Various reasons. Excess inventory. A chance to keep skilled workers employed at slow times." Walter's worry mounted as he watched Fred's skeptical expression. "So you see, we can't sell to you below our best price."

"Fucking right," said Harry, sounding as if he were giving the response to some blasphemous litany.

"Five percent," said Fred.

"Sorry," said Walter.

"No," said Harry almost simultaneously.

For a second, which dragged out to many seconds, there was silence. Walter hoped that his anxious sweat would not show. How could Harry look so insufferably bored, as if he didn't give a shit? Maybe he didn't. After all these years, Walter still couldn't be sure what his friend was thinking.

"Okay, I'll go along." Fred finally broke the silence.

"Now about the media," Walter started, feeling confident again.

"We'll supply what we can get," said Fred reasonably.

"It's got to be defined closer than that," Walter's chin jutted more than usual. "What happens if you can't get what we want?"

"I'll get you good stuff, don't worry about that. But obviously I can't supply what I can't get." Fred sounded like the soul of reason. "We don't have forty-five million dollars of media just lying around, you know." He spoke the number with awe, a sum worth worshipping. "We'll have to go out and get it—and I can't be precise about exactly what we'll find."

"Nevertheless, we've got to have some ground rules," Walter insisted.

This was the key as far as Fred was concerned. Relax, he told himself. But it was hard when you wanted something this badly. It would be the biggest deal in his life—and only just in time, too, considering how the rest of his business was running out of money. "What rules?" He added as much boredom to his voice as he could manage.

"The main thing is that it has to be mostly television."

"I can agree to that in principle," Fred said, relieved. "Say fifty percent."

The man bargains every inch of the way, Walter realized, amused. No wonder he's so successful.

"I know we're friends," Fred explained, evidently guessing at Walter's thoughts. "But I always do business at arms' length."

"Fucking right," Harry agreed.

"I'd want more like seventy." Walter said.

"Sixty," Fred said. "I can't go further than that." He kept his tone light only with enormous effort.

"Very well," said Walter at length. "But I want the rest in national magazines—no radio or newspapers."

"I agree to no newspapers right off. But I'd like to throw in some radio. I know you'll say it's flaky, but you'll just have to trust me. Twenty percent radio, and I'll make sure it's good value."

"Okay, you're on: sixty percent TV; twenty magazines; and twenty radio, and we trust you." Walter agreed. He felt tremendously relieved.

"Sure we'll trust you," Harry commented. "We can't get fucked more than twenty percent on twenty percent."

Walter and Fred both laughed excessively, each letting his tensions drain.

Harry wondered who had wanted the deal more. "I'm going to make some phone calls," he said. "This ain't the only damned deal in the world, you know."

"Next door," Fred said. "Now Walter," he added, "let's you and me put our deal down on paper."

By five o'clock Fred and Walter were finished. With difficulty they managed to extricate Harry from his telephone. Together the three went out to the pool. Martha was just rousing from her nap, happy and relaxed, but with eyes still glazed from her earlier experiences.

Judith was dangling her feet in the pool like a little girl. "Had a good afternoon, boys?" She turned to them cheekily.

"We have a deal," said Fred.

"A fair deal all around," Walter agreed. "And you?"

"We had . . ." Judith paused, watching Martha's eyes flicker, ". . . a great time. The sun really turns me on."

Harry Grass thought he heard his wife mutter "Christ" under her breath. But that was so unlike her, he decided he must have misheard.

Walter reclined in an oversized, puffy easy chair in his library. His wiry, athletic body was almost engulfed by the chair so that his legs, stretched onto the low coffee table, looked like two lengthy sticks. His thin face with its sharp nose, jutting chin and weather-beaten complexion, far more handsome now than in its weasely youth, showed anger, tension, disappointment—perhaps even resignation. But no hint of serenity. Even Bundle, the tiny fluff of white, furry mongrel whom Walter loved more than any other living thing, sensed it. She would not permit herself to sleep; and she knew full well that this was no time to start one of her frolics. Today her master would certainly not join in. Instead she rested her head on her paws and observed Walter intently through her huge clown's eyes.

Walter, for his part, watched Harry Grass pacing nervously.

"Now look, Wimp, I'm gonna put up one million bucks, and that's all I'm putting up. Not one nickel more. I don't think you should either." Harry looked and sounded incensed.

Compact and restless as a boxer, he could not stay still for a moment. One second he would be absently glancing at a book, another fingering one of the sculptures of which Walter was so proud. One day, Walter often promised himself, he would really splurge and buy himself a Giacometti sculpture to stand in the window alcove. A tall, vulnerable, bronze nude which would capture all the ethereal, elongated beauty of being female. Like Judith, but without such a predominance of raw sexuality.

Walter shook himself free from his fantasy. He had to concentrate on convincing Harry, even though he already sensed that he had no chance. "But you were the one that got us into Magnatel in the first place," he insisted.

"So what? I still think it's a fantastic deal. But Wimp, no deal's worth putting your whole life into."

"Stop calling me Wimp," Walter said testily.

Harry's pacing took him to the liquor cabinet at the end of the room. As if to give his hands something to do, he absently poured himself a stiff Scotch. Dropping in the ice cubes, he splashed whiskey onto the polished sideboard. Without bothering to wipe up the spill, he gulped down the drink. Walter watched him in surprise. Harry rarely drank, and, for all his verbal excess, he was usually meticulously tidy.

"I've called you Wimp since you were the new Polish kid on the block," said Harry, pugnacious about everything at the moment, "and I ain't changing now."

"But you are. You're backing down on Magnatel. I've never seen you do that before." Even as he said it, Walter realized that wasn't true. Quite the contrary, Harry always backed down when the going got too rough. Hadn't he left Walter hanging on that tin roof years ago; and run away from Nathan's; and . . . ? A thousand memories flashed through Walter's mind. "No," he said, bemused at his revelation, "I just figured out that's wrong. You always back down."

"Fucking right," said Harry Grass, not remotely apologetic. "I believe in bein' practical. You know I always fight to win, and I win most of my fights. But that's only because I quit when I know I'm losing."

"But—"

"But nothing. What's the point of fighting if you're gonna lose?" Harry leaned his bulk far back in his chair in protest. "Look," he said, his tone grandfatherly, "I like to make a buck as much as the next guy. And I've made more of 'em in my time than most. You and I have together. For thirty years, about, since we done that first deal. And I've taken my fair share of the risks, just like you have. But listen to me, Wimp," Harry leaned forward in his chair. "Apart from that very first deal, when we didn't have a thing to lose, I've never bet my whole stake on any one deal. There's just too many things could go wrong. Who needs it?"

"What could go wrong?" Walter demanded.

"How the flaming hell should I know? It's never what you expect. Like I said, this looks like one of the best deals ever. That's what I thought at the start, and that's what I think now."

"So why don't you put up more money?"

"Because I ain't God. Just because I think things will go one way doesn't prove they will. Maybe something no one ever thought of will get screwed up. So I put up a million and lose it. That'd hurt. But it wouldn't fuck up everything I've worked for all these years."

"And if you put up two?"

"Then I'd have to back out of half the other things I'm doing. It ain't worth it to me. And like I said, I don't think you should do it either."

"But we've got to put up four million dollars between us to bring Kashi in."

"I hear you," said Harry, giving not an inch.

Walter looked at him in disappointment. "You're sure?"

"Fucking certain."

"Then I guess I'll have to put up three. If I hock everything— the company, the houses, everything I can lay my hands on—I should just about be able to swing it."

"You're nuts, man. It don't make no sense," said Harry, incensed. "One thing screws up and you could be flat on your ass with one stroke. After all these years, after all these trials, after all these problems. Don't you see, Walter, what it would mean to start again? Maybe it was fun crawling our way into a gas station when we was kids. Or maybe it was just something we did 'cause we didn't have no choice. I don't recall. But it's different now: We're both well off. Hell, I'm further up than I ever expected to be in my whole life. I could retire tomorrow; never do another thing and live well the rest of my life, hold my head up, send the kids to school, stay out of that fucking filthy slum we grew up in . . . I ain't risking goin' back there, not for the best deal in the world, not for you, not with God himself as my business partner."

"I've never heard you make as long a speech as that in your life."

"I feel strongly about what I said," Harry said quietly. "You do what you want, Wimp, but at least you know where I stand." He smiled ruefully at his friend and walked over to the sideboard. Carefully he wiped up the Scotch he had spilled.

"That I do," Walter said. For several minutes neither man said a word. "We're different, you and I," Walter said at last, talking as much to himself as to Harry. "You've got it made, you and Martha. I can't explain it, but all I know is that it's different for me. You're right that I have enough money. But even so, inside I know I've got to keep hustling. I'm a hell of a long way from feeling safe. Maybe it's like you say, I ought to settle down . . . But I can't. I don't know why. All I know is that I have to keep fighting. Every step of the way."

"So? Fighting's what life's all about." Harry showed no sympathy. "Of course you have to keep fighting. You don't see me retiring, do you? All I'm saying is you don't have to take that sort of risk. You don't have to wrench your guts. Stay with things where if you lose, you lose; so what? Make sure you've got enough left to tell the world to go fuck." Harry was so wound up he was almost shouting.

"But I don't have one thing that's worth having. I don't. . . ."

"You don't get no respect," Harry interrupted, using the tired cliché of the famous comedian. His voice was soft again. "Don't you understand, Wimp? It don't matter a good goddamn whether you get respect or not. All that counts is you got enough to live the way you want. That's all there is."

"Then let's go dancing?"

"Huh?"

"Oh, nothing," said Walter wearily. "I know you're right, Harry. Dead right. And I appreciate your warning me. We haven't been much for giving each other advice, so I'm grateful. But the fact is, I'm going to make a run for it anyway. I truly don't know why. All I do know is that I *have* to. Perhaps it's just that if I make this deal, it makes all the rest come right. I'd no longer be a hustler. I wouldn't even be the Polish kid from Brooklyn who made a packet. Finally I'd be someone; I'd have done something to remember." He grinned at Harry. "Hell, I wouldn't ever be Wimp again, not even to you. . . ."

"A monument?" Harry sounded half-embittered, half-saddened. "You're welcome, kid. Me, I don't need no fucking monument."

"I suppose you could call it a monument," said Walter. "I don't know why I want it. I just know that if I don't try for it, for the rest of my life I'll wish I had. Some things you just have to risk."

"You're the one that used to run over the roofs," Harry laughed.

"Yeah. And remember how you all left me?"

"I remember," said Harry annoyed. "But if you're implying that I'm leaving you now, you're wrong. It's totally different. Then I ran away without warning you. I admit it. But now I'm warning you loud and clear: I'm putting up one million bucks because I think Magnatel's a good deal. But don't come crawling up my leg if things get tough. I'm telling you straight, Wimp, I'm not ever putting up one more fucking cent."

"Okay, you've made your point." Walter was getting angry at being browbeaten. "So get off it already. I won't ask you, okay?"

"Yeah, okay," Harry said gruffly. He waited a moment to let Walter—and himself, too—cool off. "So where are you going to go for the rest? You need another twelve million, right?"

"Yes." Walter agreed grimly. "Where the hell do you think I'm going. To the only place left where I've got any real bargaining power."

"Von Ackermann? And let him off the hook on Clarendon if he puts up the twelve?"

"You agree, I take it?"

"Oh, sure." Harry gave Walter a worried look. "You really want it bad, don't you?"

"Yes, I do," Walter agreed. "I really do."

"Just take it easy, Wimp," Harry said, looking even more concerned. "I'm telling you, if you try too hard on this one, you're gonna get yourself screwed."

11

The elongated black Mercedes 500, complete with bar, television set and one-way glass—of course bulletproof—drove at break-neck speed along the road bordering the Rhine. It was twilight; the folks who lived in the villages were relaxing after a long day in the vineyards or wine presses which were the area's main economy. As they strolled placidly along the narrow streets, the car's high-powered headlights picked out the young couples, dogs, bicycle riders and sauntering old folks as harshly as a policeman's beam cross-examining criminals. In the glow of the lights they looked like silhouettes of grotesques. The driver, his face impassively stern, never moved his foot from the accelerator, forcing the easygoing strollers to jump for their lives. His only concession to safety was occasionally to flick the beams as if grilling the suspects on the road.

Walter sat in the back of the car, wondering whether to ask the driver to slow down. The request would be taken as a sign of fear, a loss of face. On the other hand, the panic the man was arrogantly sowing through the small villages was an outrage. Eventually Walter did nothing, and hated himself for his indecision.

Even as the roads became narrower, the car hardly slowed. It took corners so fast that the tires catapulted loose stones from the road's surface into the hedges. Even through the closed windows they sounded like hailstorms. Fortunately there were no pedestrians here; the roads were almost eerily empty. Walter was hurled from side to side of the limousine like a loose sack of goods. But the driver was completely immobile. Stern and solid, he seemed to be an integral part of the car itself rather than a separate human entity.

At last, two hours after leaving Frankfurt, the car slowed. Moments later its headlights picked out an enormous wrought-iron gate bordered by towering granite pillars: an entranceway suitable only for a pope, a head of state—or a successful German businessman. Beyond the gate, which opened smoothly for their passage and closed the moment they were past with automatic finality, was a carefully manicured park. It was large enough for two gold courses. In the moonlight, its sweeping lawns looked chillingly empty. Walter was quite certain that, if he observed carefully, he would see prowling mastiffs.

At the end of the driveway, elegantly flanked by linden trees, was the residence itself, a gothic castle full of towers, minarets and spires. Perfectly ridiculous! Walter thought. But he had to admit it was imposing. Walter wondered again how Von Ackermann had got started.

"After thorough investigation," Walter's research head had written, "we have found out nothing about Von Ackermann before the end of the Second World War. He emerged in 1946, at about age thirty, from total obscurity into overnight business prominence."

The report continued in the informal style Walter encouraged for several pages, but only Von Ackermann's postwar exploits were chronicled. . . .

Postwar Germany was in complete disruption. The autobahns, constructed to allow Hitler to move his troops swiftly, and supposed to last for millenia, typically ended unexpectedly in jagged holes where a viaduct had been bombed out. Normal currency did not exist: Cigarettes, lipsticks, silk stockings and Hershey bars replaced money as the medium of exchange. De-Nazification courts abounded, although erstwhile Nazis were a rarity. The remains of the Hitler Youth were as beautiful, blond and Aryan as ever, but were starting to chew gum. Bars with names like Times Square and Las Vegas abounded. Soap and everything else was in very short supply.

Into this sea of shortages, administrative disruptions, bombed-out cities and unrelenting struggle, Von Ackermann first surfaced, letting it be known that he was the owner of a huge amount of unrefined animal fat. It was of very poor quality, contaminated with skin and flesh which had to be filtered out before any processing could start and again two or three times during the process itself. Nevertheless, in the absence of any better raw material, its value was so high that Von Ackermann was able to acquire a small soap factory using only part of the fat itself as the down payment. He used his new plant to convert the rest of his raw material into an abundant supply of soap. If it was not of the highest quality, that mattered little, for with the proceeds of the first few vats, he was able to buy a supply of a powerful French perfume oil and some dark pink dye, which masked most of his product's shortcomings. "Beauty Soap" overnight became a huge success.

In the early days Von Ackermann insisted that the filtrate from his raw materials be destroyed by burning. His technical advisors suggested that burying would be cheaper, but Von Ackermann refused on the grounds that it would eventually cause pollution, which he wished to avoid. At the time he was thought to be extreme in his views about pollution. Later he was considered to be ahead of his time. However, by then his interest in pollution control seemed to have waned and the large factory he had constructed in the meantime was in constant violation of local pollution ordinances.

No one ever discovered where the tough, powerful, obviously brilliant entrepreneur found the fat in the first place. But how his business expanded from there, by a series of courageous and creative investment leaps, has been the subject of a hundred newspaper stories. Once he virtually cornered the world's used-tire market and sold gigantic quantities of the tires to Cuba and Poland. At another time he bought a hundred Rhine River barges and used them to carry junked steel from a demolished armament depot in the south of Germany to the steel mills in the Ruhr. He still has large interests in the shipping business. On yet another occasion he acquired great fleets of used-up vehicles—old taxis and totally run-down trucks. Helped by a group of Armenian businessmen headquartered in Istanbul, he exported them to Turkey and thence, it was said, to both Bulgaria and Cuba. It was never clear what the Turkish group paid for them. *Der Spiegel* darkly hinted that there must be some connection between the obvious scam of exporting completely dilapidated vehicles and the vast Turkish fields of waving poppies.

There were also huge transactions made via Brazil with aquamarines; and, at one point, a series of headline-making deals involving several Picassos and a giant Monet painting found in Buenos Aires.

At first Von Ackermann conducted business out of the Frankfurter Hof Hotel, then still occupied by the American military forces. For reasons which have never become clear, the Americans allowed Von Ackermann to use a portion of the hotel's ballroom. Later he moved to an office on the Zeil, the main shopping street of Frankfurt. His office had a rear entrance onto the Breitegasse, the short street which the city administrators had set aside for swirling crowds of prostitutes. They continue to ply their trade there to this day.

Later still Von Ackermann moved his by then highly successful empire to a castle in the middle Rhine, which he was able to acquire in exchange for a large Renoir, a gorgeous Modigliani and a half-dozen minor Picassos.

It was this castle which Walter had now reached. It was lit with enough spots to make it eligible for a "son et lumière" show, and decked out with enough gold leaf, colored tiling, ornate carving and brilliant paint work to qualify it for the gingerbread award of the year. Its rococo turrets, shadowy balconies and overall air of macabre excess made it wholly inappropriate, in Walter's view, as a business headquarters. Far more suitable, he thought, as an operatic setting. A few colored spotlights and it would be ideal for *The Merry Widow;* add a thunder cloud and it would reverberate ideally to the most sonorous of Wagner.

The car drew up in front of the main entrance, and Walter alighted. Surely there must be a portcullis, he thought, if not a guillotine. But the door opened in the normal manner, and he was welcomed by a traditional butler complete with black tie and tails.

"Good evening, sir," the butler said, his English only barely Germanic. "May we welcome you to Schloss Ackermann. The Herr Generaldirektor is looking forward to seeing you. Please come this way."

The butler walked ahead of Walter across the dim entrance foyer toward studded, oaken double doors. Passing through them, Walter followed the butler dutifully across what must have been the Great Hall. It was entirely empty except for a long table against one wall. Rows of spears decorated one wall, and a series of medieval shields, complete with various ornate coats of arms, were lined up on the other.

Eventually they reached another set of heavy double doors which the butler threw open. Walter was instantly inundated by the crashing chords of Wagner's *Tannhäuser.* The heavy music reverberated in his eardrums.

Even as he was recovering from his surprise, Walter realized that there in front of him, behind another long table, its black top gleaming, sat Heinrich Von Ackermann. His host looked up from the paper he was reading and for a long moment observed Walter standing in the doorway. Neither man moved. Then, slowly, Von Ackermann reached over to a switch and turned the music volume down.

"Mr. Cort," he said, his voice seeming to express something between awe and delight. "What an honor to welcome you to my home. How pleased I am to see you."

"Thank you," said Walter.

"I thank *you*, my dear fellow, deeply. Deeply. Please enter further into my study. I am delighted you have come."

"Thank you," said Walter again, made to feel foolish by the older man's obviously insincere rhetoric. "I too am pleased to be here." The comment sounded utterly hollow, but he noted from his host's expression that he had hit the right tone.

"You must forgive the loudness of my Wagner. I revel in his music," Von Ackermann continued. "I am moved to awe. That never happens to me in business." He laughed with pleasure at his own wit.

"If not to awe, at least I hope I can move you to admiration for the business we are here to discuss," said Walter, seizing the opportunity to cut through the social amenities. "I think you will be impressed by the Magnatel deal we are . . ."

". . . trying to finance," Von Ackermann interrupted.

". . . financing," Walter contradicted firmly. "We already have most of our money. We need only the last twelve million dollars."

"My dear fellow, but of course," said Von Ackermann. "I do understand. We shall discuss it in great detail." Suddenly he seemed to remember his manners. "But forgive me," he said, looking terribly concerned. "I'm so interested in what you have to say, I quite forget myself. You must be tired from your trip. First let me have my butler, Rosenblatt, show you to your chamber." He turned and pulled a tasseled bell cord just behind his chair. "Then we shall convene for dinner in an hour. And over dinner we can commence our discussions. . . ."

Almost immediately the door opened and the butler beckoned Walter to follow. As Walter turned, the music swelled again.

After another long walk Rosenblatt showed Walter into his assigned bedroom. It was a round turret room centered with an enormous bed with white *Federkissen*, puffed high, lying on lemon yellow sheets. The effect was more of an outsize lemon meringue pie than a bed. The room was strewn with Persian carpets. Everywhere it was filled with what Walter thought of as frou frou; frilly china ornaments, Indian carved metal vases, Turkish prayer mats, African ebony pieces. It felt precisely like an expensive gift shop.

Rosenblatt inspected the bathroom briefly, bowed and withdrew.

Walter was relieved to be alone. The Schloss Ackermann was both overpowering and totally unreal. It was as if he had been transported to a Hollywood movie set. Although Walter was not particularly tired, having arrived from the United States the day before, he felt as disoriented as if he were suffering from severe jet lag. And underneath the sense of unreality, there lurked also a sense of danger. It's just Germany, he told himself. I'm paranoid about it. But the cliché, just because I'm paranoid doesn't mean they're not out to get me, kept popping into his head.

With a determined shrug he started to undress. This was all nonsense. The hot water of a good, deep bath would surely wash away his forebodings.

It was fortunate that the butler returned an hour later to accompany him to the dining room. Alone, he would never have found his way down the endless winding corridors, up several flights of stairs and through at least half a dozen different rooms. They finally reached the long hall and, just beyond it, the formal dining room, entirely lighted with candles. There must have been fifty candelabra flaming. A long table stood at the room's center, with two large upright armchairs on either side of it. There were more spears and shields on the wall, lighted with small spotlights.

In total contrast to the baroque splendor of the candled room, Von Ackermann was dressed in a standard business suit, white shirt, dark tie and polished shoes. He looked as inappropriate in this feudal setting as a knight in armor would have seemed in Walter's office. Walter felt equally out of place.

"Good evening, my dear fellow," Von Ackermann called.

"Good evening," Walter responded coolly, wishing the German would stop referring to him as his dear fellow.

"A schnaps, a schnaps," Von Ackermann insisted. He snapped his fingers and a waiter, clad as formally as if he had been serving in the dining room of the Frankfurter Hof, poured out two shot glasses of liquid from an ice-encrusted bottle and handed them to Walter and his host.

"*Prost,*" Von Ackermann practically threw the liquor down his throat. Walter, used to the hospitality traditions of the Germans, did likewise. The liquor felt fiery and tasted of carroway seeds.

"Another," Von Ackerman insisted.

"I would love one more, but my last." Walter had no intention of allowing the German businessman to dull him with alcohol.

They went through the same procedure a second time.

"Now we shall have dinner," Von Ackermann announced. The insistent warmth of his tone and the jovial smile that seemed an almost permanent part of his face were belied by the utter coldness of his eyes. They were dark gray-blue, the color of Gillette's original "blue" razor blades. Walter had to concentrate to avoid his feelings of revulsion, much as a man will avert seasickness by keeping his eyes firmly on a stationary point outside the boat. But having decided that his last hope of raising the final twelve million dollars was Von Ackermann, he would not retreat.

"So, we shall sit and eat," Von Ackermann announced. "I love food."

Von Ackermann's figure supported the statement. He was over six feet tall, with a barrel chest and an ample, sloping stomach. At sixty-five years he was not quite obese, but his cheeks had turned to jowls heavy enough to stretch the edge of his eyes and temples downward. This cast of his eyes contrasted with his perpetual smile and made the face seem ambiguous, almost sinister. The eyes themselves lacked even the generosity of self-indulgence. "Cruel" was the one word Walter could not shake from his mind as the best description of his host. Was it only his own bias?

"Seat yourself," Von Ackermann ordered. "Seat yourself and be comfortable."

"Thank you," said Walter, feeling no sense of comfort whatsoever.

Von Ackermann clapped his hands in the classic potentate manner. Instantly Rosenblatt appeared through the swinging doors at the side of the room. As quiet as shadows, two more waiters followed. They bore silver trays of smoked salmon and caviar, which they served with skillful ritual. Just the right amounts of chopped egg and onion were placed around the caviar; just the perfect few drops of lemon were squeezed onto the salmon. A third waiter, complete with sommelier's tasting cup hanging from a chain around his neck, served vodka. Like the schnaps, it too had been frozen into a block of ice.

"So, my friend," said Von Ackermann, "we indulge in the only good thing the Russians ever invented." He paused. "But not the only thing they *claim* to have invented." He laughed heartily.

Walter found his habit of making unfunny jokes particularly irritating. "The salmon is more likely to be Scottish," he said contentiously.

"Of course, of course."

Walter hoped Von Ackermann would be as agreeable when it came to the financial discussion ahead. He was just about to cut through the preamble and get down to business, even if it was somewhat premature, when the door again opened. Rosenblatt, the butler, entered silently and bowed slightly. Evidently he was announcing the main attraction. As Walter watched, two men in white smocks and chef's hats wheeled in a large, silver, heated trolley. They stationed it between Von Ackermann and Walter. As if in response to a silent fanfare, they uncovered the lid and stood back. Inside was a thoroughly lifelike roast suckling pig, so carefully positioned and so carefully browned that it looked alive. In its snout it held the traditional apple, and the expression on its face seemed one of pure pleasure at the incipient treat. It looked, Walter thought, not only as if it were alive, but also thoroughly "cute," a rather horrifying word for something they were about to eat.

"Pretty, isn't it?" Von Ackerman commented. "I will enjoy carving you a slice."

Was his unusual syntax intentional? "Thank you," Walter answered noncommittally.

"I'm sorry my daughter could not be with us tonight. She is a very brilliant woman who has studied in America and understands a great deal about business affairs."

"I am sorry too," Walter replied quickly, seeing his chance to get down to business, "because she would find what I'm here to discuss fascinating."

"Ah yes, I am aware of Magnatel. A good company."

"Excellent. And we have been able to buy it very inexpensively."

"*Have* been able to?" Von Ackermann asked. "Your English constructions sometimes leave me mystified. You mean you have *not* been able to buy it, do you not? In German we would say *"Sie mögen es kaufen können*—you *may* it to buy be able." His smile widened. "With my help," he added.

"It is so certain that we'll buy it that I keep talking as if the acquisition were already consummated. You are quite right, of course. Technically we don't own it yet. But practically we do. All we have left to do is to decide from whom to take the last twelve million dollars. Obviously we'll have no difficulty—"

"Obviously you will."

Walter was shocked. Usually in such discussions the attack came less frontally. Very well, he thought, if that's how Von Ackermann wanted to play the game, he could be just as rude. "Your *opinion* is irrelevant," he said. "I *know* I can raise the money without you. That's all that matters. The only reason I'm here is that, as we're working on Clarendon together, I believe I may make a *better* deal with you than I could elsewhere." He hoped he sounded convincing, that his anxiety to get the money, his knowledge that this was his only remaining chance, did not transmit itself to his opponent.

"Twelve million dollars and no security?" Von Ackermann dripped sarcasm.

"Twelve million dollars buys twenty percent of a company we're buying for eighty-five million. On that basis alone it would be worth seventeen million . . ."

"Ridiculous arithmetic. You have borrowed out all the assets."

"But since we'll be paying them back in less than three years, the twenty percent is worth much more than that."

"A matter of opinion."

"If you share the opinion, you will invest the money; if you do not, you will not. It is of little consequence to me."

"Now, Mr. Cort, I do not wish you to become so abrupt with me," said Von Ackermann, adopting a grandfatherly tone.

"I would like to have you as an investing shareholder in Magnatel. But if you don't want to participate, I won't be very concerned. You must make up your own mind." Walter hoped he sounded sufficiently nonchalant.

"What, then, are the terms?"

"Very simple. A total of sixteen million dollars of equity is being used to finance this acquisition. . . ." Walter started to explain the acquisition financing in professional detail. Von Ackerman nodded his understanding from time to time. After a while, still listening intently, he picked up the carving utensils and started systematically cutting up the piglet. Walter tried not to look, afraid he would see pain on the animal's face as the knife sliced away at its belly. He barely managed to suppress a shudder. Von Ackermann served each of them a huge portion while Walter finished his explanation.

"Clear," said Von Ackermann. Instead of further comment, he motioned to the wine waiter, who with utmost obsequiousness poured him a tasting portion of wine. Carefully swirling the amber liquid around in his glass, the German examined it. Then raising it to his fat lips so that it looked as if the glass were being squeezed between the vise of his jowls, he took a sip and "chewed" it in the accepted wine taster's manner. He nodded his head in approval so vigorously that the flesh of his cheeks swung back and forth, pulling his eyes even farther downward. "Excellent," he said, "simply excellent. Mr. Cort, try some."

"No thank you." Walter had decided he wanted no more alcohol, and no more orders from Von Ackermann.

"No wine?" Von Ackermann was shocked for the first time.

At least I've gotten through to the son of a bitch, Walter thought. "No wine," he repeated firmly. "I shall save myself that pleasure for when we have completed the negotiations. Then we can either celebrate your decision to join us or toast my departure to visit another investor."

Von Ackermann scowled and said not a word for fully five minutes while the servant continued to fill both men's dinner plates. In addition to the slices from the suckling pig, there was the traditional "apfel mousse," a German applesauce; sweet and sour red cabbage in a huge steaming pile; heapings of pan-fried potatoes; beautifully formed semolina dumplings with crouton centers and lavish quantities of heavy cream sauce. Walter recognized that the meal was truly a work of culinary art, however uncomfortable the mutilated piglet's eyes, still staring at him accusingly, might make him feel. He waited patiently for his host to reopen the conversation; nothing would have induced him to break the silence himself.

"Good," said Von Ackermann eventually, pointing at the pile of food on his plate with his knife. "Better with wine."

"Yes, good food."

"So you wish me to participate?"

"I would like you to invest twelve million dollars."

Von Ackermann merely grunted. "First we eat," he said, as if issuing a challenge to Walter. "Then we talk." He looked at his guest appraisingly. "I like doing business with men who know how to eat," he added. "I'm just as frightened as Caesar was of that lean and hungry look." He took a huge mouthful of food. "Enjoy!" he ordered. Walter realized that he would have to demonstrate a greed comparable to Von Ackermann's if he were to make any progress.

For half an hour the two men ate almost in silence. Each time Walter's plate started to empty, it was refilled by one of the hovering waiters. "Excellent," Walter exclaimed as he was starting on his third helping. He hoped he was able to give the word the right sound of enthusiasm.

"Indeed," said the German. "I have a very expensive cook."

Eventually, when Walter feared he would become ill, Von Ackermann leaned back in his chair. "You have a fine appetite," he nodded approvingly. "We shall get on well." He emitted a gigantic burp. "Perhaps I should apologize," he said, "but I believe in the Middle Eastern habit of demonstrating my stomach's appreciation."

"Of course," said Walter, disgusted.

"It is unfortunate that the body cannot assimilate infinite quantities of food without becoming overfilled," Von Ackermann said conversationally. "The Romans had a good idea." He paused, evidently waiting for Walter to question him.

"What idea?" Walter asked dutifully.

"The vomitorium," said Von Ackermann. "An excellent institution which allowed the enjoyment of food to continue almost indefinitely."

"Perhaps a high price to pay?"

"Not if the body is used to it. I experimented once."

"And it was enjoyable?"

"No, but perhaps one could say worthwhile."

"I think I will abstain."

"I have an alternative, however, which is entirely pleasurable. We shall be massaged."

Walter raised his eyebrows in surprise.

"By whom? When?"

"Now. By . . ." he clapped his hands, ". . . these ladies."

On cue two square, middle-aged women dressed in starched white uniforms entered the room.

"*Jawohl,*" said one in a contralto voice so deep it verged on basso profundo. Walter was aware that she was female only by the voluminous shape of her bosom and the chunky rounded hips under the starched skirt.

"*Wir sind so weit.* We are ready." Von Ackermann said. "Please accompany Herr Cort to the appropriate room." He arose and followed the second, still silent, starched figure who marched ahead of him with footfalls so solid they made the floor vibrate.

The one who had spoken turned and beckoned Walter to follow her. He did so, seeing no other choice, down the inevitable corridors. Eventually they entered a room which looked like a surgery. In the center was a high, flat table.

"Undress," the starched figure commanded.

There seemed nothing to do but obey. Walter stripped to his underpants and started to climb on the table.

"*Komplet,*" the woman ordered.

Walter shrugged his shoulders and removed the final garment.

"Lie," she said. "On back."

Walter laid himself dutifully on the hard massage table. Its surface felt momentarily cold enough to send a small shiver through his body. The woman surveyed him very much as a butcher might evaluate a piece of meat. Walter wondered what her decision would be.

Suddenly she seemed to make her choice and decide where to attack first. With bony, powerful fingers she clasped his left foot and started to knead it. At first the sensation was merely pleasant. He had often been massaged before in Thailand, in Japan—sometimes therapeutically, sometimes erotically—and he could tell at once that this woman knew her job. There was something in the strength of her fingers that told him she was most experienced. And certainly not erotic, he thought with wry amusement. But after a few seconds the feeling became far more than pleasant. As she warmed to her task, Walter began to feel an extraordinary sense of relaxation up his left side. He had heard that the Chinese believed that massaging certain parts of the feet had an impact on specific parts of the body. He had always assumed that this was mostly fiction. But there was no doubt that what he was feeling was real, and so extreme that the relaxation felt almost like paralysis, but safe and wonderfully comforting.

After a while the woman switched to his right foot. Almost at once the relaxation which had pervaded his left side eased. That side of his body now felt extraordinarily warm and soothed but also strong and energized; while his right felt as weak as if it were in a deep, contented sleep. He felt little pressure from her fingers, only the effect of the pressure.

After a few more minutes of this incredible relaxation, the woman picked up both of Walter's feet and, placing them against her ample thighs, started to press her thumbs upward into the balls of his heels. The result was even more astonishing than before. Both his arms suddenly lost all feeling. It was not an unpleasant sensation, simply a feeling of utter weightlessness, almost of nothingness, as if his arms had never existed.

"That's extraordinary," he whispered. "How do you do that?"

"Relax," she ordered, brooking no further questions.

She slipped her hands under his legs and slowly started to work her way up the back of his heels, across the Achilles tendons, on up the calf muscles. The feeling in his arms returned gradually, but with each inch she moved up his calves, a different part of his body was affected. Sometimes his hands disappeared; sometimes a piece of his chest ceased to exist. As the feeling returned to each spot, Walter could feel a sensation of heat and tingling, almost an ache, as if the spot itself, not its counterpart in his leg, had been deeply and thoroughly massaged.

"That's extraordinary," he repeated in admiration. "A wonderful feeling. You are most talented."

"Yes," she said, her voice still distant and stentorian, but, Walter thought, slightly more friendly.

"Now the stomach," she informed him.

Walter had no idea what she intended to do. He knew, however, that he did not want her to touch his stomach. It was bloated with the food he had consumed; any massage there would make him thoroughly uncomfortable.

She moved ponderously around the table until she was next to his stomach. Gently she placed her fingertips onto the skin of his belly.

"I would prefer . . ." he started.

But even before he could finish the sentence, he was surprised into silence by her fingers, which, barely perceptibly, started to vibrate. The rest of her remained absolutely still, but the fingertips themselves seemed to generate a buzzing sensation, as if they were powered by a low-voltage electric current.

Walter decided against remonstrating. Instead he gave himself over to the remarkable sensation.

As he lay back, trusting the expertise of his masseuse, he felt more like a child in the care of his nanny than his normal, suspicious self. The buzzing in her fingers increased. Even though the rest of her body remained still, he could now see the effect of the vibration on her upper arms and on her face. Tiny ripples became visible on her skin, as if a breeze were blowing cat's paws onto its surface.

The sensation on his stomach was extraordinarily soothing. As the vibrations intensified, he could feel the excess food in his stomach being compressed, as if it were being shaken down and compacted. The bloated feeling gradually eased and was replaced by a pleasant emptiness.

Then the woman was kneading his stomach as well as vibrating it. He would never have believed that such an activity could be pleasurable. Quite the contrary, he would have assumed that it would make him quickly sick. As it was, however, the kneading was one of the most delightful feelings he had ever experienced. Suddenly she stopped.

"You will now toilet," she said.

He had hardly understood the words before he felt an almost overwhelming need to defecate.

"There." She pointed to a door.

He jumped off the couch and ran to the bathroom. Within seconds he had found a toilet and emptied his bowels of an incredible amount of matter. It was over before he fully realized what had happened. A feeling of tremendous relief pervaded him. He was emptied and actively hungry. He was also amazed.

After a few moments he had recovered sufficiently to return to the room.

"Good," she said, as if praising a baby who had just been successfully toilet-trained. "Now we shall finish."

He lay down again on the massage table and quickly, professionally, she massaged the rest of his body. It was a traditional, vigorous, relaxing and thorough job. When she was finished, he glowed and tingled all over. He dressed quickly, feeling alert, strengthened, relaxed, energetic—and now very hungry.

"Now you return," she said, still without any facial expression, let alone a smile. She pointed down the corridor. "Left, left, right, right, right," she instructed. Briskly she patted him on the thigh. "Go," she said. "You are finished."

Walter reached the dining room at exactly the same time as Von Ackermann.

"Extraordinary, are they not?" the German asked.

"They are. I have never experienced anything like it."

"It is a rare art not widely known. It is only practiced in northern China. And here, at my castle."

"I am grateful to you," Walter said formally. For once it was what he meant, not what he was required to say.

"Now we shall eat further," Von Ackermann announced.

Although half an hour before Walter would have been sickened by the sight of more food, he was anxious to do so.

As the huge portions were being served, Von Ackermann said nothing. Then, when Walter had started to wonder how to recommence the business discussions, his host abruptly returned to them himself. "The investment of twelve million you suggest provides me with no security at all," he said severely, as if criticizing Walter.

"We've been through that," Walter replied. "There is nothing I can do about it. If you don't wish to participate on those terms, let's discuss it no further."

"Perhaps if I received a larger share of the business . . ."

"I could not accept that," said Walter, realizing he would but not wanting to admit to such a position too early. "But perhaps we could improve your position by including the money you owe us on Clarendon as part of your twelve million investment. It will amount to almost half a million dollars." It sounded like a big concession, Walter realized. But he had to start giving ground somewhere, and this was the easiest area since he wasn't at all sure he'd get most of the money from Clarendon in the first place.

"If you need my money, I am entitled to more of the business," said Von Ackermann, ignoring the offer entirely. "That is a valueless concession," his attitude implied. "I shall remember it, but give nothing in return."

Walter was incensed at the tactic, and at himself. Already he had given away several hundred thousand dollars, perhaps his trump card, without gaining any advantage in the negotiation. "You are already getting more than twelve million dollars of value for your investment," he said angrily.

"Only if it makes the profits you project."

"It will."

"Then why not borrow the twelve million dollars instead of selling part of the business?"

"I would be delighted to borrow the money from you," said Walter. He could see no possibility that Von Ackermann would lend the money, since that would give him even less security than being an owner. But clearly the older man had a suggestion up his sleeve.

"How quickly could you repay it?"

"We could work out a schedule," said Walter carefully.

"In one year?"

"Possibly," Walter said slowly, knowing that according to his latest projections, that would be feasible. He had been able to use the projected barter savings to induce Dr. Schatten of Magnatel's parent to delay payment of that amount for eighteen months. Since the barter savings would come in more quickly than that, he could use them to repay Von Ackermann first. Then, even if he did not have the full amount available to pay off Schatten, he could pay most of it and wangle another few months' delay on the balance. After all, Schatten would hardly vitiate the whole deal just because of a delay on the last few million.

"But what would be my advantage in lending the money?"

"I assume you have given that some consideration."

The German either missed or chose to ignore the sarcasm of the remark.

"Yes," he said. "I would be willing to accept the same twenty percent of the company—but I would expect my money back in twelve one-million-dollar monthly installments."

Hearing the words, Walter felt a surge of relief. He knew, of course, that Von Ackermann's proposal was totally unfair. It meant that he would get his share of the company for nothing. But that was not the important thing for Walter. What was important—marvelous, in fact—was that now the deal would be done. At last he was sure of it. *Sure!*

Desperately, Walter tried to hide the elation in his face and his voice. "I think you are asking too much," he started. "But, perhaps—"

"Of course," Von Ackermann interrupted, "I would expect that all assets not already pledged as security to someone else be pledged to me."

"Fixed assets," Walter interrupted. "We could not pledge liquid assets, since they are bought and sold as part of the everyday business."

"Very well. Fixed assets."

First point for me, Walter thought. All fixed assets have already been pledged to Kashi for his loan. I'm giving away nothing.

"In addition you would have to undertake not to sell any part of Magnatel to anyone until I am paid off," Von Ackermann continued. "After all," he smiled mirthlessly, "you will understand, Mr. Cort, that it is only in you that I am placing my faith."

"I appreciate your confidence." Walter stalled for time. It seemed like a reasonable request as well as a flattering one. "Very well," he agreed.

"Finally, there would of course have to be certain assurances in case repayments were not made on time."

"What assurances?" Walter was immediately suspicious.

"My suggestion is very simple. I lend you twelve million dollars, repayable in monthly installments of one million dollars each. To show my goodwill I shall charge you no interest. If you repay the money on schedule, I keep twenty percent of the stock of the company. If you do not repay each month on schedule, I take one hundred percent."

"That is outrageous," Walter cried.

"Possibly," said Von Ackermann softly, the smile fading from his face for the first time. "But then I suggest to you, Mr. Cort, that you have no alternative. So why don't we discuss it more coolly. Emotionalism in these matters rarely helps."

"Very well." Walter fought to control his wave of hatred. "As a first step, I obviously cannot give you the same percentage share for a repayable investment that you would get if your investment were permanent. My other investors would object. I suggest a maximum of ten percent of the company if we repay your funds."

They debated for a few moments and then agreed to twelve percent.

"And now, if we do not repay . . ."

"You have assured me you can," said Von Ackermann coldly. "Can I not trust your judgment on this?"

"You can."

"Then the penalty is not severe. It only comes into effect if you are wrong and cannot repay."

Walter hesitated before his next answer, and it was that hesitation that told Von Ackermann that he had won the point. "The percentage is too high," Walter said firmly. "One hundred percent is truly outrageous. Perhaps fifty . . ."

"We shall do the deal at one hundred percent or not at all," said Von Ackermann, solid in the knowledge that Walter had no other choice. "Take it or leave it, as the English say." He reached over and started to turn a knob. To Walter's consternation the music which had been barely audible through the closed study doors now started to rise in the dining hall. Looking up, Walter realized there were loudspeakers in the corners between ceiling and walls. "Think about it," Von Ackermann said, his voice rising above the music. He turned the knob further so that the music inundated the room. His smile fixed on his jowly face, he shoveled more food into his mouth.

There rushed through Walter a series of hurricanelike emotions, violent and circular. He'd done it! He'd gotten Magnatel. A three-hundred-million-dollar company. And he would own more than half of it personally. It was an unheard-of deal. Incredible! But in the very victory lay the gall of being beaten by the German. At one second he felt as if he were in the spotlight of success; at the next, as if that spotlight were pinning him to ultimate catastrophe.

And yet he knew he could repay the twelve million dollars to Von Ackermann. There was really no danger. Within a year he would have paid the German off. And he, Walter Kortinowiecz, from the terrifying woods of Kracow via the almost equally terrifying jungle of Brooklyn, would own the controlling interest in a huge international company. They would write about him in *Fortune* and *Business Week* and possibly even in *Time*. They would quote him everywhere that business was done. So great would be his wealth and power that anyone who loved him for that would be forced into such a great love it would be like loving him for himself.

Slowly Walter stood up. He walked over to where Von Ackermann had turned up the music. With a quick twist he turned it off. "My dear fellow," he said, "I'll make the deal as you request. If I don't repay your debt, you'll get all of Magnatel. But if I do, you keep six, not twelve percent. As we Americans also say, take it or leave it."

12

Bubbling with delight, Walter overflowed with plans and ideas as Von Ackermann's driver rushed him back to Frankfurt Airport. How he wished he had someone to talk to. He felt so elated that his mind bounded from one thought to another, as undisciplined as a butterfly.

Throughout the flight back to New York, his pride expanded. He'd done it! He, Walter Cort, would now own well over half of Magnatel—fifty-six percent, to be precise. A three-hundred-million-dollar company.

Half a dozen separate times he recalculated the ownership arithmetic, gloating. Six percent would go to that pig Von Ackermann; that was the only part he didn't like. But it wouldn't matter once the twelve million was paid off. Von Ackermann would only be a small minority shareholder with no power. Thirty percent went to the investors—Kashi, Harry and himself—for the eleven million dollars they'd put up. He'd put up three million, so he got eight percent of the company for that. Harry got two percent for the million he'd put up; and Kashi got twenty percent for his seven million. The thirty-five Kashi had given as a loan was different; he'd get that back with interest, but no ownership. So that left sixty-four percent of the company for Harry and him to split. He'd get three quarters, since he'd be running it—or forty-eight percent. Harry'd get sixteen percent. That was the split they always made when one of them ran a business and the other was just a co-promoter. All told, it meant Walter would end up with fifty-six percent of Magnatel. Easy control!

But the best part was what he could *do* with Magnatel once he was running it. The company had been asleep for so long. With his marketing experience and his expert staff at Walter Cort, Inc., he'd have that sleepy giant turned around in no time. He'd managed it often enough for other companies as a consultant. A year or two and Magnatel would be growing and dynamic. And it was *his!* He could hardly keep the grin off his face. He so wanted to share his achievement! How delighted Harry would be, and Fred Pogue, too.

By the time the plane touched down, Walter was bursting with his desire to tell his friends. He'd done it! He'd done it! And Harry and Fred should share in his success. They'd be so *pleased!*

The moment he could reach a telephone, Walter called Harry. "We got it," he started as soon as he heard his friend's voice. "I made the deal. A twelve-million-buck loan, repayable a million bucks a month . . ."

"Isn't that risky?" Harry, immediately cautious, showed none of the exuberance Walter wanted.

"No, goddamnit, it's not risky. It's a near-miracle, Harry. Don't you understand? We've done it. We've bought a three-hundred-million-dollar company."

"But you've got a hell of a repayment schedule. What happens if you can't repay the million a month?"

Walter's elation was crashing. "Then we lose the whole thing," he said, sounding more as if he were admitting to a misdemeanor than celebrating a victory.

"You *what?*" Harry was truly shocked. "Including my million?"

"Yes, and my three." Walter was becoming belligerent. "Damn it, don't you think we can save at least a million a month between the barter savings and everything else? Hell, Pogue's deal brings us in over two million a month right there."

"But that's needed to repay the other loans."

"Sure. But they can be delayed. Only Von Ackermann's twelve million is crucial."

"Hmm." Harry remained dubious.

"Well, don't you think we can?" Walter demanded again, becoming more and more angry. Here he'd pulled off one of the biggest business deals in history and all Harry would do was grunt and bitch.

"Should be able to," said Harry, but not very confidently. "Trouble is, things don't always work like they should."

"What other choice do we have?"

"We could forget the whole thing."

"Is that what you're suggesting?" Walter was now really furious. "Because if you are . . ."

"I ain't suggesting nothing," said Harry very quickly. "I wouldn't fucking dare!"

"Good," said Walter, still angry.

"Calm down, Wimp. I'm not backing away."

"Okay."

"Hey, and Wimp, well done." He hung up.

When Walter dialed Fred Pogue's line, there was no answer.

By the time his bags arrived, Walter's elation had evaporated and he found himself fallen from the heights of dizzying excitement into the bleakness of a lonely evening. Except for the pleasure he could count on from Bundle when he reached home, and Mortimer's solicitous welcome, there would be no one.

"If that's all there is . . ." he started to think, but he dropped the thought, realizing that if he followed it he would have to take some action. At the moment, when the world was ignoring him instead of cheering as it damn well should, it didn't seem up to him to organize things. For once he preferred to wallow in self-pity. If they would not share his triumph, why should he bother to arrange a celebration?

Head down, he walked behind the porter to the taxi stand. He had been too excited to remember to call from Frankfurt to have the car meet him. Or perhaps there hadn't been time at the airport. He couldn't remember; the excitement seemed a long way off. He crossed the street toward the cabs.

Everyone, not only Walter, stopped to stare when the gorgeous girl in the white mink placed two fingers in her mouth and let out a piercing whistle.

"With a mouth like that . . ." Walter overheard a cop start to say to his buddy.

Good God, it was Judith, he suddenly realized, waving to him hysterically.

"Over here, dummy," she yelled. "Over here."

Walter waved back weakly and veered toward her. The porter followed him.

"That son-of-a-bitch hadn't even noticed her," he heard the same cop say. "I'll be. . . ."

The rest of the speech was drowned by another whistle from Judith. "Hurry," she screamed as he grew near. "Hurry, I can't wait."

As fast as the world had emptied, it filled again. Walter was smiling now, his head high. This was more like it! Who needed the Harry Grasses of this world when there was always a Judith?

As he drew close to her, she ran a few steps toward him, her coat streaming in the gusty wind, and then hurled herself up at him. The next second she was clasping her arms around his neck, her legs around his waist, as tightly as any koala bear.

"Darling, darling. Did you do it? Did you?"

"Do what?"

"Get that company you were on about. You know, the one you keep talking about. The one that makes vibrators and things." She was entirely serious, Walter realized.

"Yes," he said, feeling a wave of emotion so strong it brought tears to his eyes. "Yes, I did."

"Great! That's marvelous." She slid down his body until she was standing in front of him, every bit of her body seemingly in contact with a piece of his. "Then I was right to plan a celebration," she said, obviously still worried about the arrangements she'd made.

"What . . . ?"

"I've got the Ferrari back there. A nice cop said he'd take care of it for me. And Mortimer's meeting us up at the Cape," she looked up at him for approval. "With Bundle," she added, as doubtfully as if she were handing her teacher an apple instead of her homework. "Then for the weekend we'll come back to New York. It's my birthday. I'll be twenty-one. And we've invited a whole bunch of people to a party. . . ."

"You're presumptuous, young lady." He wanted to sound stern, but he was too touched to make a good job of it.

"Not anymore," she said triumphantly. "I got shots."

He laughed in spite of himself. "Let's go, then," he said. "It was probably time we organized another of our events. So let's go dancing. . . ."

Walter accelerated a shade faster than the conditions of the road and the traffic could justify. The roar of the motor gave him a sense of power, of gut pleasure. As he moved the car smoothly between lanes, proud of his control and amused at the envy and annoyance he created in the other drivers, Judith stretched herself sensuously on the soft leather seat beside him and let out a gurgle of excitement. Exactly like a cat, he thought, all unconscious grace and physical vitality. He was grateful that she had met him. Besides that, he really liked having her in the car. Her excitement at the speed reflected and magnified his; and he felt no need to detract from his pleasure in driving by making conversation. You don't converse with a cat, he thought wryly, you just give or receive pleasure.

"Faster," she urged him. "Hurry."

He glanced over and saw that her face was as tight as when the coke she snorted every few hours first hit.

"Hurry," her voice was a tense half-whisper as if to urge him on without breaking whatever spell the speed cast over her. Slowly one of her hands started to stroke its way up the inside of her thighs, and suddenly he realized that she was leaning back and rubbing herself slowly and rhythmically the way she did when she showed her pornographic movies. "Oh God, I love it!" she said to him, and her hands speeded up.

The car in front dawdled in the left lane, and to the right a sixteen-wheeler, trundling along, blocked Walter's path. There seemed nothing to do but wait in line until gradually the slow car edged in front of the truck.

"No, don't slow down," she cried urgently. "Don't ever slow down. Oh God, I want it!"

The combination of the car's power and the girl rising toward orgasm beside him was building Walter's own excitement almost unbearably. She was incredible. He was as horny as he could ever remember.

"Go!" she shouted.

Without thinking, Walter slammed his foot down on the accelerator so that the Ferrari leaped forward almost into the car in front. At the very last instant he wrenched the wheel to the left. Never easing his pressure from the accelerator, he tore onto the grass median, around the car in front, and back onto the highway, accelerating away with the Ferrari's engine whining in praise and agony.

The girl suddenly went rigid, her face contorted, her hips lifted and she let out one long marveling scream of release, while Walter's own excitement seemed suddenly to burst from inside him with a totally unexpected, magnificent ejaculation.

Walter Cort, dressed in skin-tight beige chinos and a silk shirt open to his chest, greeted each guest by name. He was proud of his ability to remember names—and if he didn't know one, several of his staff were standing close by to help. "Spontaneity needs the most work," he often explained to them. Katy Rochester, looking lovely in a very expensive evening gown, made it her particular business to be helpful. From time to time she would ask Mortimer, who seemed to know everyone, for the guests' names. Then, surreptitiously but efficiently, she would write them down in a small, silver notebook together with a brief description of their clothing. "Margaret Salzer—clinging blue" or "Jim Christian—checks and Topsiders." The rest of the time, picking occasionally at her book, she would feed Walter any names he forgot.

The guests were of the widest assortment: elderly statesmen with wives weighted down by ostentatiously expensive jewelry; models with faces painted to technicolor vividness and figures so thin they bordered on anorexic; several senior army officers, rigid to the point of brittleness; a variety of young actors of perfect physical proportions and total egocentricity; a few older ones, each playing to the hilt a role he thought appropriate for the evening; and the inevitable society reporters and gossip columnists. But most abundant of all were the lawyers, financiers, bankers, advertising agents, promoters and sales executives

Walter thought might be useful to the running of Magnatel.

Harry Grass, for once dressed conservatively in gray slacks and a blazer, arrived early.

"Where's Martha?" Walter wanted to know.

"She didn't feel well this evening, but she may drop in later. Said to say hello to you. And particularly to say hello to Judith."

Walter made no comment, but he wondered what Judith was up to. He couldn't imagine that she could do anything wrong with Martha, but still. . . . "Go in and grab yourself a drink," he urged Harry.

Jimmy Leonetti, the head of API, the world combine he had rescued from near-bankruptcy only two years ago, arrived with two gorgeous girls clinging to him. "Hello, Wally," he shouted. "How're you doing? Meet two of my ladies." He patted each of them on the fanny.

"You're magnificient," Walter said. "All three of you. Magnificient!"

"This one's Maxine," Leonetti said.

"And I'm George," the taller of the two spoke for herself. There was something special about her bearing, a certain dignity.

"I'm pleased you came, George," he said. "Georgina, I suppose?"

"George," the girl said firmly.

Leonetti looked at her appraisingly but refrained from giving her rump another pat.

Walter's staff mingled among the guests, alert to all the social niceties: a drink here, an introduction there. They were even more alert to any business opportunities they might glean from the hundreds of conversations buzzing everywhere. Their boss might be flying high on his new acquisition, but they still depended on Walter Cort, Inc., for their livelihood, at least until they found themselves a job where the owner hadn't lost interest.

"Fantastic party, Walter. You've done it again," said a Brooks Brothers–attired, white-haired gentleman sipping a double martini. "Beautiful women."

"Aren't they," Walter agreed, adopting the older man's tone of benign approval. "But you should see many such creatures. Your group owns Karlee Creations, doesn't it?"

"It does." The older man's eyes hardened. "But I only see the balance sheets." He smiled coldly. "I understand some sort of figures better than others."

Katy moved toward the two men. "I would guess you understand both sorts pretty well," she said with a flirtatious smile.

The old man smiled, flattered. "Well, maybe," he admitted.

"May I present Katy Rochester?" Walter said, having no choice but to introduce her. "George White."

"Delighted," said White. He looked at Katy's dress. "I see you understand fashion," he said. "It's an Oscar, isn't it?"

"Why, yes." Katy was impressed that he would recognize the designer. Oscar de la Renta originals were not cheap. She was delighted someone had noticed. "Thank you for commenting."

"I only wish we could do as well as he does. Every time I look at Karlee's profit figures, they seem to get worse. Lucky to break even this year."

"Can we help?" Walter responded to the opportunity more by habit than with enthusiasm.

"Maybe."

"You recall we did a turnaround on Flair awhile ago. You had some connection with them, didn't you?"

"My brother . . ."

"That's right, he worked there. How is he?"

"They're doing all right."

"Perhaps Katy here and the head of our fashion division could come and see you about Karlee."

"You'll come too?" George White inquired sharply.

"Of course. If I possibly can," said Walter, knowing he would not.

"Okay," the old gentleman was saying. "But we're not paying for this whole party, you hear?"

Walter laughed and made sure his guest's martini was refilled before moving on to the next conversation. Whatever his guest said, Karlee *would* pay for this party.

". . . Need a donation for the hospital," a professional fund-raiser was saying to another guest, the well-known manager of a huge charitable trust.

"Have you sent us a proposal?"

"Of course. But you know how you treat them."

"With great consideration and sound reasons for rejection," the manager laughed.

"Precisely."

"How much?"

"We need about eight thousand," said the fund-raiser, appraising his mark.

"I'll interpret that as five."

"Will I get it?"

"You can count on it. Just send us a new proposal for five. By the way," the manager added, "I'm on the board of the Shakespeare Theatre. We could use . . ."

". . . about five grand?" the fund-raiser laughed.

"About."

"You got it."

Walter walked on.

"This new thing that I've written," he heard an effete young man with long blond hair say to a tiny old lady whom Walter recognized as New York's leading gossip columnist. "I'm certain it will be a *tremendous* success."

"Yes?"

"You *must* read it," the author insisted. "It's not for me to say, but many people are saying it shows *real* talent." He giggled, obviously hoping to be reassured.

"How nice," she said vaguely.

Was she going deaf? the young writer wondered, looking flustered. She seemed to have missed his point. "Now that *you* have written so successfully yourself," he tried again, "I'm sure you'll understand that this time I'm not being *merely* commercial. It's *much* more. . . ."

The old reporter smiled up at him owlishly. "Yes," she repeated, sounding confused. In tomorrow's column, she decided, she would say that he "spent the evening shoveling charm and sales pitches."

"Not that it won't be commercial too . . ." the writer insisted, trying to smile boyishly at the same time.

Walter walked on. Clearly the old girl was still tough as a turtle.

". . . What's a nice girl like you . . ." Walter stopped, hardly able to believe the cliché.

"Doing?" the girl asked. "I'm doing what you think I'm doing."

"Here?"

"No, but if you'd like to come to my place. . . ."

Walter wondered how she had slipped past Mortimer.

"At last, darling," Judith came over to him. "I've been waiting for you until I can hardly stand it."

"You look like a snake trying to shed its skin," he said, admiring the silk dress that clung to every curve and crevice of her body. "Fantastic. How the hell did you get into it?"

"I thought of you, darling, until I kind of got slippery all over, and then I just smoothed my way in."

How disgusting that Judith was, Katy thought, overhearing the conversation. And so obvious. Incredible how the men all fell for it. Walter was as bad as any, maybe worse. Thank god she didn't have to use her body the way Judith did. Already she was doing far better with her brains, and the battle had hardly started. Just a little planning and subtlety was all it took.

Time to leave, Katy decided. This wasn't the right arena for her to compete. Quietly she slipped away.

". . . And I say of course we must improve the bottom line," the chief financial officer of a huge cigarette company was insisting as Walter joined his group.

"But profit isn't the only important consideration," an impeccably dressed conservative young man responded, his eyes shining with conviction. "I'm with the John Deibold group. You may have read about us in *Time*. We believe that, to survive, business has to involve itself in all forms of consumer change. For example, we helped set up the Food Safety Council. We promote corporate change to keep up with the times."

"I still say that the bottom line is profits."

"Certainly, but profit has to be taken in context . . ." The younger man stuttered to a halt as Judith glided up and winked at him.

"I heard the editor of a terribly important newspaper say," she interrupted, her voice innocent, "that the bottom line generally has hair around it."

The younger man laughed tentatively. But the older one, deeply offended, nevertheless recognized a truth and blushed brilliantly, perhaps for the first time in twenty years.

By two in the morning there were only about thirty people left. Walter's staff had all left, following his long-standing order never to stay beyond midnight. He had no intention of allowing his employees to mix into his private pleasures. The older business guests had also left, driven out by the escalating music or the necessity to hurry off to Connecticut or the Hamptons.

Half a dozen men grouped in the corner chewed pills and stroked each other. Elsewhere men and women danced together or alone. Moving among the guests, Mortimer supervised.

Relaxed on a couch, with a slight, almost mocking smile of self-satisfaction on his lips, Walter enjoyed the action. This was his party, under his control, at his expense. There was no need to work at being dominant; he *was* dominant.

Judith, irrepressible, danced alone in the center of the room. Already she was giddy with coke, the evening, the music. A tall, Latin man, immaculate in a white suit and open shirt, danced near her, his eyes glued to her body. He danced very well, with understated rhythm, dignity without stiffness.

"Who is he?" Walter asked Mortimer as he passed his couch. "Did we invite him?"

"He came with the Argentine ambassador. His name is Juán Gomez Velasquez and that's all I know about him."

"He's good-looking. And Judith is dancing as if she knows he's rich," Walter said acerbically.

"A five-hundred-dollar leisure suit," said Mortimer knowledgeably.

The dancers kept a ring clear around Judith as she writhed in her second skin of shiny silk. She was so tall and voluptuous she seemed superhuman, a deity, and the onlookers her worshippers.

Walter remembered the Tigress at Raymond's Review Bar. The difference was that Judith, just as exciting, was available to him. Perhaps he should interrupt before the man got any wrong ideas. But no, time enough. Judith would come when he called for her. Walter felt confident in his ownership of all he surveyed.

A determined red-headed girl, eyeing Judith and the Argentinian with indiscriminate hunger, invaded the circle in which they danced. Her hips swung more suggestively than Judith's, but her body with its overlarge breasts seemed awkward in comparison. She was clearly the aggressor, although which conquest she had in mind, Walter could not tell. He watched to see what would happen. Imperceptibly, the Argentinian danced toward the new girl. When he was close enough, his hand moved as rapidly as the end of a rapier. Stingingly he slapped her bottom.

"Ouch," she screamed, losing all dignity and most of her sex appeal. The Argentinian, never missing a beat, started to raise his hand again, and she scurried off. The audience laughed and there were a few claps. The girl, pouting and close to tears, threw herself onto the couch next to Walter.

"That's all right, dear," he said, putting his arm on her thigh. "You can't win 'em all."

She snuggled toward him, anxious to prove that she was desirable after all, her hand falling automatically to his crotch.

"Later, perhaps," he said, not interested, but unwilling to double her rejection.

"Okay," she said, "I'll get a drink." She leaned over in full view of the watchers and kissed him hard on the mouth. He responded just enough to further salve the girl's feelings.

It would have astonished Walter to see Judith at that moment. So deeply hurt did she feel at his casual petting that, amidst all the gaiety and vamping of her dance, her eyes filled with tears.

Without breaking his rhythm the Argentinian moved around Judith, turning her with him until she had her back to Walter. He clasped her shoulders. "So you will dance with me," he said into her ear, his face half-covered by her hair. "For tonight you will dance with only me." His accent was indefinable, neither Argentinian nor European, but with a Hispano-German assurance, almost arrogance, which Judith found most attractive. "And you will wear this," he added, pulling an aquamarine pendant large enough to sparkle even in the dim light out of his jacket pocket. He threw it around her neck. "You will dance with me," he repeated. "And enjoy the pendant." If she did not do that, his look implied he would choke her.

Walter saw the Argentinian's act and was instantly furious. How could the SOB—Velasquez, was he?—try to buy his woman away? But as quickly as the anger rose, he forced it down. What the hell, he thought, Judith could make up her own mind. And he had to admit the jewel was worth more than the fifty-dollar cocaine "straws" she filched from him. He could do with some of that, he thought, and waved Mortimer to fetch the tiny silver tray with its coke spoon and jewel box of powder. Two massive blasts, one into each nostril . . .

As the night progressed, so did the wildness of the party. Pot, coke, 'ludes, any number of other pills, and always the wild music, screaming loud and louder, making the whole room vibrate. In the corner a young, almost completely wasted human, probably male but decked out in female finery, beat the bongo drums in time with what-ever music was playing. His head held rigid and his eyes closed, his fingers, knuckles and arms vibrated against the drums until his skin bled.

Walter watched not only the guests, but also himself. He felt quite separate from the surroundings, and very superior. He could observe objectively his own body, alternately racked with anger at Judith and her new man, then calmed with the knowledge that he didn't need her or anyone. He could even observe dispassionately his body's reaction to the coke, watch it shivering like a grove of aspens, every nerve aquiver like leaves when the breeze came in gusts.

Still in the center of the room, Judith continued to dance with her handsome Argentinian, inexhaustibly gyrating. She had gradually eased herself out of her dress and was clad now only in the tiniest of bikini briefs and sharply pointed evening sandals so high and thin that they seemed to keep her, as if by desire alone, floating a few inches above the floor.

Lost in the cocaine and the spectacle of Judith, Walter had a feeling of uninvolved admiration for her beauty. He felt an impersonal, generalized lust for her greater than he could ever remember before, so great it ended barely this side of violence. Through his drug-inten-sified vision, she became the very essence of all femaleness.

But underneath, still grateful that she alone had bothered to meet him at the airport, he also felt the stirrings of real fondness for the human being inside the magnificent trappings of that body. He liked her, he thought with surprise. He knew very little about her, only some of her crazier adventures—if he could believe her stories—and that she had started as a wildly ambitious kid somewhere in the dock area of London. But he really liked her. They had a lot in common, too, both starting out totally poor.

He arose unsteadily, determined to talk to her, and signaled the band to less noise. But as he did so, the Argentinian, still as impeccable as when he first entered the room, sensed Walter's approach and leaned forward to whisper to Judith. Walter saw her throw her body against him, evidently delighted by his suggestion. She fingered the pendant which glittered and bounced on her breasts.

Before Walter could take another step, the Argentinian swept the girl away, half-carrying her toward one of the bedrooms off the main living room. He slammed the door behind them.

Walter stopped as abruptly as if he'd been slapped. For a moment he felt the tumult of rejection and jealousy. But almost as fast he pulled himself under control again. No, he thought angrily, it's absurd. Don't get involved, he admonished himself; don't be vulnerable. Caring is weakness. Leave her alone. Leave them both alone. Don't follow; don't touch. Don't let your heart be touched; don't make a fool of yourself. Don't be an ass! The litany of warnings stopped him from fighting for her as he wanted to, stopped him from even admitting to himself that he wanted her for herself. She's just another woman, he assured himself. With a shrug he forced himself not to care.

He turned on his heel and walked back toward the far corner of the room, where two nubile young women were caressing an older man whom Walter hardly knew. "Come," Walter said to the two, ignoring completely their bemused companion. Dutifully they arose and accompanied Walter into his bedroom.

"But where are you going?" the abandoned man expostulated. There was no one to listen to him.

When Walter awoke much later, all that was left of the evening was a memory of arms and legs intertwining, more zingy sensations of coke, vaginas wet and clasping, fingers probing, the smell of musk and the fragrance of sweat. As he stretched in his bed, his penis stirring but far too satiated to harden, he remembered too the incredible sensation of orgasm coupled with the cold sting of the white powder on his glans; the screams of the girls as they came together reaching almost unbearable heights; the stickiness of champagne over their bodies; and at last the exhaustion which had left him only just enough energy to push the girls groggily out of his room before he collapsed into his satin sheets.

As he became fully conscious, Walter realized that the whole room now stank of stale champagne, sweat and sex. Groaning, he pulled himself out of his bed and looked at his clock. Two o'clock. He could see slits of light through his drapes. Saturday afternoon, he assumed. Perhaps it was Sunday. No, Saturday, he thought. He hadn't slept around the clock. He rose and stretched his arms over his head. Why did he always feel guilty after these excesses? They hurt no one beyond leaving a hangover; they were fun and exciting—but the next day his life seemed so dreary, so much emptier than usual. He probably should not allow another one.

Hating the stench of the bed, Walter pulled off the sheets and flung them into the corner. Feeling better at having thus improved his nest, he walked to the bathroom. Soon the stinging shower hitting his back washed away the worst of his depression. He wondered what had happened to his guests. He'd see in a moment. And then came the thought which had been nagging just below the surface of his mind, the thought he didn't want to deal with but could no longer put off: What had happened to Judith?

Walter showered and shaved carefully, put on a pair of slacks with creases like knife edges, slipped his feet into loafers of suedelike softness and threw on a crisp but soft sports shirt. He looked at the pile of bedclothes in the corner with distaste, shrugged and walked quickly into the living room. Mortimer would take care of the bedroom. He was pleased to see that the mess from the party had been completely removed; evidently the cleaning staff, organized in advance by the invaluable house manager, had already finished.

"Mortimer," Walter called. "Mortimer," his voice rose on the second call. There was no answer. Walter pushed open the kitchen door. But his house manager was not in sight. Possibly he had gone out. Unlikely, Walter thought. He rarely left the house when his employer might need him. Walter began to be worried. It was not like Mortimer to have no appropriate meal ready. Perhaps he had become ill.

Deciding he had to investigate more closely, Walter hurried up the back stairs to Mortimer's small suite of rooms, an area he rarely visited. His house manager had made it clear when he started working for Walter that this was to be his private domain and not even his boss would be welcome. Walter knocked on the door. There was no answer, but the door swung open slightly.

There, to Walter's atonishment and concern, lay Mortimer, hair disheveled, pot belly entirely vulnerable, surrounded by sheets so sordid and crumpled they looked like piles of garbage. He was snoring stentoriously. The smell that had pervaded Walter's own bed and body permeated the room. And scattered over, around and under Mortimer, like the remnants of a giant feast, were strewn the elongated limbs, slack snoring mouths, damp bodies and disheveled hair of the two girls he had pushed out of his room earlier—and the pretty boy bongo player as well. The floor was littered with bottles. At least, Walter thought wryly, when Mortimer fell off the wagon, he did it with a vengeance.

By ten that evening, Mortimer having recovered most of his dignity, the house having been purified of all remnants of debauchery, and Walter having eaten a sensible evening snack of rare steak and salad, life should have regained a certain equilibrium. In fact, however, Walter was deeply anxious about Judith. Mortimer had reported that, after an hour or so in the bedroom with Velasquez, she had emerged higher on drugs than he had ever seen her, and apparently very angry. She had scratched and screamed at the Argentinian for a while, but eventually, half-abducted, half-seduced, she had left the house with him.

"I wasn't able to intervene," Mortimer explained shamefacedly. "But . . ."

"I know. Nor was I." Walter felt equally guilty. It was an unexpected and unpleasant feeling. "We'd better call some of the others to see where they went. Judith can take care of herself all right. Still. . . ."

But after a number of telephone calls, Walter was much more worried than before. Several people described Judith as first shrieking, then dancing like a crazy woman, then weeping as if every unhappiness on earth were bearing down on her. Through it all, the witnesses agreed, the tall Argentinian had just watched—and gloated.

"He never even took off his jacket," one of Walter's friends told him. "and when they came out of that bedroom, Judith was absolutely nuts. She must have dropped every chemical in the house."

"What happened to her?"

"I don't know. Somehow he spirited her out of here. Maybe he gave her something stronger. Someone commented that she might be on shit."

"Oh, Christ," Walter explained. "Not that." With an effort he forced his voice back to normal. "Where did he take her?"

"No idea. All I know is he had a car, a great lethal, silver thing. I think there was a driver too, or a bodyguard perhaps. And Judith was babbling something about going to see the mad stars, or the mad starlight. Something like that."

"The Starlight Room at the top of the Madison Hotel?"

"Yes, she could have been saying Madison Starlight, I guess. Sorry, that's all I know."

"No, you've been very helpful. I think I'll be able to find her now." Walter hung up the phone, already planning for action. Don't be vulnerable, a small voice tried to remind him. But he ignored it, admitting to himself at last that he had become really fond of the crazy, beautiful, wild, young female.

It took Walter fifty dollars to persuade the manager of the Madison Hotel to give him information about an Argentinian gentleman.

"The count is out for the day, but the girl is still there. Penthouse number one," the manager explained. "It's the far elevator, but you can't go up there. It's against the house rules. Please excuse me now. I have to leave. I don't believe I've ever seen you here."

Walter grinned at him, waited while he left and walked quickly toward the far elevator.

To his infinite relief, Judith looked radiant when she opened the door.

"Darling," she cried. "Oh Walter, darling. I'm so pleased you're here. Wait till I tell you what a marvelous thing has happened to me."

"You lost your virginity?" Walter's relief made him silly. "You've found religion and been saved?"

"No, I'm serious. I want to tell you." She looked like an infinitely beautiful little girl. "Juán is taking me with him," she said. "Isn't it wonderful?"

Walter felt his stomach knot instantly. "Yes," he said. "I suppose so." He paused. "Are you really all right?"

"Of course I'm all right. It's marvelous, I tell you. Be happy for me."

"What's so good about it?"

"That he *wants* me! He wants me to come and live with him. Nobody ever wanted me like that before. Not since my Mum threw me out when I was fourteen."

"But. . . ."

"You didn't," she said, not accusing, but simply stating a fact. "You were nice to me, and fun to be with and all that. But you didn't want me living with you. Nobody's ever wanted me living with them."

Judith was becoming so shrill, Walter feared she would become hysterical. Astonishing how her moods changed. "Are you on something?" he asked, suddenly suspicious.

"No, only happiness." She calmed at once.

"You sound like a soap opera."

"Then don't share my happiness," she said, instantly hurt and therefore angry. Damn him, she thought, why won't he understand. "I don't care what you think," she said, full of defiance. "I'm happy."

"Are you?" he asked, doubting it. Then he blurted out. "Someone said that last night you got onto heroin."

"No," she said. "Is that what's worrying you? No, I didn't. I'd never do that." She paused, smiling broadly, thoroughly pleased now that he cared enough to be worried about her. "Almost everything else, but not that."

"You sure?"

"Particularly not now that Juan really wants me."

"Does he? Or does he want a beautiful slave?" Walter demanded brusquely.

Judith was stopped in her tracks.

"He seems a cold and dangerous man to me," Walter followed up ruthlessly.

"Oh no, he's not like that. He's warm and wonderful." But Judith's voice showed her doubt. He wasn't really warm and wonderful, she reflected. He was harsh in ways she didn't even understand. But then, men were always harsh with her. They always wanted her for her body, for the fun and excitement she gave them. They weren't ever soft, not the way she really wanted.

"Would you stay here if I invited you to live at my house?" Walter asked, listening with amazement to his own words.

"Do you mean it?" she asked, as shy as a wild young animal being offered food out of a human hand.

"Of course."

But in spite of his flat assurance, Walter realized that he probably did not. It was more that he felt himself cornered, committed to being helpful. Just below the surface he was annoyed that his fondness for her had caused this instant obligation. And the moment he asked her to live with him, he also started to feel anger toward her.

"But why?" she asked, sensing part of his complicated feelings. "How come you're asking me now?"

Walter refused to deal with that question. "I don't want you to go with Juan, that's all," he explained illogically. "I'm frightened for you. Stay here."

"But what would I do? Who would look after me?"

"I would, of course. Don't be ridiculous, I've got enough money."

"Oh," she said, "I'd . . ."

Her voice was drowned by the sound of a motor outside, first pulsing loudly and then rising to a crescendo. They ran to the balcony doorway. With amazement they watched the helicopter land on the flat roof. Sikorsky IIA, Walter noted automatically. Its door swung open and Juán Velasquez, dressed in another white suit, alighted and walked briskly toward the apartment doors where Walter and Judith were watching. Like Walter, he did not deign to duck beneath the blades only a few inches above his head. Barely slowing his stride, he burst into the room.

The Man from Glad, was all Walter could think stupidly, the Man from Glad.

"Come!" Velasquez shouted, beckoning Judith. Walter could see the shape of the word on his mouth rather than hear it in the din.

For a second the girl swayed between the two men, as if she were again writhing to the music.

Walter stood rooted to his spot, knowing that if he beckoned her with the same conviction that the Argentinian had, she would follow him. But his anger intervened. Why was she forcing him to a commitment like this? It was too much responsibility. He was willing to spend money on her, and later perhaps . . .

In the clattering roar of the helicopter, the three formed a wordless tableau.

Breaking the picture first, the tall Argentinian again beckoned Judith imperially. "Come!" he ordered a second time. He held his hand toward the girl.

As if in a trance, she moved a step closer. The single step broke the spell for her; once she had taken that, she could move easily again and she hurried toward him. He placed one arm around her waist and with the other held her elbow. Then he helped her out of the door as one might help a tired swimmer out of the water. Together they hurried across the tarmac and into the 'copter.

Walter remained immobilized. His last sight of her was as she peered through the helicopter's window. He could not tell whether her look was pleading for understanding, begging for mercy or wishing him well. All he knew as he watched the aircraft lift off the roof, diminish to a black spot and then disappear entirely, was that he was swamped by a sense of loss and disappointment more bitter than any he had felt since he was abandonded by Rebecca near the forest and, in an intertwining memory, heard that Rachel had left him.

Walter stood quite still for many minutes watching the sky where the helicopter had disappeared. She'd made her decision, he supposed. She was adult enough: reaching her majority yesterday amidst the highs of rock and chemicals, twenty-one years old with a lifetime behind her. And she'd made the choice sensibly enough, he decided, taking the man who would give her the most.

What else is there in life? Walter asked himself. What else but money and power . . . and love, fondness, even friendship? "Bullshit," said Walter out loud. "Money and power." He looked out the open door to where the helicopter had been. "Good luck, Judith," he shouted. "Be rich and happy."

From deep in his past there came to him a form of words his mother had sometimes used. "Go with God, Judith," he said softly, with infinite bitterness. "Go with God, but go."

He turned and walked slowly out of the empty suite toward the elevator. Another of his mother's distant sayings rang in his head. "Hold onto your friends," he could remember her admonishing. "They carry your luck."

13

Katy Rochester dressed very carefully this Monday morning, selecting a silk Ted Lapidus dress suit which looked entirely businesslike but which managed, so subtly that she knew she could never be caught, to be thoroughly sexy as well. It was a warm deep gold, just a shade darker than her hair, and it had a pinstripe of blue which perfectly matched her eyes. The jacket was of nubby raw silk, also gold and blue. It gave her a taller, more stately look, but at the same time, quite inadvertently it seemed, it emphasized her breasts. The overall effect, paradoxically, was to make her seem both very distant and very desirable.

At eight twenty-five Katy presented herself at Walter's door and knocked. She had timed it carefully so as to not be excessively early for her eight-thirty appointment, but early enough to get there before Caroline, who always arrived at precisely half-past. She carried two cups of coffee and a piece of Danish pastry.

"Come in."

Katy pushed the door open with her foot. "I brought us some breakfast." She was pleased to see him smile his appreciation. The expensive dress, the serving gesture, the shared breakfast—her scene had been carefully planned.

"Thank you."

"You're welcome." She broke the piece of cake in half daintily. "You'll have to help me eat it. I'm hopelessly addicted, but it's not exactly ideal for my figure."

"Not for mine either," he said, "but then what is?"

She was elated. He was responding to her cues as if he had learned his part in advance. "Ah," she said, "that's exactly what I want to talk to you about."

"Your figure?" She was really a lot more attractive than he had given her credit for, Walter decided, watching her blush. And really rather nice.

Caroline tapped on the door, interrupting at that moment. "Good morning, sir. I'll have your coffee to you in a second."

"Don't bother. Thanks, but Katy brought me some."

"Very well." Caroline wondered what Katy was up to. Now *there* was a young lady whose ambition knew no limit. She only hoped her boss would not fall for all that false innocence.

"Not exactly my figure. But yes, I do want to talk about diets, among other things," Katy continued. "I've been developing a scheme which we can start immediately, and which later will fold right into Magnatel on a worldwide basis."

"Okay," he said, trying not to sound too indulgent, "let's hear it." He was quite certain that anything she had dreamed up would be impractical. But he'd devote a few minutes to explaining why. It was his urge to teach rearing its head again, he realized ruefully. He just loved explaining things, and she would be bright enough to learn. One thing he'd have to tell her up front was that it was far too early to be developing anything for Magnatel; the lawyers were only now completing the acquisition papers.

"The whole idea actually came from you in the first place," Katy was saying. "Do you remember telling me that you and Fred Pogue had once discussed computerizing a diet so that it would be specially tailored for everyone using it?"

Walter, who could barely remember the conversation, looked confused.

"You pointed out that diets never work for the individual because they are all made for the *average* person. But no one is average."

"Yes, I do remember talking about it with Fred. I forgot that you and I had ever discussed it."

"You'd better be careful what you tell me," she said lightly. "I have total recall."

"I'll be careful," he said, wondering for a second whether there was more to her comment than he realized. Instantly he dismissed the thought. "Haven't computerized diets been done before?" he asked instead, getting back to business.

"They have," she agreed quickly. "*Woman* magazine ran one in England. And very successfully. And so have various other magazines and business enterprises."

"So?"

"But what I'm suggesting would go much further. Starting with your thought of a computerized diet, you could actually go on to computerize practically the whole person."

"I don't understand."

"Well, you could punch in their diet and eating habits, just like *Woman* did. Then you could add information about their living habits so that you could include exercises. *Woman* did that, too, up to a point. But remember, they only had one page of their magazine for a questionnaire. You could get people to fill out a whole booklet of questions on every subject to do with themselves: sports, hobbies, health, psychology, education, children, relationships, career plans, even sex."

"Would they do that?"

"Of course. People love answering questions about themselves. We once had a market research guy up at Harvard who said that people would sit still for interviews about new products for up to three quarters of an hour before they even started to object. And in this case it's a questionnaire about themselves, not about some new product. They'd be fascinated! No questionnaire would be too long."

Walter enjoyed the serious look on her face. She was like a little girl playing grown-up.

"But even when you have the questionnaire, how would you be able to give them advice?" Walter asked. "Diets and exercise seem fairly easy. But the others, from career counseling to sex, would be much harder."

"Not really. I don't think we'd find it too hard. For instance there are several books instructing people about how to deal with sexual dysfunctions. And we could do better than those because we'd know specifics; they can only talk generalities."

Walter looked unconvinced.

"Let's say she tells us in the questionnaire that she rarely reaches orgasm because he's too quick for her. He's not a P.E . . ."

"A what?"

"A premature ejaculator. Her answers have told us that. He's just going too fast for her."

"Okay." Walter wondered how on earth they had gotten onto this subject. It wasn't even nine o'clock in the morning, and here he was discussing the intricacies of sex therapy with a pretty blonde. . . . He shook his head clear and tried to concentrate.

"In her printout we'd give her specific hints on how to get him to slow down," Katy was saying. "Even actual words to say to him. Perhaps we'd even write a small article which she could purposely leave lying around as if it fell out of a magazine. Something he'd be likely to see so that he'd get the message without her having to tell him . . ."

Walter looked at her with pleasure, more interested in her than in her proposal. Her eyes were shining. A lock of hair kept falling forward, making her look girlish in spite of her expensive clothes. She pushed it back each time, and once or twice she unconsciously tossed her head backward so that her hair lined up in patterns which might have been formed by the wind.

She knew he was not paying attention to her the way she would normally have insisted. He was missing the details, and it was insulting that he wouldn't take her seriously. But for once she did not voice her objections. It was much more important that he buy her idea. If he did that, she could stand his put-downs with equanimity. If only he *would* accept it. She was determined to see that he did.

"Look here," he said, suddenly realizing that he was taking up too much time with this girl and her fantasies. "The question is, will I get an adequate return on my investment? After all, there's a big up-front cost. You'd have to write a vast book of alternatives for each of the program segments, and key in every combination of alternatives to a computer. It would be a huge programming task. Feasible, but very expensive."

"Normally, yes, it would be expensive," Katy interrupted, fearful that she was losing control of the discussion. "But not so much in this case, because for its consulting business Walter Cort, Inc., already employs both the writers and the computer programmers you'd need. And they have a fair amount of 'down time' when there's no specific client assignment available for them. You have them doing various basic research projects now when there's nothing else to do. But their time would be far better spent on this."

"Then you'd have to tell people about the program," Walter continued, ignoring her explanation. "Lots of advertising. And finally you'd have to distribute the questionnaires. You could hardly collect the cash from your customers before they'd gotten their questionnaire. So you'd be advancing more money for paper, printing, postage. Against all that, how much do you think you could get for each program?"

"Twenty, twenty-five dollars?" She put it into the form of a question, knowing that if she gave any opinion of her own, he was bound to disagree.

"Maybe, but I doubt whether too many people would buy at that price. Maybe $12.50."

"And you think the cost would be more than that."

"No, I doubt whether the book itself would cost more than two or three dollars," he said thoughtfully, "but the cost of getting started and then the expense of marketing would be horrendous."

"What if we marketed it together with Magnatel products? That's what I was thinking about in the long run. Of course, I haven't really thought it all through," she lied.

"That's a thought." Now he realized she had the spark of a really good idea. He leaned forward in his chair; his patronizing air vanished. "The program doesn't work by itself, I don't think. But when you combine it with the appliances, it could make really good sense. For example we could sell the appliances in the mail and use the computer program as the added purchase incentive."

"A $12.50 value, free when you buy blank," Katy agreed enthusiastically. This was going just as she'd planned. "Then we'd send out the questionnaire with the appliance."

Walter was impressed by how easily Katy was able to keep up with him. He'd have to stay on his toes. "Also, we could include the questionnaire with every appliance we sold at retail," he hurried on.

"And with all the Magnatel literature they mail out. That must be enormous."

"It is."

"Then couldn't we use the questionnaire to sell more appliances?" Katy asked.

Walter considered for a moment. "Yes, I think so. We'd call the whole thing the *Magnatel* computer program, so we'd get all the publicity from it behind our name. Then it would be logical that our diet program would recommend our blender."

"And the beauty segment would use Magnatel beauty appliances."

"And the section on sex . . . ?"

"Obviously vibrators."

"Obviously."

She looked at him appraisingly. Was he teasing her again? If only she could get him really enthusiastic. She was reassured to see that he seemed wholly serious. "Perhaps not vibrators," she corrected herself, "but maybe exercise machines, depilatory devices, those sorts of thing could be built into the sex part."

"Maybe vibrators, too," he said. "Several ethical companies are entering the field."

"It would need a lot of testing," she said dubiously.

"The vibrators?" He grinned at her, making her blush from her neck to her forehead.

"No, of course not," she said crossly. "The whole program."

"Of course," he agreed, immediately serious again. "But I really think we've got something worth pursuing. The sale of the appliances probably makes the whole thing economically sound."

"Particularly since Magnatel is already paying for its appliance brochures. We could include a questionnaire at practically no extra cost."

"And we could cross-promote." His own creative juices were flowing at full stream now. "Put the food questionnaire in with food appliances, and then build a sales pitch for the other programs into each computerized food booklet the customer receives."

"Sell the appliances with every segment of the computer program, and the programs with every appliance."

"We could also sample," he said, thinking of yet another new approach.

"How do you mean?"

"Well, we don't have to give out the whole questionnaire and charge people the full price. We could print partial questionnaires, say only the food section, and give them a sample of the whole program for only a buck."

"That's great," she responded instantly. "Because we'd have something to offer customers which they could send in with their payment installments . . ."

"Installments?"

"Why, yes," she said innocently. "Obviously appliances have to be sold on an installment-payment basis. They're just too expensive to sell for one-shot payment." Here was the crucial part of her sales pitch, Katy knew. She tried desperately to keep her voice casual. "Fingerhut, who's the biggest in the field, does it that way."

"But it means our money's outstanding," he said, worried about Magnatel's heavy debts.

"Not really. There are only six or eight installments and the first two pay for the cost of the appliance. Also, remember your profit is higher because there's no retailer as a middleman."

"You've done your homework," Walter said suddenly, his eyebrows raised.

For a second she feared she had gone too far. Had she seemed more prepared than she should? She held her breath.

"Do you think you could prepare a complete business plan—profit and loss and all—and then test it?"

She'd sold him. She'd won! This was a moment she'd long remember. All she had to do now was to keep cool, and keep control.

"I think I could," she said tentatively, purposely sounding unsure of herself. "With a lot of help, of course." She stopped short of simpering. "Would you let me?"

"It's not a question of letting," he said seriously. "It's a question of creating projects for yourself. You helped create this one. It's largely your idea, your vision. Naturally it's up to you to make it work."

"You mean you'll let me control it?"

"Of course. As long as it works, we move forward. If it doesn't it'll kill itself. You can start right away with the testing, so you'll be ready as soon as the Magnatel deal is signed."

"But don't you want to have control?"

"I'll have control," he said smiling at her. "I'll be watching you all the time. Which reminds me—talking of diets, isn't it about time I invited you for dinner? This evening?"

"Oh, I am sorry," she said politely. "But I already have a date." It was a lie, of course, but he had sounded so sure of himself. Well, no thanks, that wasn't for her.

"Okay," he said, hiding his surprise that she had turned him down, "then I'll just have to watch you from afar."

Perhaps he would, she thought. But he'd have to watch very closely indeed to see what she had in mind.

Caroline entered the second Katy left the office. "Did you have a good weekend?" she asked, her imagination running riot as it did every Monday.

"As far as I recall," he assured her with a smile. "All the girls seemed to think so." He was rewarded by her look of outrage. It always amused him that women were willing to do almost anything, but were generally shocked to hear those very things talked about.

Caroline turned quickly to business. "Fred Pogue wants to know whether you have a client who could use about a hundred thousand watches. He says he owns them at half wholesale."

"Has them on a barter deal, probably," Walter murmured. "Maybe in exchange for hotel rooms which only cost him half their rack rate. . . . Yes," he added after a moment's thought, "I think we may have someone for those watches. Get me Mike Jackson at Consolidated Paper. They use premiums by the ton."

"I thought they sold toilet tissue."

"They do. But they get bigger displays and more push by giving premiums with every order. I was once in Jackson's office when a buyer called to ask how much paper he'd have to buy to get a Cadillac as a premium," Walter chuckled. "Twelve thousand cases, Jackson said."

"And he bought it?"

"He did. About two hundred thousand dollars' worth of toilet tissue."

"And they got him his Cadillac?"

"Absolutely. As a matter of fact, he probably got it a hell of a lot faster than I'm getting Jackson right now." Walter grinned, but Caroline knew he was serious.

"Oh, very well," she said and hurried out to make the connection. How exasperating he could be—particularly when he was right!

"Mike, I've got some premiums you might be interested in," Walter started as soon as Caroline connected him. "A hundred thousand watches at half wholesale. . . . Of course they're good. . . . No, not hot. . . . Okay, I'll send you samples. . . . Good to talk to you." He hung up and buzzed Caroline to return. "Get Pogue to send Jackson watch samples right away," he ordered as she entered. "I think they'll go for it. What's next?"

"Those gauchos never got to Mitty."

"Why the hell not?"

"Held up in customs."

"Don't we have someone on it?"

"Yes, Samuelson."

"Then tell him to start earning whatever we pay him. Or better still, get Katy to do it."

"He wondered if you had some contacts in England," said Caroline coldly. She rather liked young Samuelson in the trading department, and she was getting to dislike that climbing Katy Rochester a great deal.

Walter eased off. "I don't have contacts with anyone who wears gauchos," he said and grinned at his secretary. "Anything else?" he asked quickly, before she could again stray from the subject.

"There's a pile of telephone calls. I'll bring them in."

"Yes, and the mail."

"Okay, if I can carry it."

For the next hour, helped by Caroline, Walter waded through the incoming mail: inquiries from prospective premium buyers; questions from consulting clients; real-estate offers; investment prospectuses nicknamed "red herrings." He dealt with most papers very fast, either throwing them away unread or barking a brief order to Caroline. "Write them we're not interested." "Ask for more information." "Yes, if they can cut the price to under a dollar." "Set up a meeting." "Let Samuelson handle this—but more effectively than he handled those gauchos." Only the more important mail did Walter bother to read carefully. Some of it he put aside for careful thought later. He only hoped he'd have the time. For weeks now he'd been snowed under by Magnatel papers.

"Joe Hargraves wants to see you," Caroline interrupted, referring to Walter's chief assistant. "There's been a problem with the API contract."

"Send him in." Walter was instantly worried. API was one of their largest consulting clients, and had been for years. They always had several different projects working there, good for maybe a quarter of a million dollars gross income a year.

Hargraves bustled in. He was a worried, round-shouldered, moon-faced man whose stocky frame was running to fat and whose forehead wrinkled almost to the middle of his bald scalp. An accountant by training, he was most at home when poring over balance sheets whose secrets he could unearth at a glance; least comfortable when faced with a creative business problem broader in scope than just the bottom line; and worried sick when he had to take personal responsibility for the outcome of anything at all.

"What's the problem, Joe?" Walter asked a shade impatiently. Hargraves always saw the black side. "Which one of our edifices collapsed this time?"

"It really is serious," said Hargraves, wrinkling his brow until it looked like the rippled sand on a wide beach. "It's been building for weeks." His voice was surprisingly high and rapid. "We've tried our best on the latest API consulting contract, but Leonetti won't buy it. I'm afraid he losing confidence in us, if he hasn't lost it already. We could blow all our business with them."

"Hold on a second. Start at the beginning."

"You know that Jimmy Leonetti, an ex-trucker—Tough Jimmy,

they call him—became president of API two years ago."

"Of course I know all that. Jimmy's an old friend."

"They pushed out the previous management, who really messed up in spite of everything we advised and helped them with—"

"Then he raised enough money to pull the company out by selling off half its cosmetic subsidiary," Walter interrupted impatiently. "I know all that; you don't have to go back to Adam and Eve." It was a phrase his mother had often used, Walter realized with a start. He hadn't heard it in thirty years, and that it should pop up so spontaneously unnerved him.

"So Leonetti asked us to propose a new study on improving API's snack business," Hargraves hurried on. "But when we did, he said we weren't offering anything new. . . ."

"Were we?"

"Well, I suppose, in a sense, maybe not."

"Goddamn it, if we weren't we don't deserve to get the job. No one's going to pay a consultant for nothing."

"Well, we tried."

"The road to hell. . . ."

"I know, I know. But if they'd given us more of a chance."

"Look, Joe, Tough Jimmy doesn't owe us anything. It's up to us."

"I knew you'd say that. And you're right. We were overworked, and we simply didn't do enough preparation."

"Do you need more help? Seems to me you had as many people on that job as you should need." Walter studied his assistant. Hargraves was a good man, but a chronic complainer. You couldn't give him everything he asked for; you'd be broke if you tried. On the other hand, if they really were short-staffed, Walter would have to do something.

"Of course we need more people; we always do." Hargraves looked at his boss whimsically. "But in this case it was different. We tried to come up with a new idea. But it didn't spark, and with the meeting date getting closer, we settled . . ."

"You should have called me."

"Yes sir. But you were working on Magnatel."

Walter moved not a muscle until his assistant had left. He should have been irate; in the old days he would have exploded. But what the hell, he thought now, it's Magnatel that really matters. That's why he wasn't concentrating, not fighting hard enough. He should have been at API. "It never works without me," he muttered. His clients just wouldn't settle for second stringers. Poor Joe. He was fine for follow-up, but he'd never make the first team. That's why he was working for Walter Cort, Inc., and not out on his own. Walter wondered what would happen when the Magnatel deal was consummated and he'd have no time left for consulting. Oh well, he'd worry about that when it happened.

"Ask the licensing heads to come in," he said to Caroline, taking his mind off the consulting problem by looking at something different. He couldn't do much about Leonetti right now, anyhow.

Licensing the names of designers, sportsmen, socialites and stars had been a new idea ten years ago, when Walter had been one of its pioneers. Endorsements had, of course, been well-known: There had always been celebrities anxious to emote for cash about how wonderful some product was. But in those days the use of a celebrity's name on the brand itself was unusual.

Walter Cort, Inc., was a medium-sized licensing agency representing nine couturiers of varying degrees of fame; five celebrities, ranging from Hollywood's best-known sex symbol to an English earl; eight sportsmen; and six companies with widely known names that could be licensed outside their own fields. As agents, the company kept ten to twenty percent of all licensing income they pulled in for their clients.

Walter normally attended the weekly reviews of the company's licensing activities. But as he walked to the conference room, he realized that he had missed the last three briefings. He hoped nothing had gone wrong in his absence.

The head of the licensing department was as tiny and optimistic as Joe Hargraves was plump and worried.

"Well, how are things?" Walter asked.

"Marvelous," said Billy Wilson. "Except for one small problem, everything's great."

"What's the problem?" Walter's heart sank. When Billy admitted to even the smallest difficulty, the situation was usually drastic.

"We've reviewed our performance to date," Billy said in a businesslike tone which, knowing his normal optimism, Walter took to be positively somber. "While we expect to pick up some new clients soon, we must tell you that with our current roster, our gross income will be nine percent below last year."

"Good God!" said Walter. "How come?"

"The main reason is that we lost Pirandello," he said, referring to one of Italy's best-known fashion designers and the company's most lucrative licensing client.

"What do you mean we've lost them?"

"The contract came to an end and Pirandello's people chose not to renew," said Billy sadly. "Of course," he added, "we still get our share of all licenses we wrote earlier. It's just that we can't develop new ones."

"But why didn't he renew?" Walter demanded. Pirandello had been a friend for years. "What happened?"

"He felt he wasn't getting as much personal service as he used to," Billy was saying. "I did my best, but. . . ."

Walter knew exactly what Billy Wilson, tactful down to his bootstraps, meant: Walter Cort wasn't there when he was needed. Even though Pirandello was not especially demanding, he did want to see the boss at least occasionally.

"I would have told you, but you were so tied up with your German deal. . . ." The telephone interrupted and Walter picked it up, knowing it must be for him. Only Caroline was allowed to break his no-interruptions rule.

"Yes?" Walter answered impatiently.

"Fred Pogue wants you to call immediately. His number is—"

"I know his number," Walter interrupted. "Thank you." He quickly dialed. "Walter Cort here," he said. "I'm returning Mr. Pogue's call."

Fred was on the line in an instant. "Listen," he said, "that cocoa deal you set up for us looks as if it's breaking."

"Why?"

"The price of cocoa beans has dropped so fast that your purchaser has gone into the open market and covered himself for cash."

"Are you sure?"

"No. That's why I'm calling."

"I'll call you back." Instantly Walter called Caroline back. "What's the number of the cocoa people?" he demanded. He scribbled it down.

"By the way," she said before he could hang up, "Mr. Jackson called to say they don't want those watches."

"Shit," he said and slammed down the receiver. How long was this lousy luck going to last? It seemed it had been going on for weeks. Without pause, Walter dialed the number Caroline had given him. "Jim Nicholls, please," he said as soon as the connection was through. "Walter Cort here; I'd like to speak to him immediately."

After only a short pause he heard the voice of his client. "I was expecting your call. Everything you heard was right. Sorry."

"You bought the cocoa?"

"Yeah, the price dropped to a three-year low. I was afraid it might shoot up again, so I covered myself for a year. Even on a barter deal, you couldn't match the price to which cocoa has dropped. At least I didn't think you could, and I had no time to find out."

"Just checking. No problem," said Walter doing his damnedest to hide his disappointment. There was no point in explaining that, at any price, barter would have improved the deal. Now that his commitment was made, why argue the point and get his friend mad?

"Sorry. I know you did a lot of work on it."

"Never mind, Jim. Really. We'll do something else together."

"Good of you to take it in that spirit." Jim Nicholls admired Walter's style.

Walter finished his licensing meeting with no good news to offset the bad, and returned to his office. He turned to the mound of papers which had accumulated. The very first one was a notice from his landlord. His rent, he saw, was about to be raised.

14

"We ran our first test ad on Friday," Katy cried exuberantly as soon as she saw Walter. It was Wednesday morning, and he had just returned from his latest trip. "The results are coming in *fantastic.*" For a Boston Rochester to allow herself such a slip in grammar the results must be spectacular, he thought wryly. And indeed Katy was almost beside herself with excitement. "We've got point two percent in the first four days. According to the projections from previous offers, that means we'll go well over one percent."

"Where does that put you?"

"At one percent we almost break even without the appliances. And at any sort of projection on the appliances, we ought to get back thirty cents for every dollar we invest."

"That *is* good."

"Let's hope it holds." She bounded out of his office, leaving behind a sense of cheerfulness as tangible as the waft of her scent.

Just as well something's going right, Walter thought, rueful now, and very aware that for some time Walter Cort, Inc., had had an almost uninterrupted run of bad breaks. Not that he was really worried. Magnatel was virtually a certainty now. He'd spent the last two weeks liquidating his assets. Every piece of property he could sell, he'd sold. What he couldn't sell, he'd mortgaged. Every painting he had collected, he'd auctioned. Every outstanding receivables, he'd either collected or factored off to a collection agency. Now, at last, at the end of the second hectic, traumatic week, he was able to add up the total amount: It came to three million one hundred thousand dollars.

Enough to consummate the deal—even if it left him practically no other asset except Walter Cort, Inc. And the way that was going, he wasn't sure how valuable it really was.

"Your car is waiting, Mr. Cort," Caroline interrupted him.

"Very well," he said with a sigh. "I'm on my way." This was certainly not an assignment he had been looking forward to. Twice before they had tentatively recommended against the acquisition by Pittsburgh Steel and Iron, one of their clients, of a small mechanical tools company. Twice before the client's middle management had asked them to dig for more facts. Now it was up to Walter to make the final presentation.

"Good morning, Mr. Cort," the pilot of his private plane greeted him as he alighted from his helicopter at Teterborough Airport in New Jersey. "We have clear weather to Pittsburgh, and our flight time will be just under two hours. I've put your breakfast aboard."

"Fine," Walter said, "so we're ready to go?"

"No one coming with you today, sir?"

"No. I'm all alone. They trusted me."

The pilot laughed dutifully. Walter clambered into the plane, and within minutes they were flying toward Pittsburgh.

Henry Streicher III, president and chief executive officer of Pittsburgh Steel and Iron, Inc., was an arrogant, white-haired patrician in his late fifties who had inherited the huge industrial empire founded by his grandfather. He had ruled it idiosyncratically but competently ever since. Earlier in his career he had spent enormous sums to run for Congress, but he had lacked the personality to pull it off. Voters tended to dislike him. Many people did. Instead, he had been appointed secretary of commerce by a Republican president grateful for major campaign contributions. Once the Democrats returned to power, Streicher returned to supervising PSI from an eyrie atop the company's skyscraper. Two walls of the office were floor-to-ceiling glass.

"A magnificient view," Walter commented as he entered. Secretly he was delighted that his own office view was even more spectacular.

"I'll give you a guided tour of downtown Pittsburgh," said the president, waving his arms toward the windows. "Do you know it, by the way?"

"Not too well, although I've visited here a number of times since we started working for you." Walter never missed the chance to emphasize how closely he was involved with his clients.

"Follow me, then." Streicher walked to one corner of the bank of windows. "Just to your right is our airport. We bought it to make sure we get priority for our planes."

"Very interesting."

"Next to that, the harbor. That's my yacht, and on the other quays you can see our ore boats."

Again Walter murmured something appropriate.

"On the left," said the president, moving along the glass wall, "is our first steel mill. Of course we have bigger ones now, but it's still profitable—although labor is a problem."

"Yes," said Walter. "We've studied your labor problems."

"Quite so," said Streicher. "Next to that is our shopping center. Originally it was to be a service to our employees, but now it's a profit maker in its own right."

Walter was becoming irritated. Partly it was his host's boasting; but mostly it was the realization that, even with Magnatel—and even if he lived to be a hundred—he would never build an empire one tenth the size this man had inherited. That took generations. And it took just as long, he thought cynically, to take it for granted.

"Next to that you see a group of tall apartment buildings," the president was continuing.

"I suppose you own those too," Walter interrupted acerbically.

"No," said Henry Streicher, not realizing the effect of his words on Walter. "Those belong to my sister."

After luncheon with key PSI executives in a private dining room, it was time for Walter's presentation. For three months his staff had been studying whether PSI should acquire Martin Tool, a small mechanical tool company. Last week they had told Walter that they were strongly and unanimously opposed to the acquisition. After hearing their reasons, Walter agreed. Moreover, he was pretty sure that most of the PSI executives now present also opposed it; he could read it in their faces and had heard the hints during lunch. These men, neither stupid nor inexperienced, knew that Martin was in difficulties. They knew too that one or several of them would end up taking the blame if it failed. Each man was determined that it not be he. Each man, too, was determined not to air his views until it was clear what the boss wanted. And probe though he might, Walter could not be sure what Streicher felt.

The men settled themselves quickly around the long, dignified, board-room table.

"Twelve weeks ago you retained my company to study whether PSI should acquire the Martin Tool Company," Walter commented urbanely, no trace of his nervousness apparent. "Today's meeting is to present our recommendations. To save your time, and to make sure there are no misunderstandings, we have prepared a short summary presentation." Long ago Walter had learned that such a presentation was essential for agreement. Documents, however well written and argued, were rarely effective in large corporations. Most senior executives were so busy attending meetings and writing their own proposals, they rarely had time to read other people's. "Since all of you are busy —and our findings are cut and dried—you can expect to be out of here by three-thirty."

Walter noticed Henry Streicher starting to frown. "Of course," he added hurriedly, "I shall stay as long as you like. I warned my pilot it might be a long wait." No harm in reminding the client that Walter Cort, Inc., could afford a company plane. "So let me commence. . . ."

As Walter talked, easily and persuasively, he turned the pages of a flip chart which looked as deceptively simple as if he had casually pulled it together himself. In fact his staff had labored over those charts, reviewing them until they were as lucid as they could possibly be. Clarity of presentation, Walter believed, was almost as important in consulting as content.

As he turned the charts, Walter studied his audience. Blank stares returned his glance. Only Streicher's face showed any expression: a barely perceptible frown, a crinkled eyebrow, momentarily pursed lips—all clues of precisely the reaction Walter had feared. Obviously Streicher wanted to go ahead at any cost. Whatever Walter said, he would never convince him how foolish buying Martin Tool would be.

But although he realized it was virtually hopeless, Walter had no thought of giving in. Persistently and systematically, he built his case against the acquisition. So what if Streicher merely became more impatient? Walter had a job to do. Making the sale became vital; nothing else seemed to matter. It became almost an affront, an insult to his professionalism, that he could not elicit agreement.

Don't become too strident, Walter warned himself. Don't oversell. Streicher will think you're protesting too much.

But looking at Henry Streicher's face, glowering more deeply each moment, Walter found it incredibly hard to hold to his own point of view without overreacting. It was as if the only way to avoid being beaten by Streicher's sheer strength was to overemphasize. Christ, Walter thought, the power of the man! Three generations of power, plus Washington, plus those untold millions. No wonder he's tough to withstand.

"And so for the key reasons cited, it is the recommendation of Walter Cort, Inc., that PSI not proceed with the acquisition of the Martin Tool Company," Walter concluded firmly.

There was total silence except for a subdued snort from Henry Streicher. Not a face changed its expression; only the wrinkles on Henry Streicher's forehead seemed to deepen.

With a barely concealed sigh Walter closed his flip chart and sat down, looking a lot more relaxed than he felt. "Well, gentlemen," he asked, "are there any comments?"

The silence in the room remained absolute. Everyone waited for Henry Streicher to speak. He was an unpredictable man, his staff knew, sometimes willing to delegate responsibility and take advice, at other times quick to fire a man for having his own point of view. No one would commit himself until the boss's mood was clear.

"Well," snapped Streicher, "what do you think?" He waved his hands at his executives. "Doesn't one of you have an opinion? Someone?" He pointed at an elderly, tired-looking gentleman, who seemed to shrink lower in his chair. "Smothers, you're supposed to be the chief financial officer around here. What's your view?"

Joel Smothers held only one view: He wanted to keep his job until he reached the retirement age of sixty for a full pension—only three years to go. "I believe," he said judiciously, "that Mr. Cort has presented an interesting idea. And I assume," he said addressing himself directly to Walter, "that you will be willing to advise us on alternatives to acquiring Martin Tool."

"If that were useful to you," Walter said carefully.

"For a fee?" Smothers asked.

"What?" Henry Streicher's voice was filled with suspicion. "An additional fee?"

Clever of Smothers to have turned the question so adroitly; no wonder he had lasted so long. "It is premature to talk of further fees," Walter said quickly.

"It is not premature to say we're not going to pay any," said Henry Streicher.

Walter ignored the rudeness. "I believe we were waiting for Mr. Smothers to give us his views," he said instead, smiling at Joel.

Balls, thought Smothers, but no hint of his annoyance showed. Instead, very calmly, he embarked upon a reasoned reply. "I believe that Martin Tool could be an interesting acquisition for PSI," he said. "Possibly there are, however, alternatives. So it seems to me . . ."

"Get to the point, for Christ's sake," said Henry Streicher violently. "You think we should buy Martin or not?"

Instantly Joel Smothers, who had not worked for Henry Streicher for twenty years without understanding the man, knew that Streicher intended to buy the company regardless of all advice. He'd be retired before anyone would have to admit it had been a mistake. For just a moment he felt pity for Walter. But the feeling only lasted a second.

"Definitely," he said. "I do not agree with Mr. Cort. I believe we should certainly buy Martin Tool."

"Does anyone disagree?" Streicher demanded.

"Definitely not." "Certainly not. "Agree completely." The voices tripped over each other in their eagerness to concur.

"Mr. Cort, there seems to be no one in the room who agrees with you," said Henry Streicher loudly. "So we shall ignore your advice. That's all. You may bill us for the work your company has completed, but no more. Good afternoon." He arose and, like an emperor followed by his sycophants, flowed out of the room.

Wearily Walter gathered together his papers, found his own way to the elevator and left the building.

"Back earlier than you anticipated," the pilot observed cheerfully.

"Right. Let's go back to New York."

As soon as they were airborne, Walter poured a stiff Scotch and opened his briefcase to work on something different. No point in berating himself; he couldn't expect to win every time. Yet he knew he could have won: not by adding another word to his presentations or changing a chart, but simply by having spent enough time with the client. If he hadn't been concentrating on Magnatel, he could have spent time with Streicher in Pittsburgh, gradually building rapport and winning his trust. Then they would never have had to have a showdown like today. As it was, Walter realized bitterly, he had failed both his client and himself. And he hated to fail.

Idiotically, he felt like a small boy, ready to cry. At the same time he felt jumpy, as if his heart were pounding, as if his limbs wanted to jump, to run, but were forcibly restrained. His mind, body, head, all of him was tense. No, he thought, not tense exactly, hyper-alert. As if now by alertness he could reverse his earlier failure.

By the time Walter landed in New York, he had drunk two more Scotches. He felt more undirected than tense, but still deeply dissatisfied, totally at a loose end.

"Thanks," he said automatically to the pilot, "a good flight." He alighted and watched his limousine approach. Near him a larger plane taxied into place and switched off its engines. The door flew open; two businessmen and a worried stewardess emerged. They looked around, evidently annoyed, gesticulating. The girl hurried in Walter's direction. "Excuse me," she called, an attractive young women, obviously upset. "Our limousine hasn't come, and my two passengers are frantic to get into New York. Could you give us a lift?"

"Sure."

"Oh, thank you." She waved them over.

Walter let the two men ride in the back, putting the girl in the front seat between Nathaniel and himself.

"Where can I drop you?" he asked over his shoulder.

"Midtown, please. Anywhere that's convenient. We appreciate the ride."

They parted at Fifty-eighth Street and Lexington Avenue.

"And you?" he asked the girl. "Will you join me for a drink?"

"I'd love a drink."

"Then we'll go to my apartment."

"You needn't wait," Walter told Nathaniel, taking the girl's bag. "I'll get Jackie to her hotel." He hoped he'd got her name right.

"Okay, Mr. Cort."

Awed by the apartment and its manservant, impressed and attracted by Walter, it took Jackie only moments to decide that she wanted to stay for one night at least.

A pretty creature, Walter thought appreciatively, and he had nothing else to do. He sat next to her on the couch. Leaning over, he gently removed her glass and set it on the table mat. No point in leaving a ring on the table. She held up her face to be kissed.

"Oh, honey, I love that," she whispered as he stroked first her breasts and then her thighs, kneading her buttocks gently. "Do that some more."

He continued working his hands gradually over her.

"Do it more, honey, do it more," she urged.

A limited vocabulary, he thought, hardly able to concentrate. His mind was on other matters: the Pittsburgh fiasco; the continuing Magnatel negotiations; Walter Cort, Inc., and its future. . . .

"Ooh, that feels good," she repeated. "Do it more."

Automatically he helped her shed her clothes. She looked quite attractive when she was finally nude, her clothes strewn over the floor.

"Now you," she whispered. "I want to see you."

Walter took off his tie and started to unbutton his shirt. He was beginning to concentrate on her at last, to enjoy. He removed his shirt.

Good God! He froze in mid-action just as he was undoing his belt. It wasn't possible. Nothing. He was not hard, not even slightly.

"What's the matter?" she sensed his hesitation.

"Nothing," he said quickly. "Nothing at all." If he took his pants off, she'd realize. "You're gorgeous," he said desperately and bent forward to kiss her breasts. His hands ran the length of her body. Surely any moment now.

"Do it more. That's *lovely,*" she said, wriggling underneath him as he gently bit at her nipplies and started to stroke her pubis. "God that's *great!*"

Nothing. He moved down the sofa so he was kneeling on the floor, his bare torso between her legs. At least she couldn't touch him like this. He licked her stomach and moved his face lower. Now it would start; it always had before. It *must.* He tugged at her labia, pulling the lips apart, enjoying the warm, womanly scent of her. Nothing still. His tongue started to flick between her lips.

"That's fantastic, honey. Fantastic!" She was moving her hips against his face. "Do it *more.*"

He realized she was on the edge of orgasm. But she couldn't come yet. He wouldn't let her; he hadn't so much as stirred. He slowed down deliberately, feeling excited and worried in equal measure.

"Don't stop," she cried. "Don't stop!" she wailed louder. "Go on, go *on!*" Very carefully he kept her at just that point, first for seconds, then minutes. After ten minutes she could stand it no longer. "Please," she begged, "please go on."

He gave her another squeeze, fascinated now by the physical animal before him, excited that he could arouse her to such passion, but outside himself, a nonparticipant. One more stroke, one tiny extra squeeze, and she was over the top, unable to control the shuddering of her body, screaming in her orgasm.

"God, Walter," she said, as she finally came down to earth. "I've never had it like that before. What did you *do?*" She lay back panting.

It was a few more minutes before she realized that he was still not ready. "What's the matter, honey? Don't you want to?" she asked, suddenly guilty about what she perceived as her selfishness. "Are you feeling blue?" The silliness of the phrase embarrassed Walter mightily.

"No," he said, "I'm fine." More than anything else he wanted her out. This was just awful. "Look," he said, "I've got some people coming in. Is it all right if I ask Mortimer to take you back to the hotel?"

She didn't know whether to be shocked or understanding. "I guess so," she said doubtfully.

"Good," said Walter. He arose, adjusted his clothing, and hurried out of the room. "Mortimer," he called. "Help Miss, uh, Jackie back to her hotel."

"Yes, sir."

Walter walked through the hall to the master bedroom and undressed slowly. Few of his girls entered here. Judith did, but then she had invaded the whole house in spite of Mortimer's best efforts. But the casual girls, like Jackie, were only invited as far as the living room or a guest bedroom. Walter had always liked his privacy; now he was deeply grateful for it.

God, he thought, what's wrong with me. He flung himself onto the bed. What a horrible day, he thought, what a horrible, horrible day.

He was terrified, fleeing in a wet wood at night, lighted crazily by the beams of a hundred searchlights. He was eight or nine, but with the understanding of adulthood. As the beams hit the wet tree limbs and trunks, they shone silver for a split second. It made the forest look as if it were illuminated by a million small flashes of lightning.

He dashed from dark to dark between the searchlight beams, ducking behind trees when the light came too close, falling flat on his face into the leaves when there was no tree to hide him.

He knew just where he was going: to the caves at the far end of the forest. It was a terribly long, perilous journey, he realized, but he had to get there, he just had to.

Happiness dwelt in the caves. As he fled between the searchlights and the trees, he could not quite remember what the happiness was, but even this far away he could feel its influence reducing his terror.

As he got closer to the caves, he became less frightened, more cavalier about the searchlights. He let their beams come closer before he ducked behind a trunk or jumped into a ditch. Once, becoming overconfident, he was almost caught. A beam actually touched the heel of his foot. It seemed to trip him and he winded himself falling. After that he was more frightened again and more careful.

An infinite time seemed to elapse as he ducked and dashed through the black and silver night, but he didn't tire or despair. The caves were waiting for him, holding their gift of inexplicable happiness.

Then he knew he was there. He sensed a halo of light which might have been morning. Ahead, the trees thinned. Only one searchlight, bluer and narrower than the rest, still probed to find him, sweeping over the empty ground in front of him like a fluorescent sword.

He dropped to his hands and knees and crawled as fast as he could across the clearing. On the far side he could see the face of the cliff. He ignored the pain in his knees. Already he could distinguish the darker shadow in the cliff which he knew was the cave's entrance.

That was when the blue searchlight caught him. It pinned him to the ground as surely as a collector pins a butterfly. He could feel the searing pain, but that was minor compared to the awful knowledge that now he would never reach the safety, the warmth he knew was in the caves.

He screamed once, a heart-rending cry of loss.

It was Bundle who awoke him, licking his face in near-panic.

Much later that night Walter sat alone in his study. There was no point in trying to sleep; the dream would return. He knew it would not let him alone now until he'd made his decision.

The study windows overlooked an empty, silent street. Clouds covered the night sky, making it as opaque as velvet. At three o'clock in the morning, even New York had ceased its bustle. The street's emptiness was accentuated by the rare night person scuttling between the widely separated patches of light thrown onto the sidewalk by occasional street lamps.

Walter was tired, but not sleepy. He had told Mortimer earlier to put through no phone calls and allow no visitors.

"Very well, sir. As long as Miss Judith doesn't come. She visits at the strangest hours."

"No one."

"I'll try." Mortimer had bolted the doors and practically lashed himself into his room, much as Ulysses had tied himself to the mast while he passed the island sirens.

As a result, Walter had remained undisturbed in his tranquil, comfortable study, but with a mind that raced and worried. Long ago he had discovered that when his life was running badly, his dream of loss and frustration would first invade his sleep and then, if he didn't deal with whatever issue faced him, would eventually plague his waking hours as well. When that happened, he had to take time out to be entirely alone. Without friends to sympathize, experts to advise or participants to persuade, he had to let his thoughts roam unchecked and allow his fears to surface. Sometimes for a few hours, sometimes for days, and once for a whole, horrible week.

Then he would permit the jackboot terrors of his youth to mingle with the inferiority feelings of his teens and the fear of failure, which had dogged all his adult life, and let them all merge with his conviction that it was only his money that kept him in demand, let him survive. Gradually he had to let his equally strong belief in his ability and strength meld into his terrors and fantasies until he had worked his way through his horrors, as he called them. Only then could he reemerge under control, strengthened, decisive about how to proceed.

So it was now; as his thoughts and feelings swirled, Walter felt himself starting to unwind. From his desk he took out a cigarette of the finest Colombian gold, neatly rolled by Mortimer. Drawing the smoke deep into his lungs, he shuddered slightly from the harsh pleasure of the feeling.

Things would keep going awry at Walter Cort, Inc., he knew, now that his real concentration was on Magnatel. Theoretically it was foolhardy to put all his eggs into that one basket, but that's where his life was leading. He'd known it for weeks now, ever since he'd gotten the commitment from Von Ackermann. Since then the acquisition, with a million details from inventory evaluation to bad debt reserves, had occupied much of his time and most of his thoughts. He'd had very little energy left over for the rest of his business. The string of failures, ending with yesterday's PSI debacle, attested to that. So he knew a decision had to be made. Was he going to take the conservative route and slow down on Magnatel, concentrating more on Walter Cort, Inc.? Or should he follow his inclinations on Magnatel and keep going for broke?

In his twenties and early thirties, he had been a quick-buck artist. Sometimes on his own, sometimes with Harry Grass, he had bought and sold merchandise and later small businesses like other men trade coins or antique cars. When he did hold onto a business long enough to run it at all, it was only to pump it up for a higher selling price or, on a couple of frightening occasions, because for a while they could find no buyer on whom to unload.

When he reached his mid-thirties, Walter had concluded, after an all-night thinking session just like this one, that his goal must be to build some dignity into his career. Gradually he had distanced himself from Harry. They still did a lot of deals together. But Harry had no part in the consulting business Walter had laboriously started ten years ago. In the last five of those years, he had partially achieved his goal. Consulting gave him great personal satisfaction—he was finally *contributing*, he felt—and at least some status.

But it was not enough. He still depended, day by day, on a new deal, a new client. With Magnatel he would have made it at last.

In the end Walter's decision came easily, almost as if he had no choice. Clearly the time had come to start a new phase of his life. Whatever the risk, it was time to stop being an advisor, a consultant, and to concentrate instead on becoming a principal. Finally he had the choice of reaching the apex of business success, and through it, security. It was a chance he could not turn down. It was time to close Walter Cort, Inc.

Walter felt suddenly exhausted. Wearily he arose from his study chair and staggered back to his bedroom. For the first time in days, he felt a sense of profound contentment.

15

Katy agreed to have dinner with Walter when the first test of her mail order program pulled 1.3 percent. By then she had refused him three times. By then, too, their business relationship had grown far closer, and she was also helping him on several aspects of the Magnatel acquisition. For one thing, he'd discovered that she spoke a fair amount of German, which was useful. Thus her refusal to allow anything more than a purely business relationship had become a source of considerable frustration to him—and of course also a challenge. As a result, he had upgraded his fourth invitation (which he had decided was the last he would issue) from his original casual assumption that she would drop everything to dine with him, to a formal request so dignified it seemed thoroughly pompous.

"I would consider it a great pleasure if you would join me for dinner tonight," he had said when she had completed her latest mail-order report. He had almost added that they could use the time to discuss the business in greater detail. That would have made it hard for her to refuse. At the last moment, however, he had decided not to force the issue. As it was, he was having trouble justifying even taking this much trouble over a date.

"I would be delighted," Katy had replied, sensing that yet another refusal could be counterproductive. It was one thing to play hard to get. With a man as accustomed to having women as Walter Cort, that was a good way to make an impression. But there was no point in going too far. "Quite delighted," she had repeated.

"Good. I'll pick you up at seven-thirty."

"I'd prefer eight," she said, setting the tone she intended to maintain for the rest of the evening. He was an attractive man, just her type physically and mentally. But her objective was far more than just romantic. That might be part of it—might even be fun—but on her terms, and under her control.

Eating at elegant restaurants was one of Walter's major enjoyments. He loved fine cooking. Even more he adored the sense of importance he felt when restaurant owners or maitre d's greeted him by name and phalanxes of waiters served him. He knew, of course, that the reason he got such obsequious recognition was that he spent lavishly and tipped well. But that was part of his enjoyment: Money meant power, and the fawning of waiters was proof that he had both.

Anxious to make a good impression on Katy, Walter chose Lutèce, possibly the most luxurious restaurant in New York. He went to the trouble of phoning personally for the reservation. Not tonight would he risk missing the best table.

But when he picked Katy up at her very ordinary apartment building and, for the sake of politeness, asked where she preferred to eat, she responded all wrong. Instead of avowing pretty ignorance and leaving it up to him, as his girls normally did, she answered firmly, "I'd love a steak. Let's go to the Palm."

The Palm Restaurant in New York was, as Walter well knew, an institution. Its sawdust-covered floors, tough, bustling, tavern atmosphere and reputation for being permanently in, attracted crowds every evening. Its enormous lobsters, superb steaks and delectable cottage-fried potatoes mollified even patrons forced to wait an hour for their tables. He would receive no special favors there. And it was noisy.

"Are you sure? It's really crowded."

"I don't mind," Katy replied innocently. The more she could keep him off balance, the better.

Walter's limousine drew up to the restaurant's thoroughly un-prepossesing entrance, a set-back doorway the uninitiated would never consider entering. They alighted, waved to the infamous-looking door-man and entered. The noise level precluded conversation; and to get from the entrance to the bar at the back they had to struggle against shoving patrons and pushy waiters. Eventually Walter managed to attract the owner's attention. "Walter Cort," Walter shouted. "For two." He extracted a ten dollar bill, hoping to shorten the wait.

The owner pushed it away. "About half an hour," he said.

"You sure?"

"I ain't sure of nothing, mister. You wanna wait or not?"

"We'll wait," Katy interrupted firmly.

"We'll be at the bar," Walter said. Turning to Katy, "What will you have?" he asked.

"A beer, please. Heineken or Löwenbräu." She pronounced the second brand in the German manner, all umlauts and diphthonged vowels. "I don't care which."

"Two Heinekens," Walter ordered. The barman ignored him. "Two Heinekens," Walter shouted over the din.

"I heard you," the barman snapped back and proceeded to serve three other guests before banging two beers onto the counter. "Four bucks," he hollered. Walter slapped a five-dollar bill onto the counter.

"Thanks, mac." The barman didn't even consider returning the change.

"You like it here?" Walter asked, astonished.

"I like the bustle," Katy said, "and the fact that everyone's equal."

"That's a disadvantage," said Walter firmly. "I've been struggling all my life not to be equal." As soon as he said it, he could have kicked himself.

"You had it hard?"

"Not at all," he said facetiously. "The world always handed me my supper. I hardly lifted a finger."

"How lucky for you." Katy pretended to take him seriously. "I thought you had to struggle for it. That would have been much more impressive."

Now Walter felt doubly cheated. "We don't all come from sophis-ticated old line families, you know." Then realizing how childish he sounded, he added, "Only the lucky ones do."

"Where *did* you come from?" Katy asked, standing very close in order to be heard over the noise.

"Poland. At fifteen. By way of Brooklyn." He laughed. "It was the logical route to the top!"

Suddenly Katy realized how very proud he was of his achievements. God, she thought, she was skating on thin ice. "You've made a fantastic climb," she said, her voice expressing awe. "Tell me about it?"

At the same moment, even though they had waited only fifteen minutes, the owner pushed his way over. "I managed to get a table for you, Mr. Cort."

"Great," Walter said. "Come on, Katy."

They were ushered to an isolated table in the corner of the upstairs dining room, where it was quiet enough to talk. The noise in the rest of the room acted as a barrier around them.

"This *was* a good choice after all," Walter said.

"After all?"

"You won't let me off easily, will you?"

"Why should I?"

"Look, I know I kind of ignored you at the start. But you must admit we're involved now and I've given you your freedom on the mail order . . ." Walter interrupted himself in mid-sentence, amazed. Why the hell was he pleading with her?

"That's business."

"And this?" he asked, trying to get back some control of what they were talking about.

She was about to speak when she saw his little trap. "Of course this is a pleasure," she said with a grin. "But that's not what it's all about, is it?"

"I have no idea what you're talking about!"

"I was supposed to answer your question, 'Pleasure,' and then you would say, 'So why give me a hard time?' But the point is, quite apart from games people play, that I want to keep business and pleasure separate. Even treating them as if they were at opposite ends of one continuum suggests they are the same type of activity. But they're not."

"What are they then?"

"Business is what we do together mostly. It's the area where you are far more successful, and much stronger than me—even more worthy, I suppose, at least for the time being. That was the point you were making at Harvard. But pleasure is when we're just two people, and the questions of status, strength, worthiness—all those comparisons— don't come into play."

"Do you really think relationships can be split that way?"

Katy looked at him sharply. "Yes," she lied. "I certainly do."

"Okay," he said amenably, "I'm game. We're equals. No business. But I imagine I'll transgress, so you're welcome to push me back down if I do."

"Oh, we can *talk* about business," she said quickly, knowing that would be to her advantage. "Just not *do* business, together."

He laughed. "I don't think you know what you're talking about."

Instantly she bridled. Then with an effort she relaxed again. No point in letting an argument start, she decided, particularly as for the moment she was well in line with her main objective of keeping control. "Maybe you're right," she said. "And to show I don't hold grudges, I'll show you a 'Dear Katy' letter I have with me. It's rather sweet, and fairly typical."

"A what?"

"When people send us their filled-out questionnaires, they often write personal letters to go with them. And they address them to the signature at the bottom of the ads—which happens to be Katy Rochester."

"Happens to be?" he asked, smiling.

"Well, we had to use some name. And get legal clearance in a hurry. It seemed an obvious choice."

"Of course."

"Anyhow, that's why we call them 'Dear Katies.' " Naturally I don't answer them myself, but they do all get answered. Some of them respond again to the replies and we find ourselves with a full-length correspondence going. Eventually, if we can't end it, I get involved myself."

"Is it worth it? Do we get a lot?"

"Sure. I think so. Not a lot in percentage terms. But quite a few thousand. And they're the really loyal customers. Some of them are obviously lonely; others just love writing letters. But either way they form a hard core who'll buy anything new we have to offer. *And* their credit's good."

"Okay already," Walter laughed. "I'm convinced. Let's see the letter."

Katy handed it across the table to him. It was very short, written in an idiosyncratic hand on pink paper.

Dear Katy,

   I've now tried your cooking, your exercise and your general health plan.

   And I want you to know, they work!

   Also, since I lost my husband, they give me something to concentrate on. So does writing to you. I'm astonished and touched that you take time

168   PETER ENGEL

to reply—or program your computers to reply—so personally.

Keep up the good work. I promise to buy your next program as soon as it's ready—unless it's on pregnancy, in which case I'll give it to my daughter.

Sincerely,
Elvira Cohen.

"But that's beautiful," Walter said, quite spontaneously. To his embarrassment his voice had a catch in it. Somehow the letter seemed tremendously universal, as if it came from a million lonely people instead of just one elderly woman with time on her hands.

"It does touch the heartstrings," Katy agreed.

They smiled at each other. It seemed as if their simple admission had broken through their reserve.

For the next two hours, as they ate their way through the steaks and potatoes, the spinach salad, the famous Palm cheesecake and finally dawdled over coffee and brandy, Katy and Walter talked at first rather carefully, then unguardedly and, at the end, passionately. Most of the time, in response to Katy's careful probing, Walter described his history. He talked nostalgically of the days before his parents were killed; touched briefly on the terrors of the forest; skirted the worst horrors of Auschwitz, which he would talk about with no one; but talked at length, with humor and enjoyment, about himself as a young man in Brooklyn. He described how he had met Harry Grass, worked with him, become his lieutenant, his implementer, his doer.

"Harry came up with the notions," Walter explained. "He still does. I decide whether they're practical. And I'm usually the one who gets them going."

"Is that what happened with Magnatel?"

"That's it. It was Harry's idea, but I'm making it happen."

In spite of warning herself repeatedly that this evening was to be purely business—and that the whole arrangement was no more than that—Katy found herself feeling a more than businesslike pleasure in Walter's company. It would not do, she told herself severely. It was fine to pretend to be attracted, however far she might have to take that pretense. But it was another thing entirely if she went and fell for this guy. She must keep her wits about her, and keep them unencumbered, too.

"Ever since I first saw you at Harvard, I've been looking forward to being together like this," Katy started. She was determined to be the manipulator, to set the pace. That way she'd be able to keep control of the situation—and her feelings—while leading him on as far as she could. "Just the two of us," she added for impact.

"I'm pleased," he said simply, feeling more flattered than the circumstances warranted. After all, why shouldn't she have wanted to be alone with him? Yet it was a relief to hear her say it.

"I've seen some of your girl friends," she said doubtfully. "They're spectacular." She had meant to keep it light, but her anxiety shone through unmistakably.

"They're different." He gave her a reassuring, slightly lopsided smile. "I've been more interested in their looks than in them as people." He saw her frown. "Does that annoy you?" For once he was not upset to have revealed something private.

"Not really," she lied. "But women *are* people, you know."

"Are they?" he asked facetiously, teasing her. But she would not rise to the bait. "Anyhow," he said after a moment, "you really are different. I don't think of you that way at all."

She smiled at him. "I think that's a compliment."

"It is." He chuckled to cover the seriousness of his meaning. "You'll be happy to know that I'm quite convinced you're a person."

It was not until their third date that Katy decided that her repeated refusals to go to Walter's apartment or invite him to hers was excessive. She was no puritan when it came to sex. Not especially promiscuous, she'd nevertheless had her share both of lovers and one-night stands. And there was no doubt that Walter attracted her.

Perhaps that was the trouble, she considered; perhaps he turned her on too much. Somehow that bothered her conscience. She'd let him kiss her a couple of times, in the line of duty, so to speak, but it hadn't felt like a very dutiful act.

But what the hell? Who said you couldn't have sex with a competitor; even an enemy, for that matter. Briefly she fantasized how Madame Rubinstein and Charles Revson might have gotten along in bed. She'd read quite a lot about them while she was working at the ad agency; two hard-headed titans of imperious will and total egocentricity. Probably they'd have spent the night arguing about who should be on top!

The only consideration, Katy told herself, was whether she would be able to keep control of their relationship if they went to bed. So far it was fine. She seemed to have his measure completely. Perhaps he was becoming fonder of her than he really meant to; but she had herself well in hand. But if they made love . . . ?

What the hell? she thought again, realizing that she wouldn't have the option much longer. He'd been remarkably patient so far, for such a hungry man. But he had looked at her quite strangely the last time she'd refused.

"Will you come back to my apartment for a drink?" She blushed in spite of herself. Damn, why did she have to use such a clichéd euphemism. They both knew that wasn't what she meant.

"Perhaps we would be more comfortable at my . . ."

"No, my place the first time," she insisted, determined not to revert to another subterfuge however embarrassed she might feel. There was no need to be embarrassed, so she would not!

"Yes," he said. "I do understand. No comparisons."

When they entered her apartment, they were holding hands. He felt as clumsy as a teenage boy and, after the horror with that damn stewardess, as nervous. Of course that had just been because he'd been exhausted. But still. . . . Paradoxically, he also felt wonderfully strong and protective with Katy. Vividly he recalled the last time he had felt like this—the day he met Rachel. And, just as with Rachel he had dared do only what she allowed, now he left it to Katy to make the first move.

She did, with gusto. The moment he turned from closing the door, she threw her arms around his neck and kissed him with all the natural innocence of a little girl thanking her daddy for a gift. Then her lips opened and her tongue probed deeply into his mouth. There was no inkling of childishness left.

With enormous relief—and gratitude—Walter felt himself getting an erection. At the same time, he realized that his desire for Katy was different. Certainly he wanted her physically, as much as he had wanted any woman. But more than that, he wanted to hold and cherish her, to protect as well as arouse her. He wanted to make love.

The bed in the corner, covered by a chenille spread embroidered with flowers, looked inhibitingly innocent, a virgin bed not ready to be defiled. Walter hesitated.

But Katy felt no such inhibitions. "Come on," she said, and pulled him after her. She threw herself diagonally across the bed and stretched her arms toward him. "Quickly."

Still thinking as much of Rachel in the park as of Katy, Walter lowered himself gently, tenderly, until he was touching the full length of her body. His legs rested on the bed between her spread thighs; the rest of his weight was supported by his elbows and by her. His face was inches from hers. He kissed her slowly, luxuriously, nibbling at her lips, teasing her mouth with his tongue, probing, exploring.

After a while, afraid that he was becoming too heavy for her, he rolled off and lay beside her, propped up one one arm, one leg thrown over both of hers. Smiling, he studied her carefully.

"What are you staring at? she demanded.

"You."

"My mom taught me it's rude to stare."

"In bed?"

"She didn't specify."

They giggled together.

"You look good," he said, still perusing. "Good enough—to coin a phrase—to snack on." He leaned over and kissed her chin, then her eyebrows, then the tip of her nose. Continuing his kisses, which were returned happily, flirtatiously, he busied himself unbuttoning her dress's buttons from throat to hem. When he couldn't manage a particular button with his free hand, she helped him. Finally, when the dress was fully open and spread on either side of her like a giant set of butterfly wings, she lifted her shoulders and slipped her arms out of the sleeves. At the same time he unhooked her bra and she wriggled out of that. Then she lay back on the center of her wings and stretched herself, her toes pointing, her arms above her head, her full breasts elongated on her chest. She looked both desirable and totally vulnerable. She was practically purring with contentment and trust, totally willing now to let him lead.

"You are feline," he said, "halfway between a kitten and a leopard."

She merely smiled at him, but with such a lascivious innocence that he was quite inundated with desire and tenderness. He leaned down and started to suck on her nipples, moving quickly from one to the other, insistently flicking them with his tongue.

After a few seconds she began to squirm and then to mew tiny cat sounds of desire. As if against her will her hands moved to Walter's head, first resting gently on his hair and then, as he continued sucking, gripping at it as if she were drowning and sought to save herself . . . "Oh, God," she gasped. "Stop. Please. It's too much. Not yet."

She was about to come, Walter realized, from just the touch of his tongue. Her responsiveness made him profoundly grateful, as if she were giving him a hugely generous, very personal gift. For a moment he considered taking her all the way at once. But then, having a better idea, he did stop. Instead he moved from his prone position to a kneeling one, his hands and knees over her legs. Leaning forward, he placed his palms on her ribcage, his thumbs just reaching her nipples, which were completely almost smooth and hard now. For a few moments he massaged them, making her writhe again. Then, very slowly, he pulled his hands down her body, pressing inward as he did so. She shuddered so hard that, for a moment, he thought she had reached her orgasm after all.

"You make every nerve jump," she said, reassuring him.

"Stay tuned. There's more to come."

"God," she said, her voice filled with desire. "I'm not sure I can stand much more. It's incredible."

Walter hooked his thumbs under the rim of her pantyhose and carefully started to peel them downward. As his hands moved underneath her, she lifted her buttocks to help him.

"Relax, I'm managing," he assured her.

"Relax! Christ!"

He continued to peel the panty downward, gradually revealing more and more of her neat blonde pubis. Finally it was uncovered completely, a golden triangle underlined, as if for emphasis, by the straight line of the rolled hose across her thighs. He rubbed his fingers acrosss her labia, close to the clitoris but not quite on it. One after the other his fingers touched her until her whole body was rigid and she was certain that just one single touch would send her over the top. Never had she felt so unutterably full. But again he stopped and resumed his task of inching off her hose. He alternated between her legs, unhurried, stopping sometimes to massage some part of her leg, her soft inner thigh, the hollow behind her knee.

When eventually he had the pantyhose down to her ankles and her whole body ached and tingled with desire, he removed her shoes, and then quickly the hose. With a sigh of satisfaction and awe he looked at her, nude at last.

"You are very beautiful," he said. He was kneeling at her feet, still fully dressed.

"Now you," she said, having trouble with her breathing.

"Watch me, then." He sat back on his heels and slowly undressed himself. She started to sit up to help him, but he refused to let her move. "Lie there," he ordered, and he was delighted when she was content to obey.

Finally Walter was nude too, his penis proudly erect and throbbing impatiently as he knelt between her feet. Placing a hand on each of her thighs, he slowly slid them up her legs. His head followed his hands slowly, so that she knew what must inevitably happen and could hardly bear the suspense.

Eventually his hands reached her hipbones and his face was so close to her pubis that she could feel his breath ruffling her hair. He stretched out his legs so that he was lying comfortably between her legs and examined her closely.

"You are beautiful," he whispered again.

"Yes," she said, agreeing with the idea. "I never thought of it, but I guess so. You make me feel beautiful."

Very carefully Walter pulled the lips apart and lowered his mouth to the precise spot between them where the tiny button of her clitoris rested, almost as hard now as her nipples. Using only the very tip of his tongue, he touched it.

"Jesus Christ, oh Jesus!" she cried out. Her body went as rigid and her hands clasped the bedclothes as hard as if she had received a massive electric shock. She felt as if her whole body was ready to overflow or explode or . . . The tension, the fullness, the tenderness, the electricity was awful, marvelous, wonderful, irresistible. "Christ," she moaned, and Walter's tongue moved again fractionally. Then as he gave her a quick series of tiny flicks, she screamed with an orgasm unlike anything she had felt or read about or fantasized. Never in all her life had she felt anything as intense.

Then he was on top of her and inside her, pumping violently. And she was screaming with one orgasm after another, as she had never done before.

After only a few seconds—which seemed like an eternity to Katy —Walter gave a great cry of triumph, relief and ecstasy as he reached his own orgasm.

So for the moment it was over. Panting with their exertion, wet with perspiration, they rolled over together and lay quietly side by side.

"You are unique," Walter said, choosing his words carefully. "I feel sublimely content."

"Me too," she said. But it was not true. Her real feelings were far too private to reveal, and far too complicated. Partly she felt surprise that her body could have such violent responses; partly she felt a warmth toward Walter which scared her. His lovemaking was too powerful; if she were not careful, it would overwhelm her. That she must never allow. Partly she felt a little guilty. But mostly she was exultant. Was she not as much a woman as any he had known? "You are a superior lover," she said with conviction. "I feel fantastic."

"Superior? Then this must be business," he chuckled, referring back to their conversation at the restaurant. "Damn, I do get confused. I thought this was pleasure."

She pretended to box his ears. Laughing, they rolled across the bed, pretending to wrestle each other. When Katy tried to squirm away, Walter tackled her; when Walter tried to hold her down, Katy scissor-locked his head in her legs. Gradually their horseplay and laughter aroused them afresh. Walter's penis, as if it had a will of its own, regained its full erection.

After a few moments she guided him toward her vagina and rubbed it against her. She was so slippery that in seconds he was deep inside her. Side by side they thrust against one another steadily as they played with each other's nipples. They reached climax together, warmer, friendlier, but less intense than the first time.

Afterward, sitting cross-legged and naked on her living room floor, they chatted like old friends as they drank brandies. At midnight Walter left to walk back to his apartment.

"It was a fantastic evening," he said before he left.

"Yes. Fantastic!"

As he left her apartment and strolled into the midnight streets, Walter was filled with contentment. He felt totally happy for once, pleased, surprised, and certain that he wanted to spend a lot of time with Katy. As much time as he could.

Katy's feelings were very different. She too had enjoyed the evening and been surprised. But as she closed her apartment door behind him, her reason for being so pleased was much more specific: She had, after all, elegantly achieved the next objective of her plan.

book two
ALL OR NOTHING

16

The black Magnatel limousine—Walter's limousine now—picked him up at the entrance of the Frankfurter Hof Hotel at eight o'clock in the morning.

"*Zu Befehl, Herr Generaldirektor,*" the chauffeur snapped to attention. "At your service."

"To our offices," said Walter proudly. "*Our* offices," he repeated, savoring the words.

Ten minutes later the limousine drew up in front of the Magnatel building. The chauffeur jumped out, seeming to remain at attention even when he was moving. He wrenched open Walter's door.

"Thank you," Walter said. The chauffeur clicked his heels so hard Walter's feet stung in sympathy.

Instead of the arrogant doorman usually on duty, the desk was staffed by a washed-out-looking young woman. She looked up slowly, her face blank. "*Kann ich Ihnen helfen,*" she asked without interest. "Can I help you?"

"Yes, my name is Walter Cort," he started, wondering whether she would recognize his name.

"Yes?"

Evidently she did not.

"I wonder if you could direct me to the *Generaldirektor's* office."

"Do you have an appointment?" Her tone indicated that she thought it unlikely.

"Not exactly. But I am expected. I'm planning to meet there with the board of directors."

"I see," she said, evidently not seeing at all and not willing to make any effort to do so.

"I wonder if you could alert the key directors." He fumbled in his briefcase for their names. "Herr Müller, Herr Leimeister, and of course Herr Dr. Schatten."

"Do you really have an appointment?"

"They are expecting me," he said, enjoying himself. "You see, I am the new owner."

177

"Yes," she said, still not understanding. "Owner of what?"

"Owner of Magnatel, dear. My name is Walter Cort. I have just bought this company."

As she looked at him, her eyes gradually widened. "You have just bought it, sir? You mean you've bought some of our appliances?"

"No, dear." He wondered how long it would take her to get the point. Even though he was rather enjoying himself, he didn't want to embarrass her too much. She wasn't so bad. Bored, perhaps, but not as arrogantly power conscious as that damned doorman. He'd certainly have to go. "No, I haven't just bought some of your appliances. I've bought the company. I am your new Generaldirektor."

She understood at last. Her face went white. *"Jawohl,"* she stuttered. "Excuse me, please. I didn't realize. . . ." She jumped up from her seat. "Is it true?" she said with amazement. She looked quite terrified.

"Yes," he said with a smile, trying to reassure her. "I am the new boss, but there's no need to be concerned."

"We had heard that there was to be a change," she said, "but we didn't really believe it."

"It will be announced tomorrow in all the newspapers."

"Then may I welcome you," she said, recovering with an effort. The tone she used was one Walter associated with oaths of office or papal blessings. "May I welcome you as the new boss of Magnatel." She made the word "boss" sound like the most formal of titles.

"Thank you," he said with another smile. "And what is your name?"

"My name is Hildegard Schmidt." She was rigid with fear and awe.

The same mixture, only slightly better concealed, was apparent in the key executives when they assembled in the board room.

"I am delighted to be here," Walter started formally, "and I look forward to a long, pleasant, and above all profitable association."

"We wish to express our welcome, sir," Herr Müller, the chief financial officer, responded with equal formality. Even though he spoke in German, he used the word "sir" in English, endowing it with the respect due a most exalted title. Dangerous men, if they were English-speaking, were to him all sirs. "May we add that we too are, as you say, delighted."

Dr. Schatten merely nodded his head in agreement. He had not said anything beyond a brief greeting since Walter had entered. Was he planning some sort of silent opposition? Walter hoped not, because Schatten could be helpful if he wanted to be. If not, well, Walter would see. It was early yet to become suspicious.

"Never too early to be suspicious," he could practically hear Harry

Grass admonish. Fucking right, Harry, he thought, and grinned.

The directors around the table wondered what their new boss found so amusing.

"Now," said Walter, "it is time to start building." He looked around the table with a stern and appraising eye. "I hope you are all as determined as I am to make Magnatel into a giant." If not, he thought, you won't last long. But there was no need to say that. The men in this room already understood the point. "Into a profitable giant." God knew, he needed the profits to pay off the debts. He got up and took off his jacket. "So, gentlemen," he said, "let's get down to work."

17

The first weeks following Walter's takeover of Magnatel were chaotic. Everything seemed to happen at once. Magnatel employees who had worked placidly for years, performing their nine-to-five jobs without thought or creativity, suddenly found themselves challenged, criticized, complimented, promoted. At any moment their new boss or one of his cohorts might appear in their office, unannounced and disconcerting.

"Why do we have seven models of hair dryers in Germany?" Walter asked the general sales manager. "Isn't that too many to keep in distribution?"

"We need a wide selection to offer the trade." The manager, a short, peppery man inordinately proud of his refined, twirl-ended mustache, had no intention of admitting that he had no good answer.

"What percentage distribution do we have by model, then?"

The sales manager hesitated. He had no figures. In fact, only recently that Helmut Schneider from marketing had asked the same question. On that occasion he had fallen back on the old salesman's trick of using a lot of words to cover his ignorance. Maybe that would work again. "You see, Herr Cort," he started, "the history of the German appliance business suggests that . . ."

"You mean you don't have the figures?" Walter remained friendly but made it clear he would accept no filibuster. "Please get me an accurate distribution check by next week. Then we can decide which models to discontinue. I'd like to end with no more than four—the top sellers, and profitable."

"Yes, sir."

Walter waved a friendly hand and smiled as he breezed out of the room. But the sales manager was under no illusion that he had a choice about getting the figures. Not that the request was unjustifed, he concluded. Perhaps the time had come when he should stop resting on his laurels and get back to work.

The response was different from Dr. Helmut Schneider, manager of marketing. A bright, professional executive who had joined Magnatel only two years earlier, he was delighted by the turn of events. Before the acquisition he had been close to quitting because of frustration. Now, finally, there would be someone who understood marketing, who would help him stand up to the sales department. To date sales had overridden every initiative, killed every suggestion he offered.

"You're right, Mr. Cort, we do have too many models. I figure we only need the three top sellers, plus one extra for the Christmas season."

"You know which ones?"

"Of course. The two hand-held models—they're profitable and sell well; I've got the figures here—and our big professional model. That's our original product and remains in demand."

"Fine. And for Christmas?"

Helmut Schneider hesitated. Dr. Schatten had specifically warned him against making any proposals to the Americans without obtaining his approval first.

Walter noted the hesitation and guessed its cause. This wasn't the first time he had sensed Schatten's restrictive hand. "Don't worry," he said. "We're just talking. This is no official proposal you're making."

"The point is," Helmut Schneider felt most relieved that Walter understood, "that we need something new. The whole market has switched toward air combs and we have nothing in that area to compete. I've been recommending for months that we launch something between a dryer and a comb. A style-dryer, I'd like to call it . . ." He paused, hoping his enthusiasm wasn't excessive. Since joining Magnatel he'd often been warned about his tendency to get carried away by his ideas.

"Go on," Walter said, matching his enthusiasm. "At last a good idea!"

Schneider grinned broadly. "I was hoping that we could launch it for Christmas this year. And then if it hits, we can leave it in the line." He paused, looking suddenly crestfallen. "The only trouble is . . ."

"What?"

"Research and development say . . ." he paused, suddenly unsure of himself.

"That there isn't time?"

"Yes, sir. They say it's out of the question."

"Do you believe it?"

"Not exactly. You see, at my last company we managed a new product launch on a similar timetable."

"Then we'll do it here," Walter said. "I'll see what I can do. In the meantime, can you get a formal recommendation prepared?"

The marketing manager became very reticent. "Well, yes, of course," he hesitated, "but I did that already and Dr. Schatten . . ."

"I quite understand," Walter interrupted. "Tell you what— I'll send my personal assistant, Katy Rochester, in to work with you. She'll have the assignment of digging around in your files; that's what she's done in other departments. If she happens to come across an old recommendation of yours, well, obviously that's no fault of yours."

"Yes, *sir.*" Helmut Schneider was delighted. This was the sort of action he had long wanted.

Katy Rochester was everywhere. Her mail-order project took up a lot of her time, but she also worked long hours on special assignments for Walter. Considering her long-term plans, she had decided, the more she knew about Magnatel, the better. Bright, cheerful and energetic, she gave Walter constant support. Frequently they traveled between America and Germany together. He was virtually commuting now, equally present and active in the gray Magnatel office in Frankfurt and in the ugly but modernistic American plant in New Jersey. Only very occasionally was she not there when he needed her.

"Sorry," she would explain. "I was seeing a printer in Grand Rapids. My office should have told you."

He always felt disgruntled when he couldn't find her, and deprived.

"Well, I missed you," he would complain.

"You just missed my body."

"That too." He would pretend to lunge at her.

At first she insisted on always getting separate rooms in the hotel in Germany; and she held onto her apartment in New York. But eventually, as they found they were spending more and more nights together, she agreed to move in with him. After all, she rationalized, she had herself and their affair under control; saving money on living together wouldn't hurt anything. Still, there were moments when she had doubts, when she wasn't so sure.

Gradually Magnatel began to respond. A new spirit of determination and enthusiasm started to build. Joe Hargraves, now Magnatel's
chief financial officer in place of the stubborn Herr Müller, who had
left in disgust, was improving the flow of management information
daily. Helmut Schneider, growing in competence and power under
Walter's tutelage, was making sorely needed improvements in marketing.
The sales manager, roused from complacency, his pride pricked, had
new energy and was whipping his sales force into a frenzy of activity.

Everywhere the company was stirring. Like some powerful bear
rousing from hibernation, it was stretching its muscles. Soon it would
be ready to start moving forward. Eventually, strong and healthy, it
would be unstoppable.

But the process could not be speeded up too much. It took people
time to adjust. Also, there was a constant money shortage. It would be
months before profits improved. In the meantime improvements had
to be made on a pay-as-you-go basis. Walter was confident that the
company would show splendid success. But in the meantime, he knew
from experience, pushing too hard too soon would inevitably be counterproductive. Wisely, having roused the bear, he left it in relative
peace for a while to warm up and test its muscles.

Thus four months after the acquisition, he was no longer frantic.
Things were moving nicely without his having to kill himself. He
remained closely involved, of course, but he could afford to keep a
reasonable distance.

He was helped in not pushing too hard by the fact that overnight
he had become a business celebrity. Charity boards, business clubs,
Washington committees—suddenly all were after his time. He reveled
in it. He had always loved to give advice, but as a consultant who
wanted money for it, he had been in a position of having to convince
others to accept it. Now, his reputation greatly enhanced and his advice
free, he was sought after constantly. And he felt wonderfully gratified
and generous in giving it. It was the first time in his life that he had
had the leisure or the wherewithal to give anything. He rarely turned
down a request.

"It's changed, hasn't it?" said Katy, looking very married as she
reclined on the sofa in Walter's living room.

"Huh?" he looked up from his newspaper.

"Everything's changed in the last four months."

"Damn right."

"Success?"

"Mostly it's you being here," he said, giving her the compliment
but not really sounding interested, and more anxious to read his newspaper than to discuss his feelings.

"No, not me. Success."

"That, too. Is it bad?"

"No, not really."

"So what are you *noodging* about?"

"I'm not really. I'm just pointing out that you've become totally different. Everything's changed."

"Is it worse, then?"

"Quite the contrary. I think it's good, basically. You're . . ." she groped for the right word, ". . . easy, relaxed, calm. . . ."

"Look," he said, "it's no big mystery. I'll be happy to tell you. It's partly that I'm finally successful, partly that I feel settled. All these years I've been grubbing around, one deal after another, one girl after another one. Now I've got both: Magnatel, and you. I don't have to worry any longer."

"You sure?" Her voice carried a strange note. He'd noticed it several times in the past few weeks. It was almost as if she wanted to say something to him but was stopping herself. It made him forget he wanted to be reading the paper.

"Shouldn't I be?"

"Of course." She hesitated, wishing she'd never got the subject started. "It's just that sometimes I wonder if . . ."

"Look," he said, misunderstanding, thinking she just wanted reassurance, "you're terribly important to me."

"Am I?"

"Katy, what on earth is the matter? What are you upset about? Are you trying to pick a fight?"

"No, but you're ignoring me."

"I am not ignoring you. We're sitting here together in the living room. I'm reading the newspaper. That doesn't mean I'm ignoring you."

"Reading the newspaper and not wanting to talk to me means ignoring me."

"I didn't particularly want to talk to you at that moment because I wanted to read the newspaper. The reason I wanted to read the newspaper is . . ."

"Don't be pompous," she said crossly.

"Love, what do you want? What's bugging you?" His voice rose.

She realized that the conversation had turned into an argument. That was not what she'd wanted. In fact, she wasn't sure what she had wanted. Perhaps just to attract his attention, to reassure herself that he was still hooked. "I'm sorry," she said contritely. "You're quite right, I did want to argue. I'm jealous of the newspaper. That's the real trouble."

He laughed at her, put the paper down and walked over to where she was sitting on the couch. Touching her face, he gently kissed her cheek. "I know, love. Sometimes it's difficult remembering that doing the mundane things together is being together, too."

"Christ, you sound like a soap opera."

He laughed again, perhaps slightly more strained this time. "I am a soap opera," he said. "I'm mushy inside. I *feel* like a soap opera. And this whole conversation is about as interesting as a soap opera."

"Hey," she said, "you're right," and laughed. "Tune in again next week . . ."

"And nothing will have changed."

". . . and the little woman will be successful."

"What do you mean?"

"We're doing it, Walter. We're getting the mail-order business going superbly. It's really getting exciting."

"You haven't been keeping me up on the figures," he said. "Tell me."

"I hardly dare believe them."

"Go on."

"You know we've been doing large-scale tests of various approaches for the last three months."

"You've mentioned it," he teased, "about a million times. You read 'Dear Katies' for breakfast."

"Well, the first tests were mediocre."

"I know it."

"I thought the reason might be that our advertising wasn't strong enough. So we got a new creative group, and we tried a whole bunch of new selling techniques." Looking at him, she realized the moment was right. Any doubts she might have had evaporated in her excitement. "So we tried radio, newspaper, direct mail, TV," she said in a rush, "everything." Good. Now he'd heard about her using direct mail and he hadn't objected. Later, if there were any questions about why she had used that instead of some medium they could buy through barter, she could be the picture of innocence.

"So what happened?" He was only half-listening, far more interested by the animation in her eyes than by what she was saying.

"We've found a breakthrough to explaining exactly what our compu-programs are. And for selling the appliances at the same time. Just as we thought originally."

"So?"

"So," she said excitedly, "the new tests look tremendous. We're getting one and a half percent, double what we need." She was astonished by how much the figures meant to her. She felt a tremendous pride in her achievement, in the knowledge that she, Katy Rochester, was creating a business, building it from scratch.

"That would make it profitable?"

"Enormously. Enormously."

"When will we know?"

"Look, here are the figures." She dove under the sofa, where her papers had been lying in wait all day.

"If that's what you wanted, why didn't you say so?"

"I don't want to attract you with business figures," she said. "I want to attract you with me." It was an outrageous thing for her to say, she knew. And outrageous that he should fall for such crap. Hadn't he heard a word of what she was about? Her anger at his absurd chauvinism almost broke through. But no, a few more months. . . .

"You *and* the business," he said, laughing again.

"Yes, but on a different basis. Remember? We said they'd be separate. Oh, you'll never understand. You're just a man."

"Well, you're not just a woman. You're *my* woman," he growled the words.

"Let me show you the figures."

"I think I want to rape you first."

"Two million bucks profit in the first year?"

"I want to see the figures!"

Her voice, her face, her whole being was exuberant as she started to point out the success she anticipated. "Look at this. Even at one and a quarter percent return—well below what our tests show—we make a fortune."

"And the investment?"

"Practically none. We can stay within Magnatel's current advertising budget. Apart from that, it's just printing and distributing our sales pitch. We can put one in with every appliance, and do a selective direct mail campaign. And the questionnaires themselves. . . ." She realized she was not being very clear, but it didn't matter. "And we needn't spend anything until we're sure of a profit. That's what so amazing about mail order. You don't have to move until you're certain."

"You're sure we can get back our investment?" he asked, somewhat confused now, but feeling so gentle and full of love that he had no stomach for tough probing.

"Absolutely, even considering the investment in outstanding receivables." There, that was the second hurdle. And he hadn't noticed that one, either. "Anyway, we'll be able to borrow against them, so we shouldn't have a cash bind." It would be smooth sailing from here on, she realized. "From the return rate we're anticipating, we ought to get at least our investment back within half a year," she hurried on. "After that, it's all profit."

"So you're saying . . ."

"I'm saying that I've checked it all out. The cash flow works out over the year. And we make fine profits."

He was enchanted by her enthusiasm, dazzled by the array of figures—the more so because they came from such a charming girl. He hardly dared examine them closely for fear of some fatal flaw. Yet he did examine them as carefully as his mind would let him. There seemed no holes, no shortcomings. She'd done her homework proficiently.

"They look good to me."

"Do you mean it? Do you mean we can go ahead?"

"How much investment will there be in total?"

"We'll send out five million mailings or inserts. If we get a return of one and a quarter percent, that will mean 62.5 thousand sales. And if each sale is for a twenty-dollar appliance plus a twelve-dollar program, that will mean about three quarters of a million in dollar sales from each mailing. We can do six a month to start, and then larger ones later."

"And make money?"

"Of course. The cost of the appliance is about ten dollars and the cost of the program about four plus shipping and handling. So the gross profit is almost fifty percent. That's plenty to cover the advertising, mailing, printing—and give us a super profit."

"It sounds marvelous," Walter said, convinced at last. "The only thing that I don't understand yet is how we can keep getting more customers in."

"Direct mail," she said, quite certain. "We can buy lists of almost any size. Then, twenty, thirty, even fifty million households."

"But the mailing costs?"

"Eventually they'll be huge. But only after we're making money. Let me—"

"Do a study?"

"Right. To plot it all out for the future." She paused. "But for the time being, it's okay to go ahead?"

"Yes," he said, his doubts evaporating before her dazzling smile of achievement. He would just have to stop being so damned cynical, he told himself sternly.

"How is the rest of the business going?" she asked, anxious to divert him from mail order now that she'd won his approval. "I haven't been as close recently as I was in the beginning."

"Satisfactory, I guess."

"You don't seem sure."

"No, it's not that. It's only that it all takes time. Particularly since we basically lack enough cash flow. We all know what it takes to move the business forward: more deals, more advertising. But we can't afford much—certainly no advertising beyond the barter deals we did with Fred—because the Von Ackermann money is pushing us so hard."

"The Von Ackermann money?"

"A million dollars a month. We've repaid four million so far."

But we're making profits?"

"Sure. But not a lot. After all, it was barely breaking even when we took over. In the first four months we've been able to make a small profit, about half a million. And it's getting better. So I'm not worried. But it will be awhile before we start making millions."

"By when, do you think?"

"By the middle of next year, we should be running a lot more profitably. Fortunately we've got time."

"Including my mail order?"

"No, that's a bonus. If you can really make as much as you think, it would help us enormously."

"I'll try."

"I know," he said, trusting her completely. "And even if it is mixing business and pleasure, I love you very much."

He was touched, if a bit bewildered, when her eyes momentarily filled with tears.

18

Twelve million Magnatel mail-order responses a month. Half a million pieces a day. Five and a half per second, even with the mailing house working a full twenty hours a day.

The response to Katy Rochester's mail-order concept was staggering. Eight months after she had started it, the computerized diet program, now expanded to fourteen separate computerized offices, had grown beyond even her most optimistic hopes. And the appliance business, which remained an integral part of it, had grown well, too. Katy had never felt as proud of anything in her life.

But her success was bittersweet. One evening, lonely and depressed and with Walter out of town, she started to reread T.S. Eliot's *Murder in the Cathedral.* " 'The last temptation is the greatest treason,' the Archbishop exclaimed. 'To do the right deed for the wrong reason.' " Katy flung the book across the room in a wholly uncharacteristic display of anger. "Goddamn," she muttered, and stomped off to bed. "Even so," she told her mirror as she methodically removed her makeup, "for whatever reason, it *is* a success."

Everyone at Magnatel viewed Katy's achievement with unconcealed delight. Walter Cort, spending most of his time on Washington committees, doing charity work, advising on boards, basked in the success. At last he could do what he really wanted with his life, instead of constantly having to grub for money. The mail-order success was the added bonus which allowed that. He would have been astonished to know that another businessman, briefed as fully as he on everything at Magnatel from cash flow to mail order, was equally pleased—both at the performance of the company and at Walter's decreasing involvement.

Each morning the trucks rolled up to the mailing house with piles of Magnatel mail already stacked on wooden pallets ready for the fork-lift trucks to unload. The mail was treated like an industrial commodity, the raw material in a manufacturing process.

Automatic conveyor belts carried it to high-speed opening machines, which ground the top of each envelope against an abrasive wheel to open it. Then mechanical fingers emptied it. In this way any envelope, regardless of size, would be forced to disgorge its contents. Finally an electric eye looked for questionnaires and forwarded them, untouched by humans, for processing.

Banks of computers kept track of every person who bought or corresponded with Magnatel. Four million people had purchased something in the last three months. Mostly these purchases were trial offers, either for a dollar or "free, with $1.00 for mailing and handling." But almost a million had purchased a full compu-program or an appliance, and many were repeating, becoming regular customers. There were even 72,000 "Dear Katies" on file.

Walter reveled in his new status of senior businessman. Very much in love with Katy, and grateful to her, too, he had never in his life felt as comfortable and confident as he did now. At last, he decided, he had outdistanced the avalanche once and for all.

"We're having trouble with the next payment." Joe Hargraves wore an even more worried look than usual.

"What do you mean?"

It was eleven o'clock in the morning, and Walter had only just arrived at the office. Yesterday he and a group of other senior business advisors had attended a White House briefing on the state of the economy. Today Katy and he had enjoyed a long, late breakfast together. Then there had been a meeting of the board of trustees at the hospital at which he had been delighted to be elected to the executive committee. He was not ready for business problems at the moment.

"Can't it wait?" Joe really didn't need to bother him. He'd shown him a hundred times that Magnatel could run very well on its own. The company was well staffed now. It simply wasn't necessary for Walter to be constantly involved.

"No, sir," the chief financial officer tried to hide his exasperation. In the old days his boss would have known all about the problem long ago, often before he himself realized there was one. Now he couldn't even be bothered to listen when one was presented to him. Several people in the marketing department had noticed this. "Katy's the only one in that house who ever makes a decision," one of them had complained only yesterday.

Yet the money situation was serious. At the beginning it had been easy to find the million dollars a month to pay Von Ackermann. The barter deal with Fred Pogue had been working well. The mail-order business had been starting but had not yet been using up too much cash. Then for a couple of months finding the money had become harder. Somehow every department of the company seemed to need cash at the same time. And the mail-order demands had really started to grow. Particularly when Katy Rochester had insisted on using less advertising and more direct mail. Postage couldn't be bartered. Last month had been a real bitch. He'd really had to scrape. Of course he warned Walter then, but he'd been ignored. Now, this month, he didn't know what to do. His forehead and scalp wrinkled even more than usual in his worry, and at the ridge of each wrinkle a tiny band of sweat glistened.

"Okay, you'd better explain," said Walter with a sigh. "Please make it brief. I have an API board meeting this afternoon and I've got to get ready."

"It's the mail-order business that's causing us the problem," Joe Hargraves said brusquely. "It's eating up our funds."

"How is that possible? It's the most profitable part of our business."

"On paper, but not in cash."

Walter shook his head in bewilderment. "But Katy tells me that we'll do twelve million questionnaire distributions this month and sell a million programs plus nearly half a million appliances in addition to our regular business."

"Four hundred thousand," said Hargraves pedantically.

"So what? We're doing fine. How the hell can you tell me we're having trouble? Really, Joe, sometimes you exaggerate too much." Walter rose. "I'm sure you can handle it," he said kindly. "I really do have to leave."

"No!" Hargraves exploded, astonishing Walter with his vehemence. This time his boss *must* listen. "I know it's profitable," Joe hurried on. "But it's the cash that's the problem. We sell the program for an average of twelve fifty each and the appliances for an average of twenty. But we collect that over six or eight installments."

"I see what you mean." Walter had to admit that the problem might be a little tougher than he'd thought at first. But certainly not enough to justify Hargraves's near hysteria. The man was the original doomster. "All right," he said, reluctantly resuming his seat. "You'd better take me through it in detail."

"We need half of the installments we collect to pay for the cost of the stuff we send out when we receive the first payment." Hargraves heaved a sigh of relief that he had finally got his boss's attention.

"Not that much, surely," Walter interrupted. "Our cost of goods is less than half our receipts."

"True. But we have handling, mailing, administration—all tied to the items we send out. When you add all those together, that's what it comes to."

"Okay," said Walter, still not convinced but willing to defer judgment. "Go on."

"That's why it's bleeding our cash. Every time we send out a program plus an appliance, we receive about six dollars—and it costs us about fifteen dollars in cash. We have to wait another two months before we break even on the cash. And we have to pay for mailing costs, advertising, questionnaire and leaflet printing—all that stuff—before we even get in our first six dollars."

"But . . ."

"I'm sorry to interrupt you, but it's even worse than that," Joe said firmly. "You see, because the business is growing every month, Katy is increasing her spending, sending out more direct mail, doing more advertising . . ."

"Of course. How else can you build?"

"On top of that we're spending over a million dollars in direct-mail advertising, because Katy insists that her program would not work if it's advertised in regular media."

"Hold on a second," said Walter, increasingly annoyed at Hargraves's behavior. "You're throwing a lot of figures around, but they don't sound so terrible. I've looked into them before." He took a pencil and made some quick notes. "The way I figure it, even if we spend three for mailing, and one on direct-mail advertising, that's only at the rate of forty-eight million a year. Since we were spending thirty before the business started to expand like this, I don't see why that's so bad. You must have done a calculation to see whether the advertising is worthwhile in terms of increased business." Walter's tone became increasingly sarcastic as his annoyance grew. These people had been consultants long enough. They should know these basic approaches. That was the trouble, of course; Hargraves and the rest had never really run anything themselves, only advised others. Perhaps Joe wasn't the right man for the job after all. He'd had some doubts for a while now. "Look," he said, starting to rise again, "the next thing to do is to find out whether our spending levels are justified. I've felt they are. But if not, we'll cut back. The point is, as long as expenditures are within our budget . . ."

"But they can't be *bartered,*" the chief financial officer interrupted, his mouth set in a straight line, his teeth clenched, his voice anguished. "Fred Pogue can't take appliances against mailing costs. The post office needs cash. Our suppliers have to be paid in cash. The printer insists on cash. The handling charges are all cash. Instead of a twenty-seven-million-dollar saving we'd assumed on forty million dollars of media advertising, we're spending almost fifty million on advertising—nearly all cash. Altogether this year we've only saved six million dollars on barter. The rest has been out-of-pocket expense. I've tried to explain it to Katy. I've written letters. I've tried to draw your attention to it, but you've ignored me."

My God, thought Walter. He *had* ignored them. He'd hardly even read the mail in the last two months. Certainly he'd kept his eye on the overall figures, and they'd looked fine on the surface. But he hadn't dug into every one of Joe's concerns. Why bother? The man was a born worrier who saw a crisis behind every tree. Surely nothing was really wrong. Besides, for the first time in his life he was truly enjoying himself, and why spoil it? Then, too, his duties in Washington were keeping him so busy. And he'd been spending more and more time with Katy, who had assured him that everything was okay. He'd been so proud of his success. So secure. . . .

"We're behind already on our payment schedule," Hargraves was continuing. "But I've been able to defer part of that." He was becoming calmer again. "That's not a real problem, because our long-term cash flow looks fine. Once we start getting in the final installments from the mail, we no longer have a problem. Then we'll be receiving the money without having to incur extra costs." He felt infinitely better now that he had shared his burden, shifted it actually off his back and onto Walter's. "No," he said pompously, "I don't anticipate any trouble in the long run."

"So why don't we borrow against the money?"

"We are. We're borrowing about fifty percent of our receivables. But we can't get more than that because it's such a new venture. I've tried every bank and factor in town. The problem is we have no proof what our bad-debt rate will be. We think it will be low, but we have no track record to prove it. It all depends upon the ultimate acceptance of the compu-programs. If consumers like them as much as they seem to, judging by the Dear Katy's we're getting, bad debts will be very low. But the lenders point out that things can go wrong. For instance, if women don't find themselves losing weight on our diets, they may not keep paying. Then we'd be in trouble."

"Don't we have tests?"

"Sure. I don't think there's much to worry about. Consumers are going crazy for the programs. But the banks won't lend any more at the moment. We're into them for thirty-five million as it is, but there's no more to get. And nothing left to pay Von Ackermann. It's him that I'm worried about."

"How much have we paid him?"

"We've paid him seven one-million-dollar installments. We've got five to go. In two weeks' time I have to pay him another million."

"Can we delay?"

"No way. I've talked to him. He is positively joyful at the possibility of not getting paid. He'll take over the entire company, he said. He chortles when I talk to him. He baits me."

"Then we must pay him."

"I know that, Mr. Cort. I know that. That's why I'm talking to you. I just don't know how."

For a second or two Walter sat utterly still. He could feel his stomach cramping; he imagined he could even feel the blood draining from his fingertips with the shock he was experiencing. His heart pumped with as much vigor as if he had just run a violent hundred meter sprint.

Gradually, as he watched his chief financial officer anxiously fiddling with the papers in front of him, observed the man's brow furrowed and shiny to the very center of his head, the immensity of the problem dawned on him. Probably more could be borrowed against receivables. What Hargraves was saying was exaggerated. But clearly that money would be needed to finance the receivables themselves. It was most unlikely that the banks would lend *more* than enough to finance the current costs. Where would the extra money for Von Ackerman come from?

Post office has to be paid. Mailing house has to be paid. Printer has to be paid. And all in cash. Workmen have to be paid. Raw materials have to be paid. Packaging has to be paid. And all in cash. Computer runs have to be paid. Media has to be paid. Freight has to be paid. And all in cash. . . . The litany pounded through Walter's head, bringing with it in equal measure understanding and panic. He would lose the whole thing. The eye beam of the searchlight had him pinned. He could struggle, but would he ever get away? He could almost feel the sudden pain of the dream he hadn't experienced in months sharply between his shoulder blades. He almost cried out. And then, as in his dream, he almost acquiesced.

Walter remained immobilized for only a few seconds more. Then it was past. As quickly as the paralyzing knot had formed, it was followed by a wave of determination that made his teeth clench and his knuckles whiten. This time he would *not* give in. Long ago he had created his own defeat, like his father before him, because it had been too hard to fight. That time he had lost everything. But in the end he had started to fight back, and he had survived. This time he would survive again. He had become a man of action, and action would save him now. In the place of panic his adrenaline started to flow. In the place of stillness there was violence.

Walter stood up abruptly. "Very well," he said. "I understand. How long do I have to raise the next million?"

"We have to pay in in ten days."

"You can make out the check now," said Walter. "Date it the thirty-first of this month. There will be at least one million dollars in our account by the time the check clears."

"Very well." Joe Hargraves had no intention of arguing with Walter in this mood. He knew, too, that Walter would somehow find a way. Only once before had he seen his boss in this sort of mood. Five years ago, when Walter Cort, Inc., hit a crisis, Walter had mobilized that inner energy that was awe inspiring to watch. That time, at the last moment, he had raised half a million dollars. Enough—and in circumstances as tough as these.

"Very well, sir," he repeated.

20

If you wanted something from Swiss bankers, Walter had long ago learned, there was no point in agreeing to go to their offices. They took a personal visit as a sign of weakness. Perhaps if you flew your private jet to Zurich to demand a loan of anything over half a billion dollars, you might impress them—not that they'd show it. But to borrow a boring million or two, which was all that Walter hoped for, was impossible unless you managed to get the bankers to come and see you.

"I believe Mr. Cort might be willing to see you at three o'clock next Tuesday," Joe Hargraves had explained to the bank executive. "We wish to establish a solid international banking contact, and this may be the opportunity. Of course we would start small, barely a million or two. But Magnatel is already a three-hundred-million-dollar company, and we are growing. So in the future . . ."

"Naturally. Of course. If we can be of any service. As you say, nothing is too small to start."

Joe Hargraves had felt cautiously optimistic—much more so, at any rate, than he had for many days. Perhaps, after all, he had allowed his fears to become exaggerated.

The Swiss bankers, as punctual as their country's watches, arrived at three o'clock on the dot. There were three of them, rotund, black-suited gentlemen with shiny faces and steel jaws, strict as schoolmarms, conservative as bishops. They stood to attention in Walter's conference room as he and Joe Hargraves entered, and then solemnly shook hands in the order of their seniority. Each had his executive title engraved on his tasteful business card, a chauffeur-driven car outside, eight weeks of paid vacation annually, a round wife waiting patiently at home. All but the youngest had grandchildren, photos of whom each carried in a wallet along with an ample supply of cash. Walter tried to imagine the process of procreation, Swiss-style, but was stymied. Perhaps they are all factory-made, he thought, with great Swiss precision.

"We are pleased you have invited us," said the leader of the delegation.

"Please be seated." Walter smiled politely. "Can I offer you some coffee?" He felt slightly foolish, as if he were trying to make small talk with a group of store window mannequins.

"No coffee, thank you." The senior answered for his colleagues. They all seated themselves carefully.

"We appreciate your visiting us."

"You are welcome. Now we shall commence?"

"By all means."

"Very well." The banker took a deep breath, settled himself further into his chair and started his speech. "We are always most interested in acquiring solid, long-term clients for our bank," he said pompously. "That is the reason my colleagues and I have studied your company in detail." As if to prove it, he opened a large manila folder and extracted several double-size sheets of accounting paper, completely filled with figures in precise, cramped columns. "We understand that you desire a loan from us to pay off certain loans to others." He looked most disapproving. Swiss banks, he implied, would never lend money to repay other lenders.

"Not really," said Walter. "We need money primarily because we are expanding rapidly, so that our growing inventories and receivables have to be financed." How had they found out about the loan repayment?

"Our information is different. We understand that you owe a million dollars a month to a German industrialist, and that you need money to make the next payment."

Walter was shocked. "Where did you hear that?" he demanded. Then, annoyed at himself for having shown his surprise, he tried to cover up by quickly adding, "That is annoyingly loose talk, since it incorporates some of the truth and then distorts it." He tried to create the impression that he was judiciously considering whether to take them into his confidence. "As I explained, the fact is," he started to trust them, "that our fundamental need is to finance our growth. We do have certain loan repayments, of course, which are a small addition to our cash requirement." Even to his own ears he sounded unconvincing. "By the way," Walter added, trying not to sound too eager this time, "where did you get all your information about us?" Could they have found their way to Von Ackermann? He would have told them, of course. Or could Von Ackermann be leaking information throughout the international financial community? Was that even possible? Walter shook himself. *I think I'm getting totally paranoid.*

"We have our sources," said the banker, obviously more ready to believe them than Walter.

"Evidently," said Walter, fighting for control, still angry with himself for letting his surprise show. He wondered why the bankers had even bothered to visit if they were so well-informed and so skeptical. Still, he decided, he might as well pitch to the limit. "Before we discuss precisely how we intend to structure this loan, and any future borrowings," he said firmly, "I should make it clear that we are discussing the same matter with two other banks and—"

"No doubt."

"And we have some interesting offers," Hargraves added.

"No doubt," the banker repeated, as identically as a recording.

"Since we need the money primarily to finance our mail-order receivables," Hargraves started to explain, "we are obviously a strong borrower."

"Why do you not discount?" the banker interrupted. "Use the receivables as collateral on loans?"

"Of course we do," said Walter, annoyed that the man was lecturing. "We have borrowed about fifty percent of our receivables."

"That is the maximum that would be feasible under these circumstances," the Swiss said, as if he were giving Walter new information. "You have no track record."

"We appreciate that," Walter said tersely, determined to return to the subject. "The question is, what borrowing terms we can work out with you. And would they be acceptable to us," he added bravely.

"Quite so," said the banker and lapsed back into silence.

"Do you have all the information you need?" Walter asked as the length of the silence started to become embarrassing.

"We have sufficient information," said the Swiss banker. He looked at his colleagues, who lowered their eyes in tacit agreement. "But we are very sorry to have to tell you," the banker continued in funereal tones, "that we find ourselves unable to lend money to Magnatel at the moment, on any terms."

There was an amazed gasp from Joe Hargraves, who looked both stunned and crestfallen. This was worse than even he had expected. That they would turn Magnatel down without even a tactful letter of excuses. The Swiss must be convinced that company had no future to so burn their bridges.

"Then why the hell did you visit us?" Walter exploded.

"We believe we may be able to help," said the lead banker, unperturbed by Walter's's outburst, "by purchasing part of the company."

For a moment Walter saw a hope. If he could sell some shares in order to hold onto the majority. . . . But no, his contract with Von Ackerman prohibited that. Still, if he could. . . .

"Of course, we would require operating control," the banker continued, "at least fifty percent."

Walter stopped listening. Politely he arose. When he spoke, his voice was quite cheerful, masking entirely his disappointment. "No thanks. We're not ready to make a charitable donation just yet," he said with a smile. "But I wish you all the best. Perhaps later, when we are even stronger, you will want to do some banking business with us."

The Swiss delegation rose. Only its youngest member looked even a shade disappointed. They shook hands as formally as before and silently left.

"Nothing," said Walter in disgust. For a moment he slumped in his chair.

"Perhaps we shall do better with the Americans," said Joe Hargraves sounding totally pessimistic.

"Maybe," Walter agreed. "Anyhow," he added, sitting back up, "we couldn't do worse."

"Hiya, Wally," the senior vice-president of First International City Bank of New York called to Walter warmly from the far end of his immense office. "How are you? Come on in. Have a cup of coffee." He smiled widely at his visitor from behind his massive expanse of shining desk, empty except for an expensive marble pen holder and a bronze plaque with its owner's name, Homer Wallace, cast and antiqued on it. Why so vast, Walter wondered, and so empty? To connote power and efficiency? Probably. And carefully planned, no doubt.

Wallace arose quickly and hurried toward him. It seemed to take him forever to circumnavigate that desk and the desert of beige carpet to shake Walter's hand enthusiastically. "Joe Hargraves not with you?"

"He had another meeting. But we'll manage without him." Walter returned the smile, the firm handshake. "Good to see you, Homer. How have you been? How's the family?"

"They're fine. Just fine."

They seated themselves in two of the group of dark green armchairs which surrounded a heavy ebony coffee table. For a few minutes they made small talk. The room, Walter noted, smelled like a library.

"I thought I'd invite Marilyn Smith to join us," the banker said eventually. "She's a new case worker. Very bright girl . . ." he hesitated, ". . . ah, woman," he corrected himself. "We have to be careful these days."

"Okay."

The banker picked up the phone. "He said to his secretary, "Would you be good enough to ask Ms. Smith to to join us?" He spoke with slow politeness, as if he were trying to imitate a courtly Southern plantation owner in all but accent.

Marilyn Smith entered, thin, angular, thirtyish, with a sharp nose and eyes too close together. Walter was surprised at how unattractive she was. But why his surprise? He hated feelings he did not anticipate. Immediately he knew the answer. A bank of this size could employ anyone they wanted. So why a woman? Only, he had assumed, because she had a friend. But no, this had to be something else.

". . . investigated Magnatel closely," the woman was saying. Walter realized that she was going to conduct the meeting. ". . . and analyzed the figures. Your own report on it was, of course, very thorough." She smiled sourly.

"Thank you." Walter tried to sound pleasant.

"As a professional, I appreciate professional work."

Walter almost said thank you again, but decided that it would certainly sound sarcastic if he tried. What an objectionable female! Ugly—not that he would dislike her for that, if anything, a woman's bad looks might make him sympathize—but Ms. Smith was disagreeable, suspicious, with a slight mocking smile on her lips which seemed to tell Walter that she doubted every word he said.

"The problem is that the net asset value of Magnatel, at only forty million dollars, doesn't provide us with much security for a loan."

"But . . ."

"Past profitability has been unimpressive, and it's too soon to forecast the future."

"On the other hand, the name . . ." Walter started again, annoyed to have been interrupted.

"Of course, under new management the company should do better," she continued firmly. "I personally have little doubt of that. But we are bankers."

"Obviously, Ms. Smith. I would hardly be here otherwise." Walter no longer able to avoid sarcasm. "The point is that the company has a powerful name. And since we have taken over, we have started to exploit it most effectively both at retail and via mail order."

"We do agree," said the senior banker with a gush of courtliness. "Yes, indeed, Wally."

"However, we're still forced to stick to the banking rules," Marilyn Smith continued. "Even though you personally have an excellent reputation, Mr. Cort."

To his annoyance Walter felt himself start to blush at the compliment. He pretended to swallow wrong and began coughing vigorously.

"You sure do have a great reputation," her boss agreed. Then, forgetting his courtliness for a moment, he added with determination, "We don't want our competitors getting in on this deal if you're going to be a big winner in the long run." He looked shrewdly at Walter, clearly trying to assess what the chances were.

"Would you be prepared to make a personal guarantee?" Ms. Smith asked.

"A what?" Walter demanded, outraged, remembering instantly the last time he had been forced to give a personal guarantee and how painful that had become. "Of course I would not. What sort of question is that? I'm not trying to finance a corner grocery store, you know. This is a three-hundred-million-dollar company."

"Your personal guarantee would make it easier for us to lend, that's all," said Ms. Smith, surprised at his vehemence.

Walter was surprised, too. Why did her request make him so angry? It was not unreasonable. He had not had such a violent reaction in years. In a flash he understood. It was the security of Magnatel that had got him involved in the first place, the security of owning a huge international company. Finally he was . . . he searched for the right word . . . solid. Yes, that was it: solid. Not as before, when he had been always precariously in limbo somewhere between his mother's distant abandonment and the glossy but entirely unstable life he had built for himself. Now here was some sharp, distrustful woman trying to take away the one thing about the deal worth having. What the hell was the point of owning it all if he had to give up his personal security in the process?

"Definitely not," Walter repeated, his tone calmer. The irony, he realized, was that he had used up virtually all his assets in buying Magnatel, so actually his guarantee was practically worthless. No point in enlightening Ms. Smith on that thought. In the end he might be forced to give the guarantee after all. Good Lord, he interrupted his own thought, I've practically decided to if she insists.

"Without your guarantee I believe we would be hard pressed to loan the company money at this time," said the woman. "With it we could go to two million at prime plus two percent. Since the prime interest rate, that paid by our best customers, has been as high as twenty percent in the last year, you might end up paying over two hundred thousand dollars a year in interest." She was entirely business-like. Her lack of emotion made her pronouncements seem as final and impersonal as those of a coroner confirming death.

Walter wondered whether he should remonstrate with her. But no, he decided. What good would it do? "Very well," he said. "I shall think about it." He tried to sound noncommittal.

Leaving the bank, Walter found himself in the canyons of the New York financial section. Wall Street, like the rest of New York, was overcrowded, energetic, violent. He stumbled into the crowd, not sure where he wanted to go. Opposite was an ornate church, incongruous among the sleek, utilitarian skyscrapers. For a moment Walter wondered whether it might offer him a haven. But no, he had no time for that. His head was filled with such a contradictory group of thoughts and emotions that it pounded, and he could feel the muscles in his neck cording in spasm. Two million dollars guarantee, when, except for Magnatel, he didn't have even ten percent of that. If he did lose to Von Ackermann, he would be indentured to the bank for life. You couldn't refuse to reimburse a bank—not if you ever wanted to go back into any kind of business.

But to be enslaved like that. . . . Walter could not confront the thought without shrinking away.

Yet if he failed to get the money he needed, he'd lose everything. Wasn't that enslavement, too?

And if he did decide to give the guarantee—and hadn't he, in his heart, already?—should he tell the bank that he was not the rich man they thought he was? He knew he would have to fill in a form asserting there had been no substantial change in his financial status since the last time they had audited him. If he admitted the real situation, even his guarantee would not get him the loan. On the other hand, perjury was fraud. No, he decided, he could argue that there had really not been a change: He had merely converted the bulk of his other assets into Magnatel. On paper he was far richer than before.

And if he lost Magnatel?

Then the bank would have to wait for its money . . . and he'd have a tricky court case on his hands. And while all that was going on, he'd have to work, and work, possibly until the day he died.

"I don't give a damn how prestigious it is," Walter said crossly to Caroline. "I'm not going to waste the next week in Washington while Magnatel is falling apart from a lack of cash."

"But . . ."

"But nothing. First things first. We've simply got to raise the money. That's paramount. I don't care if the President calls me personally."

"He did," said Caroline.

That stopped Walter in his tracks. "I guess I still can't quite believe it," he said, as much to himself as to her. He remembered how he had picked up the phone and been told that the President of the United States wished to talk to him. At first he had thought it was a joke. But then he had recognized the press secretary's voice; since taking over Magnatel he had met the secretary a number of times.

"Mr. Cort?"

"Yes, Mr. President." Astonishing what a sense of awe he felt.

"I'm putting together a few unusually successful businessmen and forming the President's Business Council. Would you care to join us?"

"Of course, Mr. President." Walter had been virtually tongue-tied. Only at the last moment before the President hung up had he summoned the courage to ask, "What is the purpose of the council, sir?"

The President laughed briefly. "Glad you asked," he said. "It's to give me advice on how to run the country. Businessmen's advice."

"Would . . ." Walter stopped, not sure whether he dared ask the question on the tip of his tongue.

"Would I follow it, you're thinking," said the President, exhibiting considerable intuition.

"Yes. Yes, I was," Walter stuttered, forgetting entirely to say Mr. President.

"Occasionally." The President laughed again briefly. "Will you join us?"

"Yes, Mr. President."

"Thank you," the President of the United States had said. His voice had sounded exhausted.

"Nevertheless, I cannot go," said Walter to Caroline now. "With Magnatel's problems and the banks . . ."

"The chairman of First International City will be there."

Walter looked at her, impressed. "Are you sure?"

"Of course."

"Oh."

"I've booked your room."

"Thank you," said Walter, grinning for the first time in several days. "Thank you very much, my dear."

"You're welcome," Caroline said, pleased. He *did* trust her judgment. She *was* more than just office furniture.

The businessmen invited to sit on the President's Business Council were impressive, affluent, sophisticated, intelligent . . . dinosaurs. Within their own companies they had reached positions of enormous power. But they had spent their entire business lives reaching those positions. So they were nearly all approaching retirement age and therefore being replaced by younger men. And they were so molded to conformity that they could think of nothing to do but gracefully edge toward that inevitable day when they would be fully retired and out.

For the time being, however, each was still accustomed to issuing suggestions in a gentle manner, and having them obeyed instantly by ten thousand employees. Each sported a marvelously tailored suit as casually as if it were a pair of jeans. Most had expensive tans, even though it was winter, with masseur-toned muscles and the skier-sailor-golfer look of athleticism in spite of their gray hair or balding pates. There were four women in the group; only four, it seemed, had climbed far enough up the corporate ladder to warrant an invitation. And all the executives there were so well connected in the business world that everyone knew everyone else.

Shoulders were slapped, greetings called, big smiles wreathed faces camouflaging real emotion. Solid, carefully modulated voices filled the room. Everyone sported a nickname. All in all, the air of complacency and self-importance was so thick that it almost—but not quite—covered the nervousness which affected almost everyone. Walter, the youngest there, and an anomaly anyway for he seemed still vibrant in the midst of these dignified anachronisms, recognized the nervousness as that same mixture of bluff, camaraderie and underlying fear he had seen in the upper reaches of many a consulting group facing an important client.

Circulating efficiently around the room, Walter greeted a senior lawyer here, a corporate president there. But for all his look of confidence, he felt like an imposter, fearful of being caught at any moment. Paradoxically, he also experienced a deep sense of rightness and pride. In spite of his problems at Magnatel, did he not deserve to be here as much as any man? The honored guest and the party crasher—why did he feel such contradictory emotions?

"Walter, you know Simon Ribinoff, don't you?" A hand slapped him firmly on his shoulder.

"Of course, Simon, how nice."

Ribinoff, one of the kings of entrepreneurial America, smiled at Walter. "You pulled a big one."

"Satisfactory," said Walter coolly. He meant it was none of the other's man's business.

"I'm admiring, not condescending. We may have something to talk about."

"I'd be pleased to talk. But we're not really in the acquisition business yet. Another three months . . ." Walter waved a hand airily, wondering how long Ribinoff would waste with him if he knew Magnatel on its own could not even raise a lousy two million.

"Nevertheless, I sense we can do something."

"Perhaps we can. Why don't you call me?" He handed the older man his card.

"Certainly. Tomorrow. My office will set it up with yours."

They parted, Walter flattered that Ribinoff, truly one of the giants would so pursue him. But to what point? He became impatient with himself for wasting time. The reception was almost over and he hadn't even seen the president of that damned bank.

The President's Business Council convened formally the next morning at nine-thirty in an enormous conference room. The oval table was the largest Walter had ever seen. In front of each place setting a small microphone insured that the valuable contributions expected from each participant would be fully audible. The forty-six businessmen, four women and assorted government participants, carrying coffee and sticky, undignified danish rolls, searched for their name cards on the table. Walter observed one senior executive, the chairman of a nine-billion-dollar corporation, surreptitiously exchange his name plate with one somewhat closer to where the President of the United States was scheduled to open the meeting.

". . . my corporation intends to make every effort to stay within the guidelines. . . ." ". . . as I told my board, anti-inflationary policy is a necessity. . . ." ". . . *pro bono publico* are not just Latin words anymore. . . ." ". . . I told Nader. . . ." ". . . productivity increases are our only economic hope. . . ." Walter listened to these snatches of conversation all around him. Platitudes! Nothing he heard was more than a repetition of tired *Wall Street Journal* editorials.

As if drifting into a dream, Walter started to observe the room from outside himself. He seemed to be looking down at all the well-dressed shells sipping their coffee, trying to impress, talking but saying nothing. The babble of voices seemed to rise like steam and dissipate as completely. Was it all a public relations effort, he wondered, without substance?

In the far corner of the room, he observed a man far younger than the rest talking to an efficient-looking young woman. Still feeling as if he were observing the room from afar, Walter moved close enough to overhear their conversation. "Please inform the President that we will be starting in five minutes," the young man was saying. "And he need only give a ten-minute introduction. After that we needn't waste his time. This crowd'll be quite content to waffle on all day about inflation. But they have no ideas what to do about it. So this afternoon we'll organize them around to recommending 'stronger guidelines,' or some similar bullshit. It's the only thing they can do anyway without taking a stand."

"In other words, everything as planned."

"Right. When the President wraps up this evening, he can make the guidelines sound like an important idea. Then he thanks them for their patriotic contribution, et cetera. And that's it—votes *and* money for his next campaign. Dead easy!" The young man grinned mockingly. "Businessmen are always the easiest."

"But Paul, won't they see through it?"

"Of course not. They may be wolves in their own lairs, but they're lambs here!"

"I'll inform the President." The young woman hurried off.

"You do have it well arranged," said Walter, no longer feeling in the least separated.

"I . . ." the young man blushed.

"Don't be embarrassed. I'm full of admiration," Walter reassured him. "And I won't breathe a word. By the way, I'm Walter Cort."

"Oh yes, Magnatel." The man was thoroughly informed. "I'm Paul Borday, the undersecretary."

"in charge."

"We facilitate. We don't take charge."

Walter laughed. "You're in charge, all right," he contradicted.

"I hope you enjoy our conference."

"I think I already have." Walter laughed again. "But you must be itching to . . . er . . . get us organized."

"Yes," said the young man gratefully. "Please excuse me."

"We'll talk later," said Walter meaningfully.

"Very well." Borday sounded apprehensive.

". . . corporate responsibility is hardly a theme I need belabor at this conference," the President of the United States was saying.

Walter noted the ring of gray heads around the table nodding in automatic agreement. But agreement to what? What *was* corporate responsibility, anyway? Paul Borday was stifling a yawn.

". . . thus the willingness of each of your concerns to elevate the commonweal to the level of your personal interest. . . ."

The President spoke for precisely the ten minutes Borday had requested.

"Thank you, ladies and gentlemen. I know I can count on your diligent inquiry into these problems. I look forward to receiving your advice. It will have a major influence on the policies I propose to Congress."

The President of the United States rose ponderously, as if he had just completed some profound statement. His face was set in that statesmanlike, chin-jutting expression so beloved by cartoonists, as if he were practicing for Mount Rushmore. As the guests rose rapidly, amid the protesting squeaks of their chairs, the President moved out of the room. It was an exit worthy of a battleship. Walter saw him give Borday a brief look of approbation.

"And now, ladies and gentlemen, if you will resume your seats." Paul Borday took over. "It will be my privilege to act as mediator for this meeting. To start, I wonder whether we could hear the views of Mr. Garner Black, chairman of the First International City Bank of New York."

The bank chairman waited until all the guests were comfortably reseated. "Thank you, Paul," he started. His voice, Walter decided, was even smoother and more laden with Southern-style politeness than Homer Wallace's. Apparently Ms. Smith had the monopoly on abrasiveness in the bank. "It is an honor to be here," the chairman was saying, "and I am pleased to share with you the views that my bank has developed about the problems underlying inflation in the United States of America." He paused to sip some water and benignly scan his audience. "The fundamental problem lies with the continuing importation of foreign capital, either as straight lending or in the form of acquisitions." He paused to add weight to his next sentence. "We must stop these Arab acquisition raids," he thundered.

Growls of assent arose around the table.

"First the Arabs sell us oil at outrageous prices. Then they use *our* money to buy out *our* companies."

Walter sat with mounting impatience. This was all rubbish—preplanned rubbish, moreover. He could hardly wait for the conference to be over. But for all his impatience, he knew now that he had not wasted his time at all.

The cocktail party that evening was in a grand reception hall of the White House. Antique chandeliers, long since electrified, lit the room. Their sparkle, and even the quality of their light, was sophisticated, brittle. The furniture, period French, was covered with blue silk. Benjamin Franklin looked down from the wall with slightly bemused disapproval. Walter felt even more out of place than he had in the daytime business meeting.

Paul Borday's evasive maneuvers were experienced and effective. It took Walter twenty-five minutes of careful stalking finally to catch him talking to two other men. "Paul," he interrupted loudly, "good to see you again. Listen, about your sister. I didn't mean . . ." Perhaps it was not the most subtle approach, but Walter knew it would work.

"You will excuse us," muttered one of the men, and the other followed quickly.

"I don't have a sister," said Borday crossly.

"I'm so sorry," said Walter with a grin. "But they do clear the decks, don't they, sisters?"

"I suppose." He smiled. "You've been chasing me all evening. What can I do for you?"

"I was terribly impressed by today's conference."

"Bullshit," said Borday. "Listen, I can only take a few minutes."

"What I agreed with most was that we won't be able to control inflation unless we can stop those damn Arab takeovers," said Walter, refusing to be hurried. "Take my own situation. You may have heard of Meshulem Kashi. He's one of my major backers."

"Fat Kashi?" said Borday dubiously. "I know about him."

"We are also financed by the Germans," Walter continued. "Von Ackermann of—"

"Christ, you get in with some strange ones."

"You know Von Ackermann?"

"Well, yes." Borday wondered whether he should have said anything.

"What do you know about him?"

"Nothing."

"Of course you do . . . Look, let's not have a stupid sparring match. If you know something, tell me." He paused. "This is no time to start 'organizing' me." There was also no time to make his threat more subtle.

"Okay," said Borday. "I get the point. You might as well know. I think you could find out anyway if you dug enough." He hesitated. "You may not like this, you know."

"Try me."

"Right. Well, Von Ackermann has a clean record. We can't prove anything against him. But the State Department thinks he is one of the main support systems for top ex-Nazis in Argentina. And the Israelis think he was in charge of the body disposal when the SS was trying to clean up Auschwitz before it was liberated. They've been investigating him for years without being able to prove anything. There's even an awful story about refining the bodies. . . ."

"Shit," said Walter, turning white.

"Between Kashi and Von A, you've sure chosen some strange bedfellows." Borday looked at Walter with mounting interest. He liked this straightforward young businessman, so much more intuitive and streetwise than the pompous old bastards who made up the rest of this political charade. "I hope you're well protected."

"It's not easy to buy a three-hundred-million-dollar company for nothing," said Walter, half-proud, half-bitter. "Particularly when the American banks won't help," he added meaningfully.

"Is that it? You need a little organizing there?"

"I could stand it," said Walter with relief. "The Arabs and the Germans are trying to take me over, and First International . . ."

". . . ably represented here by their unctious chairman . . ."

". . . wants my personal guarantee to make a loan," said Walter, playing it totally straight.

"I'll drop a hint," said Borday with a grin. "It will probably help."

"I won't forget," said Walter. "In other words, I have."

It seemed hardly possible, but Homer Wallace was even more charming than on Walter's last visit to the bank. "Wally," he called across the room, stretching out both his arms this time in greeting. "How good of you to come to see us again."

Ms. Smith's only contribution was an icy smile. She did not rise.

"You remember Marilyn Smith," said the vice-president.

"A pleasure to see you again."

"Yes," said Ms. Smith.

"I promised to give you my response on guaranteeing the Magnatel loan. . . ." Walter purposely let the sentence dangle. He looked directly at Ms. Smith.

She seemed to be having some difficulty talking and coughed to clear her throat. "We have considered the matter from all angles," she said unwillingly. "As a result, we have decided to loan Magnatel two million dollars without your guarantee."

"Oh, really?" said Walter, feigning surprise. "Well, I'm very pleased."

"Yes," said Ms. Smith, merely acknowledging that he was. In that single word she managed to convey emphatically that she was not. Walter could only hope that he would never be forced to come back to her for anything.

21

The drizzle didn't help. Starting at dawn, when Walter finally admitted he'd never get to sleep anyhow and flung open the curtains, it continued all day, evenly, unceasingly, covering the town as uniformly as if it were a mist of gray paint. Buildings glistened wetly, the drizzle oozing into their every irregularity and crack. Leaves, roadways, people, the very air itself seemed clogged, opaque, depressed. And the light never varied, remaining resolutely the color of the dirty dawn as the day dragged toward afternoon.

The air inside was almost as wet as outside; every surface Walter touched felt damp, and his clothes felt as if Mortimer had forgotten to put them into the dryer. Was it imagination or did the bed actually smell moldy? "Son of a bitch," Walter muttered, sounding petulant. "Shitty day." He hoped that saying the words aloud would erase some of their malaise; sometimes, he had found, getting a thought into the open let you tear your mind away from it. But not this time.

Worse, his self-doubt enveloped him as completely as the September drizzle covered the city. "Where's that vaunted confidence now?" he demanded of his mirror. But the image—pasty-faced, worried, frowning, as remote as a stranger—merely glowered back at him silently, refusing to become involved.

By three o'clock Walter was so pessimistic about his forthcoming meeting with Meshulem Kashi that it was an effort not to cancel it. What point was there? Why steel himself for another long, arduous negotiation when he felt in his very bones that he would fail? He'd never get the damned money. And even if he did get this ninth month for Von Ackermann, how could he get the three more after that? Why force himself when failure seemed inevitable and it would be so much easier to quit now?

"Okay, let's go," he said loudly, as if whistling for courage in the dark. He turned abruptly on his heel and strode out of the room. The movement made him feel better. His morning of self-doubt was past; he was back in action. Of course he'd raise the money somehow. If only he knew exactly how. . . .

Park Lane used to be the most elegant street in London, perhaps in the world. But now most of its luxurious houses had either been pulled down or converted to office buildings. The few remaining private homes belonged to billionaires—nearly all foreign and, in the opinion of the British butlers they employed, all vulgar. Meshulem Kashi owned a particularly fine Georgian mansion there.

Walter paid off his taxi without waiting for the change and hurried through the drizzle up the front steps to the elaborately carved oak door. His mood, much improved already, was boosted further by the door's knocker, a perfectly balanced two-foot brass nude, sensuously elongated, her surface subtly textured, an invitation to caress. Resisting that temptation, he used it instead to announce himself.

Almost immediately the heavy door was flung open and before him, arms akimbo, stood a giant of a black man, for all the world like the genie from Aladdin's lamp. "How may I serve?" The genie's lilting Jamaican accent fitted perfectly with his harem trousers and bejeweled turban.

"I'm here to see Mr. Kashi." Walter felt mildly foolish addressing a genie.

"Mr. Cort? Of course. Welcome." The genie bowed low. Walter handed him his raincoat as he entered.

Inside, Walter found himself in a large hallway as overcrowded with Middle Eastern ornaments as the inside of a treasure cave. Carpets littered the floor and festooned the walls. Giant urns straight out of Ali Baba were clustered in groups. Marvelously detailed stools and tables, intricately inlaid with mother-of-pearl, supported a vast variety of statues, golden flowers, cloisonné vases, ornamental snuff boxes, crystal goblets, ancient pottery, opium pipes, gilded leather pillows, ecclesiastical brocades. In one corner Walter saw a whole jewel chest of coral and gold necklaces; in another, a hat stand supporting a dozen ivory and silver shepherds' crooks.

The main source of light for this extraordinary collection was a score of candles in holders scattered everywhere. In addition, disorienting Walter as thoroughly as if he were drunk, there was a slowly rotating red, blue and yellow spotlight.

In the far corner, illuminated by the only steady light in the room, was a statue of a young couple, nude and intertwined. It was made of the same invitingly textured brass as the door knocker.

"Mr. Kashi would appreciate your attending him in his study," the genie interrupted Walter's astonishment. "This way, please." He started toward the door at the far end of the hall, but before he had taken more than a step, Walter heard the booming voice of Meshulem Kashi himself.

"Walter, my boy! Walter Cort." There was no sign of Kashi, but the voice reverberated like a sonic boom. "Welcome, welcome!"

For a moment Walter felt sure it came from the fireplace. He had just dismissed the thought as absurd when he realized it was not. For as he watched, the wall next to the fireplace seemed to crack. Then it swung smoothly forward. Behind, even more obese than Walter remembered him, stood Meshulem Kashi, his head encased in a gigantic turban, his body swathed in ermine robes.

"Walter, my boy, since I imagine you want me to play Father Christmas, I thought I'd come down our version of a chimney." Kashi roared with laughter. "Come," he said, "you look overwhelmed."

"Surprised," Walter tried to remain cool, "but hardly overwhelmed," he lied.

"So be it, so be it." Kashi stretched out his right hand. It barely extended beyond his own body, but he just managed to place it on the edge of Walter's shoulder. "Come with me, come with me. I'll show you more." He waddled toward his study door. Ignoring its antique workmanship, he gave it a resounding kick. It swung open with balanced ease. "Come," Kashi bellowed again to Walter. "Come, come!"

As he followed Kashi into the study, Walter's astonishment was multiplied a hundred times. The ornaments here were as numerous and magnificent as in the hall, but every single object was made of gleaming metal. The three walls before him were each devoted to a separate metal: Straight ahead was gold, to the left silver, and to the right brass, copper and bronze. On the wall behind him were the most extraordinary mixed metal sculptures.

Every piece in the room was highly polished, and every available space was filled with the metal objects: guns and sculptures, stirrups and shields, icons and urns, bed warmers and cow bells, thimbles and helmets . . . ten thousand objects, each shining with its individual metallic hue.

The lighting consisted of strobes flashing blue-white and incandescent yellow. Every flash was reflected in every metal object, making it an almost blinding visual experience—with an impact that was both physical and psychic.

Meshulem Kashi waddled to the center of the room, where, on a slightly raised pedestal, rested a gleaming gold throne. He deposited himself upon it heavily. "Ahhhh." The sound reminded Walter of the creaking of a giant oak. "Comfort at last." Kashi looked at Walter shrewdly from behind eyes sunken in flesh. "Now are you impressed?"

"Indeed, yes." There was no point in denying it; the effect of the room was far too powerful.

"All my visitors are. Even my son, who believes in fitness and discipline—neither of which I'm much interested in—thinks this is impressive."

"It is an astonishing room." Walter paused, looking for the right way to phrase his answer without seeming rude.

"But not comfortable?"

"Perhaps without the strobes?"

Meshulem Kashi clapped his hands. The electrical system responded automatically to the sound. Instantly the strobes were replaced by a warm golden light. It bathed the whole room in a soft glow, as if the metal itself had become fluorescent.

"Beautiful," Walter murmured.

"Sit down, sit down." Although Kashi had dropped his voice to a whisper, he still contrived to make it fill the room. "Make yourself comfortable." He pointed to a silver chair opposite his own. "You'll find it's softer than it looks."

Walter lowered himself gingerly onto the metal slats. To his pleasure he found that, although the chair was hard, its surface was so highly polished that the metal seemed to accommodate itself to his body. "Its smoothness makes it seem soft," he said.

"And its value makes it seem warm." Kashi rolled his laughter around the room.

Walter grinned, starting to like this immense gourmand who consumed everything from women to gold with such uninhibited gusto.

"So you want to borrow more," Kashi said, abruptly businesslike. It was a statement of fact, neither a question nor a probe.

"Magnatel is doing extraordinarily well." Walter started to lay the groundwork. He wondered how Kashi knew what he wanted.

"Of course, of course. Nevertheless, you need more money."

"That's true, but I think it's important that you understand why." Walter felt that he must not allow himself to be diverted from his pitch.

"They all have good stories." Kashi's tone sounded world-weary with disappointment. "But in the end they all want my money."

"But there's a difference between—"

"Between what?"

"Between bailing out and building."

"Of course, of course, my boy." Kashi was instantly jovial again.

"We are building. Perhaps too fast." He looked at Kashi shrewdly. "But then you . . ."

"Didn't build slowly," Kashi completed the thought. "That's what you were going to say." He slapped his gigantic belly. "In any respect," he said, and laughed again. "Quite right. I did grow quite fast."

"So we need the money because we're doing the same."

"Why me, then? I'm only the court of last resort."

"You're an investor already. It's logical."

"Bullshit," said Kashi, but he was not angry. "You're having troubles."

"Borrowing money is not that easy. After all, you hold most of our collateral."

"I hold all of it," said Kashi, reminding Walter that there was steel beneath this flabby exterior.

"Which makes it difficult—"

"How much?" Kashi interrupted.

"Two million."

"One."

"Would help for the short run."

"And what do I get?"

"What do you want?"

Kashi looked shrewdly at Walter. "Well, my boy," he said, "we all want many things."

Walter sat back, wondering what was to come.

"Now, I'll tell you this. I like doing business with friends, social friends. Friends who like . . ." he paused, seeming embarrassed.

"Who like a good time?"

"There you are. I knew you were smart. A good time. A great time. A fabulously good great time!" Kashi leaned forward in his chair so that his whole body swayed forward in his enthusiasm. "I like *every* form of socializing."

"How nice," said Walter wryly, understanding precisely what Kashi meant. "As a matter of fact," he added, deadpan, "I was planning to throw a party later this week. Thursday. I wonder if you'd care to join me?"

Kashi, delighted that his requirements were to be met, let his voice rise back to its normal boom. "Wonderful!" He started to laugh. "I'm sure we'll all have a marvelous time socializing."

"And playing games," said Walter blandly.

"And playing games!" Kashi's laugh made several gongs hanging around the room reverberate. "As for the money, don't worry about the terms, my boy. We'll work something out . . . once we're friends. After all, what are friends for?"

"For playing games?"

"Right. Fantastic games!"

As Walter left the room, Kashi clapped his hands again so that the golden glow was replaced by the strobe lights. Walter's last image was of Kashi in silhouette, a gigantic lump of dough, surrounded by a world gone crazy with shooting stars.

Walter was quickly ushered out by the genie. As he walked down the steps, the door slammed behind him. Looking over his shoulder, he saw only an elegant, conservative British house. What an unlikely setting for the extraordinary decor inside, and for its even more extraordinary owner. He had reached the bottom step before he realized that the young woman hurrying down the sidewalk was bound for Kashi's house. He almost bumped into her. "I beg your pardon," he said, stepping aside.

She raised her chin angrily but said nothing. Walter caught just a glance of the beautiful, arrogant oval face, the brilliant red lips, the blonde hair under her cape. He noted the cruelty about her mouth. As Teutonic as Von Ackermann, he thought irrelevantly. Then she pulled her coat around her throat and swept past him up the steps. Kashi must be into S and M with a bitch as hard and beautiful as that, Walter decided.

The London offices of Magnatel were the diametric opposite of Meshulem Kashi's dwelling. They were linoleum-floored, metal-walled, gray cubicles. Each cubicle housed a Formica-topped desk, an overworn chair and, occasionally, a scraggly plant brought in by its occupant, possibly to prove that even in this stifling environment some living thing could grow. The employees, rather like the furniture, were aggressively ordinary and somewhat worn out.

The largest office, until recently a rarely used conference room, had been commandeered by Walter. It differed from the other offices only in that it contained a Formica table with metal legs instead of the typical desk. Hardly a stimulating venue to think about Kashi's party; but Walter had nowhere else as convenient to go to.

Already Walter had rejected a dozen ideas. He had considered taking over Raymond's Review Bar for an evening, but had decided that would not be unusual enough for Kashi. Perhaps a gigantic sauna and massage session might be in order. The trouble with that was it could not last long enough: Everyone would become waterlogged. He had considered renting buses and taking his guest to Stratford-on-Avon to see a Shakespeare play staged in the Bard's hometown, with some Shakespearean bawdiness planned to complete the evening. Too complicated, and the bus would take hours.

Try as he would, Walter had found no particularly brilliant idea. Eventually he had decided to hold the party in the Carpet Room of the Elizabethan Hotel, a small but elegant establishment overlooking the River Thames, close to the houses of Parliament. The room, Walter knew, was surrounded by small living rooms, many with beds which could be pulled from the wall. It was unique in hotel accommodations because it was covered—floor, walls and ceiling—with Oriental rugs. Dating back to the middle of the nineteenth century, the room had a scandalous history. However, today it was little known, perhaps because it was outrageously expensive to rent—five thousand pounds for a single day and night. But it was superbly luxurious. The carpets on the floor were layered as thick as those covering the floor of the Blue Mosque in Istanbul, their color predominantly deep red, with just enough blue tones to make the overall effect purple. The walls were hung with lighter, bluer rugs; and the ceiling with lovely Orientals of beige and pastel blue. So artfully were the colors melded that the room managed to be both open and airy, and, although large enough for a hundred people, as cozy as the inside of a cocoon must feel to a caterpillar.

For entertainment Walter was arranging a series of vaudeville acts. The evening would start with two graceful but vicious Thai boxers he had greatly admired at another London party, and would continue from there.

The arrangements were almost complete. Just as well, since there were barely twenty-four hours left before the party was to begin. Only a few problems were left. Organizing the evening had started smoothly enough. Although the Carpet Room had been taken, Walter had persuaded the hotel manager to let him have it. The group which had reserved it was unceremoniously moved to the Curtain Room in the same hotel. They would not be pleased, of course, but Mr. Cort was extremely well connected; the manager had received several phone calls from several *very* important people.

The Thai boxers had been no problem. Sweetly, they had assured Walter that they were readily available. Regrettably it was their day off which meant that they would have to charge slightly higher.

But the rest of the acts had proven devilishly difficult to line up on such short notice. At first it seemed as if all those who were available Walter didn't want, and all those he wanted were unbreakably booked. But eventually, by searching, cajoling—and paying royally—he was able to line up a satisfactory program. One good act—a woman with a lascivious routine with snakes—was still trying to break her booking to accept Walter's more lucrative offer, but all the rest were arranged. Two secretaries were busy making phone calls to make sure the guests and the performers all knew where to go. Meanwhile, Walter drummed his fingers impatiently on the Formica table.

The telephone rang. It sounded as impatient as Walter felt. That should be the snake woman. He answered the phone himself.

"This is Mr. Kashi's office," said a cool female voice. "Mr. Kashi asked me to call you to express his regrets. He finds himself unable to loan any money to the Magnatel organization."

"But . . ."

"Under the circumstances, Mr. Kashi asked me to inform you that he will also be unavailable for social activities."

"But I don't understand," said Walter. "I'd like to talk to Mr. Kashi."

"I'm afraid Mr. Kashi will not be available. Thank you very much." The disembodied voice ceased. There was a click and the line went dead.

Walter sat with the receiver in his hand, feeling thoroughly bewildered. What the hell could have gone wrong? Clearly, between his talk with Kashi and now, some major change had occurred. Could Kashi have found out something new about Magnatel? But no, there was nothing wrong with the company that he hadn't known. Unless someone lied to Kashi? Unlikely. Kashi would have checked with Walter before turning him down. That left only one possibility: Someone must have pressured him. But who? And how? Obviously the man with the greatest motive was Von Ackermann. If he could block Walter from getting the money, he'd take over the company. That possibility had already occurred to Walter when the Swiss bankers had refused so arrogantly. But how would the German know? Was it farfetched to think that the Magnatel offices were bugged? Walter felt a wave of disgust at the thought of someone so invading his privacy. He'd make damn sure they were electronically swept at once. But even if Von Ackermann did know that Walter planned to borrow money from Kashi, how could he stop it? Surely the German could not be allied to the Arab. That was too absurd.

Suddenly Walter remembered the woman he had seen entering Kashi's house. Perhaps that was the connection: possibly a little friendly personal persuasion. They could have played a lot of games in the last thirty-six hours. For a moment Walter felt exhausted. He'd almost had the two million; now it was gone again. His resiliency was getting used up. How much longer would he be able to stand this sort of strain? He didn't know. . . . He realized that one of the secretaries was standing in front of him. Evidently she had said something and was waiting for his reply. He hadn't heard a word.

"I'm sorry. What did you say?"

"The snake woman called. She can't get out of her contract after all. They threatened to tie her snakes into a knot if she didn't show. She says she's awfully sorry."

"Never mind," said Walter woodenly.

"I'm afraid we're not sure what to do about a replacement. We can't think of anyone. The agent suggested a woman who does a tiger act, but—"

"That's it!" Walter shouted the words. Of course! *Whatever* pressure Kashi was under, that would get him.

"What?" asked the girl. "You want her?"

"No, of course not. Not her, the real thing." He could feel his spirits rise, his adrenaline surge. "There *must* be a way," he said aloud. The one thing that Kashi wanted more than anything else was the Tigress. She had retired several months ago, and refused Kashi's frequent requests to perform again. If Walter could only find a way to persuade her . . . Judith. The thought leapfrogged the previous one. Judith had been a dancer at Raymond's. She must know.

"Get me Brazil. At once," he said to the bewildered girl before him.

"Yes, sir. But who?"

"Brazil. Judith. Judith Katz . . . Goddamn it, what's her married name? Velasquez. Call my office in New York to get the number."

"But it's only six-thirty in the morning."

"You're right. They'll be closed. So call Caroline at home. She'll know."

"But this early?"

"Goddamn it, call her. And then get me Judith, whatever damn time it is in Brazil."

"Yes, sir." But the girl still hesitated.

"Now," Walter yelled. Then he grinned at the girl to show that he was more excited than angry. "Quick, quick," he urged.

Caroline was sleepy but efficient. Within half an hour Walter was through to Brazil.

"Señor and Madame not here," said an old voice with a thick Portuguese accent. "Gone."

"Where?" Walter asked. "Where are they?"

"Switchz," was what the old woman seemed to be saying. "Switchz." Walter had no idea what the beelike buzz of the word meant.

"Skij," the old voice said in explanation.

"Skij?"

"Sí. Switchz. Skij"

Walter had an inspiration. "Switzerland?" he asked. "Skiing?"

"Sí. Sí. Skij."

"Do you have a number?" His voice was full of excitement.

"Wait, I tell."

There was a crescendo of crackling. Walter was afraid the connection had been broken. He was just about to hang up and try again when the old voice returned. "Gzzdaad," the voice said quite clearly. "Gzzdaad."

Walter had no idea what that meant.

"Four, seven; three, two; one, one."

At least that was clear. Now the only problem was to find out which city. "Could you repeat the town, please?"

"Gzzdaad."

Of course, now he'd got it. He should have guessed. Gstaad, pronounced in Portuguese. "Thank you very much," he said with enormous relief.

"*Sí. Sí,*" said the voice. "A pleasure to say."

"Darling, darling, *darling!*" Judith's voice rose with each word. "How wonderful. Where are you? Tell me," she bubbled on. Then her voice descended to its normal level. "Tell me, love, why are you calling? Is something wrong? Do you need help?"

Hearing Judith's warm, generous voice gave Walter an attack of bad conscience so severe that he began to stutter. Had she been able to see him, she would have been amazed at how pale his face became. He had not seen her since she flew off in the helicopter, and in all those months, he had written only twice, little formal notes, one responding to her birthday wishes, the other thanking heɪ for her enthusiastic congratulations when he completed the acquisition. Now he was calling her; and she knew at once that it was only because he wanted something.

"What can I do to help?" she asked again, her generosity innocent and sincere.

"Do . . . Do . . . Do you know the Tigress?" Walter finally blurted. And then, trying to be less demanding, he backtracked quickly. "You see, I do have a little problem and I would like your help. But first tell me how you are . . ."

"Silly, of course I know the Tigress. We worked together at Raymond's. It feels like years ago, but we were good friends even before. Why? Do you want to get in contact? Is that it? I know she's retired, but I think I could track her down."

"First tell me—"

"Nonsense. Tell me what the problem is. What do you want? Love, I'm happy to help. Truly. Don't worry. I'm fine. Juán's on a business trip and I'm bored sick anyway. Skiing alone isn't much fun, and he's so jealous when I pick up men."

"Do you?"

"Of course. He needs to be a little jealous now and then." She laughed, but the sound was not girlish as he remembered but fuller, more womanly. "It's good for his liver." She paused and then added seriously, "But I don't do much with them. I don't want to offend his liver too much."

"Or arouse his spleen?"

"Yeah. Make him angry."

"You don't?"

"He's very good to me, Walter. I don't want to lose him. Not ever." Now her voice sounded as it used to when she was serious, like a little girl playing at being adult. Walter's heart went out to her. "But helping you is all right. He knows I still love you. And he knows that I love him, too."

Walter's head was spinning. "But then he must be even more jealous."

"Not of you. You see, I made that choice once when I got into his helicopter. When you wouldn't hold onto me. So I don't have to choose again. It was very difficult then. But now. . . ."

"I. . . ."

"Don't feel guilty. It was nothing you did wrong. I made my bed."

"And now you have to lie on it?"

"Of course. But it's full of feathers." She giggled. "How come even when I talk about something serious, bed always comes into it?" she asked conspiratorially. "I guess that's just the thing I do best. Now," she commanded, "what do you want the Tigress for? What do you want me to tell her? What's going on? Tell me. I love being involved in a mystery."

"One of our backers is an Arab called Meshulem Kashi. He's immensely rich. And greedy. For everything—money, food, women. But the Tigress refused him. Turned down a quarter of a million bucks to stay with him for a week."

"Phew! I couldn't have."

"Five hundred pounds if he weighs an ounce!"

"I see what you mean." She paused. "Still, it's five hundred dollars a pound."

"Well, I want to borrow some more money," said Walter laughing. "And . . ."

"And you think that getting the Tigress to come out of retirement and put on her act will change Kashi's mind? Or does she have to go to bed with him?"

"No, that's up to her. Just giving him the chance to see her perform again would be enough for my part of the deal. Particularly if her act could include something he's never seen before."

Judith laughed. "Oh, I'm sure she could do that," she assured, her voice utterly salacious. "We used to do an act together."

The disembodied female voice on the telephone at Kashi's office seemed less cool when she called back to tell Walter of her employer's response. "Mr. Kashi wishes me to inform you," she said, her voice sounding almost human, "that he has unexpectedly returned and would be delighted to attend a social evening with a Tigress." The voice giggled unexpectedly.

"It does sound rather strange," said Walter sympathetically.

The boxing ring had been positioned at one end of the room. Its canvas floor, cruel ropes and glaring white light contrasted harshly with the richness of the carpets all around. The audience, seated in armchairs around three sides of the ring, chattered expectantly. Marijuana smoke hung heavy in the white light. Dom Perignon or Perrier water were the favored drinks, although Kashi, as was his custom, sipped contently from a huge brandy snifter half-filled with Remy Martin. His extrasized chair was placed front and center.

A blare of trumpets, mixed with the squealing piping of Oriental instruments, heralded the start of the third and main event. The light over the ring dimmed. Two searchlight spots lit the black velvet curtain behind the ring so intensely they seemed ready to burn it. The audience hushed. Then, with the music reaching a crescendo, the curtain was swept back, and from behind it leaped two graceful, diminutive figures. Each was dressed in the traditional loose garment of the Thai boxer: baggy pants and a tunic belted at the waist. Each carried a grotesque mask which covered almost his entire head. Leaping and prancing, they approached the ring. With one final leap each seemed to fly across the ropes and into the ring. In unison they tossed their face masks high into the air, to be caught by their seconds at ring's edge. Still in unison the fighters shook their heads so that their hair, curled at the top of their heads, fell free to their shoulders. To the audience's delight, they were not the tough young men of the earlier matches, but very pretty girls, their faces both childish and knowing.

With total concentration each girl performed her personal rite of prayer, bending forward until her head touched the canvas floor, then chanting and swaying, a look of glazed ecstasy in her eyes. At first the ritual was much the same as the men had performed before their bouts. But gradually, as if it were a natural part of the ritual, each girl started a snakelike wriggle. With mounting excitement, the audience realized that each lithe miniature body was shucking off its baggy clothes until it emerged dressed only in a skin-tight body stocking, as perfect as a butterfly shed of its gnarled and ugly caterpillar skin.

Incredible how they could look so very innocent and so aggressively sexual at the same time, Walter thought. He was very aroused watching the girls, one in a white leotard, the other in black. The tiny ones like these always excited him the most.

Back to back, the two girls stood in the center of the ring. Slowly they gyrated around each other; it took almost a minute until each had faced in every direction from the ring. Slowly then, each moved toward her own corner.

The bell for the start of the match clanged.

The two girls approached each other, crouching forward like tiny cats ready to spring. For interminable seconds they circled each other.

As they moved, their bare feet seemed to claw the canvas; their hands, too, seemed to grow sharp claws.

The black-clad girl made the first move. With incredible speed her foot shot forward and kicked the white-clad girl in the lower thigh. The smack of contact sounded like the crack of a whip. In the same instant her fist flew forward. Catching her opponent off balance, it cracked into her right cheek.

Instinctively the white-clad girl counterattacked. Her knee, jerking forward, landed a staggering blow between her attacker's breasts. In precise unison her two hands arced in semicircles, their thumbs outstretched at right angles. They fairly whistled through the air, landing with a chopping crunch on either side of her opponent's breasts. There was a *whoosh* of pain from the girl, echoed by the *whoosh* of the audience.

For a second the fighters backed away from each other. Then, as if maddened by her pain, the black-clad girl launched herself through the air feet first at the white-clad girl's head. For a moment it looked as if her ankles would entwine themselves around her opponent's neck. Then the girl in white fell backward, breaking the grip. Both fighters were lying on the floor now, their legs intertwined, their bodies half-curved upward, each straining to overpower the other, a composite picture of agony.

As if by prearrangement both girls raised their free legs with the obvious intent of kicking their opponent's groin. The audience gasped. But neither foot reached its objective. Instead the shins cracked together with the sound of two sticks hitting. For a few seconds more the girls strained and panted against each other. Then the bell clanged for the end of the first round.

Slowly, painfully, the girls rolled onto their stomachs and away from each other. They raised themselves onto their knees; finally they dragged themselves upright and staggered back to their corners, limp little rag dolls.

"Walter, my boy," Kashi looked at his host with admiration. "I can say you have impressed me. I have never seen this before."

"Violence has its appeal."

"All excesses do."

"Not all," said Walter. "Some excesses lose all their appeal once they become real."

"I might debate it." The bell clanged for the second round. "But they start. And watching is better than talking."

The white-dressed girl looked subtly more aggressive than the black as the round opened. Her crouch seemed bent slightly further forward, as if she were the more ready of the two to pounce. The girl in black seemed more tensely coiled back, as if to protect herself.

As seemed inevitable, the white girl lunged first, snaking an arm at her opponent's left breast while, in an impressive feat of coordination, her leg aimed for her opponent's groin. But the result was unexpected. For the black-clad girl, with a response faster than the eye could possibly follow, managed to grab her attacker's arm and leg, one in the crook of each elbow. At the same moment, she jumped at her attacker, both her knees hitting with a sickening thump hard enough to be heard all over the room. The sound of the air pressed out of the white-clad girl's lungs was echoed by the shocked hiss of the audience.

The two girls fell then, as if in slow motion, onto the canvas. They seemed welded together, the arm and leg of the white-clad girl beneath riveted into the crook of the elbows of the black-clad girl above.

For a moment they were motionless, one kneeling on the chest of the other. Then with a keening wail the girl beneath clenched her free leg and arm against those in captivity and scissored the girl on top of her. She seemed like a tiny octopus engulfing her attacker. Then she started to squeeze.

Now the fight became as much a matter of will as of strength, the girl underneath seeking to engulf, to consume, virtually to assimilate the girl kneeling on her chest, while the girl above, bearing down with every ounce of her strength, tried to use her knees to crush her enveloper into the very fabric of the canvas floor.

The audience held its breath, frozen with tension. The fighting girls were motionless too. Only their panting and the sweat glistening more and more on their exposed limbs and soaking their leotards told of the enormous effort each was exerting to dominate the other.

The few seconds of effort seemed like an eon. Then it was over. The exertion was too much. With a final howl both girls collapsed, virtually unconscious. At the same moment the bell ending the round clanged. Neither antagonist moved; they lay side by side like two tiny corpses. Had it not been for the heaving of their chests, they would have seemed dead.

For half a minute they lay as if in a coma. Then gradually, hesitantly, from each corner, came a second. The two elderly men bent over the girls and tried to pull them apart. Still the audience made no sound. As each unconscious girl was lifted, it became clear that their hands were clenched together inextricably in a clasp of both victory and defeat.

"Fantastic!" Meschulem Kashi's voice, resonant as a gong in the silent room, broke the spell. "What a performance!" Instantly there was a crescendo of excited talk.

"It's not over," said Walter.

"Will they be able to fight more?"

"You will see," said Walter. "That was merely an hors d'oeuvre."

Even as he spoke the lights above the ring, empty again of antagonists or seconds, dimmed. Again the bright spots focused on the black velvet drapes at the back of the room. But this time the lights were a subtle pink—as bright as before, but less glaring. The music too seemed more melodic as it rose. Then the drapes were pulled back.

But instead of two agile kitten-females leaping, two tall, sensuous shadows seemed to glide out of the very end of the black tunnel behind the drapes. Slowly they moved into the spotlight, taking shape as they moved forward. At last they emerged, dressed in skintight silk costumes, one with the markings of a leopard, the other of a tiger.

"Holy Allah," said Meshulem Kashi, leaning forward so far that his chair creaked in protest. "Jesus Christ, it's the Tigress."

"Yes," said Walter, "and Judith."

"What will they do?" Kashi asked impatiently.

Walter just smiled at him.

"What?" Kashi repeated, exasperation and excitement mingling in his voice.

"Oh, the same sort of thing," Walter said ambiguously. "I think you'll enjoy it."

And indeed, as the room became hushed, the two gorgeous women started to perform precisely the same ritual prayers and incantations the two girl boxers had performed prior to their bout. They, too, touched the canvas with their foreheads, and swayed and chanted in apparent ecstasy. But there was a dramatic difference in the effect of the rituals: Where the fighting girls had been tiny, sexy war machines, Judith and the Tigress were utterly licentious. So powerful was their sensuality that everyone, male and female alike, was affected by it.

"They are extraordinary," Kashi whispered, his observation audible enough to elicit nods of agreement throughout the audience.

The prayers and incantations gradually gave way, as they had with the fighters, to a modified snake dance, a wriggle. But the two women were already dressed in leotards as tight as skin; surely they could not shed them as the boxers had shed their baggy clothes. The audience watched in concentrated anticipation, wondering what would happen.

Walter knew what to expect, of course, but even he could barely observe the very gradual loosening of the leotards as, imperceptibly, their seams stretched. All he knew was that at one moment the silky cat patterns of the leotards clung tightly to every crevice of the women's bodies, and some minutes later they seemed full of wrinkles and sags. Gradually the audience, too, realized what was happening.

Still dancing in exact imitation of the boxing girls, Judith and the Tigress lifted their arms and gradually writhed out of their skins. Underneath, they were nude except for tiny bikini panties, high cut on their thighs to emphasize even more their elongated, superb legs.

PETER ENGEL

Judith wore white, the Tigress black, and both wispy garments molded themselves so intimately to their wearers that the labia and the slits between were emphasized, glorified.

Judith and the Tigress stood back to back in the center of the ring. They were precisely the same height. Their figures, too, were evenly matched, both sets of breasts at the same level and proudly standing out from the slender bodies at the same angle. Both sets of nipples protruded sharply.

Very slowly, just like the fighters who had preceded them, they started to move around each other. They hardly seemed to move their feet, but their hips swayed as they turned, gliding around each other, showing themselves off to everyone in the straining audience. They smiled their enjoyment and their pride in their bodies.

The bell clanged. With a gasp of disbelief the audience realized that they intended to fight.

"Holy Allah, they are going to copy the fighters," Kashi said to Walter. His forehead was glistening with sweat, and his eyes were as round as the weight of his cheeks allowed.

"I told you it would be the same sort of thing," Walter said, and couldn't help grinning.

The two women approached each other, crouching forward as the boxers before them had done. But although superficially their posture was similar, the difference was profound: Where the miniature fighting girls had seemed ready to spit, leap and scratch like vicious kittens, these two were sullen, dangerous, ominous. As they circled each other, Walter was unable to shake the fantasy that their feet would leave claw marks in the canvass.

Just as the black-clad fighting girl had been the first to leap, so the Tigress, in her black panties, made the first move now. But where the fighter had shot out her foot almost faster than the eye could see to kick her opponent viciously in the lower thigh, the Tigress's leg moved forward in languorous slow motion. And instead of the smack of contact, there was a sigh from Judith as the Tigress's leg started to caress her lower thigh. At the same moment, in the same slow motion, the Tigress's hand moved forward and she stroked the full length of Judith's cheek.

Not by instinctive reaction but by carefully planned choreography, Judith's knee slowly raised, as if it had a life and will of its own, and nestled between the bare breasts of her attacker. In perfect unison she stretched out her arms and brought them slowly forward. All the men and women in the audience held their breath as those outstretched arms moved toward the Tigress; and every person sighed with satisfaction as they touched the breasts, fondling them until the nipples, harder than ever, turned from pink to deep red. There was a whoosh not of pain but of desire from the Tigress.

For what seemed like forever, the women backed away from each other. Then, with a cry of desire, the Tigress launched herself through the air at Judith's head. While the movement itself was fast, it still seemed to be in slow motion as Judith caught the legs and, bending forward, lowered the Tigress and herself onto the floor. There the two women lay, their legs intertwined, their bodies curved upward, in a perfect repetition of the straining agony of the Thai fighters—but with a vibrant desire to dominate by sexual desire instead of the equally vibrant desire to inflict pain.

For a long moment they lay still, caressing one another's torsos with uninhibited wantonness. Then, desperate to touch each other even more closely, they both lifted their outer legs and caressed first shins, then thighs, panting as they rubbed their legs against each other. As their legs started to move downward, they seemed to lose all awareness except of the desire for each other. Then the bell clanged to end the first round.

Slowly, reluctantly, the two women rolled onto their stomachs, away from each other. They remained there for long moments, pushing themselves hungrily against the canvas. Eventually they raised themselves to their knees. Still they seemed unable to leave each other. Finally they dragged themselves apart and moved back to their corners, their breasts heaving.

Kashi remained utterly still. His whole face now glistened with sweat. His shirt was sodden with it. "Holy Allah!" he said almost inaudibly. It was the first time Walter had heard him speak in a soft, low voice. Kashi had made no move nor uttered another sound when the bell clanged for the start of the second round.

Judith, looking so utterly wanting that it seemed she simply couldn't hold her desire for the other woman in check for another instant, made the first move. Blatantly, without thought for audience or convention, she moved her hand to the Tigress's left breast, and no sooner was she fondling it, than she rose on tiptoe onto one leg and moved the other leg gently but firmly toward her opponent's thigh.

Immediately the Tigress, her own desire now also aroused to an uncontrollable fever, pulled Judith's hand harder against her breast, and clamped her other arm firmly around Judith's foot. Then, all in one swift movement, she jumped at Judith, as if to engulf her. She half-knocked, half-lowered Judith onto the floor, and with a great groan of desire threw herself on top of her.

For a moment the women were motionless except for the involuntary heaving of their bodies. Then, with a wail of frantic need, Judith's free leg and arm scissored themselves against those the Tigress was holding—and captivated her captor.

Now the struggle became one of desire topping desire. The woman below sought to engulf, to consume the woman on top in her need, while the woman above, bearing down, seemed to want to penetrate to the very core of her lover beneath.

Walter, Kashi, every man and woman in the whole audience, was frozen with a sexual tension unlike anything even Walter, who had seen the women rehearse, could have imagined.

The two women, pressing themselves against each other, writhing, moaning, crying, rose to ever greater heights of passion. Somehow now, in their struggles, they managed to entangle their arms into each others panties until they both had been ripped clear and the women were nude.

Then, at last breaking the pattern of the Thai fighting girls, Judith and the Tigress were at each other in unmitigated frenzy. Hands, feet, mouths, breasts, all attacked one another in a sexual passion which was without bound, an agony and an ecstasy to see. Their voices rose to hysteria.

At last they were both reaching their moment of release. Clamped together as if in their death throes, they started to vibrate and scream, harder, louder, reaching a pitch of feeling so fierce they both seemed ready to lose their minds.

Then they were there: over the threshold of restraint, of humanity, into a world of feeling so intense that both of them together yelled out in terror and wonder, yelled as their bodies pounded in orgasm higher, louder, more complete than anyone in the room had ever seen in his or her life.

It was over. They fell back, virtually unconscious. Neither woman, nor anyone in the room, moved.

Eventually the Tigress, white as a sheet, tears streaming down her face, staggered to her feet. Weaving, she fled out of the ring and disappeared behind the drapes in the back of the room.

My God, Walter suddenly realized, they must have both been blasted with drugs. LSD? Speed? Who could tell? Surely those reactions had been too intense to be natural, and much stronger than would come from coke. Christ, he thought, realizing that Judith was still in the ring, apparently unconscious, how much had she taken?

Before Walter could move, however, the black genie who worked for Kashi materialized. With great smoothness and economy of movement for such a large man, he entered the ring. He scooped up Judith as easily as if she were made of papier mâché. Walking to where Walter sat, he laid the girl down on the carpet in front of him. "Sire," he murmured as he retreated.

For a second as he bent over Judith, Walter was overcome with a sense of remorse as if he were responsible for her excesses—as if he had to take the blame for her incredible sexual appetites. At the same moment he became aware of the audience's reactions: The men had become so aroused, he feared there might be a riot. But the women were just as aroused. Instead of a riot, there was a stampede to the bedrooms. As the room emptied, Kashi pulled himself to his feet and hurried to the passage beyond the ring.

"That was fun," Judith whispered so unexpectedly that Walter started back.

"You're okay?"

"Of course. I said it was fun. The Tigress is terrific."

"It seemed so real."

"Oh, it was." She ran her hands down her body and onto the top of her thighs. "Oh, my God, it was!" Her hands started to move from the outside of her legs inward.

"Stop that now," said Walter, his relief bringing tears to his eyes. "I thought you were hurt."

"*Le petit mort*, the little death. That's what the French call it," said Judith. Grinning, she sat up. She was totally beautiful, her bare breasts, the nipples still puckered and pointed, perfect. And her apparent unawareness of her own nakedness made her even more exciting. "I thought of you," she said, suddenly seeming shy. "That's one reason the feelings were so strong."

Walter was enormously tempted. She was so desirable, she wanted him so blatantly—and certainly he had no loyalty toward Juán Velasquez, her lover. Nevertheless, he hesitated. It wasn't the thought of Katy. He loved her very much, but quite differently. As far as he was concerned, sex with Judith was quite compatible with love for Katy. But if Judith were this needy, wouldn't sex lead to love, and then to dependence? Perhaps for both of them? He had almost loved her once before. And when she had left in the helicopter—as leave she always would—he had missed her. Why start again? Why risk falling even slightly in love and inevitably losing what he loved? It always happened that way. Only with Katy could he be sure.

Judith sat at Walter's feet and, still ignoring her nudity, looked up at him. Her lips glistened with moisture. "You are very desirable," she said, leaning closer to him, her whole body an invitation.

"You're so incredible," he replied, "that I daren't allow myself."

"But of course you can," she said softly and placed one hand on his knee. She lifted her face toward him, willing him to kiss her.

He was about to succumb—his face was already moving toward her lips—when he realized that Kashi was back and towering over them.

"Anything," Kashi said, his voice carrying an edge of desperation, his body looming so large it seemed to block out the light.

"I would give anything!" He was panting from passion and sway-ing slightly, possibly from the brandy of which he had consumed the better part of a bottle since the evening started. His eyes devoured Judith. "Anything," he repeated, "for the two of you to do it again. How much do you want?"

"That was my final performance, I'm afraid. I've given up that sort of thing," Judith explained primly.

"I mean repeat it for me alone," he explained, "in camera . . ."

"Letting the sperm fall where it may?" Judith kept her voice entirely factual.

Kashi stared at her with astonishment, not sure whether to be offended or amused. "Right," he boomed at last and started to laugh. Once started, his laughter seemed to gather momentum until, after a few minutes, he was laughing so hard that his whole body seemed to bounce all at once, like Jell-o, in different but synchronized directions. His face seemed about to fall apart under the vibration of that bouncing body. Eventually his laughter so overwhelmed him that he staggered back and collapsed into his chair. "Would you?" he demanded when he had finally caught his breath. "How much, how much? That's all I want to know."

Judith rose and stood between the two seated men, slightly in front of both of them, legs astride, arms on her hips, gloriously, wan-tonly nude. "What did the Tigress say?" she demanded.

"She refused. She refused even to name a price." The unfairness of that seemed too much for Kashi. It was one of the very few immuta-ble tenets of his life that every thing and every person had a price.

Judith laughed at the fat man's outrage.

"I offered her a quarter of a million dollars for a week," Kashi explained, almost petulant in his arrogance. "I would have gone higher."

"And now?"

"Now I want you."

Judith looked first at Walter and then at the immense Kashi. "What do you want me to say?" she asked Walter.

"The same deal for you," Kashi interrupted. "A quarter of a million for one week."

"I'm not pushing you away," said Walter, understanding at once. "You're free to make up your own mind." He refused to be tied down with the responsibility of asking her to stay or even of telling her what to do. Surely she would not go with Kashi. And yet, if that was what she decided. . . .

"You are as beautiful as she," Kashi said, awed at his own inten-sity. "You are the two most fabulous creatures I have ever seen." He seemed as drunk with desire as with alcohol. "Half a million for you to repeat your act with me in it."

"If the Tigress has refused, I cannot accept," said Judith.

"But the money—that's up to you alone. A quarter of a million dollars, girl. A fortune. For one week. Only fat Arabs like me can even think like that."

Judith tried to imagine what it would be like with this obese giant. Would he wish to lie on top? He'd smother her before she could escape. What a horrible thought! But looking at him, she couldn't help being intrigued as well as repulsed. The intensity of his desire was extraordinary. She could feel him wanting her as few men had before. "No," she said, after a moment's hesitation, "I think not." But there was enough doubt in her voice to give him hope. "Anyhow," she added, "I haven't got a week free—and a quarter of a million wouldn't be enough." Later she often asked herself what she would have done if he had not raised his offer. Was she bluffing—or would she have turned down the largest sum of money she had ever seen? But he didn't call her on it.

"Very well," he said, sounding completely self-confident. "We shall make a deal for tonight alone." He smiled at her, intending the look to be friendly and reassuring. In fact, the smile was so distorted by the weight of his cheeks that it looked more like an angry grimace. "I suggest the same quarter of a million dollars—but for tonight and tomorrow only." His tone suggested that he was about to complete a most favorable business deal, to make an unusually good bargain. His powerful voice emphasized the enormity of his offer. Even whispered, it would have been impressive enough to attract attention; in Kashi's habitual boom it caused the hush of real scandal to spread throughout the remaining guests in the room.

Everything about the man was excessive, Walter thought. His appetite, his lusts, his money. . . .

"U.S. dollars?" Judith asked weakly, trying to be facetious, pretending it was a joke.

"I am being serious," said Kashi, as if that was what Judith had wanted to know. "I have immense amounts of money." He paused for a moment and then added with great sincerity, "and an immense desire for you."

Suddenly Judith felt the full impact of her power—and she was amazed. How had she, Judith Katz, barely twenty-one years old, a kid from nowhere, managed to arouse this jaded hulk to such a pitch that any price seemed reasonable to him? Just as suddenly, she felt her self-confidence ebb. If she did consummate the bargain, how could she possibly be worth what he was willing to pay? How could she give enough? Then, perversely, as this wave of self-doubt swept over her, so did excitement. It inundated her. A quarter of a million dollars! What an incredible thought that, using her body and her imagination alone, she might be able to give this bloated roué so much physical pleasure, such bizarre and extreme sensation, that he would pay more for her than perhaps any man had ever paid for a woman before.

"Well?" Kashi demanded, starting to be angry, insulted, perhaps hurt.

"Well," Judith replied, her smile utterly lascivious, "I want you, Meshulem Kashi. It will be the easiest money that has ever come my way."

Kashi looked at her. For just a split second there were tears in his eyes. Then, regaining his composure, he said gallantly, "Then it will be the best money I ever spent."

Judith moved fully in front of Kashi's chair. Slowly she started to gyrate her hips just in front of his eyes. "You, Meshulem Kashi," she repeated, her thighs emphasizing her words, "I want *you.*"

Without for one second taking his eyes off her crotch, Kashi heaved himself to his feet. He seemed as powerful, as determined and as lumbering as an old bull elephant. For all his grunts and heaves, the man carried a certain dignity. And such was the intensity of his desire —and her pride of sex—that, for all their grotesque contrast as a couple, the two seemed almost fitting.

Even before Kashi was fully on his feet, the genie had glided up with a cloak and slipped it over Judith's shoulders. She swirled it about herself as he placed her shoes before her. Then she stepped into them and started to move, slowly, gracefully, toward the exit.

"And don't worry about it, Walter, my friend," Kashi boomed as he waddled after her through the Carpet Room toward the exit. "Don't worry about the money." He grabbed Judith by the hip. "Fabulous socializing!" he called. He reached the door. "Whatever you want," he called, half over his shoulder. Then he was outside and his final words drifted back into the room like the rumble of distant thunder: "Two million, three. Maybe more. . . ."

Oversleeping, then rising slowly the next day, wishing he had gone to bed after Kashi left instead of celebrating his success most of the night, Walter realized he had barely enough time to catch his plane. Ignoring his hangover and reveling instead in his feeling of achievement, he took a quick shower, shaved himself superficially and dashed for the car.

Walter caught the Concorde with only seconds to spare, listened impatiently to the usual mechanical sales pitch about its speed and, by the time the plane was airborne, was as fast asleep as he had been when the alarm awakened him. The stewardess had to shake his shoulder to get him moving when they arrived in New York, and he dozed in the back of his limousine on the way from Kennedy airport into the city.

But by the time he arrived at his office, he was reasonably rested. Three hours in bed in London, three on the Concorde and quite a number of minutes in the limousine should be enough, he decided. Moreover, his hangover had worn off and he still felt elated. He would call Katy as soon as he reached his office and tell her about the money. They were clear for at least two more months. How delighted she would be.

Grabbing his briefcase, he jumped out of the car and strode into the Pan Am Building. As always, he waved to the Guardian of the Lifts, who cheerfully returned the wave.

It was barely ten o'clock in the morning when he strode into his office. "And what are you looking so glum about, my dear?" he asked Caroline cheerfully. "Don't you realize it's a marvelous day?" But his heartiness only seemed to distress her more. "Listen," he said, sure she would perk up as soon as she heard his news. "We did it! Yesterday Meshulem Kashi agreed—"

"Then you haven't heard?"

"Heard what?" he said. Suddenly her worry infected him. "What's the matter?"

"Didn't you hear the news or . . . ?"

"I haven't read, seen or heard a thing since last night."

"Then you don't know," she said. "I'm sorry. Judith called to tell us first. But it's been in all the news bulletins this morning. Meshulem Kashi was shot in the head and killed outside his house very early this morning."

Walter paced nervously at the end of the modern, boring and impersonal conference room in the New Jersey Magnatel offices while his key executives took their seats. Everyone present felt and looked apprehensive. Greetings were perfunctory. Fingers drummed on the tabletop. Knuckles were whitened as they doodled with pens too tightly clenched. There was practically no chatter. He wished Katy were with him; he was worried about her recently. She seemed so jumpy and pale. He feared she was ill and hiding it from him. But she wouldn't be back from Germany until tomorrow. "Thank you all for joining me," said Walter when they were all seated, his tone flat. "The purpose of this meeting is very simple: We have to raise cash—and we have to do it fast. I thought we had the problem solved, but. . . ." His voice broke and his face, already gray with fatigue, seemed to become darker still. "But, unfortunately, with the death of my friend Kashi, our money source has not materialized." He paused and then continued in a stronger voice, "so it is imperative that we cut all possible expenditures."

"We have already done that," Dr. Schatten, leaner and more scraggly than ever, interrupted. The very lack of emotion in his voice gave it emphasis. "For my part I have cut everything, from dangerously reducing factory maintenance to firing our assistant receptionist." He made the statement so baldly it seemed stronger than if he had shouted in anger.

"I appreciate your efforts, Dr. Schatten. But there is always more that can be done," Walter said, trying to counter the negative tone of Schatten's comments. He succeeded only in sounding patronizing, not much better than a scout master reassuring his troop that the weather wasn't so bad in the middle of a blizzard. "You see," he added hurriedly, "it's not so much savings that I'm looking for as the creative use of money. I believe there are areas where, even though we're not spending too much, we could spend less."

"I do not understand," said Schatten. "How is that possible?"

"By spending differently." Walter felt on surer ground now. Fortunately Schatten had no imagination; he hated ideas, abstractions, as much as Walter loved them. "For one thing, we must cut out all advertising that we haven't bartered. We're still running too much paid television, for example. I know most of the deal with Pogue is for TV. But he can't deliver on our schedule. I don't quite know why. He insists we keep changing on him."

Dr. Schatten merely grunted, but several other executives nodded their heads in agreement.

"Why not cut advertising altogether?" Schatten demanded.

"Because we need it to sell," Walter said with certainty. "That's basic marketing: If you cut spending below a certain level, you cut sales more. And as sales fall, costs rise. In the end you have to raise prices more if you don't advertise than if you do. And then sales spiral down."

"But how much advertising?"

"No one knows. It's judgment."

"So why not—"

"Because its *my* judgment that we are spending barely enough as it is," said Walter coldly. "However," he continued, "we can switch most if not all our spending from what we're using now to what we can get from Pogue.

"Beyond that, there's an opportunity to barter paper and packaging goods," Walter continued, "corrugated board, that sort of thing."

"Without specifications?" Schatten asked doubtfully. "Pogue insists he has to have a free hand."

"Broad specs. So that what we get is acceptable, but not so tightly defined that Pogue can't vary suppliers. That way we can pay for most of our supplies partly or wholly in appliances. Even though it's more trouble that way, we should be able to cut our total packaging and paper expenditures as much as ten percent."

Walter realized that the meeting had become a dialogue between Dr. Schatten and himself. Schatten was conveying the impression that he represented the only power base in the company except for Walter himself. "So tell me, Joe, what savings opportunities do you see?" Walter hoped Joe Hargraves would take the hint.

"Wide opportunities," said Joe promptly, with precisely the emphatic certainty his boss wanted. "But before we get into my list, wouldn't it be better to hear from the operating people? Otherwise we'll be here all afternoon. And it's easier for us to catch you anytime than it is for our German visitors." He looked studiously at the pile of papers before him. After hours of studying them he still had absolutely no idea where a single further dollar could be saved.

"Makes sense," said Walter, admiring Hargraves's loyalty as much as he deplored his lack of solutions.

"I do have one small suggestion," said an elderly gentleman from the far corner of the conference table. "I'm afraid my department is rather small, only responsible for the mail room . . ." His voice indicated that his department was not only small but, he assumed, also boring to everyone but him.

"Not at all, Herb," Walter encouraged him. "I'm most interested in your suggestion."

"Well, it occurred to us that we could save cash by reversing the charges." He stopped as if the comment was obvious.

"I'm sorry, Herb, I don't understand."

"If we call all our branch offices collect, or send mail postage due," the old gentleman explained, "it's billed from the other end. That costs a little more, of course, but it takes two to three weeks longer for the bills to be processed. We'd save that much cash . . . Twenty thousand dollars, we estimated."

"That's excellent," said Walter. "What a fine idea. Let's do it right away."

Gradually other managers started making suggestions. An hour after the conference started, enough ideas to generate cash savings of almost four hundred thousand dollars had been gathered. Another two hundred thousand, although debatable, were also possible. Even without them, Walter thought, very pleased, the four hundred thousand had taken them a long way. And there was still barter. That was his best hope. Goddamn it! He was suddenly filled with bitterness. If only Kashi. . . . With determination, he tried not to think about it. But his mind refused to let go of the unsolved murder of his fat Arab backer. Of course Kashi must have had a thousand enemies. But it had been far too much of a coincidence. Obviously there was a connection. That German girl. Walter's mind kept replaying the scene of her walking into the house over and over, like a looped film.

Apart from the four hundred thousand, Walter's best hope of raising the million he needed by month's end was to do more barter with Fred Pogue, and to obtain some of the concessions for that right away. Fred often sweetened deals by including cash up front. Thus the meeting, to be held at the Friars Club, was crucial. Walter had reserved a private dining room.

"We haven't done what we said we'd do," Walter started as soon as Fred Pogue was settled. He was careful not to specify who had not lived up to the commitment. "So we've got to get on with it."

Pogue's face was more tired than Walter had ever seen it. While it had lost none of its mobility, its look of concern seemed to underlie every other expression, from sadness to laughter.

"You're right," said Pogue, looking enormously serious and using the hushed sort of voice Walter associated with visitors to art galleries. "You are absolutely right. We must do precisely that." His face livened up. "We must find areas where we can do barter. Areas in addition to television."

"That's exactly the point," said Walter. "I agree with you. We'll barter what we can on TV, but we've got to find some other areas as well."

"Well, we can't barter for postage stamps."

"Of course not." Walter ignored his friend's sarcasm, but was surprised by it nevertheless. It wasn't like Fred to speak like that. "But there must be something else."

"I'm not sure what," said Fred Pogue with a mixture of uncharacteristic pessimism and a sort of frenetic impatience and tension which Walter had never seen in him before. Normally Fred was such a calm man. His wonderfully mobile face usually showed only ripples of emotion over an apparently placid ocean. Now, however, he seemed deeply perturbed, as if the ocean itself were being churned up by some subterranean earthquake.

"Well, let's go through the alternatives," said Walter. "There is obviously media first."

"Of course," Fred sounded unenthusiastic. "But not more television. I've told you, first you wanted some. Then you wanted it all at once. That wasn't part of our original deal."

"Of course, we understand that."

"Print we may be able to do."

"Why maybe, Fred? What's the problem? You've always been able to do print."

"We've sold a great deal of the space inventory we used to have." His face drew itself into oblong vertical lines.

"And you can't get more?"

"Oh, I think so. Money is a little tight, of course."

"I'm aware."

"You couldn't by any chance. . . . No, of course not. Never mind, forget it."

"And paper? Don't you barter in corrugate and that sort of thing?"

"Yes." Fred pushed his hesitation aside with an obvious effort. "Yes, we do. I believe we could make a deal there. How much paper do you use?"

"Well over two million dollars a year on corrugated containers, and a lot more than that for the appliance boxes. Plus all the instruction leaflets. Then there's the paper we use for mail order. Many millions altogether. In fact, that's the spending which has siphoned off a lot of what we had planned to spend in media."

"I know," he said very bitterly.

"So you might be able to do something?"

"I think so. I believe that we could. . . ." There was another switch in Fred Pogue's voice; he was starting to warm to his theme. Evidently his private worries had been, at least for the moment, submerged.

The telephone interrupted Fred mid-sentence.

"Damn it," said Walter. "I told them not to interrupt us here."

"It's probably for me," said Fred Pogue. He now sounded brisk and businesslike. He walked over to the phone. "Yes?" There was a long pause while he listened. Walter saw the broad shoulders start to droop. Slowly the whole frame of the man sagged like a snowman melting. As Walter watched, Pogue's face turned ash white. "Yes," he said again. "I understand." He put down the receiver as carefully as if it were ancient ceramic, likely to shatter at the slightest bump. Slowly he turned toward Walter. "We won't be able to make those barter deals now," he said.

"What on earth is the matter?"

"I can't continue."

"What do you mean?"

"I thought I might bluff it through," he said. "I borrowed from a bank against my media inventories, and then sold the inventory without informing the bank. I needed the cash to keep the business going. I thought I'd be able to pay it back. . . ." For once his face was entirely still. "But they've caught me." Like a sleepwalker, he moved slowly toward the door. "I'm sorry," he muttered as he opened it. "I'm through. You can't count on me for anything anymore."

Before Walter could say a word, Fred Pogue was out of the room. The door closed behind him with a gentle click. To Walter, it sounded reverberatingly loud.

The employees in the accounts-payable room of Magnatel looked as harried, conscience-stricken and crooked as any group of bookies operating one of Big Julie's illegal betting parlors. Twenty people occupied the room, sharing it with a chaos of papers. Telephones rang constantly. Men and women shouted over them. Empty coffee cups and overfilled ashtrays littered the tabletops. Balls of rolled-up paper overflowed wastebaskets. And everyone lied.

"I am afraid we cannot pay your invoice #7428 since there is an error. . . . No, I'm sorry, I can't be specific, I don't have that particular invoice in front of me, just a notation that it's incorrect. Please check. . . . Yes, of course we'll pay as soon as you verify it. . . ."

"Yes, our records show that that check was mailed to you four days ago. . . . Please check with your post office. . . ."

"We've put in for a reclamation on that shipment. . . . Oh, you have a countersigned shipping receipt. . . . In that case we clearly should have paid the bill. I do apologize. We'll check into it right away. . . ."

"But of course we're ready to pay. I can't imagine why your invoice has been delayed. . . . Yes, I'll check into it at once."

The excuses were subtle, sympathetic. No one appeared to be lying. Joe Hargraves, parading up and down the room, watched each of the clerks like a hawk. Occasionally he would lean over someone and whisper some advice. "You could have asked them to call back in the morning," he suggested.

"But it's so difficult to get through. Our lines are always busy."

"I know." His face showed no hint of a smile.

At one end of the room, incoming invoices were sorted into several categories. New bills were simply filed and delayed for six weeks before handling. Old bills, reaching their six weeks' maturity date, were paid automatically if they were below five hundred dollars, and were automatically delayed another two weeks if they were between five hundred dollars and ten thousand dollars. All bills over ten thousand dollars were routed to Joe Hargraves's desk. For two hours a day he sorted through them laboriously. Bills from the post office, bills from the printer, bills from the mailing house . . . They piled up on him day after day. Some he simply could not delay any longer. The post office was slow to react, as inefficient in collection as it was in all things. But finally they did react—stridently—and they had to be paid. The printer, as Joe had discovered with more resignation than rage, refused to deliver anything if his bill had not cleared the bank forty-five days after it was presented.

"For Chrissake, we're only two weeks overdue," Joe had remonstrated with the printer's accounts-receivable manager.

"You're not supposed to be overdue at all."

"But everyone runs a few days over."

"You're two weeks over."

"Okay. We'll verify it. . . ."

"We'll start shipping your paper again when you've finished verifying and pay the bill."

"Fine." Joe Hargraves had bowed to the inevitable. "We should have the verification completed and our check over to you within the hour."

In spite of some suppliers' toughness, Joe's delays were paying off. Each day total accounts payable were rising, but deliveries kept coming. And very slowly, a small reserve of cash started to accumulate.

At the same time the hectic savings activities all over the world were bearing fruit. By the twenty-third of the month, there was $650,000 of cash available; by the twenty-fifth the total amounted to almost three quarters of a million. By the twenty-eighth Joe Hargraves, short on sleep, wrinkled and worried to death, had $950,000—only $50,000 short of the million he needed. The next day they scraped it together. A special messenger left that afternoon with a certified check for Von Ackermann. The ninth month had been achieved. Hargraves and Walter stood each other to a drink that evening, toasting the fact that, for one more month at least, the German wolf had been stopped just before the door.

"God, but it was close," Walter told Katy later that night. He was shaking from relief. "We only got it on the very last day, and even then we had to take some risks on the last fifty-thousand; check kiting, really."

"It's such an irony, when the business is going so well. There must be some other way. . . ." She seemed to be saying that she had infinite confidence that he'd find the way. "Surely someone could lend you the money."

"Normally, yes. But you know how tied up Von Ackermann has us. And with Kashi dead . . . No, we just have to cut back."

"But we are, aren't we? Haven't we tried everything?"

She stood in the middle of the kitchen, dressed in the slightly transparent robe he had given her. When she moved in front of the light, he could see the silhouette of her nude body beneath. It excited him, perhaps more because she seemed so unaware of how sexy she looked. Her hair was pinned up, ready for taking a shower. She'd do it as soon as the meat was in the oven.

Walter watched her bustling around the kitchen. Innocent, efficient, sexy . . . He loved her so much that he felt as if his love were a living thing, part of him and yet separate, like an invisible cat that lay purring on his chest. He wanted to hug his love. "Can I help?" he asked, descending to the mundane because he could think of no way to express what he felt.

"No thanks, I've just about got it done."

"You're so efficient."

"Aren't I."

"And woman's work is never done?"

"Not really. I don't mind it. Anyhow, lamb chops are my favorite."

"I like the smell of the rosemary."

"When it burns, you mean?"

"Almost like incense . . . a burnt offering for the food to come."

"Meringue for dessert?"

"You're sinful. When do you have the time? I thought you were busy with your mail order."

"Opening envelopes, you mean?" She laughed. "Sometimes I have to work at it all morning."

He had a quick vision of the trucks bringing in the mail, the fork-lift operators unloading the pallets, the automatic machinery slicing open the letters. "I can imagine," he said drily.

He waited a moment, unwilling to interrupt her domestic pleasures but knowing that the time had come to be firm. "Love," he said, taking a deep breath, "I know how well it's going, but you've got to cut back even further, whatever harm it does short-term. We can recover later."

"But I *have* cut. As much as I can."

"No, I mean you've got to cut out all the mailings. No further business to be generated. Stop building."

"Then we'll destroy everything I've started." She sounded desperate. "It'll never revive. It's a new business. It can't stand drastic surgery any more than any other newborn can." She wondered if she was being too dramatic. "And it's so profitable," she ended weakly.

"I know. But it's not profits, it's cash we need. You know as well as I do that every new solicitation you send out costs us more cash at the start than it brings in."

"But it makes a huge profit later."

"Sure I know that," he said with bitterness. "So later Von Ackermann will own a damned profitable company," he added, his irritation mounting.

"And if we cut back that far, we'll own an unprofitable one."

"I'd prefer that to nothing at all," said Walter, frustrated that she couldn't understand.

"You think I'm not sympathetic?"

"Are you?"

"Of course. Of course I am. It's just that we've all worked so hard to build this mail-order business. We can't just stop now in midstream." For the moment that was all that mattered.

"We *must* stop." His voice rose in real anger now. "Don't you understand, we'll lose the whole company."

She realized she was going too far, but her passion was genuine. She couldn't stop herself. "That's not my problem," she said coldly. "I'm just in charge of the mail-order business. All I know is that if we cut further, everything we've worked for will go down the drain. Our competitors will come in. Our customers will switch to them. The mailing pieces we've already paid for will be wasted."

"That's just the point, we've already paid. So it doesn't affect our cash. But we haven't paid the mailing costs. Or the costs of the appliances and the diets. Every time you get a new order, it costs us more money than it brings in for the first few weeks. Later, when they pay their installments, it's fine. But in the beginning it's a cash drain."

Of course she knew that! It was her idea, wasn't it? Her baby! But clearly he was adamant. "Very well, darling, I do understand," she said, her voice softening. "I'm exaggerating, I suppose. It's just that I'm so thrilled with our success."

"I'm thrilled, too, dearest." He touched her cheek. Words were so inadequate. What he really wanted to do was take her in his arms, reassure her, comfort her, love her.

She moved away from him, unwilling to accept his touch. She just couldn't be intimate all the time. He relied on her so. It was too much. Sometimes she thought that she was losing control completely.

"You're right," Walter said, trying to use words to express his feelings instead. "It's a brilliant feat. But we'll start it again. We'll think of something. In the meantime we have to economize." He realized how hollow his words sounded. "I do realize how disappointing it is," he said. "And I love you." That sounded even emptier. Again, he tried to reach his hand out to her.

"Okay," she said, at last accepting the inevitable. She put her arms around his neck. "Okay, I'll see it's done."

Suddenly Walter felt sick to his stomach. Never, not at the toughest bargaining session, not even when he had grappled with Von Ackermann, had he felt like this. He was shivering inside, frightened, terrified that he had hurt her. "I'm sorry," he said contritely. "I know it's difficult for you. It's difficult for me, too, love. I just don't know where to turn."

"I'll cut immediately," said Katy cheerfully. "Now I've put the meat in, so I'll go take a quick shower. You want some potted shrimp first?"

"I'm not terribly hungry," he said, feeling queasy.

"What's the matter?"

"Nothing, just a slight upset stomach." Not for the life of him would he admit how much arguing with her upset him.

"Oh, love. I feel so bad," she said. "So guilty."

"What are you talking about?" He tried to bluff his way through.

"We should never talk business before dinner. Now I've upset you."

"Don't be silly. It's just an upset stomach. It doesn't matter. Hell, if I ate the shrimp, they'd be gone, right? So throw them away and we'll both pretend I ate 'em!" He laughed, trying to keep his tone bantering.

"It's not the damn shrimp," she said, her voice full of concern. "I don't care about that. It's just that I love you and I hate to see you upset." Funny, she thought, it was really true. She did love him with part of herself, even though the other part was all business. Thank God she could still manage to keep them apart, even though it did seem to be getting harder to do.

"Go take your shower."

"Okay," she said. "I'll only be a few minutes."

"Take your time. I'll look after the meat." He wished she would leave. He was feeling worse every second.

She pecked him lightly on the cheek and pressed against him for a second. He thought the pressure on his stomach would make him vomit. Then she was gone and he could lower his head between his knees.

In spite of their conversation, Katy procrastinated on cutting back the mail-order business. It was going so well; just one more day. . . . Thus three days later, when Walter was walking through the mailing room, he noticed no reduction in activity. Where a pall of idleness should have hung, the pace remained frantic.

"Are you still mailing?" he asked the foreman.

"Yes. But we have clear instructions from Miss Katy only to use up existing materials. We're not to develop anything new."

"I see," said Walter, trying to keep the anger out of his voice. "Thank you."

By the time he got home, he was in a towering rage. "Katy," he yelled the moment he was inside the door. "Katy, are you here?"

She emerged from the upstairs bedroom looking as sweetly, sexily innocent as he had ever seen her. His heart almost melted, but then his rage burst through. "Katy, damn it, I have to talk to you."

She knew she was in trouble, of course, and guessed he had found out that the mailings were continuing. But she felt quite confident that she could control his anger. "Okay, I'll be right down," she said softly, knowing how well she could manipulate him, but no longer as proud as she once was of that ability.

Walter waited impatiently. God, how he hated to yell at her. It made his whole body tremble. He, who would fight anyone else at the drop of a hat, would do almost anything to avoid a confrontation with her. Yet there seemed no choice. Why wouldn't she understand? Why?

But he had to have sympathy. She had built such a good business. All on her own ideas and energy. He never ceased to be astonished at the maturity of her business approach. It was as if she had some hidden internal business instinct, the sort of judgment that usually takes years of experience to develop, which kept her on the right track. Harvard must be better than he thought.

How awful she must feel to have to cut back at the very point of success.

"Yes, love?" She was in the room before he realized it, startling him. "What's wrong? You sound so angry."

"We agreed you'd cut back all mailings," he said, trying to keep all the emotion out of his voice. "But they're continuing."

"Oh, no, I've cut back everything," she said. "Only the last few days to use up the materials we've already got. It wouldn't be right just to waste them. They're all dated, so we can't hold them in stock."

"No more mailings," he said flatly.

"But that's absurd, darling, we can't just throw away good money."

"We can and we must."

"But we've got to send something to the customers. It will cost us more to explain why we've quit than to continue."

"That's nonsense," he said, furious now. She had no justification.

She felt the depth of his anger for the first time. It frightened her. Had she gone too far after all? "I suppose you're right," she retreated fast. "I know I should have cut back. I'll do it right away, I promise. I'm sorry."

"Well, do it," he admonished. "We've no alternative."

"I'll do it right away," she repeated, wondering whether, after all, she could still procrastinate a little longer.

"We're short," said Hargraves, his brow wrinkling to the very top of his skull. "Desperately short."

"How much?"

"Three million bucks, counting the Von Ackermann payment."

"Good God!" Walter, who thought that the last weeks had inured him to crisis, was shocked. The sum was even larger than he had anticipated. "How the hell can that be?"

"The mail-order business." Hargraves's voice was without inflection. He was careful not to mention Katy by name. "Last week about ten million mailing pieces were sent—all they had left in inventory. And the returns are coming in strong."

"How strong?"

"They'll end up at five percent."

"Astonishing."

"Indeed it is."

"We'll make a big profit."

"In the end, yes. But for now it's a hell of a cash drain. Every one of those replies calls for a diet program, and many want an appliance as well. They only mail us in one dollar to begin with. It takes two months to get our money back on the diet and three and a half to get our money back on the appliance."

"So . . ."

"So if we do get the five percent—that's half a million replies— we'll drain over four million dollars from our cash."

"But you can borrow some on the receivables."

"Fifty percent. We'll be down two million."

"Plus the million for Von Ackermann."

"Right. And we've delayed payables, made savings, sold assets— just about up to the hilt. Perhaps we could find another half-million. Perhaps not."

"You think we've sold everything we can?"

"Everything that moves. There are only a couple of areas left to even look at."

"Then get to them fast." Walter raised his voice for emphasis. "We *need* the money; we *have* to find it. I am not, I am absolutely not going to give him this business for want of a lousy million bucks." His anger rose as he spoke. Too often nowadays his anger seemed to break away from him. It had become almost as hard to control as his business destiny. Hargraves ignored the fact that it was three million they were looking for, not one. He had understood the message very clearly.

It was Hargraves's wife, an unimaginative lady prone to sleeping restlessly, who first heard Hargraves's idea.

"Holland," her husband muttered in his sleep, or was it Holly?

"What?" she demanded, irritated and suspicious. He had awakened her from the first five minutes of sleep she'd had all night.

"Holly," he mumbled again. His wife nudged him solidly in the ribs. He mumbled something indistinguishable, which she feared might have been "fuck you," turned over, said "Holland" in a clear, strong voice, and started to snore.

"What was all that about Holland you were yelling last night?" his wife questioned him the next morning. "You kept me up half the night."

"Holland?" he had no idea. "Oh, yes, yes," he said, suddenly remembering. "Holland. Sale and lease-back. That's it; I've got to rush."

"When don't you?"

"Sale and lease-back", he repeated, looking as happy as he was able.

"Sale and lease-back" were just about his first words when he did reach his office. He was talking to Magnatel's legal advisor.

"But according to our contract with Von Ackermann, we can't sell fixed assets," the lawyer objected.

"That's the beauty of the Holland building. We don't really own it," Hargraves explained patiently. "All we have is a fifty-one percent interest in it. That's why we haven't sold it before."

"Still it's probably a fixed asset. I don't think—"

"Probably. Think. It's debatable. So we'll do it and apologize later. By then either we'll have paid off Von A's debt or he'll own the whole company anyway. So who cares whether we may be violating his contract."

The lawyer grunted morosely. "And how can you sell a building if you only own half of it?" he demanded.

"Oh, come on," Hargraves said crossly. "I don't have to explain this to you. You know as well as I do that a sale and lease-back is just a financial transaction. You sell the building and agree to lease it back. It's only a way for the lender to invest his money at a higher rate than he could get from a bank. So why can't we do it with fifty-one percent?"

"I've just never heard of it."

"Okay, then tell me, is there a legal problem?" Hargraves tried to keep the exasperation out of his voice.

"No," said the lawyer hesitantly, unwilling to commit himself. "I don't think so."

"Then let's do it, damn it. We need the money. Our share of that warehouse must be worth two million if it's worth a penny."

"Okay, okay."

"It's not okay until you've done it," Hargraves said. His secretary was amazed how stern he sounded, how decisive. He never used to be like this. "And do it fast," Hargraves added. "Goddamn fast."

"Oh, darling!" Judith ran out of the customs hall at Kennedy airport to where Walter was waiting and fell into his arms. Her face was covered with tears. "Oh, darling, I'm so miserable."

Walter held her to him, patting her shoulder. "I understand."

"And I can't even tell Juán. He loves me so much and it's all marvelous and there's all that money and everything's perfect and—"

"You can tell me, though. We're in it together." Seeing her so miserable, Walter did not hesitate to take responsibility.

"Oh, the last time I saw you I wanted you so much, and then I went off with Meshi and then he was killed and the money and . . . and I think I'm so *bad.*" Tears streamed down Judith's face.

"You *are not bad.*" He said it with more conviction than he felt. Then, thinking about it, he realized that what he had said *was* what he felt. "You give value for money," he added after a second, making it clear that he was paying her his highest compliment.

"Well, I'm a lousy hooker."

Walter stepped back and looked at Judith. "Huh?"

"I should have collected in advance. But I was much too intrigued by Meshi . . . That's what Kashi wanted to be called, Meshi." She wiped her face with the back of her hand. "He was actually a very nice man, Walter. Gentle. At least he was with me. I was surprised. I don't really care that much about the money, although it's a pity. But I'm awfully sad for him." Her eyes started to fill again. "He was sexy in a way, too. He wanted me so much, you see. I sort of liked him," she concluded naively.

"Poor sweetie," he said. "Come on, let's get going." But why was her reaction so strong? "There's more than that, though, isn't there? If you tell me, perhaps I can help."

"It's me, it's my bad luck," she burst out. "He wouldn't have died if I'd stayed away."

"But what did you have to do with it?" Walter hugged her to him as one might comfort a tiny girl, oblivious to the envious stares of every man who walked past.

She didn't answer Walter's question, but looked at him quizzically instead, her head to one side, her lips pursed as if she were wondering how far she could trust him. "I'll tell you what happened," she said finally.

"Okay."

"It was fun when we went to bed," she started. "He let me poke at him." She giggled at the memory.

"Poke at him?"

"Yes, I could push my fist practically up to my wrist right into him. Like this." She pressed her fist against Walter's stomach. "Only you're all hard. He just went in. It was really a sexy feeling."

"As if you could penetrate him?" He started to steer her across the terminal.

"Yes, I suppose. Though I wouldn't know. It's not an experience I've had." She was laughing now, her sadness overlooked.

"And then?"

"Then we made love for a while and slept." She stopped walking and Walter noticed that not only their porter but one or two other men were edging closer to listen. "Then we screwed some more. He was very good. He knew just how to move his body out of the way, if you see what I mean."

"I'm afraid I do," said Walter, trying to hide his disgust.

"We slept afterward, until about five in the morning." Her voice choked up again. "Then he went outside and. . . ." She couldn't continue.

"But why? What was he doing outside?"

"That's it." Her voice was high-pitched and cracked and her eyes streamed tears again as she rushed on. "That was because of me. Meshi said that I could have absolutely anything in the world in addition to my $250,000 as long as it didn't cost more than $5. And I said 'Pickles.' And Meshi said, 'Are you pregnant?' and I said, 'After the way you went at it last time, maybe I am. But whether I am or not, I want pickles. And that's not more than $5 and you said I could have anything I wanted in the whole world that wasn't more than five dollars and pickles isn't and that's what I want.' " She had stopped crying again and was able to continue in a more normal voice. "It all sounds silly now. But we were having fun. . . ." She was begging Walter to understand.

"Of course."

"So in the end he gave in and rang for Apollo."

"Apollo?"

"You know, his servant."

"Oh, you mean the genie? He's called Apollo?"

"Yes. He's really nice, too. Meshi likes to . . . I mean . . . he *liked* to dress him up in that funny costume. And Apollo really didn't mind. I think he quite enjoyed it."

"Go on then."

"Well, for some reason Apollo wasn't there. I guess he was out with a girl friend or something. At first Meshi started to get mad, but then I came to Apollo's rescue and it was okay. By that time I wished I had never even brought up the damned pickles, and I said I didn't want them anymore. But Meshi wasn't having any of it. He said there was an all-night store on the corner and he'd go there himself. So he got up and put on his silk robe. It's really a tent. Gorgeous material. It must have cost a fortune. Anyway he put it on and opened the door. I followed him, but not all the way outside. First he said, 'God, it's cold out here.' Then he lifted his head and raised that great voice of his so loud that practically the whole neighborhood must have heard: 'Pretty pickle! Picking pickles for a pretty pickled pretty.' . . . I'd had a bit to drink, you see."

"He must have had a bit too. I'm surprised he could even manage to say all that."

"He was great at tongue-twisters. We'd played at them earlier. He could say 'red leather, yellow leather,' so fast that it sounded like a machine gun. Try it, try it," she said, seeing Walter smile. "It's not as easy as you think."

"I know," he said.

"And then he was killed. Oh, Walter . . ."

"But that's not your fault."

"I heard the shot: a great bang, like a cannon. And I saw him fall, but slowly. Walter, it was so slow. He stood for a long time. And I knew he'd been hit even though he didn't move at all. I can't tell you how. I could see him through the open door. He sort of shivered. His whole body shivered. The fat rippled, almost. And slowly he started to shake. And then he sank. I can't really explain it. He just sank like . . . as if he were melting. Then he became a blob. Not a person anymore. A dead blob. And he sort of slid down the steps."

"How could you see all that?"

"Oh, I'd run all the way to the front door by then. It was awful. He sort of, sort of . . ." She was crying hysterically now, hardly able to choke out the words. "He sort of oozed down the steps, like a melting lump of fat."

"There, there," said Walter inanely.

"But why? Why is he dead?" Her anger broke through the tears. "What did you do?"

"I rushed down the steps to see if I could help. But I knew I couldn't. I knew he was dead even before I got to him."

"Weren't you afraid that somebody would kill you?"

"Oh, do you think they might have?"

"Well, they didn't. But it was a fool thing to do," said Walter, worried for her in retrospect.

"I never even thought about it."

"Which only proves that you had nothing to do with his death. They must have been waiting for him. Obviously they couldn't expect him to come out at that time. So they must have just been waiting. Could have been asleep, for that matter, and woke up when they heard him shouting."

"There you are . . . It *was* me. If he'd gone out later he'd have had a bodyguard with him. He always went with one."

"Couldn't have stopped a bullet. They'd have got him if they wanted to."

"But he'd have lived a little more. Had some more fun . . ."

"A few hours, perhaps. But what's the difference?"

"A little more fun," she said quietly. "That's all there is." She was absolutely serious.

"You're lucky they didn't get you too," Walter said, quite unwilling to think about the point. "You'd have been a perfect target."

"Yes, I knelt down over him and I was quite still for a long time."

"What were you doing?"

"I . . . I was praying," she said defiantly, as if admitting to having done something wrong.

"That's nice," said Walter. For a split second he remembered how his mother had often prayed. Instantly he banished that thought too.

"But who . . . ?"

"I don't know. He must have had many enemies. A man with that much money. An Arab, and with his appetites. He must have offended many people."

"But he didn't offend me," said Judith with great dignity. "With me he was a gentleman." It was an epitaph of which Meshulem Kashi would have been proud.

For a moment both of them remained silent. Then, "I think we'd better go," Walter said, realizing they had attracted quite a circle of spectators.

"Yes," she said. She turned a beaming smile on the porter, who had been waiting patiently. "Come on, Jimmy," she said. "Sorry I kept you." Dutifully, the porter followed Walter and Judith to the door.

"How come you knew his name?" Walter said.

"I asked him."

"I hope I see you again, lady," the porter said as he finished loading the bags into the car.

"I'd like that."

"You're the first human I've had all day."

". . . so you see, we're very close to the brink," Walter finished his explanation about the Von Ackermann situation.

"But you *can't* lose it," said Judith, intensely worried.

"I know," he said. "We can't. But we easily could."

"I'll see if I can get Juán to help. If he does lend you money, would he lose his investment if Von Ackermann does win anyway?"

"He might or he might not, depending on how useful—or dangerous—Von Ackermann thought he might be. If Von Ackermann refused to pay, Juán could always sue. But it would probably end in a compromise."

"Compromise. I learned how to do that years ago."

"You haven't been alive *that* many years."

"I'm over twenty-one now," she said just a shade bitterly. "And I learned about compromise before I was in my teens. Anyway," she added, brightening and determined, "we've just got to find a way to raise that extra money. How much do you think you need?"

"Not sure. Depends on the Holland sale and lease-back deal I told you about. That'll pay all our current costs and leave something over. Still we'll need at least half a million."

"Okay. Then that's what I'll try to get from Juán."

"I don't think I want you to," Walter was suddenly concerned for her. "I love you for the gesture, but . . ."

"I'm a friend. Why don't you want me to?"

He paused, not wanting to offend her. "There's no such thing as a free lunch. If you pay for it up front, you know what it costs. If you take it as a gift, God only knows."

"But that doesn't apply to me," she said, becoming angry.

"No, my love, I know it doesn't. It's just my reflex."

"Then why the hell—"

"Okay, okay," he said. "I want you to get the money for me."

"That's better," she said, mollified. "I'll see what I can do." She smiled at him voluptuously. In spite of everything on his mind, he felt himself getting hard at the thought of having Judith one more time. Incredible, he thought. No wonder men did crazy things for her.

"But why?" she demanded, switching back to Kashi's death as if they had not talked of anything else, the anguish rushing back.

"I just don't know." Walter had some difficulty following the train of her thoughts as they jumped backward and forward.

"Did they find out, did they arrest someone?" she wanted to know. "I haven't heard they've done anything."

"The London police are efficient. They'll certainly try. But it must have been very professional. They'll have trouble finding anyone."

"And I couldn't even find you," she said. "I tried to call but I didn't know where you were staying."

"I'm sorry," he said, contrite. "You must have been terribly frightened."

"I was frightened, yes. But I was more disgusted and sad and . . . angry, that's what I was. I was angry. He was so revolting when he was dead." She paused, trying to understand a concept that had not crossed her mind before. "He seemed more dead than other people because of his fatness," she said hesitantly. "It was as if, when he died, his soul fled faster." She shuddered at the memory. "I can remember every detail. Every color, too. He was lying in a double patch of brightness, where the light from the doorway hit the streetlight. His face went sort of bluish under the pink, and the veins stood out—like an orchid a boy once gave me which I left in the fridge too long. He was lying on the steps, which were gray-blue and dirty. The dirt was on him, too, as if he were already flaking to bits. The light was brighter around his head, so it gave his face, which was pulled back by its own weight, a halo. . . . Ugh, I could paint the whole thing this minute."

"Yes," said Walter. "Yes, I understand." He was astonished at how vivid her imagery was in his mind. "Have you ever tried painting?" he asked, interested, but mostly trying to change the subject.

"I did once," she said. "I was staying with this Italian painter. He didn't speak much English, but he was nice. A little temperamental, but talented. He said what I painted was primitive. When he said that, naturally I stopped. I mean he should know. So then he got mad when I wouldn't go on."

"He was complimenting you, my love. 'Primitive' doesn't mean bad. It just means that your painting was innocent, like Rousseau's."

"Yeah, he mentioned something about a fellow called Rousseau."

"Do try to paint some more. I'd like to see some of your paintings."

"Okay," she said and smiled up at him. "I'll give it another try."

Walter was relieved that she hadn't questioned him further about Kashi's death. Not that he knew much. But what he did know was frightening. He'd called the police in England the moment he heard about Kashi. At first they wouldn't tell him anything. Then yesterday, when Walter called again, the English police captain had opened up a bit.

"I'll tell you what happened, Mr. Cort, if you'll tell me all you know about Kashi. Perhaps you have some information."

Walter had agreed readily.

"But you've got to keep it confidential," the captain had insisted. "If we have any leaks, it might hurt our investigation."

"Of course." Walter had no intention of talking to anyone about Kashi anyway, not even to Katy. She was upset enough these days without bothering her with that.

"Apollo, Mr. Kashi's house man, returned shortly after the killing," the police captain had explained. "He told us that a man had telephoned to ask him to pick up a wallet he claimed Kashi had dropped."

"At five in the morning?"

"The man seemed rather drunk. He said he'd only just found it at your party, which he said was still going on. That sounded plausible to Apollo."

"Why couldn't it wait till morning?"

"The man said he was just about to leave. He'd wait fifteen minutes, or he would give it to the reception desk. Since Apollo knew Kashi kept a lot of money in the wallet—and considering the caller's condition—he thought it best to get it right away. He was up anyway, since he often doesn't sleep well. Anyway, that's his story."

"And when he got to the hotel?"

"It was empty, of course. No party. No man. No wallet."

"Lured out of the house?"

"Presumably the murderer would have broken in if Kashi hadn't appeared on the steps. He couldn't have counted on that. Do you know anyone who might have wanted to kill Kashi?"

Of course Walter had known someone, he had explained to the captain in detail.

"And you think this Von Ackermann might have actually killed Kashi?"

"Had him killed. I've no idea. But it's possible. I would guess he'd be capable of it."

"For a man with his money, would it be worth the risk?"

"What risk?" Walter had asked bluntly. "Realistically, what are your chances of catching the killer?"

"I see what you mean," the captain had admitted, chagrined. "But is he that ruthless?"

"Yes," Walter had assured him with total conviction.

"He'll do it, he'll do it," Judith screeched her delight over the telephone. "Half a million dollars. He promised."

"That's astonishing! That's wonderful!" said Walter, just as excited as Judith.

"I called him as soon as I got to the hotel. And this morning he called back and said the check was on its way. We were still chatting when the hotel sent up the messenger with an envelope. I've got it here. I've got half a million bucks for you, Wink! Oh, I'm not supposed to call you that."

"It's 'Wimp,' and for that much money you can call me anything, my love. I'm really speechless. I don't know how to thank you."

"You don't have to, silly. It's okay. And there's no strings attached," she added, reading Walter's mind so well that he broke into a coughing fit. "It's what you were thinking, wasn't it?" she said triumphantly.

"What is it?" Katy mumbled, waking up and rolling over toward him.

"It's Judith," Walter said, holding the phone so that Katy could hear. "She asked Juán whether he'd invest any more money in Magnatel and he said yes. She's got a check."

"How much?" Katy asked suspiciously.

"Half a million dollars," said Walter exultantly.

"Half a million!" Judith squealed at the other end of the telephone.

"That's wonderful," said Katy, trying to force enthusiasm into her voice. "What time is it?"

"About seven," said Walter. "You don't sound very enthusiastic."

"At seven I have difficulty sounding anything," said Katy. "But it's good news."

"Is it that late?" said Judith. "I better get some sleep."

Walter's elation carried him to his office on a cloud. They'd done it! They had money for another month—and ahead of the deadline. So they had almost six weeks to raise the next million. Somehow there must be a way. He was all set and ready to fight. Tough as his opponent looked, he, Wally Cort was still ahead on points. He hummed the theme from *Rocky*, then smiled contemptuously at his own melodramatics. He sounded like a damned soap opera, he decided. But he felt good anyway.

Walter attacked the piles of work on his desk with honest enthusiasm. His energy felt boundless. The pile of instructions to his henchmen grew. Poor Caroline was kept busy taking dictation, calling people, following up on ideas. A thousand thoughts about how to raise the next million crowded into Walter's mind. Somehow he'd find a way. After all, he had six weeks, didn't he?

His world crashed at eleven o'clock. He knew it would the moment Caroline hurried in with the telex. Her face told the story.

"What's the matter?" he asked immediately.

"It's bad news."

"Show me."

She handed the paper to Walter. Its message was very short: "Regret to inform you have changed investment plans. Am no longer willing to loan money to Magnatel. Check delivered this morning has been stopped. Velasquez."

The phone rang at that moment. At first Walter was going to ignore it, but then he guessed who it was. He picked it up as slowly as if he had become suddenly old.

"Yes."

"You got the telex, then," said Judith recognizing his tone instantly.

"Yes."

"He called me a few minutes ago," she said. *"They* warned him they'd kill him too. A man called him an hour ago." Her voice was panic stricken. She burst into tears.

"I'll be there right away," he reassured her. "It's all right." But it wasn't at all. He felt near tears himself.

"We'll just have to find another way," Walter said to Caroline the next morning, but his voice carried little conviction. "We'd better get on with it."

"Yes, sir," she said. "I'm very sorry."

"Well, get on then," he said crossly, hiding his disappointment under irritation. "We haven't got all day."

"Okay," she said taking no offense. She hurried out of the room.

The papers on his desk, his plans, his ideas—all seemed futile. Half a million dollars was still missing from this month. Even if he could raise that, how could he manage the next month as well? To give himself a respite from thought, he reached for the top of the newspapers. It was *Wall Street Journal.* He liked to look at it from time to time, a sort of punctuation to his frantic days. He glanced down at it . . . And his world, largely shattered already, crashed yet further. The article he saw on page 4 of the *Journal* read: "Fred Pogue, Noted Bartering Agent, Indicted for Fraud."

Mr. Fred Pogue, president and chief executive officer of Pogue Bartering, Incorporated, today pleaded guilty to a charge of fraudulently borrowing against assets he didn't own. These assets included television time and a number of pieces of real estate which he had previously sold to raise money for his faltering barter empire. . . .

Walter did not continue to read. He knew the story all too well. Poor Fred. He shook his head in consternation. What a dumb thing to do. And how very understandable.

24

"I didn't think I'd ever come to this," Walter said to Harry Grass. "You gave me one hell of a lecture, and I swore I'd never ask you. But I've no choice; and I figure that's when friends count . . . Anyhow, I guess you can always say no." He sat back. "That's all there is, Harry. I've explained the whole thing."

"Yeah," said Harry sourly.

There was silence as the two old friends stared at each other. What would become of their friendship? Up to this moment they had always been equally strong.

"You're begging, you son of a bitch," said Harry. "I never thought you'd sink to that."

"You're right. Neither did I."

"I don't know what to do with that."

"Do anything you please," said Walter, his anger starting to rise. "You put it into words clearly enough. You know the situation. I'll do what you want. Begging's bad enough. I'm not going to grovel, too."

"I don't want you to," said Harry seriously. "I don't even want you to beg."

"I got no choice," Walter said, his grammar slipping for the first time in years.

"You don't have *any* choice," Harry corrected him with a wide grin.

Walter smiled back weakly.

For several more minutes the two men faced each other without a word. Harry had just opened his mouth to say something when the door flew open.

"Well, have you got it all fixed?" Judith demanded, bursting in.

"She couldn't wait," Martha Grass explained, following her.

"You've been here half an hour," said Judith. "How long could it take?"

"A lifetime," said Walter softly.

"Yeah, about that long," Harry agreed.

"So it's all settled?"

"I guess," said Walter.

"Yeah," Harry agreed slowly, evidently clinching his decision. "I told him before I wasn't going to put up any more."

"You're not?" Judith's face fell as abruptly as if she'd been hit. "You're not going to lend him any? But you have to, Harry. He'll lose the whole thing."

"I know it."

"But—"

"Look, I told him I wasn't going to lend him nothin' after the first million. I told him that. An' I told him he oughtn't to do it."

"He also told me I shouldn't come crawling up his leg," Walter added factually.

Instantly Judith burst into a flood of tears. "Christ," she said, "Christ, how can you be like that? You've been friends for twenty years. Now he wants to borrow money and you've got it and you won't lend it to him. Is that all there is to friendship? Don't you care about anything but money? How can you?" She was virtually hysterical.

"Look, honey, I warned him." Harry put his arm around her shoulders to comfort her. "I told him."

"What sort of a friend *are* you," she screamed at him. "Who wants to hear your I-told-you-sos? Don't you see the man needs you? You prick. He'd help you if you needed him. . . ." Violently she pushed Harry away. "Martha," she said, "can't you make him see what he's doing?"

Martha Grass instinctively replaced Harry's arm around Judith with her own. At once Judith lowered her head, a desperate little girl, and sobbed on the older woman's breast. They looked so like mother and daughter that Harry, remembering a dozen scenes like this with his own kids, felt conscience stricken.

"There, there," said Martha feeling thoroughly unmotherly. "We do understand."

"I know *you* do," Judith sobbed, waving an accusatory finger at Harry. "But he doesn't."

"It's a lot of money, dear," said Martha reasonably.

"I know. Of course it is. That's why he needs it." Judith couldn't understand the problem. "Harry's got it, hasn't he?"

"Yes, dear," said Martha. She realized how dangerously close she was to letting her feelings show. "Sure," she repeated, pulling back and now patting the girl in a consciously motherly way.

"Well, maybe I could think about it," said Harry.

"Don't bother," said Walter, acutely embarrassed by the whole situation. "Don't bother, I don't care. That much I don't want the money."

"Oh, come on," said Harry, "don't be a shit."

"Me?" said Walter in outrage.

"You know what I mean. Just shut up. Don't make it any worse."

"Perhaps you and I should talk," Martha said to her husband.

"We don't need to talk, Mother. Anytime you want to talk, I know what it means."

"So?"

"So when you want to talk, I always end up doing what you want. So what's the point of talking?"

"Then you will?" Judith, elated, dried her tears instantly.

"I didn't say so."

"But you will, won't you?"

"Perhaps not all of it." He turned to Walter. "How much you need, Wimp?"

"Half a million to start. Perhaps more later."

"Yeah? Well I don't want none of that more later shit."

"Up to a million, wouldn't you say, Dad?" said Martha. "Wouldn't you?"

"I guess. Okay. Up to a million," said Harry, sounding rueful. "Same terms as before."

"You're great, just great. Thank you, thank you." Judith rushed over to Harry Grass and kissed him firmly on the lips. "Just great," she repeated more softly. "Thank you." She walked back to Martha and smiled at her. "Thank you so very much." She said it with great depth of feeling. Then she leaned forward and kissed Martha, too, on the mouth. For just a second her tongue probed through her lips. Martha Grass, standing rigid, felt an electric surge pass through her as powerful as when she had once shocked herself on a faulty electric socket. Her face drained of blood.

"You okay, Mother?" Harry asked as Judith stepped back. "You look white."

"I'm okay. Just a little weak."

"It's the excitement," said Judith. "She'll be all right. Come on, Martha, I'll take you upstairs to bed. I'm a wonderful nurse." She put her arm around the older woman's waist and led her from the room.

"It's nice they're such friends," said Harry to Walter as the door closed behind the two women.

"Yes," said Walter, "good friends."

"There's one thing I wanna make clear now that Mother's gone," Harry added. "I don't want to be the only one to put up funds. So anything I put up is for matching funds. I'll go as high as a million— but only as much as you can borrow from somewhere else."

The meeting with the First International City Bank of New York was as agonizing to Walter as it was pleasing to Ms. Smith.

". . . so I have decided to change my view in order to be able to borrow extra funds," Walter concluded his explanation. "I am now willing to put my personal guarantee behind a loan."

"You need the money." Ms. Smith barely tried to hide her glee.

"Of course," said Walter urbanely. "I would hardly borrow without need. Our business is growing. We need the working capital."

"What has made you change your mind?"

"Oh, our business is sufficiently strong now that I think the risk is minimal. Of course, in principle I still object to a personal guarantee. But since you were good enough to bend your principles the last time and lend us a reasonable amount without a guarantee . . ."

"An entirely voluntary gesture," Ms. Smith interrupted sarcastically.

"Quite," said Walter, ignoring her tone. "So this time it's my turn."

"Quite so," said Ms. Smith. "By the way, have you been traveling much?" she asked, apparently to give herself time to think. "To Washington?" It was no inconsequential remark.

"No, not recently. And I don't plan to go there for a while."

"Good. That's very good." Her voice was round with pleasure.

"So we'd better get down to business," said Walter briskly.

"I thought we'd done that some time ago."

"I suppose," said Walter. "How much are you going to lend me?"

"Not much."

"Possibly. How much? After all, you said you would lend me more with a guarantee."

"You do realize you would have to guarantee the whole amount."

Walter knew he would have no choice. "Certainly not," he said belligerently. There was no point in giving up too soon. "The first loan is complete. Why should I guarantee more than just the new loan?"

"Because," said Ms. Smith very softly, but very clearly, "if you don't, I shall not lend you any more money." She smiled, quietly triumphant.

"You have a way with words." said Walter. "How much?"

"Two hundred thousand."

"I would not settle for less than three fifty."

"I shall lend you three hundred thousand dollars," Ms. Smith answered, almost flirtatious in her triumph, "against a guarantee on the whole two million three."

"Very well." There was no point in arguing further, so why extend her pleasure—and his discomfort—longer than necessary.

"You will simply sign the normal No Change in Assets document," said Ms. Smith. "I assume there have been none."

Walter wondered whether she knew. Would he sign such a document? He could still see the headline in the *Journal:* "Fred Pogue Indicted for Fraud." Yes, he supposed he would. Later, perhaps, he could argue . . . Perhaps. But he needed the money now. Three hundred from the bank meant he could get three hundred from Harry, and that meant he'd survive this month, at least.

"Of course I'll sign it." He said.

"Of course."

"I need the money by week's end."

"Very well," said Ms. Smith. "You'll have it. And I hope for your sake the business is as strong as you say."

"Dear Katies" from all over America—some from overseas—poured into the offices of Magnatel.

Dear Katy,

Finally Susie, that's my daughter, got the right guy for her! And it's all thanks to you!! You give her some real good advice about how to look good and all. Now Johnny's interested at last. Which is more than you could say for that other fella. He was only interested in one thing, if you know what I mean.

It's like everything else, if you look good, you feel good, and if you feel good, good things happen to you.

Thanks, Katy.

Dear Katy,

I have been really lonely for a long time. I'm confined to a wheel-chair, you see. My son and daughter-in-law do come to visit when they can, but they are very busy. And it's not easy for them.

I try not to complain but sometimes I get depressed. When that happens I cheer myself up by writing to mail-order companies. I know it's silly. Years ago I wouldn't have dreamed of it. But now, somehow, it helps. Often it's the only thing that does.

Usually I just get back a form letter, but from you I get a real letter. I know it's real because you use my name—and not just inserted mechanically, but correctly in the context of the paragraph. Perhaps you do it with computers, but if you do you're very clever and you make me feel very special.

So let me tell you that you have done me a great service. I will

unhesitatingly buy anything you recommend. As a matter of fact, I'm on my fourth program now. Exercise is not exactly appropriate to me, but I give it to my daughter-in-law, who tells me she enjoys it. (Frankly, even though I shouldn't admit it, I don't really care whether she does or not!)
  Thank you very much.

           Sincerely,
           Virginia Bellamy (Mrs.)

Dear Katy,
  If you are a computer you're the first computer that I've enjoyed writing to. You're a positively human computer. And if computers are to take over the world, let me tell you, I'm going to vote for you as President!
  I'm not quite sure how you do it, but you seem to know all about me. You answer my questions intelligently, you refer to my foibles, and by golly you've got a sense of humor.
  I assure you that whether you're a computer or a person, you have one very loyal customer in

          Yours truly,
          Debbie Yankovich

Dear Katy,
  My boyfriend absolutely refuses to believe that you will answer this question. My problem is that I'm not on the pill and so I refuse to let him make love to me unless he's wearing a condom. He says it's all right as long as he doesn't come. I say maybe, but I'm not so sure.
  Katy, I don't want to go on the pill because I'm not sure it's good for young women like me—I'm seventeen. And I surely don't want to become pregnant. Also, I don't believe in abortions.
  Do you think that my boyfriend is justified in threatening to leave me if I don't do what he wants?
  Please help. I promise, I promise I'll be eternally grateful. Please.

              Very Upset.

All letters received by "Dear Katy" were processed quickly, efficiently, and as impersonally as milk, which starts warm and frothy as it squirts from the cow but ends chilled, homogenized, pasteurized and hygienically bottled. The giant opening and sorting machines first ordered the letters. Then they were punched into the appropriate computer program by keypunch operators, who converted them mechanically into predetermined categories of response. Finally the computer typed the replies on high-speed printers, which, with lasers, wrote faster than the eye could see or the mind comprehend. Nevertheless, quite unlike milk, which succumbs to the processing so completely that it becomes bland, white and uniform, every "Dear Katy" reply was totally personal in form and content. So sophisticated had the computer programming become that even the respondents who suspected that they were corresponding with a computer were lulled into the belief that it was a real person.

Every letter was answered. Ninety-eight percent of them were programmable and were answered by computer. The rest were answered by real people representing Katy Rochester. A few of the more interesting ones she answered herself. Every letter that went out was signed either "Katy Rochester" or "Katy," depending on whether the original letter was signed by full name or by first name only. The machine that signed used real ink.

The list of "Dear Katies" grew by almost 300 a day; it was now up to 60,000. By the end of the year, Katy believed the file would contain over 100,000 names. These, of course, were the best customers of all. As Virginia Bellamy (Mrs.) had explained, they would buy anything Magnatel offered.

The "Dear Katies" were Katy's greatest pride. She loved the feeling of being so wanted by so many people. "Certainly they're misfits," she explained one evening to Walter, "but they really need us and they really care."

"Don't you feel bad that they think it's you while it's really just a computer? Its so personal for them, but so mechanical for us."

"But it isn't. We spend a tremendous amount of time and money and thought and care on understanding these people. Of course we compartmentalize their problems and handle them on a computer. But aren't all human reactions and emotions capable of being compartmentalized? Isn't that what Freud did when he classified human emotions and invented a science? Isn't that what all of science is about?"

"I suppose," said Walter doubtfully.

"But it is!" Katy, warming to her theme, was convincing herself more than Walter. "In essence, all science consists of categorizing disparate facts into meaningful series, to understand their part in the order of things. So if psychology, or any other behavorial study, is to justify being called a science, it has to categorize, too."

"Are you saying that 'Dear Katies' are now to be elevated to a new science?"

"Well . . ." she pretended to ponder it. "It has some merit."

"Very little! Also, you'd have to grow a beard."

"Hmm," she said, stroking her chin, "a curly blonde beard. . . . But seriously," she added, "what I'm saying is that I don't feel dishonest about being mechanical, because, in a sense, that mechanization actually increases our personalism—if there's such a word."

"Katy, my love," he laughed at her, "you've just created the most ingrown circle to nowhere. Are you always that good at justifying yourself?"

"You may be right," she said, slightly rueful, slightly defensive. "But I still think I've got a point."

"Possibly, but you've lost it somewhere," he teased. "If you really think what you've just explained makes you honest, you've got a talent for rationalization that shouldn't be wasted on anything as minor as this!"

"But we do have a business," she changed the subject, determined not to let herself be bothered by what he said. "And that's for damn sure."

"Yes, darling, that we do. You've done brilliantly. And I'm delighted." He looked at her with love—a devotion, really, so deep it barely stopped short of weakness. "Yes, Katy, you've done more than I ever dreamed you could." He examined her carefully, as one might gaze on the Mona Lisa or admire a perfect Ming vase. When he spoke again, there was awe in his voice, his chin jutted with determination and commitment. No hint of weakness remained. "And I love you very much," he said quietly.

Today, however, Katy was more sad than proud as she walked through the moribund outpost of her business empire. This was where the action had been, where the mail-order business, *her* business, had shown its vitality as surely as if it had been alive. But no more. She had been able to stall no longer. "No more mailings," she had sent out the word, forced at last to comply with Walter's directive.

At the far end of the almost empty room, she observed two men apparently taking an inventory of the furniture.

"What's going on?" she asked as she approached them.

"Operation Big Sell," one of them answered succinctly.

"What's that?"

"Sell whatever ain't needed."

"But we will need these," she objected heatedly.

"Probably so," the man agreed cheerfully. "But not right now. So, we sell."

Christ, she thought, how awful. Yet it was what she had expected, wasn't it? At Harvard she'd wanted to find out what real business was like. That's why she'd joined Walter Cort, Inc., in the first place. Well, she had to admit that she was learning—and fast.

Even as Katy was walking through the empty, echoing mail room, so throughout the Magnatel empire a hundred other department heads were pacing their domains.

"Sell, sell, sell! Save, save, save." Those were the words of the minute. In every office every mind was turned to the one objective of raising money. "If it moves, sell it:" this was the catch-phrase of Magnatel's new hand-to-mouth practicality. As each price was negotiated, each sale agreed, each savings plan consummated, the details were telexed instantly to Joe Hargraves's office in New York.

Succeeded refinancing all office equipment effective immediately. Total saving $38,000 at current exchange rate.

Canada is pleased to announce they have found a tax rebate opportunity. Detailed explanation follows but accounting firm and lawyers concur deal is practical and legal. Saving C$41,000.

Switzerland, per your instructions, arranged sell special shipment hair dryers more than twelve months old and therefore technically in contravention of our quality control standards. Naturally they had been written off preparatory to destruction. Therefore sale gives incremental profit. The profit, expressed in dollars, will vary with exchange rates but is presently estimated to be $29,154.

I sold my company car. In Uruguay they're worth a lot. I got $11,000 for it after commissions.

Slowly the cash mounted.

"How far have we got?" Walter demanded for the tenth time that day.

"The latest total is just about $700,000." Joe's tab was as up to date as a network computer on election night.

"That means we can pull down all of the rest of Harry's million. One million four hundred thousand all together. We must be about there."

"Except we're still draining cash out," said Joe sourly. "As soon as it comes in, it evaporates—water through a sieve, he added, mixing liquid metaphors while he kept the company afloat.

"When will it end, then?" Walter demanded in total frustration, his voice rising. "Is there no end?"

"Next month," said Joe, his voice soft and utterly reasonable. Only his closest friends would have seen how his teeth clenched and the muscles of his jaw worked. "It will end next month, Walter."

"But why's it continuing?" Walter, near his breaking point, would not be mollified.

"Because, last month and early this, we didn't cut off mail order." He said it without inflection, careful to imply no blame. But his jaw still worked. "Next month, December, we'll start getting money in without sending anything out . . . we'll start to generate cash—as long as our business continues to do well."

"Fine. Enough?"

"Oh, no. The real cash flow doesn't start till mid-January. In December we'll only make a little. But it's a helluva lot better than the three million cash outflow this month."

"Three million?" said Walter. "For Chrissake!"

"I know."

"And that's not even counting Von Ackermann?"

"Right. We need four million in all."

"And we've only got one point four million? You have to be kidding me."

"Oh, no, we've got more than that," said Joe, to Walter's infinite relief. "I've stretched our payables to their ultimate breaking point."

"More than last month?"

"Yes, because I've promised to start paying faster next month. Our suppliers still trust my word, er . . ."

"More or less, you were going to say."

"Yeah," Joe agreed. "More or less." He did not return Walter's smile at all. "I told them we'd definitely start paying next month, and several of them gave us some extra leeway."

"How much?"

"One point seven million of the two point six we were short."

"So what we need this month is only nine hundred thousand more."

"Yeah. Except I don't buy the word 'only.' "

"No, I guess you're right. Neither do I."

That evening Walter sold the Ferrari. He got fifty thousand for it from a friend. It frightened him that he felt so little emotion about letting it go. Once he had loved that car.

Eight hundred thousand to go. The battle continued the next morning, Walter and Joe Hargraves starting again exactly where they had left off the night before. After a few moments their conversation was interrupted by a knock on the door. A young woman carrying several telexes entered hesitantly.

"Come on in," said Walter. "You've got morning telexes?"

"Yes, sir."

"Good. Let's see them. How much?"

"Another $124,000, sir. From five countries."

"That's great," said Walter, "I'm delighted. Listen, come right in anytime. Don't worry about it."

"Yes, sir." She started to leave.

"But only if you've got money," Walter called after her. She turned her head and smiled.

"That's good news," said Joe.

Just under three-quarters of a million to go."

"And ten days left."

"It's only the eighteenth," Walter objected. "We've got twelve."

"We have to get the money by the twenty-eighth to get it there in time."

"Hell, no. We can't risk that. We've got to figure out some way to get the money there faster than that. Can't we cable it?"

"It still takes twenty-four hours to clear. At least normally."

"So make a special arrangement with a bank close to Castle Ackermann, and have a man standing by so that when we cable the money, he can rush it right over. The whole thing shouldn't take more than a couple of hours."

"If it's banking hours."

"No, goddamn it. We've got to find a way to get it there even if it's outside banking hours. Look, it's possible we may have to do it in the middle of the night."

Hargraves wanted to disagree. This was just the sort of excess to which he objected. What a way to run a financial department. But no, Walter was right. When you were this tight, anything could happen. Time was just a luxury. "I'm not sure how. . . ."

"Joe, just do it."

"Yes, sir." Joe Hargraves could never decide whether to feel hurt or relieved when his boss laid down the law. On balance, he thought, relieved.

More telexes yielded news of more money. The girl rushed in to Joe Hargraves's office two or three times an hour. Five hundred dollars here, two thousand there, sometimes twenty or thirty thousand. Then she would smile and gleefully wave her telexes. Once she came in sorrowfully. "I'm afraid we've had to give $11,000 back. The car buyer in Uruguay backed out."

But she was back again only twenty minutes later.

"They sold it again," she said, as if she'd won first prize in a sweepstakes. "They sold it again!"

"Huh?"

"Uruguay. They've sold the car again. For fourteen thousand this time."

"Before commissions?" Hargraves asked acidly.

"Yes," she was surprised. "How did you know?"

"Everything in Uruguay, my dear, has commissions," he said wearily.

Five hundred thousand dollars to go. Four fifty. Four hundred to go. Three seventy-five . . . But the telexes were fewer and the amounts smaller. There were only five days left.

"Even if we could raise it this month, what chance do we have for December?" Walter asked his key helpers. He was gray with fatigue and worry. Was there any point in this absurdity, he wanted to cry. This charade of selling off every stick of furniture, every asset, even our pride if we could get a dollar for it. "Why am I so cursed?" he wanted to scream. "Is it worth it?" he repeated instead. "If we do make it through this month, what hope do we have for December?"

"Our projections show a slight cash gain, as I told you last week," said Joe Hargraves judiciously. "We might make as much as fifty thousand, assuming we hit our Christmas sales projections, which are ambitious. If we fall short of those, we won't even break even."

"And Von Ackermann?"

There was a long pause. Joe Hargraves did not want to say what he had to say. His forehead wrinkled so grotesquely that his hair seemed to stand on end. Eventually he replied, "The Von Ackermann million," he said, his voice hoarse, "the Von Ackermann million does not seem possible."

"And if we do better than our forecast?" Walter refused to hear the answer.

"Then we'll do better on our cash."

"But could we possibly find the million?" Katy, who had been listening silently, asked. "Is there *any* hope?"

"He already said there wasn't," said Walter testily. "What do you expect him to say? He's the accountant. He's not paid to be optimistic."

"Well then?"

"But *we* are. First we'll make this month somehow or other. And then I'll sell that extra in December if it kills me."

"But how?"

"And if it does kill me," Walter added, trying to make it light, "think of the insurance."

Katy looked at him, not sure how serious he was. Had she heard his implication correctly? "While there's life, there's hope," she said, testing him out.

"Goddamn right," said Walter. "And it's hope that we live on. And otherwise. . . ."

He left the alternative unstated, but for a moment he looked at her with such sadness that she could not mistake him again. Instead she returned his look with dawning horror. This whole thing had gone too far. Much, much further than she had bargained for. "You wouldn't?" she asked, appalled. "You wouldn't?"

"Oh, come on, Katy. What a foolish question. Of course not. And if I did, you'd never know."

Three hundred thousand. They might still make the eleventh payment if their luck held. Two hundred and seventy thousand. Four days to go. Twenty thousand more came in. A quarter of a million to find. . . .

It started to snow in New York the next morning, a heavy wet snow that weather forecasters predicted would amount to eight inches. Traffic ground to a halt at the very mention of it. So far it was only slush, spraying pedestrians as they scurried along the sidewalk, coating the bottoms of cars and buildings with a skirt of brown muck.

Walter jumped a dirty puddle on Park Avenue. Why did none of the drains in New York ever work? A car, aiming to beat the light, hit the edge of the puddle and threw up a cloud of filthy water. Walter tried to dodge but his pants were soaked anyway. "Oh, shit," he said loudly. No one so much as raised an eyebrow. He continued to slog his way across Park Avenue. It had been better when he had the cars, he thought, but they were all gone. Nathaniel now drove a gigantic Cadillac for a sinister-looking black man. Walter turned left down the avenue and hurried toward his office. Damn, it was getting late and he couldn't afford to waste a minute. He started to jog.

Three days to go, was all he could think. Today, and three more. Then he had to have the rest; a quarter of a million to go. The figure kept pounding in his head. Although he was already panting, he started to run faster.

By the time he arrived at his office, Walter was thoroughly wet, from snow and slush on the outside and from sweat, which he could feel pricking under his armpits, from within. His face, which had become paler and more drawn over the last weeks, was bright red at the cheeks and at the nose, making him look consumptive. Caroline regarded him, full of concern that he was working his way up to a heart attack, or at least an ulcer.

"What's in the mail today?" Walter called out, even before reaching his office.

"Twenty-two thousand dollars more of telexes," she said, "and a query from the Kashi estate wondering whether we are selling any of the assets pledged as collateral on their loans."

"I'm surprised it took them so long."

"They would like a complete accounting of what we've sold."

"Good, give it to them," he said, smiling cynically. "Tell Hargraves to prepare it when he has time, and send them a letter to that effect. Explain that we'll do it as fast as we can but that it will probably take us four to five weeks to work out a complete inventory. And tell them that, in the meantime, we can assure them that we haven't sold any of the assets pledged to Kashi as collateral."

"Is that true?"

"How the hell would I know? He had a lien on all the fixed assets, but not on the operating ones."

"What about desks and things, and machinery? We've sold lots of those."

"Debatably he had a lien. But we could argue that they are not really fixed and that we sold them in the normal course of business. It would be a matter for a court case."

"But if they wanted to sue us. . . ."

"They could hardly do that before the end of the year. By that time we'll either be starting to repay their loan or Von Ackermann will have the whole thing." He wondered briefly what the lawyers would say. Was it fraudulent to sell pledged assets? He didn't care. "Okay," he said, "let's get down to work."

"Yes, sir," said Caroline, deeply worried for him even though unsure quite why.

"First get me your English friend on the line," he said. "I have an idea."

"Mitty?" she smiled as always when his name came up.

"That's it."

She hurried out to make the connection.

"Raymond," said Walter as soon as he heard his friend's voice. "How are you?"

"Marvelous, old chap, just wonderful. You're having fun with Magnatel?"

"Enjoying it enormously," said Walter dryly.

"So what can I do you for?" said Mitty in his ridiculously over-refined British accent.

"We've got a few hair dryers left over. Our sales are terrific, but we've got a newer version out. I'd be willing to make a deal if you are interested."

"Always interested, old chap. Hear you need the money."

"Doesn't everyone?" said Walter, trying to keep it light. There was no point in lying to Raymond Mitty. He was far too well informed. But there was also no point in seeming needier than he had to.

"How many do you have then?"

"Up to fifty thousand," said Walter promptly. "Cost, about twelve dollars; wholesale, just under twenty dollars; and they retail for between twenty-five and thirty dollars in this country. They come in various colors, and there are some other model variations which are minor and don't effect the price. We'll give you all the details, but I thought we might discuss over the phone whether you're interested."

"Always interested, old man. Like to help out a friend."

"You're not helping me out," said Walter quickly. "You're buying good merchandise at a price so low you'll make another killing."

"Depends, doesn't it, on the actual price." Mitty was quite unaffected by Walter's sharp tone.

"We'll let you have them for cost plus 20 percent."

"Fourteen forty?" His voice expressed his utter astonishment. "You don't mean U.S. dollars?" he asked, unbelieving and trying to clarify.

"Too much?"

"Not if they're made of gold."

"They're not, I'm afraid," said Walter reasonably. "But after all that's only a little above our cost. And we do have freight and storage and handling and all that."

"My dear fellow, of course I sympathize. I know how difficult it can be. But I'm sure you must realize I just can't pay you more than I can sell them for. Actually, as you're a friend, I'd be willing to buy and sell at practically no profit to me. But a loss . . . I'm terribly afraid my partners wouldn't go for it, don't you see?"

"Raymond, I'm not asking you to make a loss. Do you want to buy 'em or not? Give me an offer."

"Love to, old man. Five bucks apiece, I should think, is what we could sell them for. Probably make you an offer of about $4 each."

"You're trying to tell me $200,000 for the lot?"

"Sound a bit high, doesn't it?" said Raymond Mitty, as if he'd gone too far in his original offer.

"For fifty thousand units," said Walter, his voice echoing the incredulity Mitty had shown a few moments previously. "That's the most absurd offer I ever heard. And then, no doubt, you'd want me to pay the freight."

"Of course."

Normally Walter would have enjoyed the bargaining process. But not now. This was no longer a game. He wished Mitty would get serious. "Look, let's get to business, shall we?" he said coldly. "I'm busy. You can have them for eight dollars F.O.B. New York."

"Five," said Raymond Mitty.

"Seven."

"We'll split the difference. Six dollars a shot. You pay the freight."

"We've already split—all your way. I want seven. And you pay freight."

"Okay, I'll pay the freight, but I won't go above six, old man. That's my limit."

"You're on," said Walter, "but there's a wrinkle. I need the money fast."

"I know," said Raymond Mitty.

"You know too goddamn much."

"I live by it."

"So?"

"Costs me more that way, you know."

"Bullshit," said Walter.

"But I'll do it since you're a friend," said Mitty, completely ignoring Walter. "Tomorrow morning you'll have the money. And I'll pay freight. But five dollars a unit, old man. Take it or leave it."

Walter remembered all too clearly the last time he had heard those words. They made him so angry now he almost turned the deal down.

"A quarter of a million," Mitty interrupted Walter's thoughts. "Tomorrow before noon."

Christ, Walter thought, what a position to be in. But he had no choice. "Very well," he said wearily. "Two hundred and fifty thousand dollars. It's a deal."

"Marvelous, old chap. Lovely. Done. It's a joy doing business with you. See you around, old chap. Bye, bye."

"Good-bye," said Walter. He hung up slowly. There it was—a month saved. He'd lost money on the deal, of course. But he had the $250,000 in cash. Thank God, he thought. He felt as weary as if he'd run a marathon. He rested his arms on his desk and slowly lowered his head onto his arms.

Walter Cort was still sitting hunched over his desk, head on his hands, waves of relief washing over him so powerfully they made his stomach tremble to the point of nausea, when Caroline tapped hesitantly on the door. She entered without waiting for a response. "Are you okay?" she asked, panicked when she saw her boss with his head on the desk.

"Yes," said Walter. "Yes, I'm fine." Lifting his head, he smiled. "I'm great, Caroline. We've done it for this month. I just sold Raymond Mitty a quarter of a million dollars' worth of appliances. The money will be here tomorrow. We've done it," he said, his voice starting to revive.

She hated destroying his elation. "I'm afraid it's not all good news," she said.

"Now what? What's wrong now?"

"Leonetti called from Inter-Land Trucks. He wants to get paid."

"Everybody wants to get paid. What's new?" said Walter.

"He's very serious," said Caroline. "He said he'll get an injunction for sure if he doesn't get his money tomorrow. He says that as our trucker, he can get the court to block all merchandise in our warehouses until he's paid. I told Mr. Hargraves. He said Leonetti's right. He probably can close us down if we don't pay him."

"How much?"

"About two hundred thousand. I told Mr. Hargraves, and he said to tell you."

"Very well," said Walter angrily. "Get me Leonetti on the phone.

No, wait. On second thought, I'll get him myself. What's his number again?" Walter dialed the number as Caroline told him.

"Leonetti Investments," a dulcet voice answered.

"I'd like to speak to Jimmy Leonetti."

"I'm not sure whether he's in, sir."

"Tell him it's Walter Cort, sweetheart. And tell him I'm in a flaming goddamn rage, and tell him he's in. Got it?"

"Yes, sir." The voice sounded less dulcet.

"What do you want?" Leonetti's voice came shouting into the telephone seconds later. "Great to hear you're in a rage."

"What's this about your wanting money?" said Walter. "You know we're going to pay. Why the high-handed stuff?"

"Oh," said Leonetti, the anger leaving his voice. "It's just that we have extended as much credit as we can manage."

"What the hell are you talking about? You've let us run sixty days overdue for months."

"I know it. We've changed our policy."

"Bullshit, Jimmy. What's going on?"

Jimmy Leonetti coughed uncomfortably. "Pressure," he said. "Irresistible pressure. I'm sorry, Walter. That's all there is. We can't ship unless you pay."

"For Chrissake."

"You're $202,000 overdue."

"We've been running that much for months."

"Then pay," said Leonetti, an edge coming into his voice. "I've told you, we're under pressure from some of our international clients. I don't know what you've done to them, but it seems we won't get our boats unloaded if we cooperate with you. Pay up, Wally. That's all."

"International clients? Where?"

"What difference?"

"I want to know."

"Hamburg," said Leonetti, and hung up the phone.

"Shit. Goddamn son of a bitch." Walter slammed the phone onto its cradle. Ten minutes ago he had the money. Now he was missing two hundred grand again. Where would it stop? When would it stop? He picked up the phone and dialed Joe Hargraves's extension. "Listen, pay Leonetti's goddamn bill. Its $202,000 overdue."

"But we don't—"

"Don't argue, just pay it," said Walter and hung up wearily.

The weather forecasters had been half-right. By evening eight inches of snow had indeed fallen. They had been half-wrong, too, for it had never got as cold as they anticipated and no snow remained on the ground. It was all slush now. Sidewalks, roads, gutters, everything was full of gray, lumpy ice water. Cars splashed wakes like speedboats, while pedestrians hugged the buildings trying to avoid the spray. The streets were almost empty. And still the water, half-snow, half-rain, fell.

Sodden from repeated splashings, Walter didn't even try to avoid the puddles or the spray. He simply sloshed through the late-evening swamp back to his apartment. It would be cold there, and empty. Katy was away on a business trip. Funny, he wasn't quite sure where. Trying to rustle up more business, he assumed. She had said she'd be back tomorrow evening. And he had made no progress at all with the money. Mitty's check had actually arrived this afternoon: $244,000, as it turned out, after certain transfer deductions the Englishman had taken. He could argue with Mitty, of course, about the missing six, but not if he cashed the check. That would be deemed proof of acceptance. And he had no option but to cash it.

So he still had $208,000 left to find.

Six months ago he was a tycoon. Now, alone in his apartment, with only Bundle to keep him company, it seemed he was a pauper. Two hundred and eight thousand dollars. Six months ago he could have written a check without hesitating. Now it seemed utterly unattainable. "If my friends could see me now." He remembered the words of the song. That had been boasting of success; but it seemed just as applicable to the edge of failure where he now teetered.

Holding Bundle in one hand, he walked over to the cabinet to pour himself a brandy. "Silly puppy," he said, looking at her draped over his hand, as floppy as if she were just a piece of fur. "How can you be so trusting? If I dropped you, you'd probably kill yourself. Bundle, take care. You cannot trust. . . ."

The little dog merely wagged her tail infinitesimally.

"Yes, I suppose you're right," said Walter smiling down at her. "You're bred to trust. Not me, though." Still holding her in the palm of one hand so that her little legs and her head drooped over on either side, he poured himself a brandy and returned to his seat.

He placed the little dog on his lap, where she let out a sigh of contentment, twitched a couple of times and fell fast asleep.

Now what? Walter thought. What can I do now? If only it were as easy for me as for the dog. He ran his hands over the arms of his chair and felt a certain contentment at the luxurious softness of the leather. It reminded him of the Ferrari. There was nothing left to sell now. And even if he did find the remaining $208,000, what about next month?

He remembered that his friend, who had bought the Ferrari, had said he could borrow it back occasionally. Walter might take him up on that. He could always take it down the coast road by the cliff, driving faster and faster, straight off the road, until it floated. . . .

He imagined it would be like a Disney cartoon, hanging there suspended in the air for long seconds before the inevitable force of gravity caught and plunged the car down to. . . . To a million-dollar life insurance policy, he thought ruefully.

It was a thought.

Black clouds tore across the charcoal evening sky over Schloss Ackermann. The wind whipped at the trees, changing their shapes from stately to grotesque. A single spotlight illuminated the castle's ornate main doorway and the turret above it, leaving the rest of the castle suspended, black and gloomy, in the stormy sky. Occasionally the moon appeared briefly between the racing clouds and cast an eerie light over the park, making it look even more desolate and causing the guard dogs to bay.

A black limousine pulled up the driveway to the castle, driving very fast and spraying gravel. It screeched to a halt in front of the main entrance, and the driver blared on his horn. Then he catapulted out of the car, wrenched open the back door and clicked his heels in Teutonic salute, his back rigidly at attention.

Almost immediately the front door flew open and there emerged from inside the castle a tall, attractive, blonde woman. She stood in the doorway, illuminated by the outside spotlight, and stretched out her arms in greeting.

From inside the car, elegantly wrapped in a long mink coat, emerged another blonde, tiny in comparison, and sweet-looking. She hurried up the few steps to the door.

The two women embraced formally, the tall one bending low over her visitor as if bestowing a blessing. "So welcome back," cried Helga Von Ackermann to her ambitious ex-roommate, Katy Rochester.

"So! We have him." Von Ackermann was pouring champagne when Katy came down from her room half an hour later. Next to him, Helga in a floor-length white gown looked coolly regal. They stood beside the fireplace, in which a great pile of pine logs flamed and crackled. The fire's reflections danced over them. Paradoxically, Katy noted, the firelight made Helga look even cooler than usual and made her father seem sinister, even dangerous, not warm and friendly as they might have. Perhaps it was just her foolishness, she thought. "Drink, my dear," Von Ackermann handed her a champagne glass. "Toast the success of our schemes. Have they not worked just as I predicted?"

"Just as we planned," Katy's voice was cold, lacking the jubilation of her host. But she lifted her glass together with Von Ackermann and his daughter, downing it as they did in one draft, and then holding it just below eye level for a few solemn seconds.

"So, dear Katherine," Von Ackermann said, his voice replete with satisfaction, "in one year you move from Harvard student to the ten-percent owner of a worldwide enterprise."

"That should be worth millions to you," Helga agreed. "You've moved from poor back to rich."

And from an innocent if ambitious beginner to a cold and successful double-crosser, Katy thought. "Yes," she said, showing none of her feelings.

27

Two hundred and eight thousand dollars to go.

A pittance compared to the three-hundred-million-dollar company Walter owned. Or almost owned. But for all that, close to unattainable—or maybe quite impossible.

And only three days left before the end of November.

Walter writhed in his bed. It was not even light yet. He looked at his watch for the tenth time that night. Six-thirty. Finally time to get up—even though he had slept hardly at all and was, as he ruefully reflected, as ground down and exhausted as a lump of old hamburger meat. Still, it was better to get moving than to lie here, his brain racing pointlessly, skittering from hairbrained solutions to self-pity, from despair to groundless optimism, to resignation, to nightmares about Katy:

How would she react if he were poor? Would she be as disgusted as he with his failure?

He pushed off the covers, careful not to disturb Bundle, rubbed his eyes, wondering what it was that made them feel so gritty on mornings like this, and dragged himself to the shower.

Even if he could raise the rest of the money for this month, what about next? It was the basic thought which had stopped him from sleeping. What about December?

Yesterday he had calculated—and recalculated three times—the chances of making the additional million by selling more merchandise for Christmas. The answer, each time he figured it, was the same: almost no chance at all. Even the current forecast was ambitious: Christmas sales were projected to be twenty-two percent ahead of last year. At that level cash flow finally turned positive—$50,000 to the good, Joe Hargraves estimated. Which left him nowhere, Walter thought bitterly, still $950,000 short. In order to pull in that sort of extra cash, sales would have to be a whopping fifty-six percent ahead of last year.

"Impossible," he muttered as the shower stung his back. But not quite, he thought. It *could* happen. If his planned promotions worked phenomenally well, and if the weather held, and there was no transit strike, and department store sales boomed. . . .

Of course sales weren't cash. But they *were* receivables—money owed him by established retailers. Unlike mail-order receivables, these could be factored easily enough. He could borrow at least three quarters, maybe eighty-five percent of them right away.

But fifty-six percent! Joe Hargraves said flatly it was impossible. Everyone else thought so, too. So did Walter, for that matter.

But it *could* happen, Walter thought again. He turned the shower off abruptly. It could! "To hell with it," he said decisively. "First November."

"Two hundred and eight thousand to go." Walter was in Joe Hargraves's office. With its simple leather furniture and spare wooden desk, it seemed a more businesslike setting to discuss the desperate cash situation than his own. He faced Joe across the desk. "We just have to find a way," Walter insisted.

"I know," Joe agreed. "But where?"

"No idea."

The only sound Walter could hear was Joe's fingers nervously drumming on his blotter. It was of expensive tooled leather, Walter noted, quite out of keeping with Hargraves's normal frugality.

"My wife gave it to me for our tenth anniversary," Joe said, following Walter's eyes and reading his thought. "It's not for sale," he added, attempting humor.

"Is anything left?"

"Nothing we can think of. The telexes are still coming in, but only a few hundred dollars at a time."

"I've nothing, either. Even the car's gone."

"I know."

"And borrowings? Can't you think of anyone?"

"There is one source," Joe said reluctantly. "But . . ."

"Who?"

"But I'd no more borrow from him than sell my wife's wedding ring."

"Hey, that's not a bad idea," Walter said suddenly.

"Sell my wife's—" Hargraves's voice showed the start of anger. Work was one thing, and God knew he was loyal to Walter. But no one, not even Walter who had helped him so much over the years, attacked his family.

"No, of course not. I meant sell jewelry. There's the diamond ring I bought Katy. I never thought of it."

"You could ask," said Joe to keep the doubt out of his voice.

"She's not here. Off on a business trip somewhere. I'm not sure where she went. I assume her office knows."

"Women are funny about things like that." Joe was being very careful. "She might not be willing." Never, he was thinking. That little lady would never agree to give up something she owned. "I'd ask her first if I were you."

"No time," said Walter decisively. "Ask your girl to get me Muscowitz, would you?"

"Your jeweler?"

"Right. I bought the ring from him; I'm sure he'll buy it back."

Joe made no further comment, but the click of his tongue made his opinion plain.

"Wally, what can I do for you?" Abraham Muscowitz's accent was Jewish enough to be part of an ethnic joke. "You want I should find something else pretty for your Katy?"

"No, Abe, thanks. As a matter of fact, I want to sell you something this time."

"Fine. I buy. I sell. Whatever you need. Just show me the merchandise and I'll make the offer. You want I should come to your place? No problem."

"You know the merchandise. I want you to buy back that diamond ring you sold me."

Walter could hear the old dealer suck in his breath. "But that's bad business for you," he said in a shocked voice. "You only had it six months. So if you sell now, you lose money."

"I realize that."

"I don't like doing this," said Muscowitz, sounding as worried as he felt. When clients wanted him to buy back goods he had sold them only a short time before, there was always a problem. Maybe they paid ten thousand dollars, so they wanted back at least nine. But there was his profit in the ten, and probably a salesman's commission, and all his office overhead. You couldn't run a business in jewelry without making at least keystone, in other words setting your selling price at double your base cost. Some jewelers made 1.2 times keystone or even more.

"I *expect* to lose money on the deal," Walter interrupted the jeweler's thoughts. "But right now I need some cash. Later I'll be happy to buy it back, and lots more stuff to go with it." He tried to sound convincing. "So how much will you offer?"

"Well, the situation is . . ."

"Look, I know about your markups," Walter interrupted. "I don't expect to get all my money back. But after all, you and I have done business for a couple of years now."

"Nothing like this, Walter. That piece you bought Miss Katy was a beautiful item."

"So what will you buy it back for?" Walter's voice started to show his irritation.

"Perhaps I could manage about forty thousand." Seeing no alternative, the jeweler started the negotiation.

"No," said Walter blandly. "You're thinking about the wrong piece. I mean the diamond I bought to give to Katy. Remember? Six months ago. I paid you $77,000 for it." It was always the same, Walter was thinking. Whether it was Mitty or Muscowitz, the bargaining always followed the same pattern.

"I tell you something. You can't sell what you only just bought and expect to make money."

"Who ever said anything about making? So far you're offering me a $37,000 loss," Walter snorted, pretending exasperation. "Look, if you don't want to do business, just say so."

"Okay, Wally. So on this one, I don' wanna do business." The jeweler turned the tables adroitly.

"Fine. So I'll go somewhere else. There are other places where I can sell—and buy." Walter felt he had no option but to call Muscowitz's bluff.

"You're not goin' to get no better deal nowhere." The old man could not allow as good a potential customer as Walter Cort to go to the competition. It wasn't every day that a man bought a major gem and then sold it back a few months later. If he could do that sort of business a few times, he could retire. "I'm tellin' you, forty thousand's a good price."

"Not good enough."

"So, since you're a friend, I'll go higher. No problem. What is friends for? How much you want I should give you?"

"Seventy thousand. I still lose 10 percent on the deal. And you're back where you started, except you made seven thousand bucks free and clear. And the value of the diamond and its gold setting has rocketed in the last months."

"A friend, Wally. I said a friend. At that price I'd be a benefactor. My rabbi would think I'd joined another temple." The jeweler laughed uproariously at his own joke. "Maybe I could go to forty-five," he said generously. "For a . . ."

". . . friend," Walter completed the sentence. "Forget the friend, already," he continued, picking up part of the jeweler's Yiddish lilt. "Better I should be an enemy."

"You are a friend," Muscowitz said seriously. "Tell you what— I'll give you twenty-five down and twenty-five in three months."

"No." The word burned from Walter. "That's no good at all. I need cash up front."

"A little debt that needs fixing?"

"Something like that."

"Happens all the time. No problem. You want cash, I pay cash."

"Okay," said Walter. "That's better. So let's get serious. Sixty thousand. Come on, make up your mind, I'm busy." Walter tried to bully his way to a conclusion.

"Fifty. That's it. I'm out of my mind at that. But it's because I like you."

"Done," said Walter. "Fifty thousand cash. And I'm still your friend." He hung up the phone and smiled at Joe. "A hundred and fifty-eight to go," he said with satisfaction. "Joe, I'm telling you, we're going to get there."

"It's craziness." The accusation was violent. "Even if we do, we don't have a hope next month. You're commiting suicide."

"We'll see," said Walter grimly. "Now, you were saying about the only borrowing source left?"

"I don't think you—"

"You mean the sharks, I assume. Big Julie."

Big Julie refused to do business in Walter's office. The luxury made him uncomfortable. And however often Walter reassured him, he always felt that the electronic equipment scattered there provided far too much opportunity for making secret recordings—by parties unknown, or by Walter himself, for that matter. Julie had suffered from rampant paranoia about bugs ever since the Feds almost managed to put him away as a result of one they had cleverly planted in a public phone booth he had been unwise enough to use regularly.

Walter, for his part, never felt comfortable in Big Julie's office overlooking the garbage trucks. It felt dangerous there—and it smelled horrible.

"We'll meet at La Strada," Big Julie ordered. "It's on Queens Boulevard, halfway between youse and me. Good Eye-talian food."

"I know the place." Walter recalled there had been a shooting there some time ago.

"I know the owner good."

"Bet you do. But Okay. One o'clock."

"Not today or tomorrow. I've got the weekend trucks to supervise. How about Monday?"

Walter realized immediately that the excuse was foolish; Big Julie was simply pushing for an advantage, wanting Walter to admit that he couldn't wait that long. None of Julie's clients ever could; no one went to a scalper if he had time to raise money through regular channels. But Julie wanted to test just how desperate Walter was.

"Fine," Walter said evenly, far too experienced to fall for such an elementary ploy. "But I'm afraid I can't make it next week. Got to go to Germany on a deal. How about the week after?" He prayed Julie would not call the bluff. "I'll probably need some more by then anyway," he added, trying to sound slightly bored.

"Don't wanna make you wait that long," Julie said gruffly. "When there's business to be done, get on with it. That's what I always say."

"As you like," Walter was only just able to stifle the relief in his voice. "But it would have to be today or tomorrow. I'm tied up Friday." Was he pushing his luck too far? He held his breath.

"Lunch today. One o'clock's okay," Julie replied. "I'll cancel everything just for youse."

Walter hoped Julie couldn't hear him let out his breath. "See you at Strada's," he said.

La Strada featured well-kept vinyl and chrome, with occasional plastic flowers. The noise level was high but, as Walter noted when he entered, the tables were far enough apart to make evesdropping difficult. The patrons were obviously well-to-do, mostly swarthy men in superbly cut suits accompanied by overdressed women with too many jewels and too much makeup. Most of the women seemed older than the men, but a few were quite young and aggressively attractive. A few pairs of older, almost grandfatherly men sat in the more isolated booths. No one seemed to look at them but, Walter noted, they were impeccably served by the maitre d' and the proprietor himself.

Big Julie was waiting at a table in the corner. Before him was a carafe of red wine. He was far wealthier looking and better groomed than when Walter had first met him years earlier, but the same underlying force was still clearly evident. Julie was not, in fact, as large as he appeared. But he was brutally tough. At fifty he kept his hair with the same brush-cut he had when he was a youthful gang leader, and it still suited him perfectly. His shoulders were so wide that his bull neck seemed in perfect proportion. And his face, which was large and round enough to seem bland on another man, was made hard and spare by the muscular jaw and the steel-blue shadow of beard.

"Wally," Big Julie called loudly across the restaurant the moment he saw Walter enter. "Over here." He waved his hand vigorously.

"Hello, Julie."

"Great to see youse." Big Julie gripped Walter's outstretched hand in both of his. "How you been? It musta been almost two years."

"Doing fine. Just fine."

Both men knew it was a lie.

"And you? How's the trash business?"

"We're up to three hundred trucks now. Some of them real big compactor mothers. One of 'em can crush a whole factory's crap in just a few loads so it ends up with just a pile of huge bricks. I never woulda believed it. I still recall the old days when we had to shovel everything in by hand."

"And you're still making money?"

"Sure. Big money. On all sortsa things."

"Protection like you used to?"

"Nah. Don't do that no more. The government runs their own protection racket."

"How d'you mean?" Walter laughed. "It's not like you to let the Feds put you out of business."

"It's all them rules. You hearda OSHA?"

"Occupational Safety?"

"Yeah. That crap. They got so many rules, no one could follow them all. An' then there's the city inspectors, too. An' the State. Between them, they got every manufacturer over a barrel."

"So?"

"So if the businessman don't fall in line—money, voting, whatever—they just use one of the rules to close him down. It's a far better racket than I ever had."

"So what do you do instead?"

"Lending." Big Julie grinned meaningfully at Walter and leaned back in his chair. "But let's have some food first."

They both ordered a pasta dish, which was ample and excellent.

And the Chianti Classico that Julie called for was superb. Under other circumstances Walter would have loved the meal; as it was, he had difficulty even swallowing.

"Okay, feller. So what's on your mind?" Big Julie looked up from his meal. "You don' look like youse enjoying the food."

"Nothing too serious. But as I said, I need to borrow some money for a month or two."

"Why?" The question hit as hard as a bullet.

For a moment Walter considered telling his host it was none of his business. Be arrogant as hell, that was probably the best way to go. But, of course, it was a risk. Big Julie might refuse to play. At the last moment Walter lost courage. "It's to finance our receivables at Magnatel," he said. "We've been growing so fast that we're low on cash."

"How you gonna repay?"

"Next month the installments on the last two months of mail-order sales come in. So we'll have the cash."

"How does it come in?"

"How d'you mean?" Walter played dumb.

"Don't be stupid. You know what I'm asking. In what form does the money you collect come in?"

"You know the answer yourself. Small checks. Money orders. Some cash. Five, ten, maybe twenty dollars at a time."

"So we could lend you money the same and you could bury it?"

"I could. But . . ."

"That would make our lending rates more reasonable."

"Not very reasonable, though." Walter smiled.

"Look, Wally, you know what we do and how. If you want money from us, you gotta pay. Our risks is higher than other lenders have."

"Yes, I know. And you know I don't have another choice or I wouldn't be here."

"Sorry to hear that. I never like to see my friends forced to come to me." Big Julie sounded genuinely solicitous.

"So how much will you lend me?"

"How much you need?"

"One hundred and fifty-eight thousand."

"Phew!" Big Julie whistled through his teeth. "You do have a problem."

"Only temporary."

"Sure. That's what they all say. But it's too big for me."

"How much, then?"

"I could go to a hundred, maybe. But I'd have to make a couple of calls at that."

"Bullshit," said Walter calmly. "Since when did you ever have to check with anyone?"

"You're right." Julie grinned at him. "I forgot how long we known each other."

"Then a hundred it is? You won't go higher?" Walter was secretly delighted to get that much. Big Julie and scalpers like him normally kept their loans small and widely spread. After all, there was a limit to how tough they could get with any one borrower: They could only kill him once.

"Yeah, one hundred."

"And at a reasonable interest rate?"

"Depends."

"On what?"

"On what you call reasonable."

"Try me."

"Forty percent."

"That's not bad," said Walter, hardly daring to believe it. "The prime rate's been over twenty."

"A month," said Big Julie.

"What?" Walter was genuinely angry. "You're nuts. Forty percent a month? If you don't want to lend me, that's fine. But don't fuck me around with no 40 percent." Walter's intonation regressed twenty years in his rage. He remembered the first time he had done business with Julie. "You was always tough," he said. "But not stupid."

"Okay. Okay." Big Julie was surprised at the outburst. "I didn't mean to go too high. Forgot youse was one of us, not the city dude you look like."

"Well, remember it," Walter felt mollified.

"Okay. We'll do it for 20 percent a month for two months."

"I don't need it for two months, only six weeks. So I'll agree to the twenty percent, but only once for the whole period. You give me the hundred tomorrow. I'll give you back one twenty January 15."

"Done," said Big Julie. "Except I'll give you eighty now and you give back the hundred the fifteenth."

"I need more."

"Then go to someone else. That's it from me." Julie took an enormous mouthful of pasta and pushed away the plate.

"And if I want to delay any?"

"Then we collect."

"Shoot me?"

Big Julie waited with his response until he had finished his mouthful. "Hell no," he said eventually. "We gone modern. Now we compact you."

"Seventy-eight left to go," Walter announced to Bundle. It was nine at night and, try as he would, Walter had been unable to raise another nickel all afternoon. The little dog wagged her tail as if to say she understood. "Now what?" He walked to his desk. Until last month he had owned a handsome Wooton roll-top. Now a cheap flat-top of nondescript origins served. He picked up his address book and started to turn the pages. Was there anyone left to approach?

After an hour Walter had found only three names he had not yet tried. But it was too late now; he would call them first thing in the morning. They might be good for something.

There was a quiet knock on the door.

"Come in," Walter called.

Mortimer, as proper as ever, entered. "Is there anything I can fetch you, sir?"

"No. Thank you, Mortimer." Walter's voice sounded worn out. Mortimer was the last of the luxuries left from his old life, he realized. Up to now he had been essential in getting the furniture sold, and in showing the house on the Cape to prospective buyers. A few weeks ago it had finally been sold. Anyway, considering their increasingly hectic schedules, Walter and Katy needed someone to run their lives. Even so, if they didn't make it through December, there'd be no choice.

Suddenly Walter realized Mortimer was talking to him. ". . . know how difficult things are," he was saying. "And so I've decided to offer my help."

Walter, looking up at Mortimer in astonishment, realized that the butler was smiling at him warmly. How incongruous that smile was! Mortimer, ever the correct serving man, had never before permitted himself such a liberty.

"You helped me once when I was pretty far gone. And I've been very grateful," Mortimer continued. "Even more than that, you trusted me from the first day. I'll never forget that." He seemed suddenly embarrassed, unsure of how to explain himself. "So I thought I might repay the favor," he rushed on. "I've got some money saved, you see . . ."

"Oh, no, Mortimer, I couldn't." Walter's voice cracked. A lump formed in his throat. "You . . ."

"I want to," Mortimer interrupted. Tactfully ignoring Walter's consternation, he leaned down and straightened out a pillow on the sofa. "I've thought about it, and it's something I'm determined to do."

"But . . ."

"I realize that any money I lend you might be lost. But I'll risk it. The only reason I have it in the first place is because of you. You've paid me most generously, and I have nothing much to spend it on." He paused and, smiling again, added, "And no vices left to burn it up."

"Don't you think you'd better sit down?" Walter asked. It seemed quite wrong for Mortimer to continue to stand, butlerlike, while offering a loan.

"Oh, no, sir. I don't want our relationship to change. Even if you can't pay me for a while, I'd like to continue to work for you. You see, I know you'll bounce back even if Magnatel does go wrong."

Briefly Walter wondered how Mortimer knew. But then Mortimer knew about everything that went on.

"I keep pretty close to what's happening," Mortimer explained, as though reading Walter's mind. "I know you're in a crunch." He made a wry face. "And I know what a money crunch feels like. I've been there."

"Yes. I suppose."

"By the way, Big Julie called and said you could pick up the loan any time today." He looked at Walter reflectively. "I did business with him once, before I came to you," he explained. "Not an easy man."

"No. He's not," said Walter, understanding.

"So I thought maybe my money would help," Mortimer concluded. "I've saved quite a bit." Awkwardly, looking thoroughly embarrassed again, he stepped forward. "Here," he said, "I've had the check certified so you can get the money right away." He handed Walter an envelope. "You can do whatever paperwork you think is right later," he said hurriedly. Abruptly he turned and quickly left the room.

Slowly, the lump now burning in his throat and tears stinging his eyes, Walter tore open the envelope. For a moment he couldn't focus on the check inside. Then, his eyes clearing, he read the figure. He ignored the tears which spilled over his cheeks. This must be all the money Mortimer had in the world, the savings from the entire time he had worked for him. "Twenty-eight thousand dollars, only," Mortimer had written in his meticulous handwriting. The signature, just as legible as the rest, showed his true name, Harold M. Stein. It was the first time Mortimer had ever allowed Walter to know what it was.

Fifty thousand dollars to go. It was Walter's first thought as he awoke. And just today and tomorrow to find it.

But this morning his confidence was high. He knew he would make it. If Mortimer had that much faith, then everything was possible. "Come on, Bundle." Walter sat up and tousled the little dog. "Time to attack. It's seven o'clock already and you're still fast asleep." He jumped out of bed while the little dog, sensing her master's ebullient mood, yapped delightedly.

"Fifty thousand. That's all we need," Walter called to Caroline as he rushed in. For the first time in days he'd eaten a hearty breakfast. He felt brittle, as if his well-being couldn't last, but wonderful.

"You got more, then?"

"Twenty-eight thousand. From Mortimer, yet."

"From Mortimer?" Caroline was shocked. "But how . . ."

"His savings. He volunteered—and insisted."

"He must be—"

"Nuts?" Walter asked cheerfully.

"No, I wasn't going to say that," she said, wondering whether she could scrape up any money herself. "He must be very loyal."

"Yes," said Walter, instantly serious. "He is. Very."

"What now? You've called everyone you know, haven't you?"

"Practically," he agreed, coming quickly down to earth. "But there must be someone left."

She looked dubious.

"I was thinking of Jackson at International Paper. You know, the guy who was going to buy all those watches. I know where I can buy a few more cheap. Perhaps he'd buy a load."

"I'll get him."

"Also, the old fellow who owns the Karlee garment group. Perhaps some consulting work."

"You mean George White. You never followed up with him. Do you think . . ."

"It's worth a try."

Doggedly Walter and Caroline worked all morning. But they met with no success at all. "No, thanks. We've no need for watches," Jackson explained. "No, we've appointed a different consultant. Didn't think you were available. Sorry." "No, I'm afraid we have no investment portfolio at this time." "No, it's not the sort of deal we lend against." "No. . . ."

By two o'clock Walter was back in despair. Nothing. Fifty thousand to go, and in a third of the time left to him, he had raised not a penny. Not a single telex had arrived all morning. There was no place left to turn. He started to pace the room, as claustrophobic as a polar bear hemmed into a metal cage.

Joe Hargraves, looking his worst, brow wrinkled, clothes disheveled, entered. "We've got to send off that check," he said. "There's only tomorrow left."

"We're almost there," Walter said. "Only fifty thousand left to find." He tried to make his voice sound cheerful.

"But where?" Joe Hargraves's desperation was evident. "I've tried everything."

"So have I." Walter couldn't hide his hopelessness.

The two men faced each other silently. There seemed no further path to explore.

Billy Wilson, formerly Walter's licensing expert and now public relations manager of Magnatel, burst into the room with all the exuberance of Mickey Rooney catapulting onto a stage. "I've done it," he yelled. "I did it!" He was giggling like a child.

"What?" Joe and Walter, both startled, demanded in unison.

"The Japanese. They'll license it." Billy Wilson was incoherent in his delight, practically jumping up and down. "They'll license the name Magnatel," he crowed. "For light bulbs."

"You mean they'll pay for the name to use on their light bulbs?"

"Right. A straight licensing deal. Six percent on the first million of sales, declining to 2 percent in the long run."

"That's . . ."

"The best deal I ever made."

"When?"

"That's the super kicker. They'll pay the first installment of the fee in advance. Right away. The check's coming over from their New York branch this minute."

"How much?" Walter sounded more stunned than anything else.

"Like I said," Billy Wilson chortled. "Six percent on the first million. Sixty thousand dollars."

28

When Katy awoke in the main guest bedroom of Schloss Acker-mann, she should have felt elated. November 30 was the day she would achieve her goal: By night she would own ten percent of Magnatel—ten percent of a three-hundred-million-dollar company. Her share would be worth at least eight million dollars the day she received it. And soon far more, for when Walter was finally beaten, the money crunch would end and the company would boom. By this evening, barely a year and a half after she left Harvard, she would have reestab-lished the Rochester fortune. What it had taken her father a lifetime to dissipate, she would have restored in only a few months.

On top of that, as soon as Walter was out, she would become Magnatel's president. That was part of the deal. Even though Von Ackermann would be chief executive officer and would no doubt keep her under pretty tight control, it meant she would be seen by the entire business community as one of the most powerful women in industry.

Money and power—what more could she want? After a few years in that job, she could go into government, a university, the diplomatic corps—anything. She'd be able to call her own tune. Then let her relatives sneer. . . .

The day seemed perfect for celebration. Her friends Von Ackermann and Helga awaited her downstairs, no doubt ready to have a huge breakfast. Across the room, elegantly furnished with Louis XIV furniture, she could see through her balcony window that the rain had stopped and the winter sun was making the manicured park beyond glisten invitingly.

Instead, Katy felt guilty, nauseated, disgusted.

She flung herself back onto the bed, knocking the huge down pillow which served as sheet, blanket and comforter half onto the floor. She tugged it back roughly onto the bed. Why the hell wasn't she happy? All was fair in business, wasn't it? She'd known all along what she was doing. So what if Walter lost out? Win a few, lose a few. Hadn't he done as much to others? He wouldn't starve, after all, He could always start Walter Cort, Inc., again if he wanted to. She'd even lend him the money if he needed it.

"Oh, shit," she said and threw herself angrily onto her stomach, as if that would help her shake off her gloomy mood.

Nothing helped. There was no point in staying in bed. The sick, sinking feeling in her stomach was as persistent and painful as a migraine.

In contrast, Von Ackermann, already seated at the dining table, was in exuberant good spirits when she came downstairs. Since it was a Saturday morning, he had donned the gray Loden jacket and green pants and suspenders of a landed gentleman. Katy could hear Beethoven's Pastorale emanating from his study. "Good morning, my dear. Good morning. We hope you slept like the *Prinzessin* who used to inhabit your wing of my Schloss—the *Prinzessin* with no pea in her bed, naturally." His face was wreathed in smiles, although Katy, frowning dourly, noted that even in this genial mood his eyes remained cold.

"Thank you. I slept soundly."

"Good, good." Von Ackermann nodded effusively. "I am so delighted when you, as my guest, enjoy a good night's sleep."

"Thank you," Katy repeated. She always felt ill at ease with Von Ackermann's excessive concern for her well-being.

"Today is the day we finally win, is it not?" Von Ackermann chortled his pleasure.

"Indeed." Katy tried to sound enthusiastic. Underneath she continued to feel miserable.

"Then let us have a good breakfast. Helga will be down shortly."

He banged on the bell next to his chair. "I enjoy victory even more on a full stomach."

Rosenblatt, the butler, appeared silently. "Yes, sir?" He was identically dressed as when she had seen him the previous evening, as if he had never gone to bed at all.

"Breakfast," ordered Von Ackermann. "We want a large breakfast. Orange juice. Eggs. Would you like them fried, Katy, or *Eier im Glas*—eggs in a glass—the German way?"

"I think I'll do without the eggs, thank you." Even the thought of them turned her stomach.

"But you must eat, my dear. Come, eggs are good for you."

"No thank you," Katy said firmly.

"And *Gänseleberpastete?*" the butler prompted.

"Yes. Certainly. Goose liver pâté is perfect. And some slices of ham."

"Very well, sir. And of course croissants."

"And perhaps some Swiss cheese. And coffee. Or would you prefer tea, Katy?"

"Coffee is fine."

"Very well, sir. I shall bring it right away." The butler glided out of the room.

"Are you not feeling too well, my Katherine? Perhaps it is the excitement. But you should eat."

"Now, father!" Helga swept into the room. She was dressed in a floor-length silk morning robe, which swirled about her as she moved. Her blonde hair was pulled up into a deceptively simple coil at her neck. She looked classically beautiful, the ultimate sophisticate playing at innocence. "Father, you must not bully my roommate." She seated herself opposite Von Ackermann. "Remember, Americans don't know how to eat. They toy with their food. Most of it's synthetic anyway." She smiled at Katy while her father laughed. "Katy, you have a case of nerves this morning," Helga said with certainty. "It is natural."

Rosenblatt entered, followed by the inevitable waiters—different ones from last night, Katy noted, and dressed in white instead of black. As often as she had been here, she could never recall seeing the same waiters twice. Either Von Ackermann's staff must be huge or the turnover very rapid. The butler issued orders almost inaudibly, but the waiters evidently understood, for they served quickly and correctly. Katy was reminded of a master shepherd controlling his sheepdogs.

"Wonderful," said Von Ackermann. "Now we shall eat."

The chimes, indicating a visitor at the park entrance, interrupted Von Ackermann just as he was picking up his knife and fork.

"Now who would that be?" he asked, instantly wary. "We were

expecting no one. Especially not at this time on a Saturday morning." Unexpected visitors were always unwelcome, his expression indicated. "Rosenblatt, find out at once who that is," he ordered.

The butler was already leaving. "Yes, sir, of course." His tone conveyed that there had been no need to issue the instruction.

"I cannot understand who that might be. If it were a tradesman, the guard would have sent him to the back entrance. So it must be someone to see us . . . Katherine," he asked sharply, "you were not expecting someone?"

"No, of course not." Katy was intrigued by her host's reaction. Even Helga, she observed, looked less calm than usual.

Rosenblatt, having telephoned the guard at the front gate, returned. "It is a man from the Deutsche Bank," he explained. "He wishes to see the Herr Generaldirektor personally, but he refuses to disclose his purpose. He merely states it is urgent. Our gatekeeper assures me that his credentials seem in order."

"Very well, send him up," Von Ackermann's voice was cold now and the expression on his face turned stony.

"Yes, sir."

While they waited for the visitor to drive up to the castle, Von Ackermann ate heartily. But it now seemed a mechanical act. He no longer appeared to receive pleasure from the food; even when he commented on how good it was, Katy got the impression he was saying it as a matter of form. When he exhorted her to eat, she remained silent.

Eventually the dining room door opened. "Herr von Schmidt-Scheiner," Rosenblatt announced.

A suave, middle-aged gentleman in a business suit and dark winter coat, carrying a black homburg, entered. He clicked the heels of his well-shined shoes and bowed slightly from the waist.

"Herr Direktor Von Ackermann?"

"*Jawohl.*" Von Ackermann arose and walked toward him. They shook hands formally.

"It is my pleasure to deliver to you," said the visitor, "through the International Rapid Transmittal Service of the Deutsche Bank, a certified banker's check in the amount of one million dollars from Mr. Walter Cort of New York. Would you be kind enough to sign this receipt." He handed Von Ackermann the papers and, extracting a gold pen from his inside pocket, proffered it. As he did so, he again clicked his heels and bowed stiffly.

Von Ackermann barely managed to control himself until the bank emissary had left. Then he exploded. "You said he was finished. Finished!" he roared at Katy. His face, contorting with rage, turned beet red, while his knuckles, pressing onto the table, were clenched white.

Katy, watching him with more surprise than fear, wondered whether he might not just have a stroke there and then.

Helga, although reacting without violence, was equally angry. Her face had become cold, hard, immobile. Katy could not help thinking that she looked like an angel of death. "What happened, Katy?" she demanded in a tight, controlled voice. "You said he could not possibly raise this month's money."

"I don't know. I can't imagine. I was convinced he was all played out." Oddly, she did not feel the anger and disappointment she should have. "I can't believe he managed it," she said. "As far as I could tell, he had no money sources left, nowhere to turn."

"But he found it. He found the money," Von Ackermann thundered. "Where?"

Katy looked as bewildered as she felt. "I simply don't know."

"Can he find more?" Helga asked.

"I'm certain he can't. He's sold everything he owns. Even his car's gone. The company hasn't got a nickel left. And he's borrowed from everyone he knows."

"You sound as if you admire him," Helga said suspiciously.

"I do," Katy answered simply. "He's put up a hell of a fight. I'd never have dreamed that he could make it again this month. Sure I admire a fighter. But that doesn't mean I want him to win."

"I should hope not," Helga agreed. "You have a lot at stake."

"Can he raise the million for December?" Von Ackermann interrupted. "That's the only question. His voice sounded even more guttural and dangerous than Katy had ever heard it before. "Will his damned *Yiddish* friends bail him out yet again?"

"I've no idea who helped him this time," said Katy, shocked by the outburst of anti-Semitism. "But I'm certain he'll never find the final million. You can rely on that."

"I trust that you are correct," said Von Ackermann, imbuing the words with a threat so heavy it seemed to hang in the air—a bitter, toxic cloud of hate.

"And if I am not?" Katy had to press the issue, had to find out what he meant.

"Then we must find a solution. I would have to take decisive action." His tone was bland now, without any overt emotion. But although his words were ambiguous and his voice matter-of-fact, not even a child could have misunderstood the threat of violence.

"What sort of action?" Katy asked in horror. The full cruelty and ruthlessness of the man was becoming clear to her. How could she have missed it before? How on earth could she have been so naïve?

"Like we used to arrange," Von Ackermann was saying, "a final solution to our problem."

Katy felt herself drawing back into her chair, shrinking away from Von Ackermann and his daughter as from two monsters. "But you couldn't," she said in a weak voice.

"Why not, my dear?" Helga asked coldly. "We would only do what was logical."

"Because . . ." almost desperately Katy searched for a reason. She had to protect Walter, she realized. Even if they were just bluffing with their threats, she couldn't take the risk. But they weren't bluffing. Suddenly she realized what had happened to Kashi. All along, if she had ever allowed herself to think about him, she would have known. The clues had been there the whole time, staring her in the face, only she hadn't allowed herself to contemplate the thought.

"After all, our solution worked satisfactorily before," Helga was saying, "when the Arab refused to cooperate."

"Because Walter has a million-dollar insurance policy on his life," Katy said, almost shaking with relief that she had remembered such a logical reason for not harming him. "If he died, his estate would pay the million. That's just about the only way the money could be raised."

"That would take time, would it not?" Von Ackermann considered the information as he would evaluate any other business data.

"No," Katy said, trying hard to sound just as businesslike. "It's a special policy designed to pay off very fast."

Helga was studying Katy relentlessly. "You are concerned for him, are you not?" she asked.

"Of course," said Katy, realizing that she dare not lose the trust of the Von Ackermanns, for fear of her own safety now, too, but quite aware also that she would only get away with lying to them if she stayed reasonably close to the truth. "I don't want any harm to come to Walter. I don't like violence . . . unless it's necessary," she added, forcing her voice to be calm. Desperately she hoped they would continue to have faith in her. God only knew what they would do if they thought she was switching sides. "Anyhow, it won't be necessary, I'm certain he can't find the money."

"How fast?" Von Ackermann asked, ignoring her assurance. "Surely not in less than a month?"

"I'm not sure, but I think so." Katy tried to answer as she would if the subject were not murder and she were not filled with horror and fear. "You see, the policy was designed to provide immediate cash to cover any short-term problems caused by his death."

"Fortunately, it's Christmas," said Helga. "That would delay them."

"Of course," Von Ackermann agreed. He smiled, relaxing for the first time since the bell had announced the bank messenger. "So if by mid-month our friend is coming too close to getting the money, we can make a decision without worrying about the insurance."

"So it seems," said Helga. "Is that right, Katy?"

"I think so." With an enormous effort Katy made her voice sound equally relaxed and confident.

"Then eat, my dear," Von Ackermann encouraged her. He took a huge mouthful of ham and chewed contentedly.

"Remember, you must watch him every day," Helga admonished, apparently satisfied that Katy was still on their side. "If he starts finding any money, you must let us know at once."

"Of course."

"You *can* find out, can't you?" Helga asked.

"Naturally she can," Von Ackermann interrupted, his mouth still full of ham. "He tells her everything. It is the most bizarre situation I have ever seen. My little Katy is quite brilliant. She is stripping her opponent of his clothes. Everything. Like the best professional. As well as I could." He swallowed the rest of his mouthful with a giant gulp. "And through it all, he loves her passionately," he roared with laughter. His whole body shook and tears of mirth streamed out of his eyes. He wiped them away with a red silk handkerchief which he extracted from his hip pocket. "My little Katy!" he gasped between his laughter. "You are beyond compare. Like Mata Hari, perhaps. To have your enemy love you while you destroy him. That not even I have achieved."

Katy never knew how she managed to bear the remaining hours at Schloss Ackermann until it was time for the chauffeur to drive her to the airport. She could hardly breathe, choked with her disgust. But manage she did, spurred by the knowledge that if the Von Ackermanns guessed her changed feelings, she might never reach America alive, never have the chance to warn Walter of the danger he faced.

Nor could she later recall anything about the flight back to New York except that the stewardesses seemed to hover solicitously, constantly asking her how she felt.

Walter, in the meantime, was becoming more and more worried. Why hadn't she called? Where on earth was she? When she left three days ago, he'd been so preoccupied with finding the money for November, he'd barely paid attention when she told him where she was going. They both traveled a great deal these days, visiting department stores or drug-chain headquarters, working with salespeople, pushing for business. Then yesterday, when he'd finally got the money off, he'd called her office to find where she was, anxious to tell her the good news. But they'd lost touch with her. Apparently she'd left on a trip to Chicago, but when they tried to call her, the hotel had no record.

At first Walter had assumed that her secretary, a new girl Katy liked but who seemed pretty dumb to him, had just become confused.

"Let me know as soon as you find her," he'd told the girl crossly.

But when no word of Katy had come by last night and then by this morning, Walter had become seriously alarmed. It was two o'clock in the afternoon now, and he was vacillating between near-panic that something must be terribly wrong and thoroughgoing annoyance that she had not called.

When Katy finally walked in a few minutes after two, he felt a surge of relief. "Where the hell have you been?" he demanded, his concern turned to anger. "I've been worried sick about you."

"I'm sorry," she said contritely. "I. . . ." She hung her head, looking pale, contrite, heart-sick.

Instantly Walter realized how miserable Katy felt. "Oh, love, you haven't heard!" He rushed over to her. "There's nothing to worry about. We made November." He threw his arms about her and hugged her. "It was close, but. . . ."

"I know," she interrupted. Then, remembering that she still had to explain herself, added, "I called in to keep up with it."

"Then what is wrong?" He was full of concern. "Aren't you well?" He started to help her off with her coat.

"I'm fine," she said, hardly knowing how to look at him.

"You don't look it," he said gently. "Do tell me. I know something's wrong."

"It's nothing." But it was clear that he didn't believe her. And clear, too, that she would have to tell him. Only she couldn't, she simply couldn't. "I'm just worried," she said weakly.

"Please don't worry, love. We'll find some way to make the last payment. I've no idea how," he tried to sound lighthearted about it. "But there must be a way."

"Do you think so?"

"Even if we lose, I'll look after you somehow," he said, not wanting to answer her question directly.

"But lose to Von Ackermann?"

"I know it hurts," he said. "But what can we do? We can't very well kill him, can we?" He grinned at her, and she thought the unintentional irony of his remark might make her burst into tears. "Anyhow, I would never have found you if I hadn't got involved in this deal. You would have left the company and I'd never have seen you again. So if I lose everything—and keep you—it would be the best trade I ever made." Again he smiled at her, a brave smile hiding his terror. Would she even stay with him if he were poor again? Oh God, what would he do if she left? "And you never know," he added, still in the same forced, cheerful tone, "I might get hit by a truck. . . ."

"Oh no," she cried out in horror, knowing exactly what he was thinking. "Don't say that. Don't. I couldn't stand it. I can't. . . . Oh my God," she moaned and broke into racking sobs. "Oh, what have I done?"

Walter was completely bewildered by her reaction and terribly shocked. "What is it, darling? What's wrong?" He tried to pull her toward him. "It's all right," he soothed. "What did I say? I'm sorry."

"No," she cried. "No, it's not you. It's me." She pushed him away, sobbing convulsively. "Oh, I'm so ashamed. I've been terrible. Oh God, I'm so sorry. If only I could roll it all back . . . Oh, I'm so sorry," she wept.

"But for what? What have you done? What could you possibly have done that's so awful? I'll understand, Katy," he insisted. "Tell me. It's all right. I love you." Again he tried to put his arms around her, to comfort her.

"No," she said, fighting against his sympathy, pushing him away as determinedly as if he were smothering her. "No, you can't understand. You couldn't. No one could. No one . . ."

She was almost hysterical, Walter realized. "Katy!" he said sharply. "Katy, listen to me."

"Yes." She fought for control. "I'm sorry." With an enormous effort, she managed to achieve a measure of calm. "I'm all right now. And I know I must tell you. You have a right to know." She took a Kleenex from her bag and wiped her eyes. "Just give me a few moments." She replaced the Kleenex and took out her makeup kit. Turning half away from Walter, she patted the makeup around her eyes, covering their tear swellings, and then applied lipstick. It was as if she needed protection before she could tell him. "I'll be ready in a minute," she said. "Then I'll explain. I only hope. . . ." For a moment her voice broke, and Walter thought she would start weeping again. But with another great effort she held onto her control. "I only hope you will not be hurt too terribly."

"By what?"

She wouldn't answer him but completed her makeup instead. "Now," she said when she was done, "let's sit down in the study."

Meekly, full of foreboding, Walter followed her into the study. He sat on the sofa where she indicated, while she placed herself opposite him on the leather chair.

For a moment she studied him silently, the sense of loss in her, and of horror at what she had done, swelling and flooding over her like the water from some huge reservoir after the dam had broken. In those moments, too, the contrast between this man, whom she had now lost so irrevocably—and broken and endangered besides—and Von Ackermann became almost unbearably painful. A wave of love for Walter swept over her so powerful that she had to grip the sides of her chair to stop herself from jumping up and throwing herself at him. With equal, overwhelming passion she was filled with loathing for Von Ackermann, for Helga, but above all for herself.

"I have betrayed you all along," she started, her voice low and shaking. "I have worked for Von Ackermann to destroy you. Helga, his daughter, was my roommate in college. I get ten percent of Magnatel if Von Ackermann takes it over." She spoke mechanically, as if she were reciting. *Father, forgive me for I have sinned,* her tone seemed to mimic. So deep was her pain that she dared let none of it show for fear that she would lose control and drown. "All along, I have played a game with you, pretending to work for you, pretending to love you. It has all been a lie. Even the mail-order business was a trick worked out by the Von Ackermanns and me to use up the cash.

For many minutes she continued her recitation, explaining it all, extenuating nothing, excusing nothing.

Even when she told Walter how Von Ackermann was responsible for Kashi's death and warned him that his own life—and now hers— was in danger, she refused to excuse herself. She should have known.

When she was finished, she sat, hands on lap, head bowed, drained. She felt dirty and degraded, full of self-hate, and completely devoid of hope. I love him, was all she could think. How ironic—and pitifully sad—that she should discover that only after she had destroyed all hope that he could ever again love her.

Throughout Katy's recitation, Walter's position never changed. The casual observer might have thought he was relaxed, listening with interest to what she was saying. The closer viewer would have realized that his whole body had become rigid. Each of his muscles was clenched against another, like so many steel vises. His breath emerged in rapid, shallow gasps.

The silence which followed the completion of Katy's confession seemed to last interminably. For her part, Katy was devastated with shame. For his, Walter was filled with a million swirling, battering thoughts and emotions he could neither sort nor comprehend—but which, above all, he simply could not accept. He was in a state of shock as total as if Katy had died.

"All this time?" he asked at last, his voice a whisper. "All this time you were working for him?"

"Yes," she said, filled with self-loathing. "Yes. Every one of your employees, even thousands of Magnatel customers—they were all loyal to you. Only I, who pretended to love you, only I who *do* love you, I now realize, betrayed you. Only I. . . ." She was sobbing again, no longer hysterical but weeping quietly. The tears streamed down her cheeks unheeded. She knew her heart was breaking.

Walter could remember so clearly how his mother had told him to leave the house and hide in the woods. He could hear her quite distinctly, as if she were sitting in the chair where Katy was weeping. "Run. Hide. Trust no one."

"I still love her," he wanted to say. But his mother was no longer there to hear him. He remembered how they had dragged her off as he lay flat in the ditch. She had not even screamed.

Slowly, as if he were carrying a heavy weight, or as if the air had become as thick as water, he rose. Without another word he left the study. As if in a dream, he took his coat from the hall closet and opened the front door. Bundle barked once, but he ignored her. The little dog's tail drooped. Walter stepped outside and closed the door firmly behind him. As he walked down the steps from his house into the cold gray city, a snowflake landed on his face.

The few snowflakes fluttering down turned gray in the New York air even before they reached the ground. It took two hours before enough had fallen to be seen on the roadways and sidewalks. By that time, too, the patches of vegetation which dotted the city—the boulevard in the center of Park Avenue, the trees and bushes decorating the frontages of the more elegant office buildings, the churchyards on Fifth Avenue and Wall Street—were dusted with the light gray, shimmering powder. Pedestrians were hurrying more than usual and ducking their heads to keep the flakes out of their eyes.

By late evening it was snowing in earnest. Heavy flakes were falling perpendicularly from the low-hanging sky and forming thick layers on the ground. The snow reflected bluish under neon lights and gold under incandescent ones. Cars, oddly muted by the snow, moved carefully but nevertheless skidded at corners or when starting at traffic lights.

Somewhere in the city Walter plodded on as if he were hurrying toward a goal. In fact he was quite aimless. His dark coat was covered with snow; his hair was plastered with it. Unlike the few other pedestrians bent against the storm, Walter kept his head up, oblivious to the snow stinging at his eyes. The pain in his heart overwhelmed every other discomfort.

At midnight, sodden, freezing and finally exhausted, he turned into a small hotel. The clerk looked at him suspiciously when he asked for a room. But when Walter wordlessly gave him a five-dollar bill, he changed his attitude and accompanied his exhausted but evidently well heeled guest to one of his better rooms. It was a spartan affair furnished with a red vinyl chair on partially worn linoleum, a single bed with sagging mattress, fly-specked lace curtains in front of opaquely dirty windows and a dank, moldy-smelling shower stall, toilet and washbasin. Walter, oblivious to his surroundings, said nothing. He shrugged off his overcoat, letting it fall onto the floor. As soon as the manager departed, he flung himself fully clothed facedown onto the bed. He fell at once into a near-coma of exhaustion and despair.

The snow continued without abatement for thirty-six hours. By that time fourteen inches had fallen. Creakily the city's snow-removal system started to fight back. But with surly employees and hopelessly antiquated machinery, it was quite inadequate to the task. Unsnarling the city would take days.

The whole eastern third of the United States was blanketed by the blizzard. From Presque Isle in northern Maine and Chicago in the West, to Washington in the South, the snow bogged down traffic, messed up deliveries, kept shoppers at home and gave the retailing industry one of the worst weeks in years. Any chance Magnatel might have had to exceed its Christmas sales forecast was obliterated.

Joe Hargraves sat in his office, his chin resting in his hands, and gazed at the snow. What a shame for Walter, after he'd tried so hard, he was thinking. He wondered what Von Ackermann would be like as a new boss. A colleague who worked for one of his other companies said he wasn't so bad. Of course, it would have been better if Walter had won—he was great to work for. But you had to be philosophical about these things. The German might turn out all right. Where was Walter, anyway? He hadn't seen hide nor hair of him in two days.

Mortimer chose to shovel the snow on the balcony. He could just as easily have left it untouched, since no one ever went out there in the winter. But it offended his sensibilities to leave a task like that undone, and anyway, he needed to do something physical to keep his mind off his worry over Walter.

His first indication that something was seriously wrong had been yesterday at noon, when he had asked Katy where Walter was. It was so unlike him to be away without letting Mortimer know how to contact him or when he'd be back. Katy had burst into tears and rushed from the room. He still didn't know much more. But from her reaction and Mr. Hargraves's resigned expression when he hurried over this morning to see Katy, it was obvious that things were terribly wrong.

Presumably they couldn't raise the final installment.

But where *was* Walter? Was he just nursing his wounds, wanting to be alone? Or had he been in an accident? Mortimer had checked with the police and the hospitals, but they had no record of him. He shoveled harder. What the hell should he do? Wait without interfering; start the police searching? He wished he could have a drink.

As for Katy, she had been beside herself ever since Walter left. She had not left the apartment, praying without hope that he might call, brooding or crying, never ceasing to berate herself for her disloyalty. Then, this morning, driven to a hopeless flurry of activity, she had hauled poor Joe Hargraves to the apartment and demanded that he find a solution.

The poor man had merely shrugged hopelessly. "It's impossible, Katy. With the snow we'll be lucky to hit our forecast, let alone beat it."

"Then we must find the money some other way. I just can't sit here and let him lose everything. I can't!" Even knowing the risk to Walter, she knew she had to do something. It was the only way he might forgive her. And anyhow, she simply wouldn't tell the Von Ackermanns; she'd swear Walter couldn't find the money. They'd probably believe her, and they wouldn't risk the insurance paying up if they didn't have to. By the time they realized, she just hoped it would be too late. There'd be no point left in killing him. As Helga would say, it wouldn't be logical.

"Forget it," Joe had shattered her thoughts completely. "We couldn't raise another ten thousand if our lives depended on it."

Finally, unable to stay home another second, she decided to go to the plant.

As Katy walked through the door of the mail-processing room, she was surprised to be surrounded by activity. She had assumed that, with no new mailings going out for the past few weeks, there would be little mail coming in. But the place was in pandemonium.

"What's going on?" Katy called over to the foreman. "The place is going crazy." She was not really interested, but she had to do something to take her mind off Walter's plight.

"Damn right. Haven't seen it like this for weeks," the man called back. "It's the Christmas mail. We're getting cards by the thousand." He grinned at her. "Mostly for you."

"Oh, sure," she said mockingly. "Everyone cares for me."

The foreman grabbed a handful of cards as they emerged from one of the opening machines and handed them to Katy. "Here," he said, "look for yourself."

"Happy Christmas, Katy," the first card read. "Thank you for making my year a lot better. You did me good." The writer had drawn sprigs of holly around her card.

In a daze Katy opened another one, and then another and another. As she read the blessings being poured onto her, her eyes filled with tears.

"Katy, you have been so warm and friendly and helpful to me. Thank you and have a wonderful Christmas."

"Dear Katy, "Thank you for everything you've done for me. I hope you have a very Merry Christmas and a really healthy and success-ful New Year."

"Katy, God bless you. . . ."

"Katy, I really wish you were my daughter. And remember, if there is ever anything I can do for you. . . ."

That was *it!*

As the idea hit her, Katy felt its impact as powerfully as if she had collided with a physical object. For a moment she was too stunned to move. Then she was galvanized, hardly able to contain her excitement. "How many do we have?" she shouted to the foreman.

"What?" he looked bewildered.

"How many Christmas cards are coming in?"

"Dunno," he said succinctly. "They'd know in the office. But they're coming in heavy. Five, ten thousand a day."

It *could* work, was all she could think. It had to work. Before she had even finished formulating the thought, she had turned and was running for the door. If only they could move fast enough. It was December fourth already. There was so little time left.

Katy entered the mail-room office still at a run. It was occupied by a skeleton staff. She dodged between the desks, fairly scampered over to the supervisor's office in the corner and burst in violently. Having no work, he was relaxing with his newspaper. The man was so startled as Katy rushed in that he dropped the paper and jumped to his feet, almost upsetting his chair.

"Sorry, Harry," she panted, "but I've got a crisis."

"Okay," he said, recovering at once. "It'll be good to have some-thing to do."

Thank God he was solid, she thought, one of the best people she had. "How many 'Dear Katies' do we have on file?" she demanded.

"Just over a hundred thousand. And there's a heavy load of Christ-mas ones coming in. About ninety-five hundred a day. Lots of duplica-tion with our file, of course, but some of them will be new."

"And the loyalty file—how many *A*s do we have?" Katy was referring to the computerized list which grouped all Magnatel custom-ers by the number of times they had purchased. *A*s were customers who had bought at least four times.

"Over half a million. And another million or so *B*s." Those, Katy knew, were customers who had bought at least twice.

"How big a mailing could you get out by the fifteenth?" Katy's face was bright pink, glowing with excitement.

"I thought we weren't sending out anything."

"Never mind that. I've got an idea. How many?"

"Well, half a million if we started right away. What do you want to send?"

"No," she said, her words tumbling over each other. "That's not enough. A letter. I want to send out at least a million."

"Do you have it?" he interrupted, starting to get caught up in her enthusiasm.

"Not yet. I'm going to write it right now."

"Okay. Then I'd better call the printer and tell them we want a rush."

"Yes," she said, enormously gratified that he wasn't arguing with her. "Fortunately we've just paid their bill, so they'll deliver."

The supervisor picked up the phone and started to dial while Katy hurried to the nearest typewriter. "And tell them to—" she started to say.

"Get the lead out?"

"Yes," she agreed, smiling for the first time in days. "Tell them at least that."

Katy's hands flew over the typewriter. The letter, already largely formed in her head, seemed to transfer itself onto the paper automatically, as if her hands were simply the mechanical extensions of some preprogrammed computer.

Within minutes the letter was completed. Katy pulled it out of the typewriter so fast that she tore off a corner. Quickly she read it through and made some minor corrections. "I've finished," she called to the supervisor.

He was just completing his phone call. "What took you so long?" he asked with a grin. "The printer says they can have a quarter of a million letters tomorrow and the balance by the end of the week if I can get the original over to them right away. Is it really done?"

"Here," she said, handing it to him. "See if you think it's okay."

He took the paper and started to read, a frown of concentration on his face.

"*Dear* __" the letter started. He nodded his head, knowing that the computers could add the correct names into the letters as they addressed them.

I'm Katy Rochester—the real person, not a computer program. I'm writing to you because I'm in desperate trouble and I need your help. I've never done anything like this before—and my boss, Walter Cort, who owns Magnatel, has no idea I'm doing it now. He'd certainly stop me if he knew. But I have no one else to turn to. . . .

My trouble is that, as a result of something I did, Walter is going to lose Magnatel unless he can come up with a final payment of one million dollars by the end of this month—lose it to a devilishly clever German businessman who tricked me into betraying Walter.

Oh God, how I wish I hadn't fallen for the trick. But I did. And now if Walter doesn't come up with the money, he'll lose everything he's worked for. Everything!

He'll be as poor as he was twenty-five years ago when an American GI rescued him from a German concentration camp and brought him over to America.

I don't have room to explain exactly what happened. But one thing I can promise you is that the reason we're short of money isn't that Magnatel is doing badly. Quite the contrary, it's actually doing too well. We've expanded so fast that we're out of cash. And we can't borrow anymore from regular sources because the contract with the German businessman ties us up in knots.

The point is, if you'll lend us the money, we'll have no trouble repaying you within a few months. I'm certain of that.

So here's my request. Please, will you help me save Magnatel for Walter? Please loan us anything you can spare—maybe just a dollar. In return, I promise on everything I hold sacred that I will repay you double within six months. But please send the money right away. We've got to have it before the end of the month, and the Christmas mail will cause delays. Please hurry.

If by any awful chance Magnatel can't repay your loan—which I know it can—I'll repay it myself somehow. Not in six months, because I don't have any money of my own, but somehow. Even if I have to work the rest of my life for it. I promise.

Probably Magnatel will be able to repay your loan before six months. But even if we only keep your money one or two months, we'll still repay you double.

Please, please help me help Walter. I was the one that got him into this mess. And I'm the only one who can get him out of it. He's tried everything else, and he would never beg anyone like I'm begging you. He's much too proud. For that matter, so am I, normally. But this is different. I just can't let him down. If I do, he'll never want to see me again. And I couldn't stand that. You see, I love him so very, very much.

> *Thank you.*
> *Katy*

"Christ!" The supervisor's voice sounded husky. "I never read anything like this before."

"Will it work?"

"I have no idea. Perhaps. What if it doesn't?"

"Then. . . ." Katy's eyes glistened with tears. "It has to work," she said simply.

"Okay. Then let's get going," said the supervisor. His voice still sounded rough, and he had a great desire to ruffle Katy's hair as he did to cheer up his own daughter when she was sad.

"It just has to," Katy repeated softly.

Katy drove back to the apartment at a furious pace. There was one more thing she had to do to protect Walter, and she couldn't do it at the plant. She had to be somewhere private when she called the Von Ackermanns to tell them what had happened, somewhere that no one could possibly overhear. If only she could make them believe her story. She refused to dwell on what would happen—to Walter and to her— if she could not.

She dialed Germany from Walter's study. Mortimer would not disturb her, and she still had no idea where Walter was. It was late afternoon in New York, which meant it would be midnight at Schloss Ackermann. The butler answered the phone.

"Is that you, Rosenblatt?" she asked, recognizing the voice but wanting to be certain.

"Yes, of course, Miss Rochester. May I help you?"

"Listen, it's urgent. I have to speak to Helga right away. And to Herr Von Ackermann. Are they there? It's an emergency. Are they asleep?" She purposely rushed on, wanting him to report to his employers that she seemed near panic.

"They are both here, and still in the Herr Director's study. I will connect you at once."

It took only a few moments before Katy heard Von Ackermann's voice. *"Jawohl?"* he said. "Katherine, is that you? What is wrong?" He sounded both impatient and apprehensive.

"I'm on the line too," said Helga. "What is it?"

"Walter's found out," Katy started rapidly, letting her words tumble over each other. "I don't know how he found out or how much he knows, but somehow he's discovered that I'm on your side."

"So?" Helga interjected. "What difference does it make? He would have found out soon enough in any case."

"Sure. But then it would have been too late. As it is, he's used it to pull a hell of a stunt. It's a last-ditch stand, all right, to get the money. But it could work. I don't think it will, but it might—and it makes me look like a total idiot." She let her voice rise. "The bastard ʼed my name to send out a sob-story letter like you wouldn't believe. ʼs made me the laughing stock of the world. I just found out about ʼo late to stop it. I'll kill the son of a bitch. I'll—"

"Stop!" Von Ackermann's order silenced her. "I cannot understand you. Now be calm and explain."

"I'm sorry. I'm just so flaming angry."

"Proceed."

"Well, I just found out that Walter has written in my name to everyone who ever wrote a personal letter to Katy Rochester. In the letter he has me asking them to loan him money to save Magnatel."

"Mein Gott." The words were the first involuntary exclamation Katy had ever heard from Von Ackermann.

"What does the letter say?" Helga demanded.

"I'm not quite sure. I only have a preliminary version," Katy explained. "They're sending it out now but I wasn't able to get a final copy. I tried but they're keeping me out of the plant and—"

"Read it." Sharply Von Ackermann stopped her again.

"Yes." Katy shuffled for a moment and then read the letter. Purposely she kept only the general format the same, changing or leaving out the more persuasive sentences. Also she omitted all reference to a "German businessman." No point in making Von Ackermann angrier than necessary. As she read, she made her voice become increasingly outraged. "Just listen to *this,*" she would interject as she came to a piece about herself. "What nerve!" Finally she was finished. "He's an absolute . . ." She paused, apparently searching for the right epithet, ". . . an absolute *shit!*" She seemed to be practically stamping her foot in anger.

"Its not a very good letter," said Helga matter-of-factly. "It's just a tear-jerker, all right for your soap operas, but no use when it comes to the real thing. Moreover it suggests that Magnatel is in real trouble even though it denies it."

"What can we do?" Katy demanded, refusing to be reassured.

"I don't think it's going to work. He's desperate all right, but no one will lend him money on that pitch," Helga continued calmly. "Americans are far too wary. I don't think we have much to worry about."

"I'm not so sure," Katy disagreed. "It *is* a tear-jerker, as you say, so it may raise sympathies. There are always bleeding hearts out there ready to support anything that's sentimental enough."

"Not so many when it comes to cash," said Helga with certainty.

"I hope you're right," Katy still sounded doubtful. "But can't you make *sure.* Can't you stop him?"

"There's nothing illegal that I can see," Helga said. "Nothing to justify an injunction."

"No. I didn't mean that," Katy pretended to be out of all patience. "I mean like you said before, Herr Von Ackermann. You spoke of a solution. . . ."

Von Ackermann, who had been silent for some time, evidently considering the same question, answered decisively. "That would be out of the question now that the situation is so public," he said. "Far too great a risk."

"But . . ." Katy pretended to want to argue.

"And it might build sympathy for Mr. Cort, giving the opposite effect to the one we want."

"Moreover, it is not necessary," Helga repeated stubbornly. "I am convinced the letter will not work."

They talked for a few more minutes, Katy gradually allowing herself to be convinced by them. Finally, they said good-bye.

"Don't worry," were Helga Von Ackermann's final words. "Believe me, it won't work."

Dear God, thought Katy as she hung up the phone. Thank you. She had saved Walter's life, from the Von Ackermann's at least. Now if only she could find Walter in time and tell him what was happening. And if only Helga was wrong.

Were Americans so slow to trust? No! Katy would not believe it. And the letter was more than a tear-jerker. Much more. It was a plea for help. Honest and sincere. She meant every word of it.

Surely the money would come in. It had to. One and a half million letters would be out by the end of the week. Only 67¢ average from each person who got one would bring in the million. Helga had to be wrong. She *had* to be!

Oh, please, Katy thought, oh please, please. Please let Helga be wrong.

The first nine letters in response to Katy's appeal reached Magna-l even before her letter went out, contributions from members of the iling room staff. Twenty-two dollars in all. Katy was so grateful that thanked each of the contributors personally, pleasing and embar-
ϱ them enormously.

he money from the outside, however, could not be expected

until the third day. Even without the Christmas rush, few responses to Magnatel offers arrived before the end of day two, and at this time of year the mails were notoriously slow.

Katy arrived at the plant early on the third day, unable to contain her anxiety. Already the place was bustling, the first delivery of the day being unloaded from four post-office trucks parked at the receiving bays.

The foreman saw her enter and came over at once.

"Good morning," she called. "How many replies are we going to get?" she tried to make the question playful. They often bet each other on response rates. Her attempt at lightheartedness failed completely, though, and he took her entirely seriously.

"Dunno. Never seen a letter like that. Could go gang-busters— or nothing."

"Thanks a lot!"

"Anyhow, we won't get much today, and we won't even know how much till this evening."

"But—"

"You didn't code it different," he explained, "so we have to sort through all the Christmas cards to find any money."

"Oh, please try."

"Of course," he said, understanding how full of anxiety she felt. "What we can do is keep a running tally so at least you'll know how we're building."

"Okay," she said. "And keep your fingers crossed."

"I will," he said, smiling at her with sympathy. *"And* I'll touch wood." He started to leave, then stopped. "There's no need to wait here," he said kindly. "We can call you if you want, or you can call in anytime."

"Thanks. But I think I'll stay. I couldn't relax anywhere else anyhow."

"Okay." He hurried off.

The first mail delivery brought only fifty-one replies, the second almost two hundred. Single dollars, sometimes two, three or five dollars in a letter. Occasionally someone sent a check for ten or twenty.

As Katy watched the tally, her worries mounted. There were twenty-four days left in the month. To raise the million she needed just over forty thousand dollars a day. By noon the tally had reached only nine hundred and five.

She nibbled at a sandwich for lunch, appreciating the foreman's consideration in ordering it for her but totally uninterested in food.

By three another thousand replies had arrived, and the tally had reached about two thousand dollars. But Katy was now thoroughly dispirited. Even though she knew not to expect much the first day, this was terrible. Maybe, after all, Helga was right. . . .

"Telephone call for you, Katy," the foreman called to her. "Take it in my office, it's quicker."

"Thanks." She hurried over, relieved to be doing something, and picked up the receiver.

"Hello. Katy Rochester?"

"Yes. Who's this?"

"Jim Carpenter of the *Post*. We've just heard about the letter you sent . . ."

Of course, she thought, this was something for the press; a letter like this would be highly newsworthy. For a moment she felt resentment. It's a private affair between my customers and me, she wanted to say. But that was foolish. The press could help. The more people who heard about her appeal, the better. She should have thought about it herself. She hadn't even told Billy Wilson.

"Yes, of course," she said quickly. "What do you want to know?"

"Well, could you tell me about it?" the reporter asked, sounding wide-eyed and naïve.

Katy had not had much experience with the press; reporters made her nervous. "I suppose so," she said doubtfully. "It's really just what it says, though. I'm not sure I can add much."

"Why do you need the money?"

"Just as I wrote. It's because we owe a million dollars at the end of this month to repay . . ." A flash of fear stabbed at her. "*I* wrote," she had said, admitting it was her work. What if this was no reporter at all. She wouldn't put it past Von Ackermann to set a trap. "I mean, that was written over my name," she corrected herself quickly. "Listen, can I call you back in a moment? I'd like to go to a quieter telephone."

"Sure." He gave her his private number.

"Thanks." She hung up, her heart pounding. If it was Von Ackermann, she had a lot of explaining to do. For one thing, how had she managed to get back into the plant. Quickly she looked up the main telephone number of the *Post*. There was no point in calling him back on his private line. That could be a trick, too.

"*Post*," the operator answered brusquely.

"Jim Carpenter, please."

There was silence, then a series of clicks. Katy held her breath.

"Jim Carpenter here."

Thank God. She recognized his voice. "Okay, I'm with you now," she said.

"Called me back through the switchboard," he observed. "Checking up on me?"

"I must have got your number down wrong."

He ignored her excuse. "What are you afraid of?"

"I'm afraid that this is going to be a short conversation unless you start asking me some useful questions," she said tartly. "Now what would you like to know about my letter?"

"You were telling me why you need the money."

"To repay the last installment of a debt." She felt back on safe ground.

"And the letter's true?"

"Well, yes," she said. "We do owe the money." She knew that was not the answer he wanted, but it was safe.

"No, I mean that you love Walter Cort."

This was it, she knew, the question and the answer was what the paper would print. "Katy Rochester denies love for Walter: Magnatel appeal a hoax" or "Katy's love deep and real. Fights to save man she adores." One way the newspaper would destroy the impact of her appeal; the other way Von Ackermann would learn of her double-cross. God knew what he would do then. Perhaps nothing, but she dare not risk it. She should never have agreed to talk to the press at all. "Look, it's very personal," she said carefully. "The letter says more than enough." She was choosing her words carefully, making them as ambiguous as she could. "I'm not the sort of person who would declare my love publicly. And I'm certainly not going to say any more than was in that letter."

"But you are living with him."

"Yes."

"Then you do love him?"

"Look here," she said frostily, "I've answered all about that. Can't you think of something else to ask."

"You're very touchy."

"No. Just busy. This is your call, you know. You can end it anytime you want."

"I'm sorry," he said, evidently realizing he needed a lot more from this difficult woman to satisfy his editors. "Let's move on."

"Fine. But I haven't got much time left." Better stay on the offensive, she decided.

"How's the response coming?"

"Weak, so far," she said, hoping he would print that. "Very weak. If it doesn't increase soon, Walter Cort will lose the company for sure."

"Do you think—"

"I don't know," she interrupted. "Look, I've got to go. Sorry." She hung up abruptly. If only he would print her last point. Von Ackermann would read it and be reassured. And her correspondents—all those "Dear Katy" writers—would try harder to help. At least she hoped they would.

By four the tally had risen to three thousand dollars. Three quarters of an hour later, just before the receiving room closed for the night, it was up to just under four thousand. Better, but still less than a tenth of what she needed per day.

Katy sat listlessly in one of the offices, studying the figures and her fingernails with equal, pointless intensity. Her index nail was chipped, she noted. She'd have to do something about that. Why bother? She curled it under her hand. Four thousand dollars. Even if the returns picked up tomorrow, there seemed so little hope for the million.

"We're just about ready to close down," the foreman reported to her. "And the tally's just about up to date. We've processed almost all the mail."

"Not a good day."

"It's early yet. You can't tell."

Possibly, she thought. But probably he was just trying to cheer her up.

The telephone rang and he answered. "It's for you," he said after a moment.

"Who is it? If it's another reporter, I'm not in."

The foreman spoke into the phone again. "No," he said after a moment, "it's not a reporter. It's the receptionist downstairs. She says there's someone to see you. An old lady in a wheelchair, apparently, who's come to answer your letter in person. She insists on seeing you even though the receptionist said you probably weren't here."

"Better send her up," Katy was intrigued. "They can get the wheelchair into the freight elevator like they did for Sid Koblenz in your control section when he hurt his back."

The foreman passed on the instruction and hung up. "How d'you know about Sid?" he asked. "And his name."

"I often talk to him. He's a hard-working fellow who doesn't let his problem interfere. He's got two kids, you know."

"Yeah," said the foreman, pleased with her. "Of course *I* know, but it's good you do." He started to leave the room. "I've got to finish closing the place down. I'll be back before I leave."

Katy was alone only for a few minutes before there was a peremptory knock on the door and a determined, aristocratic-looking elderly woman, blue-haired and carefully made up, wheeled herself in. She made her wheelchair seem like a mobile throne. "I'm Mrs. Bellamy," she announced, her voice deep and Bostonian. "Mrs. Virginia Bellamy. You almost certainly do not know my name, because the computer has handled that. But I am one of your fan-letter writers."

"Mrs. Bellamy." Katy jumped to her feet. "I'm so glad to see you."

"Thank you, my dear. I got your letter, and I wanted to help. But I'm afraid I'm a somewhat suspicious character. So I thought I'd better make sure this wasn't a gimmick to get my money. Also, I wanted to see for myself that you're a real person, not *just* a computer."

"Oh, I'm a real person, all right."

"So I see," said Mrs. Bellamy drily. "A very pretty person, too." She examined Katy's face closely. "And very worried, judging by the rings under your eyes."

"Yes," Katy said softly, extraordinarily moved by this sensible, determined woman. "Very."

"Tell me." It was half an invitation, half an order. "I have a son, you know, who's often in trouble. So I'll probably understand. And it helps to talk."

Perhaps it was Mrs. Bellamy's Boston accent, the accent of the Rochesters for generations, or her bearing, which mixed common sense, strength and sympathy in equal measure, that affected Katy. Or perhaps it was simply that Katy was so overwrought and miserable by this time that she couldn't hold onto her control another instant. Whatever the reason, Katy's lip quivered momentarily and then, to her own astonishment, she burst into tears.

Silently Mrs. Bellamy held out her arms to Katy, who struggled around the desk toward her, kneeled in front of the wheelchair and laid her head on the welcoming lap. "There, there, my dear. It's good to cry," soothed the old lady. "What you have done must be very wrong and therefore very painful."

"Yes," Katy sobbed. "It is."

"But you are putting it right, aren't you? And with great resourcefulness."

"I don't know. The money didn't come in today. Not nearly enough, anyway."

"It's only the first day, they told me downstairs. Tomorrow will be better. Anyhow, you *are* trying. When he sees that, he'll forgive you."

"No, he won't," Katy cried harder. "Not after what I've done. I don't even know where he is."

"I read your letter, you see," said Mrs. Bellamy. "So I know what you feel. He'll understand, too, when he reads it. You'll see."

"But I betrayed him." Katy's sobs were abating.

"Of course. We all do that to each other occasionally. It's how we repent that matters. An old clergyman once told me that. It was the only intelligent thing I ever heard him say," she added drily.

The dig was so unexpected that, in spite of herself, Katy giggled. She lifted her head to look at the older woman.

"Feeling better?"

"Oh, yes. I'm so sorry."

"Nonsense. I love giving sympathy. It makes for a nice change." Mrs. Bellamy said briskly. "When you're like this . . ." she banged the arm of her wheelchair impatiently, "you generally are on the receiving end. It gets to be a drag."

The word sounded so incongruous coming from this impeccable senior citizen that Katy laughed again.

"Anyhow, I'm satisfied you're no computer!" Mrs. Bellamy smiled down at Katy, still kneeling next to her. "So I'm prepared to give you a loan. Up you get now," she added sensibly, "before someone walks in and embarrasses you. After all, we've got a business transaction to complete."

"Okay," said Katy weakly. She arose and returned to the desk.

"Now I don't want double my money or anything like that," Mrs. Bellamy said with determination. "Just normal interest. But I would like a receipt. I assume that is satisfactory."

"Of course. But you're entitled to double. That's what everyone else gets."

"Possibly. But I'd prefer not. Just give me my receipt, and I'll be on my way."

"Yes," said Katy, still far too surprised by the whole visit, by her reaction, by Mrs. Bellamy's kindness, to think of arguing. She placed a piece of paper in the typewriter and wrote out a receipt, leaving the space for the amount blank. Mrs. Bellamy looked on approvingly. When Katy was finished, she took the paper out of the typewriter and handed it to her visitor. "Will that be all right?"

Mrs. Bellamy examined it. "Fine," she said. "Just fill in the amount and sign it."

"Yes," said Katy meekly. "How much shall I make it out for?"

"Ten thousand dollars," said Mrs. Bellamy in her flat Boston voice.

The next day's first delivery was so large it did not get counted until noon. Twelve thousand dollars. By the time the plant closed, two hours of overtime late, the tally was thirty-six thousand. The next day brought almost forty-five and on the Monday following the weekend they received ninety-six thousand, five hundred and three dollars.

A woman from the Bronx sent in twenty-five dollars. "I am Mrs. Elvira Cohen," she wrote, "who has written to you sixteen times this year. You've answered each and every time. So I figure I owe you. And don't bother about when you repay, Katy, it's all right. All I hope is he really appreciates what you're doing for him."

A group of nuns from Minnesota collected thirty-two dollars and sent the money together with a prayer for Katy's well-being. "Please remember to get married to him as soon as possible" they admonished. "Otherwise everything good you're doing will be in vain."

A twelve-year-old girl wrote to say she had framed Katy's letter. She sent fifty cents.

By three-thirty on December 10, the tally, including Mrs. Bellamy's loan, stood at $191,000.

Walter slept for twenty-four hours. At one point he managed to rid himself of his clothes. At another he staggered to the toilet. But apart from that, his mental and physical exhaustion dominated him. He could not—did not want to—ever awaken again.

By the second day he found himself shivering with cold, physically as ill as he was mentally distraught. For two more days, while his body raged with fever, he slipped in and out of consciousness. Sometimes he would be terrified by nightmares; at others he would simply lie on his bed for hours with neither the strength nor the incentive to move. Once or twice, as the shaft of light pinned him and the pain in his chest became unbearable, he cried out. But no one heard.

It was the manager, worried at not seeing his new guest for so long, who roused him on the fourth day by knocking loudly at his door. "You okay?" he demanded.

"Yes." Walter's voice sounded weak.

"Sure?"

"Leave me alone." Walter's fever had receded by this time, but his body was still exceedingly weak, and his only desire was to be left alone, strictly alone to sleep, to forget, in the semi-darkness.

"Sure, buddy." The manager used his passkey to enter. If this was some kook trying to kill himself, he could do it somewhere else, not in his hotel. He had enough trouble with the police as it was. "What's the matter with you?"

"I'm okay."

"You look terrible."

"What the hell business is it of yours how I look," Walter's anger at being disturbed momentarily overcame his lethargy. "Get the fuck out of here."

"Okay, okay." The manager retreated to the door, convinced his guest was very much alive, however ill he might look. "Sorry I bust in."

"And get me some food," Walter croaked at his departing back. "And a paper."

"Yes, sir," the manager said disgustedly. "Just like the Ritz." It was always the same; as soon as you did one little thing for them, they expected to be waited on hand and foot.

"I'll pay," Walter managed to say, his voice weakening. He felt awful, but some spark of resilience had been renewed. He couldn't just stay here forever.

"Okay." The manager was instantly amenable. "I'll get you a McDonald's."

Katy made her decision and returned to the apartment early on the afternoon of December tenth. She had not heard a word from Walter for four days. "Mortimer, we *have* to find him," she said the moment she entered.

"Yes," he agreed. "But where to start?"

"The police? Hospital?"

"I've tried. There's no record of an accident and he's not in a hospital. In any case, they would have contacted us by now. He had plenty of identification on him. The only thing left is to report him missing and start the police searching."

"Did he have any money with him when he left—enough to leave the country?"

"Probably checks. And he'd have had a credit card. He could have left if he'd wanted."

"You think the police are worth a try?"

"Frankly? No, I don't. They've got so much to do, they'll never look for an adult male missing only a few days. Especially not in this case where . . ." he hesitated, looking for the right way to phrase it.

"Where there's a damn good reason for him to leave," Katy finished the sentence for him. "You're right," she agreed reluctantly. "But we've got to do *something.*"

"I know. I'm just as worried as you. But what can we do?"

"Oh, God," she cried.

"He'll call if he wants to."

"I know." The tears welled up in Katy's eyes. "And otherwise he won't."

"That's right."

"It's what makes waiting so awful."

The manager put the hamburger and the paper on the floor next to Walter's bed and grabbed the ten dollars Walter had managed to extract from his wallet. "Keep it," Walter said.

"Thanks. You okay?"

"Yes. Now leave me alone."

"Sure, buddy. Whatever you say." The manager left in a huff.

It took Walter another half-hour to gather enough energy to reach for the food. Eventually he pulled it and the paper onto the bed. Leaning over, he could just reach the light switch by the door. He flicked it on. The bulb hanging from the fixture cast yellow shadows over the dingy furniture.

"Christ," Walter muttered and opened the bag. The smell of the hamburger almost nauseated him, but when he saw the container of Coca-Cola, he became suddenly thirsty. With trembling fingers he pushed the straw through the slit in the lid. Then he took a large mouthful. It felt cool and delicious. The pause that refreshes, he thought wryly, and took another mouthful. As he swallowed it, his eye fell onto the newspaper which had opened at page three.

"Woman tycoon seeks donations for man she loves," the headline read.

But it was the subhead that hooked him: "Katy Rochester sends one and a half million begging letters to save her lover's mail-order empire."

Mortimer was making an omelette for Katy when the telephone rang. Not that she wanted anything to eat, poor thing. But he had to make sure she kept her strength up somehow. He jumped for the phone.

"Hello?" He heard Katy's voice answering from the other extension. She must have been sitting and waiting for the phone to ring.

"Come and get me, please," Walter said in a weak voice. "I read about it in the *Post* just now. I'm quite ill. At the Ace Hotel. Second Avenue and Thirty-first."

"Yes, darling. At once."

Mortimer and Katy almost collided running for the front door.

When they found the hotel, Walter was in the lobby, almost unconscious. He had used up all his strength reaching the telephone. The manager was relieved to see him being taken away.

By December fourteenth the checks and dollar bills and bank orders were still coming in with every mail. Twenty thousand dollars by eleven o'clock. Another fifteen in the afternoon mail.

A young man wrote from Houston Street in New York to say, "My lover has lost ten pounds from following your diet and it's made our love life *much* better. So I'm sending you five dollars from myself— and five from him."

A matron from Ohio wrote to say that she had always hoped her daughter would turn out to be just like Katy. She enclosed her check for eighteen dollars, one for every year her girl had lived before dying in a car accident.

A teenager sent a photograph of his girl friend. "She thinks you're just great, Katy. So I thought I'd send you her picture. Isn't she pretty? Do you look like her too? If you do, I wouldn't know which of you to like most!!!" He sent in one dollar with his note.

By December twentieth the tally was up to half a million dollars. Walter was still weak, but getting better. Mortimer and Katy had wanted to take him to the hospital from the Ace Hotel, but once he was in the car he had recovered enough to insist on being taken home.

Now Katy, who was living at her own apartment, called Mortimer every day. "How is he?" she would ask each morning. "Is he well enough for me to see him?"

"Not yet, Miss Katy," Mortimer had said for the past ten mornings. "A little longer yet." With difficulty she had controlled her impatience, trusting Mortimer's judgment. "But he's getting better," Mortimer would assure her.

"Does he ask after me?"

"No, Miss Katy. I'm afraid not yet."

On December twenty-first Mortimer finally said he thought it would be all right.

"Have you asked him?"

"Yes."

"Oh, what did he say?" Katy hardly dared ask.

"He said you could come."

"Is that all?" She fought to hide her disappointment. What did she deserve, after all. What did she expect?

"Yes, Miss Katy. He thought about it for a while. And then he said yes, you could come." Mortimer paused, trying to find a way to explain to Katy the look he had seen on Walter's face when he mentioned her name. "I think he meant he'd rather like to see you," he said at last.

Katy was so terrified entering Walter's study that she just stood outside the door, quaking.

"It's all right, Miss Katy," Mortimer reassured her.

She smiled at him weakly. Still she could not bring herself to open the door.

Mortimer leaned past her and pushed it open. "There you go," he said. "I'll be in the kitchen if you need me."

Katy walked into Walter's study with no idea of what to expect. He was sitting at one end of his sofa, his feet up on the other, reading a paper. His face was gaunt from his illness, its skin so white it seemed thin, almost transparent. Her heart leaped with tenderness at the sight of him. How beautiful he looks, was her only thought.

For a moment he didn't realize that she had entered, and she observed him silently. Then, sensing someone, he looked up. He saw her and smiled.

As long as she lived, Katy would never forget that smile, filled with such joy and love, such relief.

"You're beautiful," she said. She moved toward him, feeling so full of emotion that she hardly knew what she was doing or where she was.

"I'm fragile," he said, smiling at her. "You're the one that's beautiful. But thank you anyway."

She fell to her knees in front of the sofa, where he sat. "I love you," she said. "Oh, I love you so very much." How inadequate the words were to express how deeply she felt. "I *love* you," she repeated hopelessly.

He took her hands in his and held them tightly.

"Can you ever forgive me? I'm so sorry. Oh, so sorry. More than I can possibly ever tell you."

"Yes," he said. "Yes, I've forgiven you already." He spoke slowly, trying to explain his feelings to himself as much as to her. "At first I knew I couldn't. That first night, as I walked through the snow and ended up only half-conscious at that flea-bag hotel, I was so bitter there seemed nothing left to live for. It was an awful thing you did to me. I was overwhelmed by it. But then, as I became sicker and wanted nothing more than to die, my hurt and anger started to separate."

"Darling . . ."

"No, I've got to explain. It was as if I had become a spectator. I was involved, all right, raw and miserable, but on the outside . . . As if I were watching a movie which made me cry, without my being part of it . . ." He hesitated, unsure how to express the unreality he had felt, the *outsideness*. "What you did just stopped being part of me," he explained, his voice soft. "You—the Katy I loved and lived with—became one thing; the betrayal became another: different, foreign, a wickedness that attacked both of us."

"Oh, my love," she whispered, her voice breaking. "Oh, my darling." She pulled herself forward, closer, feeling so full of him that she just couldn't bear not to be in his arms. "And now?" she asked.

"Now I love you with all my heart," he said seriously.

She was on the sofa beside him now, touching his face, stroking his body, wanting all of him with a passion she had never felt before in her whole life.

When they kissed, it was a homecoming and a new start for each of them. At first the kiss was gentle and chaste. Then, as his tongue started to probe her mouth, she felt such an elation that her whole body seemed to melt. When he touched her breasts, she was filled with a desire so strong she almost reached an orgasm instantly.

"Please, darling," she whispered, pulling at his shirt, imploring.

"Yes. Oh, yes." He started to unbutton his shirt.

Quickly she undressed him and then herself, pulling her clothes off with a terrible urgency.

"Yes," he said again softly, as she lay down on the sofa beside him. "This is what I want."

As he entered her, she cried out, feeling her orgasm start. Clutching him, hardly moving, she seemed to come for minutes, for hours, searing to him. And when only moments later he reached his peak, she felt as if she must burst. Every pore of her seemed to be in orgasm simultaneously so that she could feel herself pulsating with one violent contraction of love after another.

When finally they subsided, still clasped close, lying on the sofa like innocent children, their faces were covered with tears.

By Christmas day, which Katy and Walter celebrated with laughter and joy, the money count at Magnatel had reached almost eight hundred thousand dollars.

"We're going to make it," they told each other jubilantly.

By the twenty-sixth the tally was eight hundred and twenty. On the twenty-seventh another fifteen thousand came in. Eight hundred and thirty-five . . .

Suddenly they realized that the money coming in had slowed to a trickle.

"We'll end at eight fifty," Walter said. "Maybe eight seventy-five. But we'll still be short."

"We can't be." Katy's statement was absolute. "We just can't."

Katy and Walter, recovered from his illness, left the house early on December twenty-seventh determined to find the hundred and fifty they needed. All day long they visited or telephoned every human being they knew, fighting for money with implacable determination. There was more at stake now, for each of them, than just Magnatel. Their happiness, perhaps even their lives were on the line, it seemed. Beating Von Ackermann had become for Katy a rite of purification. If they lost, she would feel forever sullied by what she had done, self-consigned to the shade of guilt and remorse. If they won, fighting together side by side, she knew she could forgive herself.

Katy managed to raise eight thousand dollars from a family trust which rightly belonged to a cousin, but which she conned the trustee into loaning to her.

Walter borrowed three thousand from Consumer Finance, and Katy, struck by the idea, promptly borrowed three more from another branch.

Walter managed to talk Joe Hargraves and his wife into lending the company twelve thousand, and Katy persuaded the shop steward of the mailing clerks' union to loan fifteen thousand from the pension fund.

By evening they were both exhausted. Walter looked so haggard that Katy became frightened that he would have a relapse.

"You must rest, darling," she fussed over him. "I'll get you a hot chocolate."

"Never mind that. How much did we get?"

"We raised twenty-nine between us," Katy said. "And the mail brought in another thirteen. That means we have . . ." She scribbled some figures onto a pad. "One hundred and thirty-three to go."

Walter groaned. "And three days to get it."

"Yes," she said, slumping down next to him.

"Do we have a chance?"

"Of course," she insisted bravely, but unable to keep the hopelessness out of her voice. "We'll search for more tomorrow. And Joe is searching, too. Even Judith, you told me."

"Yes," he agreed. "But you know there's nothing they can do. How about you? Do you have any ideas left?"

"More will come in the mail."

"Maybe another ten or even twenty. But not the hundred plus we need. I meant beyond that."

"No." Her shoulders sagged.

"Nor do I."

"Is that it, then?"

"We'll keep trying."

"Of course," she agreed. "That's all we can do."

Another nine thousand dollars came in the mail the next day. But neither Walter nor Katy was able to raise another penny.

One hundred and twenty-four thousand to go.

Tomorrow was New Year's Eve. If they could find the rest of the money, that was the day they would have to travel to Germany. Katy made the plane reservation just to be on the safe side. She felt quite tragic as she did so.

On December thirtieth the mail brought in only five thousand dollars more.

One hundred and nineteen to go. Walter and Katy breakfasted late. They had nowhere left to go, no one to call. Mortimer was out. They were alone.

"Did you try Harry Grass again?" Katy asked.

"Twice," said Walter succinctly. "He bit my ear off the first time, and chewed it up the second."

Katy smiled weakly. "I tried Martha, too," she said. "But I didn't get as far as you did."

"And Joe Hargraves?"

"He's given up completely."

They were just finishing their breakfast when the doorbell rang.

"Probably a bill collector," Walter said. But he couldn't help feeling a tiny surge of hope. Maybe for once it would be good news.

They both arose and hurried to the front door. Taking a deep breath, Walter opened it.

"Darling. *Darling!*" Judith stood there looking as excited as a child at the circus. "Darlings!" She rushed in, laughing and jumping for joy. "Look, look," she cried, waving an envelope. "Look. It's come. It's come!"

"What has? What is it?" Walter asked, quite mystified.

"The check," she said. "The check for you." She handed him an envelope.

Quickly Walter opened it. Katy leaned over his arm to watch. With clammy fingers he extracted a check. "One hundred and fifty thousand dollars," he saw. It was made out to a Miss Janet Simpson. On the back it was endorsed to Walter Cort and carried a bank guarantee stamp.

"But who . . ." Katy started.

"Where did this come from?" Walter demanded, stunned.

"From Kashi," said Judith triumphantly. "He left it to Jan in his will, and it's just cleared probate. I persuaded her to endorse it to you."

"But who the hell is Janet Simpson?"

"The Tigress, of course." Judith burst into a peal of laughter.

New Year's Eve is called Sylvester in Germany and is widely celebrated. *Glühwein,* a hot and steaming mixture of red wine, fruit juice, cloves and sugar, is drunk before the fire, and poppy-seed tarts are consumed in massive quantities.

At Schloss Ackermann the celebratory event was vast. Five hundred guests had been invited. Their cars were parked on the gravel circle in front of the castle and stretched far back down the driveway itself. They were opulent cars for the most part, giant black Mercedeses, sporting BMWs, an occasional Citroën, a Ferrari, even a Jensen and a couple of Rolls Royces.

Looming above the cars, the castle was lit by a thousand candelabra and from outside by a hundred spotlights. Even the park was illuminated. Every tree within fifty yards of the building was equipped with its own spot; and the driveway was illuminated from gate to castle entrance by two rows of flaring torches. The composite effect of all the shimmering, dancing lights in the black night was of an enormous wedding cake, vulgar and extravagant.

Inside the castle guests milled, the men uniformed in tuxedos, the women swirling in long gowns and aglitter with jewelry. There were bowls of Sylvester wine steaming in every room. In addition, a dozen waiters circulated with champagne glasses brimming on silver trays, while yet others offered whiskey and cocktails.

In the main dining room the long refectory table was loaded to groaning point with a lavish array of food. At its center an ice sculpture of a stag held at bay by hounds glistened realistically amidst pine branches artfully arranged to suggest a winter forest. All around silver dishes were filled with venison and wild boar, shrimp and brook trout, red cabbage and delicate green lettuce. At one end of the table were two huge roast turkeys, each capable of feeding a dozen men. Next to them was a pile of roast starlings, each worth no more than a crunchy mouthful or two.

At one side of the table two cooks in tall white chef's hats carved for the guests. And beside them a phalanx of waiters stood ready to serve any guest who looked even remotely hungry.

Three separate bands of strolling players and a full dance band filled the castle with music. As the guests left their cars and walked toward the main entrance, they were greeted by raucous German polka music, thumping rhythms played by red-faced men in lederhosen. Then as they entered the main foyer, the idiom changed and an effete-looking group of minstrels in medieval costume played madrigals.

On the large balcony, converted to winter use by a glass wall, the older guests sat comfortably sipping their drinks and listening to a strolling group of violinists, while in the great hall next to Von Acker-mann's study, a full dance band played disco and rock for those couples, prancing and gyrating, who were determined to welcome in the New Year with frenetic gaiety.

Heinrich Von Ackermann, dressed in a superbly cut dinner jacket of deep maroon velvet, paraded among his guests. He glowed with geniality and contentment as he greeted an important businessman here, a powerful politician there. To the women, whether married, elderly and rich, or young and climbing, he was graciousness per-sonified. Next to him wherever he went, sometimes holding onto his arm, sometimes just standing beside him, was his daughter Helga, extraordinarily beautiful, serene—and ice cold. She laughed with her father, greeted his guests with him, shared in his triumph. For let there be no mistake, both their expressions implied, this evening was a victory celebration. They had won, and Walter Cort had lost. A worthy oppo-nent he had turned out to be, but still a loser. That he had fought well only made their victory the more delicious.

"We shall make our announcement at ten-thirty," Von Acker-mann said to Helga. "By that time all our guests will be here."

"And still reasonably sober."

"Precisely, my dear. As always, you understand me."

"Yes, Father. I believe I do." She smiled at him. "The micro-phone is all set. I checked it myself earlier."

Katy Rochester and Walter Cort arrived at the main gate in a chauffeur-driven Mercedes. Both car and driver were unexceptional. It was shortly after ten o'clock, so they were among the last of the guests to arrive. The driver stopped the car beside the guard.

"Ihr Ausweis, bitte. Your pass, please?" the guard requested.

Katy Rochester rolled down her window. "It's me," she said, letting the guard recognize her.

"Fräulein Rochester. *Natürlich.* Please proceed."

The car moved sharply forward. It continued right up to the main entrance. Katy, dressed to perfection in a Dior gown of smooth taffeta the color of burnished gold, alighted. Walter, conservative and slim in black tuxedo and waistcoat over a tidy white dinner shirt topped by a black silk hand-tied bowtie, jumped out of the other door and hurried around the car to take Katy's arm. He was carrying a bulging leather doctor's bag.

Nonchalantly they entered the castle together.

"Miss Katy. What an unexpected pleasure." It was Rosenblatt who greeted them. "We were not expecting you."

"I know."

Rosenblatt raised his eyebrows a mere fraction. "And Mr. Cort, is it not? You are even more of a surprise."

"Yes."

"Would you wish me to tell the Herr Direktor of your arrival?"

"Perhaps not, Rosenblatt," said Walter. "At least not for a few moments. We would like to surprise him."

"Of course, sir. But—"

"Only for a few moments, Rosenblatt," said Katy. "Please."

"Well, perhaps." The butler had always liked Katy. It could do him no harm to wait a few minutes before announcing them.

"Has Mr. Von Ackermann made a speech yet?" Walter asked.

"No, sir. It is planned for ten-thirty, twenty minutes from now. The microphone is set up in the Great Hall."

"Thank you. Then that is where we shall see him."

Rosenblatt looked at Walter and Katy. They looked so totally happy. It was not a frequent expression at Schloss Ackermann. "Then he has not won after all?" he asked softly.

They looked at him in surprise.

"I know much of what is going on. After all, the only reason I stay here is to learn," the butler explained. "I am very glad for you," he added and turned away quickly.

"I wonder what he meant," Katy said.

"Never mind. Let's just concentrate on staying out of sight for the next fifteen minutes. Then we can join in Von Ackermann's announcement."

"I'm longing to see his face."

With a final flourish the dance band ended its number. "Ladies and gentlemen," Rosenblatt spoke into the microphone, his words reverberating throughout the castle. "Please be good enough to come to the Great Hall. Herr Direktor Von Ackermann wishes to make an announcement." He stepped down from the microphone.

A babble of curiosity greeted his words. From all parts of the schloss, guests hurried toward the Great Hall. They crowded in, pushing each other for a good view.

Von Ackermann mounted the dais at the end of the hall. He looked imposing, strong, enormously confident, truly a powerful force. Leaning down, he helped his daughter onto the stand. She was slimmer than he, but as tall and in her own way just as imposing. They made an impressive pair standing together behind a small table on which lay the microphone.

Von Ackermann picked it up. "Ladies and gentlemen," he started. "I have invited you here not only to share a celebration in honor of the New Year, but also to celebrate with me a great business victory. I wish to announce—"

It was at that moment that Walter Cort emerged from the crowd and jumped nimbly onto the platform. Before Von Ackermann or his daughter could react at all, he grabbed the microphone. "He wishes to announce," he said in ringing tones, "that today he has become the permanent owner of six percent of my company, Magnatel."

"But you haven't—" Von Ackermann started to expostulate.

"I am here today," Walter continued, "to deliver in person the final installment of the money I owe." He paused to hold up the doctor's leather bag. "One million dollars!" he shouted. *"Eine Million!"* With that he opened the bag and tipped it upside down onto the table in front of Von Ackermann and his daughter.

The money cascaded out, dollar bills, certified checks, bank drafts, even coins.

"One million dollars, as you are my witnesses," he called to the crowd.

Not knowing what they were seeing but assuming it was all part of Von Ackermann's victory, and caught up wholly in Walter's enthusiasm, the crowd started to clap.

Walter held up his arms for silence. "One more thing we celebrate," he shouted to the crowd. He beckoned to Katy, who came to the dais and held up her arms. He pulled her up next to him. "One more thing. The best of all," he called out exuberantly. "This is Katy Rochester. My partner and lover and friend. From tomorrow on, and for the rest of my life, she will also be my wife."

The crowd cheered.

Walter and Katy jumped down from the platform. The crowd parted for them as they made their way to the exit. And it continued to cheer until long after they had left.

EPILOGUE

The wind howled so loudly that it completely drowned any sound made by the dark, powerful figure as he climbed the estate wall and jumped to the ground on the other side. And the rain pounded down so hard that it washed out his footsteps almost as soon as they were formed.

Even the dogs that normally roamed the grounds alert for every foreign sound or smell took shelter in their kennels, cowering from time to time as the lightning hit close and the thunder cracked so viciously it seemed alive and ready to attack.

So dense was the sheet of rain that, even when the lightning flashed, the man could barely discern the castle to which he was stubbornly making his way. Head down, large, ungainly, determined, the man lumbered steadily forward. There was no need to hide himself, even though he had left the thicker part of the forest now and was making his way across the more open park area. Even if someone had been looking, he would have been invisible, black-clad in this black night. In spite of that, probably from force of habit, he used the occasional trees as cover whenever he could.

"Holy Allah," he murmured, and then in the same breath and in the same perfectly refined English accent, "holy shit."

As he ploughed his way forward, buffeted by the wind and the rain, he seemed both as clumsy and as inexorable as an ocean-going tug. His face, fleshy but strong, seemed as set and immobile as the carving on any boat's prow. His eyes, hooded against the rain by heavy, almost sleepy eyelids, nevertheless glinted alertly, darting here and there, watching intently for any hint of danger.

The flashes of lightning showed the man that he had now come quite close to the castle. Only a few more yards and he should reach the gravel in front of the main entrance. Yes, there it was; he could feel its rough surface under his feet. He had never been here before, but he had studied the map for hours—and many times in the last six months he had imagined this scene. Six months was a long time to plan and wait for just the right circumstances.

Steadily, he moved across the gravel to the front door. Above him loomed the mass of the castle itself, its towers and balconies invisible except when the lightning tore open the night's fabric.

Reaching the door, the man pulled back the hood from his face, revealing a swarthy skin and black, wavy hair. His nose, large and arced, gave him a haughty, aristocratic look. He was about thirty years old, built like a football forward, with large amounts of solid muscle which might disintegrate to flab if he fell out of training. But he was clearly very much in training. There was a tautness and tension about him which made him seem tough, ominous, dangerous. He lifted a grapefruit-sized fist and tapped with incongruous gentleness on the door. Instantly it swung open.

"Welcome." The butler Rosenblatt bowed his head in greeting. *"Shalom."*

"Hardly that, my friend. I do not come in peace."

"You will create peace in my heart," Rosenblatt replied. "There is peace in justice, it seems to me." He watched his visitor, who towered over him. "Are you sure this is how you want it to be?"

"Yes. I am sure."

"Your race is nonviolent."

"I am not typical. I do many things wrong. I am trained to violence." He grinned at the butler. "I even consort with Jews," he said. "That is hardly commensurate with the views of my race."

"You are a thoroughly bad lot," Rosenblatt agreed. His voice was warm. "I want nothing to do with you. In fact, it's quite out of the question that I know you, have even seen you, least of all here . . ." He turned on his heel and walked toward a door at the side of the entrance hall. *"Shalom,"* he said again as he left, closing the door firmly behind him.

The large man watched the door close. For a moment he remained entirely still. Then, with no trace of hesitation, he turned and walked ahead through the grand hall of the castle. Only one light shone in the hall, so that as he walked, the man cast an ominous, leaping shadow over the shields and spears which decorated the hall.

When the visitor, sinister in his black clothes, pushed open the door of the study, its sound, like the earlier noises he had made as he climbed the wall and crossed the park, was drowned out entirely. But now it was not the wind and the driving rain which covered the intruder's entrance but the swelling, sonorous chords of Beethoven.

Von Ackermann never noticed as the door to his room opened and closed. His eyes were closed in contemplation; there was a satisfied smile on his lips; his hands rested contentedly on his belly.

When finally he did open his eyes, induced to do so by some indefinable sense of no longer being alone, he was startled but not frightened. *"Was wollen Sie?"* he demanded. "What do you want?" He started to reach for the bell beneath his desk.

The large visitor hardly seemed to move at all, but suddenly he was holding Von Ackermann's wrists. Briefly the German tried to struggle. But it did him no good; the grip was of steel.

"Keep still," said the visitor, now clearly recognizable as an Arab.

"Who are you?" Von Ackermann demanded. "What do you

want?" But although his voice remonstrated, he did what he was ordered and kept still, very still.

"I am a son," said the Arab, and there were tears in his eyes. Those tears frightened Von Ackermann more than the giant fists clamping over his own. Despair, revenge . . . those were the emotions he knew to be the most dangerous.

"But I don't understand . . ."

"Just a son," the Arab repeated, "but of an unusual father."

"But what do you want?" Then Von Ackermann finally understood. And with understanding came terror. "Oh my God," he whispered. "Your father. . . ."

"Yes. Of course you know."

"Please don't hurt me," Von Ackermann whispered, his cheeks shivering as if the wind from outside were tearing at them right here in his study. "It was a mistake. . . ."

"Yes."

"I'll do anything to make it up to you. I swear. I'll pay you anything you want. Anything."

"Yes, you will pay," said the son. "You will pay."

Von Ackermann opened his mouth wide to scream. Faster than the eye could follow, and before the German could utter a single sound, the Arab had pushed a wad of something pink and shiny into that open mouth. The scream turned to a grunt, a grunt of horror and submission and despair.

"German industrialist slain," the headline shouted. "Suffocated on Bar of Beauty Soap." The article below it explained:

> A leading German industrialist, Heinrich Von Ackermann, was murdered last night in his castle near the Rhine. The killing was especially brutal and macabre because the victim was suffocated by a bar of his own company's brand of soap.
>
> Known as "Pink Soap" since shortly after the war, when it was one of the first soap products launched in Germany, it was the foundation of the vast Von Ackermann empire. . . .